PRELU

The gathering storm turned the twilig
as lightning flashed, illuminating the regulars lined up along the Italian
waterside bar. Its sharp light cut through the smoke-filled room as movement
homewards beckoned for one of them.

A young waiter struggled outside to close down umbrellas no longer
serving custom whilst hopelessly at the mercy of a wind whipping them to
demonstrate the futility of human impudence against Nature's rule.

An impeccably dressed carabiniere lent against the bar, relishing a walk
home, where he would cook his favorite dish, a pleasure reserved for his one
day off. Before departing he threw down a final Cinzano, turned, adjusted his
trench coat collar upwards and headed for the door.

"That boat outside is still drifting untethered," shouted a man entering, in a
suit that had seen better days.

"Boat? What boat?" answered the Sicilian officer, adjusting the black cap
neatly placed on his head.

The barman, aware of the lawman's imminent departure, hollered.

"You've got to be kidding. Didn't you notice it on the way in?"

The ill-suited man faced the policeman directly and glowered.

"Isn't this your department, Fantozzi, to solve mysteries around here?"

Fantozzi looked up grudgingly and replied.

"Tomorrow maybe, but tonight I've a date with spaghetti alla carbonara."

The barman shouted across the room.

"Aren't you in the slightest bit curious, Guido?"

Without turning, Guido blurted back.

"Loose boats are the boatman's problem," and skirted past the suit.

The man, facing the bar, addressed Fantozzi.

"Maybe in Palermo, but here we expect the carabinieri to do their job."

An awkward silence followed, quickly filled with the barman's attempt to
lower the temperature.

"Go on Guido – just a quick look, keep everyone happy and then you're
home."

He winked overtly at Fantozzi's questioner as Guido pulled the door open
with unusual authority and twisted round to his interrogator's back and spat
his response.

"In Palermo, sir, our boatmen tether their boats securely."

1

The door slammed shut behind him.

He made his way to the waterline, the wind whipping waves, spume spitting onto polished black shoes.

Retreating back a few paces he looked to left and right, making sure no one witnessed the pedantic process of taking each shoe and sock off in turn. Feet naked, trousers rolled up to avoid a soaking; he made his way gingerly towards the tossing skiff. Realizing he still wore his cap, he turned and threw it with precision over the shoes and socks behind him. Turning attention back to the craft in the water, he waded in.

The wind edged the boat closer. Confident of aim and balance, he raised both arms and lunged forward into the boat. The stiffening wind withdrew his target and Fantozzi fell headlong into the water. Spitting out cold, clear water, he scrambled towards its prow and clambered over.

Another flash illuminated the interior, revealing an Enfield revolver, lying on the bottom of the boat. He froze, looked left, right and left again catching the outlines of an empty wine bottle. Another longer flash exposed a handwritten note. As the boat bobbed up and down, he reached in, grabbed it and began to read.

A loud clap of thunder followed by peel over peel rolled across mountains and lake as stronger waves, indicated he could not expect to enjoy a quiet evening.

DREAMS AND REALITIES

Dreams

AND

Realities

VOLUME 1 OF THE FREEDOM CYCLE

JONATHAN L. TRAPMAN

First Published, August 2016

ISBN No: 978-0-9926383-2-0
Dreams and Realities - Volume 1 The Freedom Cycle

Cover design: JTS
www.jonathantrapman.com

Living Zen Books
publish
JONATHAN L. TRAPMAN

Other works by
JONATHAN TRAPMAN
and
VIRVE TRAPMAN

DIVINE WISDOM
First ever English translation
10th century Sufi poet and founder
HOJA AHMED YASSAWI

JONATHAN AND VIRVE TRAPMAN
ENGLISH TRANSLATION
Kreet Rosin's
YOUR EVERY FEELING CREATES YOU

www.livingzenbooks.com
www.thefreedomcycle.com

FB: www.facebook.com/TotoTheBook

ELLO: www.ello.co/thefreedomcycle

Dedicated to Captain A.H. Trapman and my parents John and Lois Trapman, without whom there would be no story......
To all who search for truth, peace and unity

CHAPTER ONE

L eaning back in a rounded rosewood chair, one arm resting nonchalantly on the long oak table beside him, the correspondent was bugged by a niggling fact refusing to clarify. Having completed the work envisioned as his get out of penury ticket, he stared up at the gilded golden ceiling above. Its blue sky and cotton bud clouds teased his imagination transport itself beyond the raging storm lashing Arcadian steps outside leading to the New York Public Library he presently occupied. He struggled to stay present.

Ferret-like referencing, stitching and compiling of facts, compelling words, chapters and information had brought this definitive book on dogs to life. A rain-soaked April evening in 1928 became a potential prelude to a future free from the leaden weight of scraping by. It heralded a pursuit of happiness craved, for so long. Well over two years expended on this project, had enabled him to uncover family links to the Carolinas, which had expanded his knowledge of the family's past and encouraged him trace roots and origins. This parallel research developing his own family tree fitted comfortably into travels back and forth to Europe researching dogs and humans alike. Yet as he sat there something was missing, something so important he readily threw away the opportunity to daydream.

What was it, he asked himself. What have I missed in what's written and researched?

He read and reread the manuscript, scanning notes on the family; over and over perusing each paragraph. Time passed, so much so he forgot it altogether. All he knew for certain was the missing link lay in the family research.

That bugged him.

"Excuse me sir, I apologize for disturbing you but we are now closing."

The correspondent, deeply absorbed, did not register the senior librarian's voice. Raising his voice slightly the librarian tried again.

"Sir, we're closing and I must ask you to pack your things and leave."

He placed a gentle hand on the writer's shoulder who jumped, alarmed at the invasion.

"I beg you sir, we need to close, and may I ask you quickly collect your research and leave."

Brought into the present with a jolt, the man realized his absorption and obliviousness to the librarian.

"But I must find what's missing, I must, it's here somewhere – or more to the point it's not...."

"Sir, you can return tomorrow at seven when we open and continue. As a concession you may leave all these references in place and I shall personally see to it that nothing is disturbed."

The correspondent became agitated.

"It has to be here, it has to be..."

"I'm sure it is," the kindly librarian attempted soothing the troubled researcher's plight, "but have you not got family to go back to and spend the evening, take supper with?"

Like a bombshell, the researcher felt his mind explode realizing what was missing. He turned, stood up, took the shoulders of the head librarian in both hands, one on each, and shook them with joy.

" My God, thank you sir, thank you."

The other man, stunned at the sudden gesture, the intimate action and complete ignorance of what induced it, allowed the elated man, still holding his shoulders, to continue.

"You see it was just that, you hit it on the head. You helped me find the missing piece."

Unaware of the shock the librarian now registered, Captain Albert Henry William Trapman, ex military, erstwhile foreign war correspondent for the London Telegraph, seeker after fortunes and dreamer of better things to come, let slip his hands from the librarian's shoulders and took the man's left hand in both of his and shook it vigorously.

"Thank you so much, sir, for letting slip the magic word family.

Funnily, I have no family in this great city with whom I can share an evening meal. I have even less money to even purchase one, but all these are mere incidentals compared with the gift you've just given me and the knowledge my family from the deep south hold an important and missing piece of my puzzle."

The librarian remained stunned, perplexed and riveted to this extraordinary fellow who, before him, was as radiant as he was loud in these hallowed halls of silence. Under ordinary circumstances, such an outburst would never have been permitted. However the truth was that they were the only two left in the building, so he felt less impelled to quieten his visitor down. In confusion as much as shock, he switched off his automatic internal responder.

"You see it's the family I've missed, it's the family that's the key and it's my family I must pursue," explained the effulgent researcher.

4

Letting slip the handshake, he beamed wildly at the books and shelves around him, lifting arms outstretched in grateful supplication to one and all. At the same time honoring the librarian and all the ghosts who had begun to drift into place as the living withdrew. Hastily gathering what seemed important, along with the finished manuscript he looked triumphantly to the heavens and gilded golden ceiling above.

"Thank God for dogs and family," Captain Trapman cried.

The librarian remained stunned.

"Thank you for allowing this carnage to remain as is, sir and I'll return at seven. For now I must allow you to close shop and be about your business."

The librarian was not only bemused, mystified and thoroughly relieved as he watched the Englishman skip, like a child, out of sight but more importantly glad he could now close the doors and his evening on one of the strangest encounters he had witnessed in all his years in the New York Public Library.

He leaned over scanned the contents of research left with his photographic memory, remembering each piece and placement of the referenced detritus. He prided himself on attention to detail and was certain that in spite of the craziness he had just witnessed, he would honor his word that all would be exactly in place and ready for the Captain returning in the morning.

Noting it all he turned to go.

Across the library, Albert Trapman reappeared.

The librarian's heart sunk.

"By the way, I never introduced myself, though we've spent so many months together across these tables. I'm Captain Albert Trapman and you are?"

"George Evans, Captain," he mumbled.

"Excellent, George, excellent and please, call me Toto."

George Evans, senior librarian at the New York Public Library had no time to query the man's sobriquet. He did what he would automatically do in times of mental confusion. He took off his spectacles, looked at them quizzically and began cleaning the lenses with a finely pressed silk handkerchief. He noted he might ask that question at a later date.

Captain Trapman meanwhile disappeared into the raging storm outside.

5

CHAPTER TWO

A black-swathed sea of figures moved almost motionless. Inner turmoil battling outward restraint.

A golden casket scythed through this ocean of grief, towards a candlelit trestle before the altar in the Anglican church. Nestled behind the metropolitan bustle describing London's Knightsbridge Kensington borders, the church became a fitting place of somber ceremony for one of its own.

A chill November day in 1932 and a sharp shower became the backdrop for the grief within, where an elderly woman, her veil covering deeply lined and saddened features, self-consciously endeavored to check sobbing sadness,while a tenor launched divinely inspired resonance throughout the church, to accompany the playing out of a final adieu of a life lost before its time.

No-one noticed the entrance of a tall, fleet-footed young man creep through the rear porch entrance, remove a rough tweed cap and seek the refuge of a back pew. Kneeling down, he silently paid his respects. The chasm of vacant pews between him and the tightly packed congregation up front described perfectly the divide between his own island of sorrow and the rest.

His thoughts raced across a landscape of shared memories, times together, the bond of brotherhood. The young man's aloneness swept into a receptacle of sorrow, vibrating deep within. His soul consumed by an other-worldly presence accepted an unknown force holding him, soothing him as an inner voice softly bid him still.

All is very, very well, it coaxed.

He recalled many walks both had taken across gorse-strewn headlands and silver strands of sand. Talks of ancestors escaping deprivation and poverty, seeking freedom and release in the promise, dreams and riches lying across the ocean. The times his companion shared tales of family whose journey took them half way across the world, supporting revolution and change.

Smokey Greene, riveted to the pew, felt himself part of something he cared little for, yet shared with his now departed friend. Twenty-three years separated them, now inconsequential within what seemed too brief a sum of years. Waving aside a torrent of unspoken questions tearing round his youthful head, Smokey did what he always did, left it to brew waiting for answers to appear in their own good time. If nothing else he was a patient soul, an essential quality for an emissary to come. Painful experience and hard-learned truths would be the scholarship he must experience on his journey to mystic sage.

For now, loss absorbed was shared with a tribe of unknown relatives, friends, compatriots and colleagues, all touched in their own way by the departed's eventful and unique existence.

Smokey silently thanked him for each moment of their time together. Vowing to be true to his memory, he swore to uphold his promise given.

As gratitude and love consumed sorrow, a subtle expansion and entrance of surprising joy entered.

He took this moment as cue to withdraw as quietly as he had entered.

CHAPTER THREE

The storm lashing the streets of New York of an April night four years earlier had absolutely no effect on Toto's spirits. He was as high as a kite with exhilaration even prohibition could not bring down to earth. His enthusiasm drove him on as he crossed Bryant Park heading towards Broadway and West 44th. The park, almost deserted save for a handful of passers by, invited intemperate weather and the wraiths of haunted souls frequenting this potter's field. Toto was having none of it. He may have felt the presence of the displaced, yet tonight's mission was to get to the Hotel Astor, hoping to cadge supper off one of his journalist buddies. Wrapped in a trusty mackintosh, he raised its collar against the weather and marched forward.

Rain pelted down unremittingly, incapable of diminishing the enthusiasm felt having finished his book. He was joyful for George, his friend and ally at the library, for giving him the key he believed would be far bigger, far more important than any downpour. Where it led at that precise moment remained a complete mystery. Appreciation for the librarian's kick-start to discover more with even greater impetus sheltered him from the stormiest external influences.

Present penury had for now been assuaged by intuition. If life had taught him anything, it was to trust that. Tonight was about hitting home runs.

From an early age it had been an experiential truth. It was responsible for his nickname, Toto.

His mind floated back to that sunny morning at Cavendish, the English country house in Suffolk, where he had spent his early years. A far cry from the stormy New York parkland he presently traipsed across, yet no less tangible than the cutting bite of the rain across his face.

He saw himself, the young four year old, in his bedroom on the first floor. Talking, as he so often did, to Toto, his invisible friend. That morning, while in deep discourse, his father, fresh home from another merchant business trip, hid himself on the landing outside the lad's bedroom, wishing to surprise his son. Aware of his father's game, he carried on as if oblivious.

His invisible Self assured Albert that as long as he always remembered their bond and its presence, the boy would never be alone. Albert's father – privy only to his son's side of the conversation – was shocked when the boy turned and spoke.

"Papa, you can come in now, he's gone away again."

His father William slowly crept into the room to witness the boy standing in the middle, in pajamas and a smile to warm the coldest heart.

All these years later Toto still felt the warmth and thrill of rushing into his father's arms. How he landed in a tumble-down sort of way into long legs. He was a giant of a father in all senses of the word.

"How is my young warrior then?" William asked, as he whisked Albert into strong arms.

The young lad looked piercingly into his father's eyes, enjoying the dizzy heights experienced by adults.

"Papa, you're home, tell me about the Indians and buccaneers again."

His father hugged him, realizing there was no escape from recounting oft told tales. Adult Toto remembered the pleasure his father took in retelling a rich repository of adventures the boy absorbed like a sponge. His adult self appreciated the imagination it cultivated and how it had helped direct him to land in New York City, albeit strapped for cash, yet using skills creatively and professionally as a journalist.

He chuckled to himself, in spite of the rain working hard to bring him back to the present remaining focused on the childhood memory.

"Firstly Albert, you've not introduced me to your friend."

Albert struggled in his father's arms, faking escape.

"Not so easy young man till we've been introduced."

William had often heard Albert in conversation with his invisible friend, always accepting this as part of the process growing up for a child.

"Papa, Toto's gone. He'll not be back yet."

"Toto?"

"Yes Toto, Papa."

"So where did this friend Toto come from, Albert?"

Settling down on the floor, he looked his son in the eye and asked again.

"So where did this friend Toto come from, Albert?"

"He's me."

"You?" William replied, with some consternation.

"Toto says that," the boy replied.

"Toto says what, that he's you?"

"Yes, he's my friend."

Intrigued at the boy's precociousness, his father continued.

"Is this a real friend or just one of your imaginary ones?"

"Real, of course. None are imaginary," Albert responded slightly hurt at the insinuation.

"So can I meet him, Albert?"

"No, he's gone."

"So we'll never meet him, your mother and I."

Adult Toto remembered the concern he felt at this question and how he had paused long and hard searching for a suitable way to describe the conundrum. As a child it had been so clear yet for adults so mysterious. All these years later he still felt proud of his reply.

"He's me, so you've met him."

His father was staggered at his son's logical jump. A process, he considered, way beyond tender years. Nonetheless he entertained the boy's imagination.

"So perhaps we should be calling you Toto then."

"Can do."

"Are you saying Albert you'd like to be called Toto from now on?"

"Can do," the child repeated again.

His father was nonplussed. Wishing to ease his incredulity the boy added. "Mama knows Toto."

"Mama has met him has she?"

"Yes," mother Eliza confirmed, timing her entrance to perfection.

"So he's introduced you to Toto then?"

"Well not exactly, he's just gone away according to Albert," her husband replied, greatly confused.

Eliza's exquisite knack at extricating her husband from the masculine mire of incomprehension was what adult Toto had adored about her, alongside her ability to resolve the irresolvable. He always felt it would have stood her in good stead for the diplomatic corps.

"Why don't we call Albert Toto from now on. That makes Toto happy, Albert happy and you and I can go downstairs and take breakfast."

With that wisdom and diplomacy, from that day on everyone in his family and those considered a close friend called Albert Trapman, Toto.

Even today in his fifties, Toto recognized his intuitive self as the very same Toto of his youth. Never parted, always there, despite so many years forgetful of this constant companionship. Another thing he had utterly forgotten was the gas lamp designating the edge of this side of Bryant Park and the beginning of Sixth Avenue. Not even a refined intuition would have prevented the painful meeting of skull and metal. If nothing else it brought Toto back into the present swiftly yet more painfully than he would have wished.

"Bugger, what the..." he cried out to a deserted space of darkness littered

11

with encroaching street lighting, swiftly cupping head in hands, unaware of the exact nature his inattention had procured.

"Look where you're going, mister," cried an unsympathetic voice from the gloom.

His foolishness felt compounded just long enough for the rain to become irritating. He marched briskly off to the Astor and a free meal.

Rounding the corner to the hotel, the opportunity of a free meal presented itself stepping out of a sleek Rolls-Royce Phantom accompanied by an editorial counterpart from the New York Times he knew well. Adolph Ochs, renowned publisher of what was now considered one of the best and most respected newspapers in the country, shuffled toward the entrance, followed by Jerry Graves, his file editor.

Toto manufactured the accident.

Swiftly adjusting his wet dog look with help from one of the hotel's windows, he dispensed mackintosh onto his arm and bumped lightly into Graves.

"Most terribly sorry," Toto began.

The commotion had Ochs turn, immediately recognizing its cause.

"The British may rule the waves but their navigation leaves much to be desired, especially from an Army man" he chortled.

In spite of his seventy years, the magnate still retained the sense of humor Toto always relished. Graves immediately ceded to his boss's welcome of the encounter and brushed himself down, patting Toto on the shoulder.

"Good to bump into you," he exclaimed with unnatural irony.

All three entered the hotel, Toto sweeping in on their coat tails.

"Albert, what a pleasure and since we're in casual mode I insist you join us in The Grill Room for supper."

Fait accompli, thought Toto, accepting the invite. Ochs kept the conversation going.

"About that slim volume of yours. Is it ready to be featured in our review?"

Toto, eager to share events, diplomatically suggested he bring them up to speed at the table.

Three quarter way through the meal, with Toto sharing the completion of his book and delivering his take on the supernatural qualities he found dogs possessed, his peripheral vision caught a familiar face making its way along the center aisle. He focused on his tale, as the others craned their necks to catch his dramatic delivery.

"You see I believe a dog is able to sense those who carry bad character and those who are friendly, when it comes to us humans. We all get vetted through some sense or other when meeting these highly intelligent beings."

"Certainly need my own dog to sift unreliable sources across the news desk," quipped Graves.

"You'd need a wolfhound," Ochs responded without a pause, then chided.

"Jerry, let Captain Trapman finish this fascinating insight, please."

Picking up his thread, Toto caught the approaching figure closing in. He paused, looked up, as the elderly stranger wearily reached their table. Toto's suspicions confirmed, he stood up abruptly and extended his hand. The others turned round.

The stranger ignored the hand, while the others immediately recognized his identity.

" Nikola, Toto," the researcher greeted.

"You think I've lost my marbles? You of all people should know I never touch the unwashed, never know where it's been, so drop that hand," Nikola Tesla brusquely corrected the researcher.

He swiftly scanned the rest of the table.

"So what, you now scheming with scribbling wolves?"

Toto trying hard to cover the inventor's directness made his introduction.

"Gentlemen, I introduce the great Nikola Tesla."

The others, hands well out of sight raised themselves slightly from their chairs.

"Good evening," they both chirped in unison.

Ochs assured Toto the visitor was a well-known quantity.

Tesla gave them glancing acknowledgement and directed himself at Toto.

"These news hounds continue to under-report my genius."

Graves shifted uncomfortably in his chair as Ochs, perfectly used to this behavior from the inventor stood.

"Mister Tesla, I am well aware of both your inventions and idiosyncrasies and congratulate you on the former. Would you care to join us?"

"Dine with those supporting my enemies. Thank you but never."

"Please Nikola, do join us," Toto implored.

"You know me better than that. I'll leave you to keep these hounds under control. You know much about the breed."

Toto laughed nervously, more out of embarrassment for Tesla's huge foot he felt had been placed in the way of potential support, than his own embarrassment.

"At least your man Van Anda had passion for the sciences and a kind pen towards my work, while you lick the boots of plutocrats who make sure my truths never truly get reported," Tesla rebuked the newspaper magnet and editor.

At that moment a waitress arrived at the table and addressed Tesla.

"Can I serve you sir, or are you with these gentlemen?"

Tesla turned letting his bad temper land on the unsuspecting employee.

"Yes, you can – go home and feed your brats."

The reply hit her hard. She struggled visibly to hold back tears retreating swiftly. They all felt it. Tesla remained oblivious to it, including his manner.

"This place is infested with vultures and cockroaches. Two have just tried stealing my latest patent over dinner and you press hounds support their criminality. Toto, visit me. I'm off."

Tesla stormed towards the exit.

The researcher turned towards his fellow diners beginning an apology.

"No need Captain. The fellow has a reputation to uphold. Remember, we're press and that comes dressed automatically with a hard nose!" Ochs laughed heartily and Toto responded, excusing himself at the same time.

Graves turned to his boss.

"Do you suppose we've a poodle in the Captain?"

On the street outside Toto caught up with Tesla, by now getting a good soaking as the rain poured down. The researcher opened his umbrella shielding the inventor from the downpour.

"Why were you so bad tempered back there, I've never seen you so furious."

"They're all sluts to the whores of banking and wealth. None of them have an idea how energy works, how the very fabric of the universe pours through each crevice of time and space," the inventor spluttered, deeply hurt.

"You need these guys on your side Nikola, you need the American people to know your true worth. Why go out of your way to aggravate them?"

"On my side?" Tesla shot back. " Just like those two trying to rip off my patents over a trout and vegetables?"

"I'd no idea. How was I to know?"

"There's much you don't know, dear friend. That will be your downfall. The rats infesting this ship have too much invested in it to jump."

Tesla felt himself shrink under the endless battering he had endured. Toto targeted reassurance.

"There's money here. Investment capital, we can find it together," he pleaded.

Tesla looked at him, at his incessant hope and forced an honest smile.

"Your father was a good man, kind, as you are. He connected me with good support. When we three met those years ago things were different. Today greed, selfish interest and the rape of Earth's natural resources have changed all that."

"Show them another way with your..."

"What use are eyes to blind minds and oil barons with no desire to comprehend free energy?"

"Carnegie, Rockefeller, Morgan, Vanderbilt, Warburg. They crow about philanthropy," Toto urged.

"Philanthropy for them is self serving. The inventor is merely another cow to be milked. To spend useless hours bemoaning these truths only diverts me from the absolute necessity to harness all I channel. I must pass this to those coming after. Why waste precious time with back biting bankers, backers and vested interests. They'll never know the thrill coursing through the human heart as the inventor's creation rises from the ether, unfolding form and life. Such emotions make a man forget food, sleep, friends, love, everything. That's why I leave funding up to George Scherff and Robert Johnson."

"I remember Johnson but George, I've not met."

The two of them had arrived at a junction. The umbrella having done its job and the rain stopped, Toto closed it. Hardly a soul was visible on the sidewalk.

Tesla turned to Toto.

"Then come round to my laboratory and be introduced. It's just around the corner from the library."

"I will do," he reassured the inventor.

"One more thing," the old man cut in. "Gold's not in dollars or bars, it's not in the glory of power, these things mere selfish acquisitions of men seeing riches for themselves, blind to the needs and dispossession of their fellow man. They're the curse on humanity, leeches of all that's wonderful, glorious and magnificent about the human in the search for self."

Toto pondered his friend's words as Tesla parted and crossed the street. Stopping suddenly midway, he turned and shouted back to Toto.

"Remember, progress can only start in the mind, not the laboratory."

A passing carriage cut him from view as Toto was left scratching his head. Looking back to find Tesla, he was confronted by an empty street.

He shrugged and made for home.

CHAPTER FOUR

A commotion in the street below awoke Toto from a deep sleep. Collecting his papers he was back at the Library minutes before its doors opened.

As good as his word Toto's new friend George Evans had allowed the papers left strewn over the table on the far corner of the Main Reading Room, to be undisturbed.

He settled down to paw through notes and copious references. Despite every note and penciled diagrammatic, he knew precisely where to start.

With the help of one of the staff he began looking through files on Southern families he knew were direct descendants of William and Eliza, his mother and father. He specifically searched references to his forebear John Moore. Perhaps it was something to do with the wealth this man had accumulated, more specifically, that Moore's father had accrued that helped focus Toto's research.

Might some good fortune trickle down through the ages and land me in clover? he wondered.

He wished.

John Moore's father had arrived in the Carolinas in 1699 and with considerable wealth. He had purchased over 3,000 acres of plantation, turning it to cotton and sugar cane, a crop with which his brother had made a fortune in Barbados. Having lost his first wife Margaret, Moore remarried Rachel, who bore him a son, John on July 4th, 1726.

As Toto looked at all the papers alluding to this young John Moore it became apparent the man was highly skilled and becoming wealthier by the day, marking himself truly to be his father's son. He noted wryly the date of birth, the fourth of July, merely because of its import in the national psyche. Through shrewd deals, climbing the social ladder, clever negotiations and contacts, by 1775 the now resourceful Moore had become a member of the Provisional Congress in Charleston. This all enthralled Toto. That they were of similar age, separated by centuries, made him warm to the congressman. Out of the blue he asked the assistant whether records of wills of congressional members of other states were held there in the library.

The assistant hurried off to scroll through private files, not normally available to the general public. On his return he informed Toto there were such records.

Together they scoured the retrieved files. As he turned the page, the assistant's eye caught a side entry on a copy of Moore's will.

"What's that?" Toto asked.

"It's a reference to the Library of Congress in Washington, which seems a bit strange."

"Why so?"

"Because normally this detail would be held locally."

Toto was intrigued.

"Especially in light of being the will of an ordinary, though rich, citizen of the South. Why do you think they'd annotate the will as it's strange a copy of his will would be here in the North, even though he was a member of the Carolina Congress?"

"Precisely because he was a Congressional member, sir, as I said," the clerk replied courteously.

The young clerk, assiduously polite and as modestly dressed as his meager wages ensured, took a well-used kerchief from his jacket pocket and wiped his brow. The woolen brown jacket, worn elbows and scuffed collar, had the air of a hand-me-down from a family member no longer in need. Conscious of its provenance and with the awkwardness of someone dressing more from necessity than effect, he answered Toto.

"I'm not experienced in these things but a similar anomaly a few months back turned out to be governmental, filed under matters of state in the Library."

"That's definitely caught my interest. Perhaps being a member of Congress, state-wise, meant he was tied to national government affairs."

"That would be strange even if it was the case as it was rare even then. We're looking at the gentleman's last will and testament, which is more curious. Why would documentation associated to this Mister Moore be annotated to his will and found also in National archives?"

"Perhaps..." Toto began.

The assistant broke in and repeated.

"Perhaps if it had monetary implications attached to it pertaining a national issue."

"Of course, you're on the money there," Toto answered. "It'd mean there was an interest to his surviving relatives he wanted taken into consideration, perhaps."

Toto began to get excited. Could this be the missing piece he had felt was not present the night before? Was this perhaps part of a legacy money trail to hidden riches?

He had an idea.

"Is it possible seeing if this annotation helps us further?" he asked the assistant, pointing to a numbered reference.

The other mused.

"It may give us a clue. Let me check with Mister Evans."

Yes, thought Toto, George Evans his new friend was sure to know.

Before too long the young assistant came scurrying back in as silent a manner as to not break the library's sacred silence code. Toto chuckled to himself as he saw the librarian as excited as he was in discovering the outcome. Breathless, from restraint, he leaned over Toto to deliver the verdict in a conspiratorial whisper.

"It seems the annotation refers quite correctly to state matters whose reference denotes it being recorded in the Library of Congress. It does also mean, due to the alphanumeric string, the period in question would have been 1778 or 1779 and filed under loans."

"Fascinating," Toto responded as he struggled to contain his rising heartbeat.

More than fascinating but keep cool, he told himself.

"The bad news is," the librarian added.

Toto focused entirely on the next words he was to utter.

"The bad news is you're going to have to go to Washington to see the detailed entries there."

If that was the bad news then roll on the good news, he thought.

"I'll go straight away," he informed the assistant and without further ado and a lucky break at Penn Station he was on his way to the capital before lunch.

The Library of Congress had always been a magnificent piece of architecture for him and Toto was no stranger to its hallowed halls and contents. Another visit there he considered a pleasure more than a burden of duty. The fact it could hold family secrets up to now under wraps, was all the more reason for hightailing it over to Washington.

Armed with the references, he was escorted to the basement and encountered aisle upon aisle of stored archives. He stood waiting for the steward to retrieve two large ledgers that arrived and were duly opened.

Impatient, he watched as each page was folded back until the relevant page was reached. It revealed statutes on a War Loans ledger issued and entered on the order of General George Washington on behalf of the Continental Independent Army. The assistant read it aloud:

A loan in the amounts of cash and other loans, to the amount of fourteen thousand pounds in gold deposited on the days of February seventeenth, March third, July twenty first and September eleventh in the year seventeen hundred and seventy eight by John Moore II of

19

Moorelands and St. Thomas Parish in the State of South Carolina. Subsequently issued through indents said loans herein specified are by order of Congress, to be considered war loans and repaid with interest until so settled, at six percent per annum...

Some notes pertaining to Revolutionary claims were also found but Toto knew he had what he came for.

He calculated that – one, there was decent money owed the Moore family; two, he felt his fortunes changing before his very eyes and thirdly, it was incumbent on him to track down and realize these 'Moore Millions' awaiting him from his philanthropic forebear.

His whole life had been worth every cent of failure, dead end, calamity, pitfall and disastrous relationship he had journeyed. The bitter pill of divorce from Isabella, his Italian wife, who birthed his estranged son Adrian sweetened.

His mind raced ahead, calculating with utterly insufficient information, the effect of such a windfall. To his credit he checked his mental engine and turned to the library clerk.

"This entry implies a considerable amount to be due to whoever made claim on this IOU, would it not?"

"I'm badly qualified to ascertain that. However notes here do allude to there being reference of this in both the House of Representatives Library and in the House Manuscripts Library in the Capitol itself. To my knowledge it means a qualified authenticity to this claim has been lodged."

"In your opinion, for someone to proceed further would it be best to approach Congress itself?"

"Yes sir, that's an appropriate step to initiate, however the originals are lodged in Charleston, therefore best get hold of those from the Loan Division of the State of South Carolina. This seal copied here dates them as November 15, 1829."

With copies instructed to be sent to him at the Alpha Delta Club in New York, Toto knew Charleston to be the next stop. Toto became a man on a mission. That mission he saw as resolving, in as short order as possible, any poor economic state he presently was forced to cultivate.

He made his way back to the metropolis determined to pay his nephew Willy a long overdue visit.

Wilhelm von Meister, elder son of Toto's sister Leila, was soon to become an important cog in a wheel of fortune Toto saw turning to his advantage.

CHAPTER FIVE

The Trapman family arrived in England in the winter of 1860. The trip was instigated after William Trapman had married his young bride Eliza Rose. His suggestion they honeymoon in Europe reflected the troubled political impasse in America, where Confederate and Union camps momentarily paused for breath in an ever widening rift that would soon, he adjudged, make life unacceptable for him and his new wife.

As the Prussian Consul in Charleston, South Carolina at that time, his movements like many Southerners became the focus of intense government interest. Most everyone suspected of alliances with European interests were carefully monitored, especially as uncertainty around whether European associations favored the Confederate cause more than impartiality, made those such as the Trapmans prime suspects for collusion. Anyone sailing from the States to Europe at that time would have been interpreted as being in the pay of the South and therefore spies.

With great haste and as much covert movement as they could muster, William and Eliza boarded an English ship transporting them on the honeymoon cruise to England.

As newly-weds and in spite of a ten year gap between them, William's besotted affections for his bride cast diplomatic decorum to the four winds, helped by the warm winter breeze greeting them as they stepped aboard the English vessel in Charleston harbor.

The captain, pleased to afford the couple his boat as vessel for their maritime crossing, made sure they were given the best cabin available.

The acting consul had been particularly careful to arrange the drawing down of all his funds. Various property and lands, more difficult to arrange disposal of at short notice, were entrusted to reliable contacts with orders to liquidate them quietly, out of sight of government interest.

His contacts within the Southern Confederacy and their secretive European networks, meant he also carried documents that, if discovered would have certainly proved to Union eyes collusion with the Confederate cause. Securing these and large assets he carried on him, the couple settled for the honeymoon crossing.

Washington, alerted to the consul's plans ordered a detachment of govern-ment officers race to Charleston and attempt boarding the vessel as it made for the open ocean.

Successfully boarding the vessel before it hit full ocean they made it clear the couple masquerading as newly weds were enemy agents.

The captain, no less directly asserted his command declaring as a foreign interest, under a foreign flag and in international waters, they had no jurisdiction. Demanding anything other than leaving the vessel would be considered a violation of international and maritime law. He did, in the spirit of cooperation allow a cursory search.

It was then William discovered hidden qualities his young wife possessed. He witnessed not only her mettle but an undisclosed talent for theatre and masquerade. In later years these traits would bless their offspring with character, creativity and the love of the arts.

For now they would save their skin.

Prior to boarding William had handed Eliza certain papers relating to family and business, some sensitive enough to become a problem if discovered.

Eliza, in her role of spy tucked the apportioned documents discreetly about her person, hidden in voluminous folds of the travelling dress she wore.

As the officers made towards her and her husband, she struck a pose of confident comfort and a display of coquettish frivolity, making full use of her voluptuous nineteen-year-old assets. Settled into a deckchair, with accomplished nonchalance, she placed her feet upon a hassock in front of her. Within this innocent piece of furniture she had earlier placed the collected documents she was unable to hide about her person.

The officers, with considerable embarrassment, tried to carry out their duties. She turned on her charms and sweet approach.

Their embarrassment became their weakest link, provided the captain with a perfect excuse to call a halt to the inspection and allowed crew and passengers witness the government officers leaving the boat empty handed.

So as not to invite further unwelcome interest in his vessel or charges, he ordered full sail for Liverpool and a course etching a future of promise, joy and the complete unknown for both Eliza and William Trapman.

CHAPTER SIX

New York in the late spring of 1928 showed every sign of visualizing the American people's belief they never had it so good. Money was everywhere, overt ostentation and rampant celebration washing away austerities of the previous decade scarred by the bloodiest self-inflicted conflict mankind had experienced. Captain Trapman had left his mark on that conflict by not only having successfully survived the mass slaughter, an achievement in itself, but also, through his love of things technological. His own small mark in history came through mobilizing and proving the effectiveness of bicycles as a potent war asset – noted favorably in the corridors of power.

He reflected on the bicycle's usefulness as he pedaled happily down Broadway to a rendezvous with his cousin Willy von Meister, whose acuity in things financial allowed him to not only settle in New York City but to grow a highly successful business as merchant in an eclectic field of trade.

Willy's mother, Leila, at the turn of the century had married Wilhelm von Meister, close friend and confidante to the Kaiser and a respected military man in his own right.

The love and affection his mother inculcated in the Royal Court of the Kaiser, through her particular beauty, diplomatic graces and to say nothing of her consummate musical talent on piano and guitar, allowed young Willy to surround himself with individuals and groups of such wealth, creativity and connectivity, he came to learn valuable lessons in dealing money, trade and negotiations on both a political and cultural level, something rarely afforded others his age. For Leila, whose own family benefited from a position both as outsiders in a strict Victorian social structure and acceptance into such circles by merit of not being British, such navigation became second nature.

Following the defeat of the German Empire in World War One, Germany's economic collapse and economy brought hyperinflation, chaos and confusion to the country, young Willy saw fit to ask his parents leave to emigrate to the States. Leila, in her wisdom, saw an opportunity she was loathe to let her son miss out on. So Willy arrived in New York in the early months of 1923. When visiting in 1925, his parents witnessed a son making the very most of a decade, literally bursting at the seams with wealth, growth and the precise opposite to what had taken hold back home.

It was this ongoing savvy business acumen that today Toto found

23

irresistible and mesmerizing as he entered his nephew's offices. Plush furnishings, heavy oak and cherry desks for each of the three secretaries he employed, surprised Toto. He was amazed at the treatment of opulence Willy afforded these workers. However it did not end there. The two salesmen Willy engaged, far older than their boss, had separate offices and each of these finely individualized to each one's taste. Willy knew the secret to keeping good men. It was to make their life not only comfortable but also replete with aspiration. So his commitment to bonuses was, if nothing else, thorough. As for his own space, he chose to share it with his naval architect whose sole task was to create and construct vessels to expand the young man's trading base not only across the States but also back into Europe and his roots.

As Toto was ushered into Willy's office, Stafford Jennings, the firm's naval architect excused himself allowing the two men time alone. Noticing his hasty retreat Toto exclaimed.

"Willy, please don't feel Mister Jennings needs to leave on my account."

"Indeed not Captain Trapman," the architect assured the new arrival, "I know from old you two fellows get more done without the added distractions of set squares, rulers and cussing in the background."

"Thank you once again Stafford for your consideration, you're well aware you are considered family under all circumstances, " Willy reminded him.

"I know Willy and most appreciate it, however I'm duty bound, with Rose coming into town, to avail my wallet of its regular sortie administering womanly desires in Bloomingdales."

"Never starve a woman her desires," Toto quipped as Jennings took his leave.

Willy beckoned Toto onto a comfortable leather settee across from his own desk, enjoying his uncle's humor.

"So what do I owe the pleasure of your visit, are the smoky rooms of the press club too choked for you?"

"I have to admit I've spent little time in those steamy rumor mills. I came to bring the news I've finished the book," he announced proudly.

"Well done old man, that's an achievement."

"Less of the old," Toto chided, knowing full well the thirty-three year age difference between them merited the remark.

"I'd have you know," he retorted, "I was in Baghdad before you were even a thought in your dad's bag."

The two men broke into fits of laughter. Family they may have been. Great friends they certainly were.

"So, how can I help you and what's the real reason for your visit today?"

Toto envied and respected in equal measure the sharpness of his nephew's perception. At six foot seven literally he looked up to the young man. Willy's business sense, earned Toto's admiration and hopes to emulate the Young Turk. For now he brought his nephew up to date on the Washington visit, the appearance of a debt owed and asked for advice and assistance to further these ends.

"Absolutely, I've some fine attorneys who'll know just the right people to call upon when the time's right. That's a given. As for information, seems you need to get down to Charleston and sniff around the state legislature."

Toto agreed.

"You're going to need a fair bit of proof one way or another to waken the dormant debt if that's what it turns out to be," his nephew noted astutely.

"I'm going to need all my skills," Toto replied confidently. "The loan's marked down at six percent compound a year until repayment. I'm no math scholar but it could end up to be a tidy sum over a hundred and fifty years."

"Well, certainly worth looking into, that's for sure. However several bridges need crossing before we can reach a meaningful figure," Willy responded with caution.

"Your mother assured me she could rally support as and when in Europe with her aristocratic and political connections" Toto informed him.

"I've several influential folk here very willing to repay not inconsiderable help I've rendered them over the years."

Willy smiled reassuringly. Toto was visibly relieved at how things were developing.

He leaned forward.

"Sun Tzu's advice in The Art of War: *Victorious warriors win first and then go to war, while defeated warriors go to war first and then seek to win.*"

"Well said, forewarned is forearmed. I imagine you're going to need a not inconsiderable stipend to further research and presuming your embarrassment to ask, here's $300 to get the ball rolling."

He pushed the notes across the table.

"Willy that's incredibly generous.

"Take all the time you need. Crucial days ahead and we need to gather the right information. Thankfully you're just the man for the job." Willy replied.

Toto admired his nephew, in spite of his comparative youth. He was up to speed on everything most his age hardly gave a fig for. Toto appreciated the business acumen and prescience his nephew exuded. For Willy payback was making Toto as comfortable as possible in his endeavors, whilst at the same time remaining truly fascinated at his uncle's life experiences. He had a soft spot for an heroic uncle. He was indebted also to the Trapman clan for many connections afforded on his arrival. Without William Trapman's extensive range of business connections in New York and throughout the Eastern and Mid States, Willy would have had to use even more of his business acumen to get him to his present ranking in the business hierarchy of this extraordinary metropolis.

Toto for his part thanked his father for inviting him, as a seventeenth birth-day treat, on one of his several business trips as a merchant, to the States. It sparked an enduring love and admiration for the New World, its potential, possibility and dreams to exploit. All in all he was grateful for the close family bonds, trust and fraternity existing throughout this extended family, some-thing both parents had lived passionately since their own migration from these shores to Europe.

CHAPTER SEVEN

The maiden voyage of the S.S. Lucania in September 1893 from Liverpool to New York carried several noteworthy elements with it including a boatload of economic aristocrats plying their pleasure and business from one side of the ocean to the other in a style parallel to the ostentation and luxury the Cunard Line built into each new and better craft. The macrocosm of life, in this age of Victorian industrial wealth, was mirrored on board through absolute separation in class of travel, as well as purpose. Last ditch attempts breaking free of poverty in Europe, in pursuit of a New World of golden dreams, burned brightly in the consciousness of emigrants holed up in third and fourth class, as much as the diamonds and gold adorning wrists, necks and foreheads of self-made or inherited wealth frequented first class.

Within the bowels of the vessel, an attempt at a new Atlantic speed record held no interest for a newly signed on stoker. He cared nothing for accolades. Having left the shores of the Black Sea and a meaningless life of poverty, raw sweat and toil was the currency he traded to deliver him into the arms of riches and sweet revenge. Many levels above a birthday promise of passage, gifted by his father, was to change a young man's life forever. That both young men were oblivious to their intertwined destinies was an even greater gift for both of them.

William Trapman and son Toto watched as their luggage was swiftly whisked from sight by porters of the line.

Toto's eyes were on stalks, blown away with the commotion, pomp and mayhem making the occasion so memorable.

"I'm so happy to be here," he voiced.

Hardly had the words left his mouth when a gentleman in a fine dark suit with dark blue epaulets hung with discreet gold tassels, gold buttoned jacket and white-gloved hands made his way to their side. With well practised precision he removed his right hand glove and greeted the merchant businessman.

"A pleasure to have you with us today, Mister Trapman. May I invite you and your..."

"My son Albert Henry. He's traveling with me this time," William replied completing the steward's sentence.

The steward smiled and graciously accepting William's generous tone.

Turning to Toto he offered a finely manicured hand to the young man. Toto flushed at the importance of it all.

The head steward's sole charge was the well-being of all first class passengers. As an astute and observant employee he took a keen interest, as well as pride, in recognizing and supplying every febrile need to his well heeled charges. Shaking the young man's hand he could tell he was someone who got his hands dirty rather than dilettante youth. He noted it as commendable.

"Master Albert, a pleasure to meet you."

"My son's a keen follower of new technology, I'm sure you'll allow him a glimpse of the new engine."

"It'll be my pleasure to escort Master Albert on a comprehensive tour of the Lucania."

Below them, an impressive display of horse-drawn carriages, steam transport omnibuses, all kinds of trades vehicles making last minute drops of provisions and essentials, hawkers and dockside traders eager to relieve travelers of their funds bartered on. Others managed last minute purchases for steerage that wheedled their way to a new life.

A massed brass band entertained their imminent departure.

"Look at that party weaving its way through the melee," William pointed out as Toto squinted against the morning sun.

A colorful display of activity caused by the passage of a young man, near his age, sporting a brilliant white travel suit. Alongside him were servants, handlers and four struggling porters, almost crushed under the weight of their charges. Atop the luggage was the largest gift-wrapped box Toto had ever seen.

"What have they got there?"

"Well if I know Neily, it'll be something quite unusual," his father replied.

"You know who it is?" Toto queried, amazed at the breadth of his father's connectivity.

"Oh most certainly, the one and only young Cornelius Vanderbilt, inveterate traveler and collector of rare and mysterious artefacts. No doubt just returned from Paris. I cannot imagine what he found there but I'm sure we'll soon find out. He's not much older than you and if memory serves me he's on his way back to Yale."

"How do you know that?"

"Toto, my connections in Paris warned me this extravert member of a great family was due to be returning on the same ship, so it'll certainly make for an eventful journey. I'll introduce you when things settle down."

Toto was thrilled. He could not believe his luck all these incredible people, events and adventures just stacked up keeping him utterly occupied for the duration of the trip.

What must New York be like if all these characters are swelling the decks to get there?

His imagination was ever ready to over deliver.

"When can we meet him?" Toto demanded.

"In good time young man."

The ship having sailed found both William and Toto comfortably settled in the first class smoking room surrounded by the opulent splendor of an Elizabethan paneled theme featuring a first ever addition on any liner – an open wood-burning fireplace.

They relaxed near the hearth, alongside others mingling, getting used to the comforts the vessel offered. Suddenly the doors opposite swung open and in walked Vanderbilt, alongside a most attractive young woman hanging on his arm. As he sauntered up the room between rows of chairs and tables, his eye automatically fell on the fireplace.

William caught it and stood up. Toto followed suit.

"What a seriously pleasant surprise to have you join us Neily," he acknowledged, as Vanderbilt approached.

Mimicking an aristocratic English accent, Vanderbilt replied.

"My dear Trapman how splendid to see you. Let me introduce my friend, Grace Graham Wilson," the young socialite replied, carefully stepping sideways to fully present his female companion.

Toto was in awe. William, more accustomed to these niceties was politeness itself.

"Miss Wilson, an honor and gracious gift to have travel with us. I marveled at the beauty of our conveyance to New York, yet that pales against the beauty in front of me."

Vanderbilt smiled broadly and turned to address Grace.

"William, my dear, comes from a long line of Prussians brought up to recognize only the most beautiful aspects of life and the first to acknowledge them."

"I see that." Grace responded with a wicked smile, addressing William directly.

She found it hard to contain her amusement.

"So William, my dear new Prussian friend, I'm honored to be likened to an ocean liner, albeit an even more beauteous spectacle."

Toto flushed with embarrassment for his father as much as for his own shock of interpretation.

29

His father however delicately approached Grace, took her hand and bowed.

"The architecture of each could not be more different, yet beauty is in the eye of the beholder and yours blows everything else out of the water."

Grace loved the flattery.

"I'm happy," William continued, "to see young Neily has understood an unalienable truth. There's so much more to wealth than mere dollars and gold and I rejoice he's found a veritable Eldorado in you."

Turning to Vanderbilt, she remarked.

"Neily, you're blessed with wonderful friends."

She turned to include Toto in her remark making him blush again.

William invited Vanderbilt to join them.

"Now tell us about the other jewels you found in Paris."

"Be aware our little excursion was undercover and secret," the young socialite disclosed.

William smiled.

"When have you ever managed to keep anything undercover, with the press you carry and as for secrets you well know that is our business!"

Vanderbilt ushered Grace toward a chair Toto discreetly pulled forward. He looked up at William's son and offered his hand.

"Happy to introduce myself: Cornelius Vanderbilt – well Neily to my friends – and since I consider your father one please follow suit."

Toto smiled and shook hands. His desire to equally impress caught him out as he replied.

"A friendship gladly received and reciprocated. Albert Henry William Trapman, though my friends, at least my family that is, call me Toto. An honor to make your acquaintance, Mister Vanderbilt, I mean Neily," he stammered.

"The pleasure's all mine, Albert."

"Please, call me Toto, since we're now friends," the young man insisted.

"Toto it is then."

Something in Toto told him this would become someone he could definitely get on very well with. The same devil may care attitude around elite circles.

"How remiss," Neily interjected. "May I introduce you to Grace."

Grace, already sitting, leaned forward in the chair as Toto took a step towards her. He bowed gracefully and put out his hand. She offered hers and receiving it, he lent forward and lightly kissed it. He learned fast from his father's chivalry.

She withdrew it with decorum as a slight grunt emanated from his father's chair behind. He straightened immediately. Neily brokered the moment.

"William, your son has caught the Prussian gallantry we hear so much about. Are you certain he's no Hussar?"

They all laughed uproariously.

"You must have picked up a lot more than sand from our French holidays, young man." William quipped.

As lunch was called, Vanderbilt ordered champagne for all and announced his birthday would be celebrated on board. Toto beamed.

"It's mine as well," he cried.

"Well that seals the bond," Neily chimed.

Toto got his trip round the ship. The purser escorting him below revealed the throbbing heart to the Line's latest technology.

Men sweated away with shovels, spanners, mopping rags and brawn to maintain the ship at high speed and serious progress. Toto felt embarrassed passing lines of stokers shoveling feverishly. The contrast between the Englishman's suit and naked torsos and belted pants heightened his awkwardness.

Had it not been for the inattention of one stoker whose shovel load lost balance and rhythm, the young visitor would have passed unnoticed. The ensuing collision of passenger and worker drew anger from the purser, embarrassment from Toto and an unwanted incident for the Line.

"Damned inexperience," the foreman cried out in German as he weighed into the debacle. "Get off and put your back into work."

The young German-speaking stoker looked at the foreman with such disdain and hatred; Toto felt moved to apologize. He quickly dispelled it, seeing the hatred shot at him from the man.

"It's my fault I'm sure," he pleaded in his best German.

His fence mending carried little weight.

"No sir, these people come here to work for free passage. There's no blame on your part."

Turning to the stoker he shouted to pull himself together and continue.

It made Toto again most uncomfortable to see cold clear, vengeful spite shining through the stoker's eyes. He shivered and moved on as quickly as possible.

The laborer resumed his toil, cursing the weakness the wealthy carried, vowing his life one day would show the true power money and its force could wield.

Preparing for the Vanderbilt birthday bash, William looked into the mirror of the closet adjoining their cabin. He caught himself smiling at the thought of how proud his own father would have been witnessing his grandson.

Toto poked his head around the door, as his fingers wrestled hopelessly with his wing collar.

"Why are these things so dashed difficult to manipulate," he sighed as his frustration got the better of him. "I never seem to get the hang of studs, collar and shirt all lining up."

"Lack of a good private school education, young man." William grinned looking at the helpless youth, reveling in his toil and trouble.

"Look Papa, it's too cruel to just stand there and laugh at my plight. Surely you could show me how I can do this once and for all."

"You reminded me of a similar time I had with Grandpa."

"So you know how humiliating it is to be so at sea with this."

Toto caught his own pun and burst into laughter. William joined him.

"If that's how the evening starts, I reckon we're in for a good night," Toto replied.

Straightening his son's collar, adjusting the shirt, he stepped back and admired his offspring.

"I'm very proud of you ," he began, meeting his son's gaze, "and, like your mother, we've always held the highest hopes for you. I have no favorites among you all. It's that I believe you, of all our children, have a special calling and gift."

Toto stood silently before his father.

"I want to present something to you, to keep, carry and when blessed with your own, pass on. It's something handed down to me by my father and by his before him."

Toto felt honored and allowed his father continue.

"Our family as representatives of the Prussian people, in the capacity of consul elect have honored that privilege through bearing this token. It's a mark of our responsibility to not only Prussians but the world. A symbolic representation marking our endeavors toward the goal of harmony, peace and understanding of all peoples, cultures and races. As ambassadors for our emperor, we represent equally an ambassadorship of a greater empire, humanity. It's why, as a family, we're blessed to live beyond constraints, norms and expectations so many societies impose. We're outsiders. We enjoy freedom many are utterly unaware of, yet equally crave. It's the freedom of spirit beyond religious constraints, the freedom developed through understanding we're all ultimately one stock, one body, one being."

Toto allowed the words to flow through him as if they were his very life-blood. He accepted them as parched earth accepts a longed for shower in the heat of summer. It triggered the realization as to why he chose to be here. His whole body radiated happiness.

Turning to the desk beside him, William opened a small oak draw under the left side of the table and drew out a long, thin box, plain and undistinguished. Turning back, he flicked a small clasp and proceeded to lift the lid. Toto remained spellbound. His curiosity wanted to lean over and see behind the lid hiding the contents. His father caught his expectation. Looking down on the symbol of continuity, he slowly picked it up between his thumb and forefinger. Lifting it beyond the lid, Toto caught sight of a small rounded silver coin held within a thin silver design, connected to a stubby, silken ribbon whose colors had faded with age. The heirloom folded into William's upturned palm as he presented it to his son. Toto noticed the silver medallion had an engraved symbol etched into it with words embossed around it.

He lifted it from his father's palm and looked closer. Around the edge of the coin was an inscription in Latin. The design holding all this comprised three interlaced and pointed ovals. The symmetry of the object fascinated Toto.

"It's beautiful father, a perfect design."

The young man examined the piece and turned it gently in his palm.

"I can just about make out the inscription," he turned it again to catch the light and began to read.

Fax mentis incendium gloriae lux ergo liber sum.

Toto lifted the piece and looked across to his father.

"Within the passion of glory lies the torch of mind whose light is freedom."

Toto was in awe at the inscription. His father marveled at the young man's classical prowess. Stepping forward he took his upturned hand in his. It would be many years before Toto became aware of the true significance of the inscription.

"What's it really mean, father?"

"That, young man, is something you'll come to learn one day as I did and those that came before us have done. I'll offer you this much – once you come to understand the meaning of the triquetra, which is the symbol holding the inscription, its meaning reveals itself."

In his impatient youthful exuberance Toto wanted a fuller explanation, yet knew his father well enough to know that would not happen, so he did the next best thing.

He guessed.

"All for one and one for all?"

William laughed.

"Too much Dumas methinks. But let's say you're on your way, as we should be, if we're to get to the party on time."

The following morning on the quayside of New York harbor, a boatload of newly acquainted friends, hardened travelers and excited seekers after a new life made their separate ways having disembarked. No one noticed, from a lower deck exit, the hurried escape of a young stoker relinquishing his labors of seaboard sweat. He carried a small suitcase, wore a presentable suit and polished leather shoes. Neither would they have associated or credited him with being party to having delivered them all there in the fastest crossing time the Line succeeded in achieving.

He in turn cared nothing, if that was the case. His sights were set on a determined path to wealth, at whatever cost. An end to generational poverty born into back in Europe. Sweeping past an extravagant river of fur, fuss and frivolity he vowed vengeance and his own forced entry into this elite.

Toto, distracted by a welcoming brass band's rendition of Sousa's Liberty Bell, turned. He recognized the features of the stoker he had bumped into in the engine room and felt a similar shiver to one experienced back in Liverpool catching sight of two shady disappearing men in black on the quayside. The lively march diverted him dwelling on the connection, as the stoker disappeared into a crowded quay.

CHAPTER EIGHT

Armed with funds from Willy, Toto landed himself in Charleston on what turned out to be a relatively comfortable summer's day more akin to temperate English weather than the southern states.

His mission: to seek out records of the Moore family and the provenance of the loans John Moore looked to have made to George Washington and the Revolutionary Army whilst holed up at Valley Forge. The assistant at the Library of Congress had suggested he try the Loan Division for the appropriate papers. That was a good move in a day or two but for now he wanted to contact Mabel Webber who he had corresponded with.

Mabel Webber was the much-respected editoress of the South Carolina Historical and Genealogical Magazine. Her research abilities were legendary and as Secretary to the South Carolina Historical Society, Toto knew he could fast track a lot of investigation with such a professional.

It was not long before he found himself at the door of 88 Beaufain Street in Charleston. The impressive two storey twenty-year-old house exuded Southern chic. As a townhouse Toto loved its feel and if he could have transported it back to England and a favorite plot he had earmarked beside the Thames, then he would be a happy man. But for now his knock on the door brought Miss Webber, a studious yet kindly looking lady to the door.

"Captain Trapman, how nice to meet you after all our correspondence. Do come in. I've set up some tea on the veranda," she informed him at the same time as beckoning him through a narrow corridor towards the side room, opening onto a veranda, looking over the garden.

"I've done some research as you instructed and have come up with some very interesting information that we can discuss over a cup of tea."

Toto felt at home here, away from the bustle of the New York sidewalks and frenetic business centers.

"How very thoughtful of you to help my acclimatization into the South with some English tea, Miss Webber."

"Please call me Mabel, Captain and though tea is the preferred brew of you English folk, we here in the South throw it back as men do their whiskey!"

Toto smiled.

"Such a pleasure to share with someone as knowledgeable as yourself Albert and I know we'll have great fun working on this together."

"We shall," Toto agreed. " What are your views, if any, on the whereabouts of indents existing on the loan I wrote you about. The one John Moore made to the Revolutionary Army."

"Ah, yes. Most interesting that and what a benevolent man your forebear was. How timely to get the whole movement out of what would have become certain defeat from lack of funds and a demoralized army. I personally hold this whole period dear to my heart, so when you furnished me with all the details, I can tell you I took an inordinate time away from other matters to look into it more."

Toto deeply impressed with her devotion, felt guilt over her time and ensuing costs.

"Now I don't want you worrying about my time. This is such a pleasure for me I can promise you whatever time it takes."

"That's most generous. You have my gratitude." Toto acknowledged, relieved there would be no extra expenses.

"Well I've not been wholly truthful with you, Albert as I've been helped quite considerably by someone you'd love to meet."

Toto's sensors pricked up.

Interesting, he noted.

Thoughts of an aged professor of history filled his mind, along the librarian model he worked with in New York. Hopefully he would turn out less two dimensional than the assistants, dusting off a few volumes for him, over the last months.

"Luckily, just before you arrived, my helper popped in and needed to study some reference material I have. Let me get you two together. Stay seated, I'll only be a moment."

Toto imagined how with all this help he could be done here in Charleston in a couple of days. Eager as he was to advance his investigations, he wondered how he could further this resource.

Looking across the lawn he daydreamed possibilities. Marveling at the lush richness around the house, the ample wildlife and bird song filling the warm morning air, an intrepid mouse boldly shot across the lawn on a mission to a far bush, for cover and rest. He enjoyed the peace emanating from this spot and felt he could have been back at Riverdene, his brother Louis' country house in England. It was all a long way away. Mabel's caring nature reminded him of mother Eliza and made him homesick. The intrepid rodent's progress brought him back, yet in no way prepared him for what happened next.

A shrill song from a bird in a nearby tree drew his attention. He searched, discovered a loggerhead shrike, resplendent in black, white and brown plumage, celebrating another excellent day in song. The bird song stopped, the creature's head tilted as its interest fell on the mouse's progress. Toto observed. The bird flew off the branch and in no time at all swooped down on the unsuspecting rodent, violently spearing it with its beak, collecting it in its claws and flying off. The mouse knew nothing as the shrike knew breakfast had been served. Toto shocked at the violence he witnessed, felt blood run from his face. In spite of witnessing atrocities far greater in the trenches during the war, something about this cruelty behind beauty triggered trepidation and horror. How was it such frailty and beauty could turn to such violence.

It was Mabel's return to the veranda that brought him back. His expression of shock, as he turned to acknowledge the new arrival was accentuated at what greeted him.

"Albert, meet Anne Gregorie, my assistant. Anne, this is Captain Albert Trapman, who sent us the notes on his forebear."

Toto cleared his throat and clumsily offered his hand.

"A pleasure to meet you," he managed, hurriedly covering his emotional tracks.

The shrike's offensive unsettled him enough to be lost for words, as much as being presented a woman in her late thirties, unquestionably attractive, flowing auburn hair and eyes to pierce his very soul.

"I see you've already witnessed the bloody jaws of nature in the heart of the urban tranquility of Charleston," Anne replied, noticing the Captain's pallor.

"I'm sorry – I don't follow you," Toto responded lost traveling a sad and misty road in his past.

"You've just witnessed the tender looking shrike go for the kill as we came out. A good example of the apparently harmless turning swiftly into the hunter," she added for clarification.

To compound his shock he faced a woman, considerably attractive with eyes sharp as the beak freshly executing its dark art, showing a perceptive acuity the like of which he never witnessed.

"You saw that?" he asked incredulously.

"Well of course, how else can I interpret your ashen look at meeting me, I hope it's nothing to do with my looks," she teased.

Unfortunately his train of thought completely missed her lighthearted response landing full center as an observational truth. He felt as mortally wounded as the poor mouse yet for the life of him it made no sense.

How was it, he screamed inside, *this southern belle whose sharp eye would have matched any sniper in the trenches, had compounded the terror he'd witnessed?*

Grossly out of proportion to reality, all he heard and saw in front of him was Louise, his childhood love who broke his heart. He found sufficient presence of mind to answer her question.

"Well no, of course not... I mean you look well... I've not seen... You're very pleasing to the eye for someone expecting to see a retired professor of history," he finally blurted out, with an honesty he never contrived to release.

"Now that's a relief, Captain," the assistant replied, as she took hold of a third chair and sat down.

Toto remained standing, as much in shock as stunned surprise at the sharpness of the woman.

"The history part you got right Albert, the retired part is far from happening as Anne is currently working on her doctorate."

"With my master's under my belt I'm looking to complete my doctorate in history. Interested in all things historical, when Mabel asked me to help her out with your little puzzle, I saw its potential and didn't hesitate." Anne confirmed.

"Please sit," encouraged Mabel ushering a transfixed Toto resume his seat. He did so and instinctively went to lift his teacup.

"I see from the little I've unearthed on this John Moore, your ancestor, he lived part time in Saint Thomas Parish."

"He did indeed," replied Toto, feeling the settling influence of the tea.

"A mere twelve miles from here as the crow flies or even the shrike, if it's hungry," Anne could not resist adding.

Toto caught the humor and relaxed more.

"I'd planned to go visit, see if records were worthwhile," he suggested.

"We had the same idea," added Mabel. "There are several places of interest there."

"I might suggest," Anne added, "I accompany Albert up to the Mooreland plantation and we can gather all the information we find and correlate it into the report."

Without hesitation Toto agreed and they both decided to take the train the following day.

Miss Webber, never one to admit consummate match-making skills, felt the two younger partners in this teamwork would get along admirably in the field. Professionally confident, anything else was far too early a call, even to her trained eye.

CHAPTER NINE

Toto's childhood had been fertile grounds for developing adult imagination, an adventurous spirit and reckless dreaming. Inept dealings and failures in romance could never be laid at the door of his first wife, whose desertion and abandonment of their only child Adrian he had instigated by fleeing to South America after the war. To face his own truths, ghosts and emotional baggage must entail a journey back to his relationship with Louise Pointeau, whose connection to his family got triggered by the death of her father, whilst holed up with William Trapman, during the Prussian Siege of Paris in 1870.

A long-standing agreement between the two men noted if anything happened to Michel, William would take her in and raise her as his own. The bloody, brutal and complex situations both William and Michel faced during the siege made the latter's journeys around the city dangerous yet essential. As a Prussian in Paris, alongside the besieged and starving French, William cut a curious figure. An anomaly Toto would come to understand many years later.

The most valuable currency in a starving city is food. William held a king's ransom stock of ham. One such side of ham became responsible for Michel's untimely demise at the hands of fellow Parisians. They literally killed for something to eat. True to his word William took Louise into the family.

After Toto's birth, she was given companion and nursemaid duties around the growing child. By her eighteenth birthday she found her duties keeping her young ward occupied as a delight and preoccupation. She enjoyed his imaginative, lively and inquisitive nature. She saw much of her own patterns reflected in him. Toto equally had developed a love and affection for his half sister, that all accepted as sibling fondness.

It was an event in early May of 1887 that Toto, in spite of tender years, was to experience a new dimension, initiating a chain reaction that was to carry profound consequences forward.

Louise easily accepted Toto's connection with his inner world. It mirrored her own ways of dealing with her life tragedies.

He, for his part, adored her, always feeling safe and secure around her. Over the years their relationship bonded ever closer. Many hours of mutually silent shared companionship sealed confidences and trust.

Having related the real reason for her presence in the family, a secret never shared, and her father's tragic end, they sat beside the River Stour coursing its way through the family's Suffolk home. Toto watched a lazy line cast to trap an unwary trout, reflecting on her story. She, her back towards the water, played with the wild flowers and grasses. Suddenly falling backward, she bowled him over and the two of them tumbled and rolled towards the river bank.

Louise, hands full of grasses, let them fall all over his face. Instinctively he grabbed her blouse to prevent them both ending up in the river. Louise rolled back in the opposite direction, taking him with her. Coming to a halt with her on top, she smiled and their eyes met.

Hers sparkled as the river deposited multitudes of reflected diamond droplets into them. He felt joy pour from them. Her look of frolic melted into incandescent softness. It took him back to the warmth and memory of his mother's breast, the most natural feeling of association he could imagine. Louise caught the feeling and accepted it as offering silent assent in that shared moment.

She let the brunette waves of her unrestrained locks tumble across his face, pursuing the wild grasses. Inevitably her lips followed.

Long familiarity of each other never overtly conceived an intimacy fast approaching in that moment. Yet in no way did it feel anything other than the most natural response for them both. He felt her soft breath on his cheeks, as she offered tender lips. He instinctively received them with an awareness transcending his age.

Flooded with completeness and memories of something indefinable yet true, the kiss shared sealed an ancient promise. Catching the scent of juniper dancing between them, an heroic pulse made his youthful heart miss a beat. A split second of eternity held its breath as they held theirs, before both rolled over and lay silent, complete, beside each other in the long grass.

The magic of Toto's first kiss carried itself with him into the family's regular summer holiday in Dinard.

For almost fifteen years they gathered in this popular resort on the north coast of France. Toto at eleven could not have been happier having his brothers and sisters, including Louise, keep him company at the rented villa they always returned to. One evening Toto, Louis and Arthur were walking along the sea front. Louise had taken time to meet with friends.

The three brothers joked and swaggered along the front with the dusk of a late July evening bathing the resort in a magnificent orange glow. The sun, having set a few minutes earlier, encouraged a display of ever changing, deepening hues of color across the sky. Glass in the windows along the villas lining the strand took it in turns to reflect this natural palette.

They stopped and gazed at the spectacle.

"Just magnificent," Louis uttered.

"Like someone brushed the whole horizon with a golden stroke," Arthur admired.

"We missed the green flash, though," Louis replied with a tone of sadness.

"Green flash? What's that?" Toto asked.

"Ah!," sighed Arthur. "An enigma, that one. It's said if you watch the horizon closely at sunset, you can see, the very moment the sun sets, a green flash appear as quickly as it disappears."

"How's that?" Toto asked eagerly, shifting himself closer to Arthur.

"Flashes for an instant then it's gone. Blink and you miss it."

Louis looked at his brother.

"And you dear brother, missed it."

"Louis that's not fair, you would have done the same had you been as distracted by the beauty brushing passed me."

"What beauty?" asked a mystified Toto.

Louis leaned over to his youngest brother and wrapping his arm round the boy's shoulder hugged him reassuringly.

"Your brother Arthur's infatuation with a dancer on a boat trip."

"Did they kiss?" Toto asked.

"Yes and more, but there's a path to reckless endeavor and your brother took it with this siren."

Toto was intrigued.

He saw an opportunity.

" I can tell you about a girl's kiss."

Both brothers looked at the child, then at each other. Both raised eyebrows.

"You do?" they replied in unison.

"They've soft lips and smell sweet as juniper."

Toto felt himself grow in stature revealing, to his elders a secret, having never before passed his lips.

"Soft lips, by George," Arthur repeated admiringly.

"Yes soft and beautifully rounded."

"Rounded?" Louis responded.

"Rounded and beautifully soft even," Toto repeated as he drifted back to the moment of his amorous enlightenment.

His brothers realized Toto must have passed a youthful rite of passage.

"Now that, dear Toto is cause for celebration, is it not brother?" Louis asked, turning to his brother.

Arthur nodded. "Indeed it is. Toto, you've taken our breath away with such an admission, so all that remains is to welcome you into a very select club of three we've now become. What d'ya say to that, young man?"

"Club of three, what's that?" the initiate enquired.

"The FKC. The First Kiss Club, where only those admitting their first kiss are welcomed as honored members."

Arthur and Louis stepped up to their brother and either side of him, locked arms and swept the boy off his feet, proceeding to march off down the promenade towards the casino.

Toto felt pride brighten his whole being unlike the sweeping deepening purple dusk now giving way to starlight and a gathering half moon.

He could not have been happier. In the arms of his two heroes whisked away to manhood and a future including the love of his life. He was complete and utterly at one, with his brothers and with the one who had brought him this moment of bliss.

Gazing up at the sky above, the heavens stretched beyond the horizon.

Each star came close and touched him. He let himself merge into the bold constellation of Hercules imagining how this warrior felt as he slew his old victim Draco, slithering across the sky to the north, grateful his father had taught them the names of the stars. He reveled in it.

Swinging, supported between two warrior brothers, this young hero felt strong and secure. Casting his eye towards Virgo he wondered where his beloved Louise was at that moment. He so wished to share his feelings with her.

Yes, he thought, Virgo is truly my beloved Louise.

At that moment his brothers swung him higher bringing Toto back to the present.

"Stop!"

His cry taking both of them by such surprise, by its volume and suddenness, they nearly dropped him there and then.

"Stop, you two," Toto repeated.

With a thud they brought him back onto his two feet.

Toto's five foot two inches perfectly aligned itself between the two towering six foot plus proportions either side. They walked towards the town center.

In the shadow of a nearby building a couple of young lovers took advantage of the warm evening completely oblivious to the three men.

As they approached, Louis, with English propriety and Victorian sensitivity, steered them avoid this intimate scene.

Arthur ribbed his brother.

"Moral Louis. Where's the man about town in you?"

"Come, Arthur," chaffed Louis," I'm no Brick Lane voyeur, and anyway these French have a right to their amorous activities with a little privacy."

"Of course old chap, it's just I couldn't help noticing what a fine filly she was even from here."

"Judging the rump, brother, as usual," Louis regaled. "What will it take to teach you finer points?"

Heading away, Toto could not resist glancing at the couple in the shadows.

As he caught a glimpse of the two, the girl turned, catching an inference of their presence. Her face briefly caught the gaslight.

Toto felt embarrassed caught looking. For a brief moment their eyes met.

Toto's life stopped. His heart froze. He felt something precious drain from his being. An eternity passed before he could turn away avoiding the nightmare witnessed.

Louis quipped his brother was learning too much, too fast. His voice echoed a million miles away. Toto registered nothing. All he felt was a hollow, vacant, deathly void. Its provenance cut him to the quick.

His complexion, indistinguishable in the dark, paled to a sickening hue. The two giants either side of him became chimera in a canyon beyond reach. The lonely and cold place growing inside him screamed separation, aloneness and loss running the gauntlet of fear across his heart and into his soul.

His brothers missed all Toto experienced. The unmistakable eyes he caught belonged to Louise and they crashed into his confused consciousness, shattering his core.

How could such beauty become such a voracious predator to his heart and very existence, he thought over and over.

It felt like the lion slaughtering the lamb.

The kiss beside the Stour loomed, chasing his love into hell. Toto turned and ran. He belted back to the villa then veered off towards the beach and the cover of darkness. Racing down to the sand, his feet hit the soft sand and threw him into its gritty grasp. He rolled over and over, convulsed in pain, stopping short of the advancing tide.

He lay on his back broken-hearted. Deep, heavy sobbing gave full vent to sorrow as the breaking waves reflected the boy's broken heart.

The constellation of Virgo blurred through tears streaming down his tortured face. It felt like they were washing away every memory of beauty and happiness accrued in one short and joyful life. His head sank deeper into the sand and as if taunting him, the elongated form of Draco burnt itself onto his vision through watery, salty sadness.

He felt the hero in him defeated, pierced through the heart and cursed. The Dragon's twinkling form winked cruelly at his fate.

He was bitterly alone, forlorn.

The rising tide, in an act of cleansing, swept up and over his feet and legs. He involuntarily pulled them away too late. Cursing waterlogged shoes instinctively he blamed Louise for his plight.

Horrified at his own venom, he loved her, hated her, loved her, he knew not what. He wished it all disappear to wake from this nightmare, in his warm bed, sun pouring in and she welcoming him to a new day together.

He closed his eyes. Perhaps it was not Louise.

He jumped up and rushed to the house.

Mounting the stairs, the back door to the pantry opened silently as Louise re-entered from her night off. Cut short, knowing full well a catastrophe had befallen young Toto spotting her.

On her way to her room, Toto's door was ajar. She glimpsed him turn from the long mirror, in his pajamas, unable to reach her door before his opened and he burst onto the landing.

His joy at seeing her disarmed her, caught her off balance.

"I'm so happy to see you, Louise. "

Louise careful with her reply was now uncertain whether Toto had been the one she saw earlier.

"Just got in. What have you been doing?"

"We walked along the beach," Toto related, anguish easing.

" You?"

Louise paused too long, her face betraying awkwardness. His feelings re-injected with poison.

"Met a friend," she answered attempting casual.

"Friend?"

"Yes, Hervé."

Toto remembered the boy. He had been there when they played tennis.

He'd noticed the boy's interest in her.

"Was he with Mathilde and Florence, then?" Toto asked, hoping the young man's sisters were with them.

"No, we met alone," Louise committed.

Toto visibly blanched.

Her plan to tell him in the morning was falling apart.

His heart sank for the second time that night. Foreboding overtook him.

"Let's talk about it," she said beckoning his open doorway.

"Talk about what," Toto asked, not wanting to know the truth.

Louise led him into his room.

"Come, sit down," she indicated, pulling up a chair.

"Talk about what?" he repeated.

"Tonight," she replied.

Toto felt dread expectation turn to solid leaden certainty.

"Hervé and I have been seeing each other regularly. We're very fond of each other. Can you understand?"

Understand? he thought, *what is there to understand — betrayal, desertion and mortal wounds inflicted?*

"Understand you've tricked me?" he burst out. "Understand you love someone else?"

Louise saw the dam bursting as the boy's tender heart cracked.

"It wasn't meant to be so..."

"Not meant to be. Yet you held him, kissed him, love him and... and...."

"I love him as I love you," she implored.

"How can you, how can you love both of us? You and I are special, you told me, you told me," he repeated feeling hurt, disappointment and anger rising all at the same time.

Unable to decide which took priority, he was left floundering in emotion.

"I love you Toto as a sister loves a brother."

Toto looked at her with incredulity.

"Like a brother?" he asked. "Like a brother kissed on the lips?"

Louise suddenly realized a moment of depth and tenderness beside the river had changed their relationship from Toto's point of view irrevocably, raising it to a level of commitment a young woman some eight years older than he ought to have been aware of. Her act of intimacy became a misjudgment whose repercussions had potential to destroy a fragile young heart and scar a life.

Never her intention she scoured her heart to mitigate damage.

"You'll always be my dearest friend."

Toto looked up as if she had just told him she died. Her eyes filled with tears. His did likewise. He wrestled to stop his own dam bursting first.

It was the first time he consciously cut his emotional response. It was the hardest act of control he ever felt.

He heard himself reply.

"You're no friend, Louise, you lied to me. You've deceived me."

The bitterness in his voice cut her like a dagger.

"That's not true. We've always been friends. We share our secret world."

"Secret world? Secrets you take to Hervé. No, we no longer have secrets."

Toto felt distraught, his childhood quarterized with avenging anger.

"How can you say that Toto? They were ours and ours alone. You're the only one sharing them with me. That's how it'll always be...."

"Until you share them with him," he interrupted her.

"Never."

"Never, like our friendship," he fired back, unable to utter the word love.

"Toto, that's not fair," she pleaded.

"None of this is fair," he cried. "You've betrayed me. I can't forgive you."

Louise felt tears bursting from within. Her father's loss flooded back, the futility in finality. Despair drove a wedge of fury between what once was beauty.

"Now you're being overdramatic," she reminded him desperately.

He was in no mood for conciliation. He took it upon himself, protecting the last vestiges of a broken heart, to pull back from any more emotional engagement.

Standing up he looked at her directly.

"I'm tired Louise and want to sleep. It's enough. Go!"

His voice shuddered and reverberated within her. It was a voice of another class. The tone of a learnt way of interaction presiding over a particular social division. A bell tolled for her. The death knell on a life she knew she must now leave.

Shattered she stood and fixed Toto in the eye one last time.

"I'm so sorry, I never meant it to be like this. In spite of what you feel now, I'll always love you."

Toto looked at her. Behind his tears he glimpsed a dissolving dream. Yet something within reassured all was very well. It assuaged anger and bitterness, yet his own sense of self recognized finality. A moment defining inner turbulence and mistrust of women.

Toto's world in its shattering expanded; an expansion rushing headlong toward him like stampeding elephants. The dreamer forced to integrate or alienate the world around him.

CHAPTER TEN

South Carolina produced a delicious summer morning. Toto's arrival at the railroad station in lightweight cotton trousers, short-sleeved shirt and sports jacket had been spot on. He awaited Anne's arrival, pleased with his sartorial decision.

Her appearance in a summer dress confirmed his decision as well as illustrate his companion to be even more attractive than he remembered from the previous day. He tried hard convincing himself it was just a trick of the light until she came right up to him at the ticket office with her long slender neck coyly inviting the full flowing carefully brushed sweep of auburn hair around to one side of it. It had the effect of lengthening an already slender neckline. Her full, perfectly formed lips puckered slightly as she hugged the files she held in her right arm. Those lips held a memory from way back. The over attention he gave to the pressure exerting on her breast made him create a swift distraction to his wallet.

Convinced her sharp eyes caught this overlong gaze he hoped it was too early in the day for her skills to be fully operational.

She was no amateur and took his attentions as flattering.

Well, she told herself, *he's an attractive military man.*

She then surprised him.

"Luckily I persuaded a good friend to allow us use of his four wheels, so step outside and a fine example of Mister Ford's best will get us there."

She was not kidding he thought, as he was presented the latest four-door variety of the Model T.

Although failing to have informed Toto of her consummate organization skills he remained impressed at the whole turn of events.

"Women drive here too?" Toto remarked as they set on their way.

"You bet. A Southern girl needs to be prepared for anything," Anne quipped.

"And that you certainly are."

"Do the women drive in England in these emancipated times?" Anne asked.

"It's catching on. Seems what starts here ends up there."

They both laughed.

"It's taken the heady twenties to unleash their undoubted power onto the road and hopefully into the boardroom."

"Steady on, getting behind the wheel and in front of the board are two very different places with many hurdles between them, not least of them, us men. There's also much to point against the merits of women in places of power."

Rather than feeling slighted Anne took the challenge head on.

"Really Albert, and what do you feel they might be?"

"For a start, the resistance of the status quo."

"Well said, and what else?"

"Are they man enough to hack it?"

"In the biological sense, impossible. However from the point of view of character, totally."

Toto warmed to the character Anne revealed, feeling there might be more than just mutual, professional interests working here.

"Are you as feisty as this with everyone," he dared ask.

"Mostly everyone, except my tutors at University who always take me for a woman rather than the serious historian I am. My thesis on Gamecock Sumter will teach them a thing or two."

Toto was impressed. He knew Sumter's nickname from research.

"Sumter's one huge hero of mine. What a life, what a man."

Anne lit up.

"His life's incredible. Great adventurer, fearless of the new, undiscovered, uncharted ways. His trip into Cherokee territory."

"Meeting Ostenaco, the Indian he broke himself financially to bring over to meet King George." Toto added.

"What a hare-brained idea that was! The impulse of it. Then all you English went crazy over the Indians with the great Joshua Reynolds painting him. I love that man's work." Anne enthused with passion.

"Reynolds?"

"Yes, I've painted since a young girl, as a hobby you understand, but all the same I love it."

Their trip to Mooreland was turning into a revelation for Toto. Here was a woman, her own person, an artist and researcher, knowledgeable, passionate and as adventurous as he could ever imagine.

He recognized many similarities with Sumter in himself, especially the near penniless state in which he arrived back in South Carolina. Rubbing far too close to home he decided to take these thoughts no further.

"Our Carolina Gamecock," Anne said drawing the conversation back to Sumter, "rose swiftly through the ranks during the Revolutionary War. Moore must have known him since he was Brigadier General of the South Carolina militia."

"Moore gave his huge gift to the cause in seventy-eight and nine, therefore the South Carolina Line must have benefited some way or other," suggested

Toto.

"Washington used a lot of that money to re-equip the troops at Valley Forge, then help Colonel Greene down here," Anne shared.

The talk of Sumter kept the two of them occupied until they had reached their first destination.

Both adroit and efficient, it was not long before Toto unearthed the will of John Moore. What they wanted were references to, better still, indents proving the Revolutionary gift Moore made of $14,000 in gold was real.

Not hitting the jackpot, they acknowledged a quest involves a lot of digging for a small nugget. They headed off to the Parish Church.

They arrived as the verger was leaving. He stopped as they drew up and got out to meet him.

"We're looking for records you may hold," Anne begun, "for the Moores of Mooreland. Do you hold files helping our search for family records?"

"How interesting you ask. The name's very familiar," the verger replied happily. "Clearing out the vestry the other day I came upon references to a John Elias Moore. It referred to a place in the vault which evidently was reserved for his family effects."

"Can we visit the vault?" Toto asked, sensing a great lead.

"Not possible."

"Why?" Toto inquired.

"Because it's been sealed for over a hundred years. I've never heard of anyone getting into it."

Toto's disappointment was apparent.

About to suggest they head home, an old man, looking every bit the part of a slave-encrusted ancient bard, appeared from behind the church. With a stoop in his weary body earned from a lifetime of toil, he slowly made his way towards the group, with the aid of an old, well-worn, beautifully carved walking stick. As he reached them, the verger turned to meet Old Abe.

"Just the man!"

Abe looked happy to be recognized. Not quite hitting his hundredth year, Old Abe, as he was locally known, was renowned for his acute memory. Many swore him to be closer to two hundred. The two researchers smiled sure this walking ancient might hold the golden key to their day's search.

"These good folk all the way from Charleston are asking after a John Moore. We think he used to have a family locker in the vault, do you recall?"

Old Abe looked across at Toto and Anne and with a wicked look only the oldest and wisest men could elicit and answered.

"You young chillun looking for Master John? Good man he was and proud."

Toto wondered if the old man's wits were still intact. He could have hardly been around and known Moore personally.

"S'pose you think I lost my mind?" he rebutted, picking up Toto's thought.

And without waiting for a reply continued.

"Folks round here all tell of the generous nature of the man, though before our time, feel we know him personal from tales told."

That made better sense and they waited for a pearl to fall from the ancient lips.

"Yassir, John Elias were a good man. Loved us niggers, like family, contrary to others was treating us. Abraham, his son black as I, yet his beloved alright."

"Fascinating," Toto whispered to Anne.

Old Abe continued.

"When he sent Abraham to bury the treasures, were a sad day. Got ambushed by red coats. John Elias still made sure his love of the boy was remembered. That's why secret things were kept in the vault."

"We know," interrupted the verger. "The vault's been sealed for years under the church."

"Parson, you're right as sure. Been sealed for longer than I remember and I got years on you."

The two researchers held back a chuckle.

"Talking 'bout the vault at parsonage you need look for."

Old Abe's remark threw the verger completely. In his twenty years he had never come across a parsonage vault.

"Now Abe, you're telling me things I never knew."

"That's what years is for, inform an' educate youth," he cajoled the verger with a mighty wink.

"Well we're listening."

"As I said, go to the parsonage, find the vault."

Before turning to leave as silently as he came he looked deep into Toto's eyes. Something connected. The researcher felt scrutinized in the most profound way by the sage.

"You've the look of Squire Elias, young'un," Abe confirmed. "Could almost be related."

Toto felt a shiver course through him.

"You're right," Anne broke in. "This gentleman is related to John Moore."

"Now always right am I when comes to folk," rejoiced Old Abe. "Listen close."

Again he looked Toto directly in the eye.

"You carry the feeling and spirit of Moore. Bring his legacy to life. The path to victory littered with dead. Accept your fate so they die not in vain. Around your neck, meet the devil face on, call his bluff. Face him square, then chains of treason bust an' all will know truth and purpose. Honor the gift your family gave."

With that he swiveled round and hobbled off .

The three of them took a few moments recovering from what the old man imaprted. Toto heard more than a little trepidation. Anne felt it.

"I think we've just been informed of the real treasure. As always never where you expect it. We need to get back to Charleston."

"First to the parsonage," the verger insisted as he leapt into the back of the car. The verger never felt Abe made any sense but was certain the two visitors had to get him to the parsonage.

They were soon there.

Entering the house, their guide ushered the two researchers into the back, where a door opened to steps to a basement area. Hanging on the wall inside the basement entrance was a candleholder, complete with candle. Lighting it, he led them down to a musty and dark space.

By the flickering light of the candle, it looked deserted. Almost as large an area as the house itself, there was no trace of anything usefully stored. Carefully the verger scanned each wall.

Having completed a full three sixty degrees it was Anne who spied, with her sharp vision, a slight anomaly in the stonework close to the ground. It looked as if it had been constructed as foundations.

"Stop, just there," she insisted, moving nearer to take a closer look.

Keen eyes had worked their magic again, Toto thought and was, once again, surprised at this woman's attention to detail.

Sure enough a slight edge to one particular stone, when scraped, revealed a space just big enough for one finger to enter. The brickwork dissolved and allowed four fingers to clasp the stone.

"Extraordinary, what are the chances of spotting that," Toto exclaimed.

The verger looked on with intense interest.

"I never..." he began.

As he spoke Anne pulled away a whole section of stonework. An opening not much larger than a couple of square feet had been created. The candle lit the space, a privilege it had not benefited from for over a century. It revealed the dust-covered form of a wooden casket. Anne reached in and pulled it out. Copper stripes followed the shape of the box from back to front and reminded Toto of one of the pirate chests of his youth.

The verger broke the silence.

"If we find doubloons in that chest I'll eat my fine hat."

The other two laughed as the black number he sported looked the least edible object anyone could imagine.

"You open it as it was your forebear who placed it there," Anne acknowledged, passing the casket to Toto.

The casket was unlocked. He lifted the latch and opened the lid gingerly. The other two bent over expectantly.

Inside were several papers, in reasonable condition. A seal rolled lazily as he lifted papers from beneath it. A lion rampant was engraved on the seal. A thin silver paper cutter nestled into a small leather bound copy of the Bible. Beneath that were more parchments, folded immaculately and sealed with the lion rampant. As he lifted them out another smaller roll remained. Lifting it he instructed the verger hold the candle closer.

Toto carefully unwrapped the ribbon round the parchment. Opening it a dried sprig fell onto the floor. Anne collected it and held it in her palm. Toto read the note in front of him.

This addendum to my final will and testament, granted my hand this third day of March in the year of our Lord seventeen hundred and eighty eight bequeath and request my son Abraham be recognized a free man and inherit the enclosed seal and pendant. I ask my son and heir John Elias to act on this request on finding Abraham, issue of my relation with his mother Sarah a freed slave of Mooreland, as are all my workers. I ask certain valuables laid out in other papers be placed in store at the vault in the parish of St. Thomas along with papers Abraham carried before his disappearance in the summer of eighteen hundred and eighty.

"That's dynamite. Moore flew in the face of Southern slavery. Looks like he was one of the first to recognize their rights," Toto suggested, staring at the codicil. "And the seal, still here, never found Abraham."

"The mention of a pendant, that's not here either," noted Anne. "The mystery deepens and still doesn't answer the question: where are the indents relating to the monies Moore handed to Washington and the Revolutionary Army?"

Toto took the candle and shone it deeper into the crevice. He found nothing.

"Doesn't look like the other pieces made it. What if the indents were amongst those pieces?" he asked rhetorically.

Anne knew all wills and related matters could be found back in Columbia.

"We best visit to the Loans Department in Columbia."

Toto mesmerized by the gem of history they had uncovered, agreed.

Gathering what they found, they made their way out of the parsonage to the vehicle.

Before getting back in, Toto turned to look at the building housing the relics of his ancestors. Many questions revolved in his head, not least of all how these contents still remained hidden. Silently thanking his ancestor he got into the vehicle as the verger walked home.

As they drove off Anne realized she still had the sprig in her hand.

"Take this. It fell from the casket," she said handing it to Toto.

He took it and scrutinized the twig.

"You know what that is?" she asked.

"No idea."

"A sprig of juniper. Funny it was placed there" she mused.

"Native Americans used juniper for health issues. Moore near death and poorly, perhaps Sarah, Abraham's mother, thought it might help. She would have known local remedies and her love would have tried to save him," she suggested.

The mention of juniper shot Toto back to Suffolk and his youth. Something very familiar hit him. His drift did not pass unnoticed.

"Any thoughts?"

"Yes, I mean no, well yes many years ago I caught the scent of juniper and…"

He stopped himself from the detail, fast realizing his memory would expose the fateful day by the river and ensuing disaster. He also felt the dormant emotion this dead sprig triggered – something way too personal to share, even for a beautiful and savvy woman such as Anne. He hurriedly found a cover story.

"Juniper protects and is an attribute of Hermes."

Anne looked none the wiser.

"My classical history is negligible against my American."

Toto clarified.

"Hermes, or Mercury as the Romans called him, aided Odysseus and Perseus on their heroic journeys," Toto replied.

"Looks like that twig could be a useful talisman for us both. Best keep it as it may help our own heroic task unearthing this story." Anne suggested.

Toto felt the relief of not getting too personal.

"Odd thing what Old Abe told you. *Meet the devil face on, call his bluff. When you've faced him square, the chains of treason bust an' all will know truth and purpose.* What do you make of it?" Anne asked.

"Frankly, I haven't a clue. Sounds like an exciting conundrum and another puzzle."

"Maybe the puzzle itself, Albert" Anne suggested lightheartedly.

"I'll bear it in mind. Who the heck the devil might be. There's a mystery."

Toto enjoyed Anne's company and had not felt quite so upbeat for a long time. He found her attractive, intelligent and extremely sharp when it came to digging up references and leads. An excellent ally for what he had in mind. He decided to broach its outline the following day.

Anne Gregorie was Georgia born and her family held similarities to the Moore's plantation heritage. Unlike the Moores, her family were far less wealthy and no grand gift was donated to the revolution. It was her educational qualifications that established her personal worth and resulted in first class honors. She had never encountered a character such as Toto. His worldly nature and eccentric outlook fascinated, perplexed and interested her in equal measure. She had yet to be exposed to any serious relationship, more through dedication to studies than any desire to attract suitors. What appealed to her at this point was finding another so passionately involved in work she understood and loved. It made her look at Toto through receptive eyes.

The following day in Columbia they headed straight for the records office and the Registry of Loans Department.

Anne's connections soon had them rifling through records around John Moore. The first find was Moore's will and notes filed by John Elias, his son.

Toto gingerly explored these.

"These look interesting," he commented, turning the pages.

"What's this?" he exclaimed beginning to read out loud.

"...the fate of Abraham, son out of wedlock to my father John Moore never arrived at the parsonage in St. Thomas Parish, where under orders from our father he was to have deposited assigned package of deeds, notes and indents relevant to the loan of monies made to the Revolutionary cause. We have reports of their being attacked by British troops, who ambushed the cart and oxen carrying both men..."

Toto paused at what he had unearthed.

"It suggests the indents were in Abraham's possession. Depending on the type of indent, it could mean presentation alone recoups the loan," predicted Anne.

"Explains why nothing ended up at the parsonage. Can we find the originals?" a deflated Toto admitted at what Anne said.

She picked up his disappointment and placed her hand on his. Looking at her directly she sensed his fear. She dismissed her reading and withdrew her hand.

"With the skills we both have I'm certain we can track down where they've got to. Finding out whether a repayment has been logged would give us our first clue."

Toto lightened considerably.

If anyone could find out, Anne could, he thought.

With Miss Webber's help, the success of their threesome would be bound to grow. He took back her withdrawn hand. To confirm his acceptance of her approach he took her other one as well.

"With you and Mabel we three can crack this one and go places. Where shall we start?"

Anne felt an unusual flush. Her heartbeat quickened noticeably. This was an unexpected part of a journey she had not prepared for. Unusually, she felt it a pleasant one. Unable to work out whether it was the challenge of upcoming complex research, the enthusiasm of her new-found colleague or something more personal she merely allowed her practical side to kick in.

"We first need to find what survived General Sherman's scorched earth policy," she declared with obvious outrage.

Her anger at this Civil War desecration of what she held to be her own treasure house was apparent even to Toto. He loved that passion. He related to it completely.

"Felt the same fighting the Greeks. Made me so mad I resigned and sided with the poor bloody Greeks."

Anne looked at a man who not only showed similar fire but gave up his career out of ethical conviction.

"That must have taken some guts," she proffered.

"I don't know about guts but I remember how bloody certain I felt my writing to be a far better sword than the slaughter the Turks inflicted on the wretched Greeks."

"Even got a gong from the Greeks for my actions," he added, remembering the honor.

"A true appreciation of your commitment?" Anne suggested.

"The Chevalier Order of the Redeemer was a rare honor for a non Greek. The written word's a mighty adversary against inhumanities carried out by empire. So empowering to know there are ways to affect change, influence and order."

"You're sounding more like a founding revolutionary each day," Anne responded with endearment towards the captain.

On their way back to Charleston she continued quizzing Toto, fascinated with his motives behind his research.

"Something's been troubling me since our initial meeting."

Toto turned towards her.

"When we first met at Mabel's one of the things you shared and reiterated today was getting out of the army and using your pen as your main weapon. Admirable, yet what puzzles me is why do you still use the title Captain?"

Toto smiled mischievously, admiring the attention to detail.

"Having taken the side I felt deserved support, for me it was still combat. I rightly earned the title Captain and my pen being my weapon it felt right maintaining the Captain."

Anne pressed him.

"Is that not a little affected?"

Toto took no offence at her remark and answered.

"I'm sure you've gathered by now I like theatricals."

She nodded and smiled at an obvious fact.

"The retention of the title has worked in my favor more than once," he continued. "As war correspondent it creates even more legitimacy to investigations. Even helped interest swell authoring *The Dog* under that name."

"That explains a lot," she replied.

"As to why I'm keen to continue this research, it's unfinished business."

"Unfinished business?" Anne interrupted him.

"Yes, unfinished business," he repeated. "Something I found in those files we looked through today I didn't reveal."

Anne was eager to hear Toto's revelation.

"One document concerned the will of Moore's son. His widow was the executrix of the will. She began petitioning Congress for repayment of monies lent. This alone convinces me the whole loan is extant and whoever can force repayment of this money there's a rich reward. I propose we work together and with connections in both Washington and New York, start to build a case to present to Congress for repayment of these loans."

"There's interesting work here. Professionally of course, it holds huge interest for me."

"Personally?" Toto shot back impulsively.

That took her off guard. For the first time he noticed her confidence falter. She knew it landed them into an area she for one, kept off limits, yet she felt his directness deserved a response.

She stalled.

"What do you mean by that?"

"What I mean," replied Toto confidently, "is how do you feel about us working together?"

"Very comfortable," she replied with some relief. "I've enjoyed our partnership so far. I'm sure you can benefit from my precision in gathering the information we'll need. In the same way I can benefit from," she paused before adding, " Your expansive vision..."

Toto caught it immediately and threw back.

"Are you attracted to dreamers with vision, then?"

"Most definitely, no I am not," she shot back. "But if those dreams could find a clear way to reality then it makes the dreamer more of a visionary and that's what I'm attracted to," she confirmed.

"Are you setting out markers here?" he asked impetuously.

"That sir, is for you to wonder about and for me to decide."

She most definitely had caught Toto's attention and she knew it. She determined if she was going to sally forth on an adventure in the area of relationship then the campaign would be conducted exclusively on her terms.

Toto knew little about these game plans and even less their implications. All he heard was the music, smelt the roses and the hint of a symphony in composition as the southern summer evening air lured him into yet one more adventure.

This time the journey would land the big fish and if that meant settling for retirement in his ancestors' state on the arm of a southern belle, then surely his father would be smiling down on him from wherever he now traded his time.

CHAPTER ELEVEN

Back in New York, Toto was keen to meet Willy and report progress. First of all a report had to get to England and Germany, where his elder brother and sister lived respectively. Serious funding required their support. To prove to his elder siblings this idea was solid and substantial would also be useful.

Since leaving England, a failed marriage and relinquishing paternal responsibilities of his young son Adrian, he had been determined to prove himself worthy, heroic and successful. His goals were driven watching the obvious success achieved by both brother Louis and his two elder sisters, Leila and Rose.

Leila, Willy's mother, whilst schooling in Germany, had met a dashing young Prussian officer who, as part of an inner core of friends within the royal circle and the Kaiser himself, brought Toto's sister into contact with echelons of society her somewhat bohemian character might not have otherwise encountered. Her beauty, character, musical prowess and charm swept her into these royal circles, marriage and subsequent delivery of her first born, Willy, to whom the Kaiser himself had asked to be godfather. This enabled the establishment, within her new family, of connectivity to European aristocracy both prior, during and following the Great War. As well as affording her unique insight, during the War, into how the enemy operated and where fact and fiction drew their boundaries, she became a most useful eyes, ears and lead generator for the rest of her family. Willy's desire to emigrate to the States after the global debacle of World War One and ensuing chaos brought about through hyperinflation in Germany, allowed the long arm of connectivity and ancestral ties to be re-established in the New World. It offered Willy a future of successful business and wealth denied to many, left back in Europe. Conveniently for Toto, it offered an excellently placed ally alongside him in New York supporting and sponsoring his own developments.

Toto's elder brother Louis, having shown acumen at business, followed his father's merchant leanings and carved a good living for himself, marrying a youthful love in the form of Hettie, an operatic diva of incredible potential and settled into suburban life in England like a duck to water, whilst traveling profusely through both Europe, Russia and across the States.

His other sister Rose, the first to marry, did so in style becoming part of an illustrious and ancient Scottish lineage taking her north of the border to a life of wealth and devotion to a loving husband.

As the youngest sibling, Toto's favored status from both parents gave him an education in London. He looked up to and admired his brothers and sisters. His imagination fed and watered both by his father's storytelling and elder brothers' adventures. Childhood connection to his invisible friend increased a young and fertile mind. Frontiers between dreams and realities were crossed with few border checks.

Formative years spent in the Suffolk countryside, his closeness to Louise, his deep affection for sister Leila, were major pillars in his relation to the feminine. Elder brother Arthur's diplomatic ambitions created a towering hero for youthful Toto. His shock suicide in Dinard, in the early 1890s, alongside the brutalizing effect of Louise's treason, compounded by his mother's failing health, heavily impacted Toto's youthful psyche. His mother suffered so much from the suicide, the whole family decided never to return to Dinard.

As tortured a path as it laid out, one bright return came with Pau in the South West of France, their new holiday destination. Here Toto had the good fortune to meet and develop what became a lifelong friendship with Lord Burnham's son Harry.

Opportunities offered by Burnham, owner of the London newspaper he presently represented, afforded Toto a channel for his creativity and writing. His focus, following Arthur's death, fell on joining the military. Childhood antics on the playroom floor with tin soldiers became reality.

Military excursions distracted him from failed relationships, and sister Leila's desertion to marriage in Germany. Making it up as he went along, proved invaluable to Toto.

His passion and knowledge focused on a new technology, the bicycle and developing it as a masterful weapon of speed and efficiency in military campaigns. His prescience visioning these two-wheeled vehicles as major assets in war was the main reason his superiors recognized his value.

So impressed were they, a commission along with several dozen bicycles was initiated to aid Lord Kitchener's efforts in facing down the Boers in a second war exploding in South Africa.

That they had engaged him as a spy went way over his head. Campaign success enabled Toto to return to England with much credit to his name. It created also a marked card in secret intelligence service files.

Finishing his report, seated in his room at the Alpha Delta Club in

Manhattan, he drifted back to that Southern African excursion. The fateful journey where he and his bicycle scouts, using the train to shorten their mission, bundled into an armored carriage on special mission and reconnoiter. Beside him a young journalist kept them amused with tales of previous campaigns. Toto remembered how impressed he was with this Morning Post correspondent. How similar two paths had been. The meeting both men would remember – one for being taken prisoner and the other for narrowly avoiding it.

As he sat, his report finished, cup of tea beside him, he thanked Winston Churchill for being part of that adventure and what became, one of his successes on his own score card – the growth of the Bicycle Battalions of the British Army. The high-powered contacts he and the family accumulated over the years, he guessed, were ripe for calling in favors. That would await the outcome his funding document would elicit, sealed into a large brown envelope and handed to the concierge.

As he turned to walk from the club, he noticed a young man, dressed in dapper suit, fresh faced with eager eyes, looking lost. He approached.

"Excuse me, can I be of assistance?" he asked.

The young man looked up happy to be recognized.

"I'm searching for a friend who agreed to meet here," the stranger replied.

"Do you have the name of this fellow?" Toto asked helpfully.

Avoiding the question, the stranger continued.

"Meeting him here on a matter of investment."

Toto looked somewhat askance. Not sure whether he had the right address or even ears to catch what he had just asked. He dug deeper hoping to help.

"You *were* meeting in the Alpha Delta Club?"

"Oh, yes indeed – enemy territory."

Letting that sink in, the man continued.

"The gentleman assumed we meet in the lobby here at midday."

Pulling out an expensive timepiece from his waistcoat, Toto noticed the man's hand fumbling with it as he checked the time."

"Ten minutes past, late as well," he grumbled.

"I'm sure he'll be here soon. Perhaps you'd prefer if we asked the desk look out for him and you can wait in the lounge," Toto suggested.

The young man looked harassed. He looked Toto directly in the eyes.

"I'm so sorry my man, most impolite, not introduced myself."

There being no reason to expect that that, since Toto merely recognized someone needing assistance, all the same he accepted an introduction.

"John Rockefeller Prentice, pleasant to meet you, sir."

"Captain Albert Henry Trapman, reciprocated."

"Captain is it, military man and English from the accent?"

"Right on both counts but one somewhat dormant."

"Always happens to you people. Land in New York, lose your identity and hey presto, American."

"I meant the Captain part," Toto corrected with a smile and added, inquisitive as to his name. "With a name like Rockefeller you must have illustrious relatives."

The young man blushed.

"Happen to be a grandson to what we here like to consider our aristocracy, but damn it, man, that's another story."

Little did he realize he had ignited Toto's fuel of passion.

"Consider it unconventional but I feel our meeting was not by chance. May I suggest we wait for your friend in the lounge. I'd like to field a couple of questions."

Keen to clarify his intent, he added.

"The reason becomes self evident."

"Not at all unconventional, Captain. When have we Americans been the conventional type," Prentice agreed, with oily condescension.

They entered an elegant functional lounge where chat, contemplation, newspapers and magazines, for the largely literary membership's benefit, helped feed tomorrow's column inches. Much factual reporting, follow ups and editorials were generated here, be they financial, celebrity or political As a journalist Toto was well aware the benefits newspapers offered promoting vested interests, lobbying or partisan imperatives.

Settling into voluminous armchairs, made from the rich leather of Texan steers, Prentice zeroed into Toto.

"What particular part of our aristocracy do you wish to delve?"

Toto loved American directness. No dancing and prancing the way the English avoided through parrying, protocol and false reticence.

"I'm engaged in completing a book on dogs."

Prentice, somewhat taken aback, saw no segue yet listened politely. Those were his orders.

"While researching canine and human connection, I happened to discover my family to have been more than mere visitors. Researching Carolina breeds; I fell upon information linking my forbear's gift of gold to the Revolutionary cause."

The gold part, like a magnet, caught Prentice's attention. He leaned forward, stroked his chin, with a nonchalant gesture and remained riveted to Toto's delivery.

"This gift looks to have landed on the statute books and remains as good a loan outstanding today as it was then."

Prentice Rockefeller's genetics to sniff out opportunities in turning a deal kept him alert. His present impoverishment, due to excessive gambling looked like landing him in an opportune place. As a gambler, a poker face is a huge asset, however present penury was proof he in no way carried one. Even Toto's enthusiastic delivery did not miss this shortcoming.

"Still considerable research to be done, however, as in all things American, good legal advice, especially when it comes to money, is essential. Bumping into you may offer guidance to top attorney advice."

Toto looked across in that disarmingly innocent way he used when playing a weaker party. It had the desired effect.

"As you can imagine, the family retains the very best support in this area and I'm certain I can resource one of our many arms of legal advice to help you."

Prentice adjusted his position in the armchair, assuming a patriarchal posture, utterly presumptuous for his age.

"What sort of advice are you are looking for?" he queried.

"Initially, guidance on the strength of the case for war loan repayment and whatever hoops and hurdles need negotiating."

The young aristocrat warmed as he sensed potential partnership.

"You mentioned this was a gift, Captain. Does that mean it is considered a war loan?"

"Absolutely. Against protestations from my forebear, it was ordered entry as a loan. Moreover, a loan accruing interest at six percent a year until it was repaid."

"Interesting," murmured Prentice under his breath. "As of today do we know whether it's been repaid?"

"Apparently not," replied Toto. "Still accumulating year on year, though at this stage I have no idea of its precise worth. Undoubtedly considerable."

"Undoubtedly," Rockefeller agreed. "Here's my card, I shall speak to the family and find the best direction we can point you in."

Toto handed Prentice his own card, with the club's address. Prentice looked at it with a wry smile.

"So we have a war correspondent member of one of our great fraternities, do we?"

"Merely by association," Toto hastened to add, curious as to how the stranger knew him to be a war correspondent as his card gave no indication, but replied.

"The literary roots of this place are conducive to my work," he added and with no hint of irony, "and one tends to meet the most interesting types here."

Prentice rose to the compliment, his vanity always on the lookout for a booster.

"Seems your friend failed to show," Toto reminded Prentice.

"My friend, well, he must have been delayed or diverted. I'll leave it and contact him later," Prentice, flustered, hurriedly covered himself.

Toto caught it and made another mental note.

To further cover himself Rockefeller added.

"Was to have been a potential tap for the Skull and Bones but perhaps too much information within the enemy camp?"

"To a foreigner like myself divulging that means little. As aware as I am there's rivalry between these fraternities, I'd suspect I know as much about their internal machinations as you know about the rules of cricket," Toto joked.

Prentice laughed ignorantly, knowing damn well he knew nothing of the game.

"Give me three strikes, a glove and ball and I'm with you," he answered, "You English have a rare gift for inventing the most idiosyncratic pastimes."

"At least we gave you golf," added Toto in the spirit of one-upmanship.

"Seems your forefather gave us independence," joked Prentice.

The two men played a well-oiled game of false bonhomie. Both knew the rules, yet one, shaded from the other's true intentions, allowed naïveté to assume new friendships were afoot.

For his part Prentice believed his charm had covered the real reason of the accidental meeting. Pleased with his work, he made a hasty exit. He had discovered the Englishman's gullibility around social jockeying and marked his card accordingly.

Toto left the club while Rockefeller, mission accomplished, smiled broadly and ventured off in pursuit of an imaginary cab.

CHAPTER TWELVE

Willy von Meister ran a successful business practice with trade connections between the States and Europe proving connectivity was key to good business, not only of profit but also knowledge exchange.

For many the heavy mix of bigger, better, brasher delivered a mortal blow to their personal compass. To the smart it created opportunities surpassing their wildest imagining. Willy was savvy enough to recognize, socialize and fraternize with those shrewd enough to fulfil the American dream. He had learned early the rub-off benefits mixing with the successful and self-made.

His own import business grew exponentially alongside a willingness to use critical thinking, intuitive prompts and a healthy dose of respect from his peers who saw in him a rising star. Rising stars in this firmament were by necessity watched closely and followed. Where success was sown, rewards and riches were signals to a good harvest. With every harvest substantial knock on fortunes could be made from distribution of bounty and proximity.

Although somewhat premature, Willy's intuition found his uncle's passion and pursuit of ideas worthy of his attention. He was reminded of those times where he himself had gone off at tangents of fancy only to be shown a barren harvest. So even if Toto's research led to no more than unearthing some fascinating connections and discoveries, his small investment would be worth the joy of supporting family, albeit extended.

Toto looked comfortable and very at home as he sat opposite his nephew in the latter's office. Willy enjoyed the debriefing he was given on the Carolina excursion. It seemed his uncle had also hit some pay dirt with the on-site research team, handed on a plate, for his efforts. The young Anne and her interest she developed for Toto would serve them both well, he recognized that. Toto, at this stage, felt disinclined divulging deeper thoughts on this teamwork, not least because he was still uncertain himself. Yet for Willy, dots connected within the delivered reports were enough to conclude more lay within the relationship between Toto and Anne.

Mention of meeting Prentice had Willy appreciably brighten.

"This Prentice seems to have been a gift from the gods for us."

"Absolutely. Sort of felt I had to approach the stranger in the club. Something nudged me to make a move."

"You realize the Rockefeller factor packs a punch in this city," Willy suggested.

"Could be influential. Leila's connections will help too."

Not only as an investor but how he might help with connectivity he possessed was on Willy's mind.

"I imagine after Anne and Miss Webber have tied up genealogical threads in a week or so I'll have enough information to lay a case for starting legal inquiries and looking into loan repayment. It'll require legal minds."

"The very same legal team helping the Rockefellers, happens to help our company. I'll get onto them and make sure you see them as soon as possible."

"Great," replied Toto. "The puzzle's coming together nicely."

"Let's say we get positive feedback from the attorneys, how do you see forward momentum?"

Toto was way ahead and glad his nephew posed the question.

"The more people know of this the more support we can garner. As something of a media aficionado I'm looking to get the press generate a building story along the lines of rightful returns from a grateful government to an equally grateful people. Heart strings of payback and gratitude undoubtedly will appeal to a press constantly searching for a good patriotic thread."

"I like where you're going," enthused Willy.

"Good relationships with the New York Times helps and I'm onto that."

Toto paused as an idea formulated. He pondered letting it settle.

Willy summarized.

"You'll talk to the press, I'll arrange a meeting with the attorneys and why don't we get off and see the new Eisenstein film hitting the theaters."

"Splendid idea."

Toto wondered. Willy was talking films.

Yes, he decided.

"The invitation moves me to share an idea. What if we create a script around John Moore's gift to the revolution, dramatize it and get Hollywood to bring the tale to the screen. Certainly raise our profile and upgrade the whole War Loans case."

"A great publicity scoop. An excellent idea. Who'd direct it?"

"The new Fox studio venture would easily bite. Didn't you tell me a while back, in business if you want action, decisions, and in this case, lights, camera and action, then head to the honchos, not the hills?"

Willy chuckled, admiring his uncle's acuity and astute mind.

"A student of the game indeed."

"Follow the honey," Toto added.

"With Rockefeller, make sure the sting's not in the jar," Willy cautioned.

"Noted," Toto acknowledged.

CHAPTER THIRTEEN

America in the 1920s reflected a release valve for the war years of austerity, with a clarion call to riches encouraged through individual endeavor. The gold-plated opportunities brought every size, shape and culture to its shores. Like bees to honey, New York served as one of the nation's major entry points.

A diaspora of dreams reached into every nook and cranny immediately upon disembarkation, keen to examine the entrails for future wealth potential. One such entry onto this fevered accounting ledger, arrived in the form of a near penniless stoker, Aaron Kuterkin. His ability to have secured a place in the engine room of the Lucania's maiden voyage promised the start of a new life in a new world generating success on a scale he had previously never dreamed. In the intervening thirty-five years from arrival to heading up his own brokerage firm, the dream makers had been handed their very own poster boy lodged solidly onto the national credit ledger.

Kuterkin, once settled and setting his sights on ambitious riches, quickly determined his birth name could never survive the transition. As with so many immigrants, the name game became an all-important part of creating new identities. Throwing off all aspects relating to inured poverty was a necessary development within the dream factory. Name changing became the passport to reinvention. Thus a Khazarian Kuterkin became an acceptable Germanic American Kersh.

His roots, vague even to him, bonded strongly to the waves of Central European migration. The mix, enriched through Jewish moves east meeting Khazarian moves west found Kersh's family unusually moving from Krakow to Prussia, rather than vice versa. Born in Krakow, the poverty epitomizing their daily gruel was carried with little hope of betterment into Prussia. Young Aaron spent formative years surrounded by foreign and vindictive energy. At eight years old, witnessing his mother brutally raped and left for dead in a filthy back alley in the suburbs of Berlin, he swore to avenge the murder of this one spark in an otherwise wretchedly dark existence. His tenuous link to love stolen, he rid himself of any empathy remaining.

Prussians never registered on any value scale for the émigré, then or now. Love today was as foreign to his consciousness as the newly arrived immigrants he had left years ago on Staten Island.

Sitting in his opulent office at the heart of Wall Street, where the stench of open sewerage, rotten food and threadbare clothing were as distant shadows to another world as his fortunes were to his penniless beginnings. What was present was the overbearing perfume on his visibly vampish secretary marking her accentuated entry.

She laid her fulsome left buttock brazenly on the edge of a highly polished oak desk and lent over her boss. The bunch of letters she brought with her she used as a feather to tickle the stockbroker's chin, before dropping them unceremoniously on the desk.

Kersh's response was brutal. Grabbing her wrist, he twisted it and drew her towards him. She moaned, enjoying the treatment. Kersh merely got off on the suffering he inflicted and cared not one jot whether she in turn took pleasure from the pain. He had never been in the pleasure game. He looked into her eyes.

"Now get your god damned ass off the table and back to your desk," he ordered, twisting his hold in confirmation.

She hissed in exasperated futility, like a snake ensnaring its prey. Her tongue, close enough to his cheek to wipe itself across his face, went through the motions without contact. Her ensuing smile carried both pain and pleasure as he flung off his grip, and she in turn stumbled back onto two feet.

As if nothing untoward had happened she asked.

"Is there anything else you would like Mister Kersh?"

The brutal broker could not hide the arousal she always elicited. For six months it had been so. He knew he was tiring of it and that meant change.

"Yes Vilma, tonight - eight - my place."

Vilma Thudd smiled salaciously, tucked her short skirt back into place and strutted triumphantly from the room, swinging her nineteen-year-old butt invitingly. She not only took Kersh's treatment as a twisted sort of affection, but also felt the elation of privilege, having prime access to his sexual predilections. Her cheeks went unnoticed as Aaron Kersh opened one of the letters she had left him. Scanning it swiftly he memorized the content, stood up and whipped a camel hair ankle length coat from behind the door and headed out.

Sweeping through lines of clerks and junior brokers, each glimpsed a head they knew well to respect. Not only did it hold information and knowledge on making fortunes, that paid their wages, but it could also instigate immediate dismissal, penalty for not being top dog. Kersh relished being top wolf.

Had Toto bumped into Kersh that day on a sidewalk he would never have identified him as the same stoker, disembarking all those years ago from the Lucania.

CHAPTER FOURTEEN

Toto's New York buzzed. The helter-skelter rise and crescendo of money making, deal splitting, wealth creating, excess partaking and partying, dazzled him.

Heightened discrimination each step of the way, on any quest riding the tides of fortune, was paramount. In Toto's case, passion had a sneaky way of overriding and disregarding discrimination. Willy understood these subtleties while others failed to act on truths taking them, like lambs, to the slaughter.

Slaughter was the last thing on the researcher's mind as he stood on the piazza of Grand Central Station, under a vast clock, so often used as a rendezvous point, awaiting Anne's arrival, following his inviting her to the metropolis. He relished how they hit it off with shared love and passion for mutual interests alongside Anne's easy wit. He wondered if this might turn around an altogether barren period, following forlorn endeavors in the Amazon basin that included a badly managed affair.

Funny, he thought, as he stood like some silent sentinel, amidst a preoccupied and milling crowd, *the tinge of sadness so often felt before a new romance was absent.*

He took it as a good sign old wounds had healed. He smiled inadvertently to himself.

"I'd recognize that smile at a hundred paces," a voice broke in.

Toto looked up and focused on Anne's sweet smile. He offered outstretched arms in welcome. An affectionate embrace was buried in the profusion of humanity deep in its self-absorption.

"You just sneaked up on me!" Toto exclaimed, brushing off embarrassment his inattention created.

"Just an image of stillness, standing so pensive, as the world flowed round you, a rock in a surging river. Quite a picture!"

How poetic. He loved that. Holding her gently in his arms, careful to be not too forward, he studied her beautiful face framed in a cream crisp cloche hat, beneath which previously longer hair had surrendered to a bobbed cut, the like any Hollywood star would be proud. Clear features, pearl cheekbones offset a stylish look he acknowledged as dramatic change. The white fur neckline of a sleek coat, not only protected her from the cooler temperatures but made a definitive fashion statement. Under it she wore a light fulsome long skirt, cream and peach honoring southern roots. Anyone in the know would have to acknowledge this southern belle had nailed metropolitan fashion.

God, he thought, *she's certainly done her research.*

His admiration grew.

"You're a picture shining from under that cute hat."

"Cute? You realize this is the height of fashion."

Anne tweaked his nose with finger and thumb. "This is New York after all and if I'm meeting your chums, I dress to impress."

"Of course, but it isn't the most important part of the package."

"You get the complete set or none," she smiled.

Toto himself felt complete as he took her arm and they swaggered off the piazza to the busy street outside.

They arrived at a small family hotel off Fifth Avenue Willy had organized. The Prussian owners perfected discreet charm with sensitivity, especially where it concerned couples.

Toto guided Anne to the lounge, and as he checked in the clerk handed him an envelope.

"Quaint spot," Anne remarked, as she surveyed the homely, luxurious decor.

"Certainly is. Willy's idea, as friends own it. He'll be here shortly. Far more worldly wise than me in these parts."

Far better off financially, Toto thought.

Anne related her journey as he played nonchalantly with the envelope in his hands.

"You going to open that envelope you've been juggling while I've been talking," Anne asked.

Toto, caught out, blushed and was again reminded of her sharp eye. The waiter delivered a sarsaparilla and lemonade to their table.

"You remembered my love for sarsaparilla, Captain Attentive," she quipped as Toto took out the letter and read the note.

He smiled. A crystal ping of glass heralded the start of an adventure.

"All good?" Anne asked, sharp as ever.

"Splendid, well not altogether," answered Toto.

Anne looked concerned.

"What then?"

"Seems Willy's not joining us. Says he'll see us tomorrow."

"More time for us," she encouraged.

Toto looked up grinning like the cat that got the cream. It was not the cream of her suggestion, more Willy confirming all expenses were covered.

CHAPTER FIFTEEN

Nikola Tesla had arrived in the United States early in 1884, his expertise in telephony and electrical engineering landing him an assistant's post with famed scientist, Thomas Edison. However the treatment the young Croatian-born immigrant was dealt by an egomaniacal and wildly jealous proprietor swiftly encouraged him to set up his own facility. To that end his brilliance attracted plutocrats and venture capitalists such as Westinghouse and J.P. Morgan, allowing him develop an extraordinary portfolio of patents that were revolutionary, challenging and visionary. They were to become his nemesis, turning backers and self-interest against him. His vision and creative genius threatened the empires and profits of backers wishing to own, control and charge for all they deemed fit.

The *War of the Currents* with old adversary Edison brought him directly into the American consciousness. His success at the Chicago World's Fair in 1893 was an event both William Trapman and son Toto witnessed at his personal invitation.

It was this meeting Toto shared with Anne, as they crossed Sixth Avenue into Bryant Park on their way to the library. Negotiating the now familiar lamp post previously responsible for waking him from inattentiveness, he was anything but inattentive to his companion hanging on every word of his tales from his past.

"You went with Tesla to Chicago and saw it all?" Anne queried.

"At that age I thought I'd landed in science heaven with all the lights and spectacle on show, millions of bulbs twinkling illuminated the entire exhibition, quite breathless. Met so many new people, including Westinghouse, who in spite of his wealth, was very polite and engaging. It was there I was introduced to Frank Baum; the rat on hearing my nickname stole it for his dog in The Wizard of Oz."

Anne was impressed with her engaging guide, feeling the affection experienced in Charleston growing as they talked. Outside of familiar surroundings it was easy for her to release emotional resistance. As Toto got into his storytelling stride, he missed these telltale signs.

A handy bench offered a break from walking. They both sat as she asked.

"This inventor Tesla seems quite a character. Why didn't I hear more of him in school?"

"All his battles with both Westinghouse and Morgan rocked their ivory towers, made them fear loss of profits, exploitation and power. Free energy became heresy."

"The question is: free energy, where's the profit in that." Anne asked.

"Precisely what Morgan convinced himself – pulling funding from Tesla's Wardenclyffe. As I understand it from Nikola, none of them appreciated where he came from, how he envisioned profit in free energy. Oil in the ground, that's tangible and a controlled tap. Get people extracting free energy and whoosh profits crash to zero."

"All a bit beyond me, I'm still getting used to the magic of turning a switch and getting light," Anne admitted.

"Seems it's beyond many. I'd love to ask him how he saw it work. Good inventions always seem to be way ahead of the curve. Learned that with bicycles during the war."

"I can feel the visionary inventor playing in you and you know what?"

Toto turned to her.

"What?"

"I'm mightily attracted to that."

Her frank admission took Toto by surprise.

"Really? I'd never have taken such a studious mind to be attracted to the inventor mind, especially as I recall at Mooreland you insisted not being attracted to these types."

"For a researcher, you're something dreadful forgetful in the facts department. I suggested vision had to be grounded, as dreamers need reality. The inventor marries the two perfectly. It's why I like such individuals," she swiftly corrected him.

"Well dang me if you're not only right, but may be attracted to more than one," Toto stammered.

Anne looked quizzical.

"One what? Whatever do you mean?"

Toto looked past her at a familiar figure approaching them. His thrill at this unexpected visitor got him to his feet. He looked down at her and asked.

"What were we talking about, before you reminded me of preferences?"

"Your inventor friend Nikola."

"Correct. Like magic a meeting is but moments away."

"How so?" Anne asked.

He moved behind her.

"Nikola?" He cried to a massive group of pigeons surrounding a now kneeling hunched figure in their midst.

"Is it you?"

Anne looked round to see a tall, well dressed, suited man with an outstretched palm full of breadcrumbs, crouching amidst a host of wild pigeons, white, grey and silver. He looked up as Toto hailed him. His expression visibly brightened.

"It *is* you," Toto exclaimed. "What a delightful surprise."

The scientist slowly stood up, holding in his hand a beautiful white pigeon and the remains of the feed he dispensed.

"I see you're also with your beloved," he replied, leaving both Toto and Anne embarrassed.

Noting their embarrassment, he continued.

"This beautiful creature," he said looking down at the pigeon, "is the love of my life and regularly come to feed her and her friends."

Toto recovered enough to enquire.

"You're fond of bird life in the park?"

"Fond?" Nikola looked puzzled. "More than fond of this treasure, more than any man's feelings for a woman. Neither a joke nor lie."

Anne stood bemused, as Tesla continued.

"For you, Toto, this beautiful young lady may well be the object of your fancy, yet since I've not been introduced I cannot say. However, what I do know is this bird's more precious to me than any other being. My visits here are to be with her, feed her and hear her divine song."

Nikola's directness focused both Anne and Toto towards an admission neither had yet broached yet now lay in the open. Buying time, Toto hastily introduced Anne to the inventor. Her voice was enough for Nikola's ear.

"Ah, the resonance in that voice, the sheer vibration of the harmonic in your speech confirms one thing. You're a very sensitive magnetic personality."

Anne visibly blushed. Toto shot a look in her direction.

Tesla continued.

"The energetic harmonic of the voice tells us all. It relays fear, love, our very being. Just as the call of these magnificent creatures men call pests. People know so little yet arrogantly inflate their own breasts through ugly egos."

He brought the dove towards them, pointing to its breast.

"She merely displays her full beauty while her heart beats truer than any human."

Anne was captivated by Tesla's observation and sensitivity.

"I note your own sensitivity," she replied smiling.

"Takes one to recognize one," he replied. "It brings joy to an old heart to see the good captain has his rank and file sorted."

Toto laughed hiding embarrassment. He could never have expected such an encounter to be so poignant, yet it broke the ice.

"A huge compliment coming from you. We were talking about you moments ago. Glad you pitched up."

"Pitched up?" Nikola replied. "This is my regular rendezvous with my dove. She affords me inspiration and insight."

As the rest of the flock trotted off or flew away, his favorite remained, unafraid and static on Tesla's hand. He placed her gently onto his left shoulder.

"You look a true science pirate," Toto joked.

The bird cooed softly as they all sat down.

"No need of boats, I've something far more useful."

"Of course, that vertical mechanical bird of yours," Toto guessed.

Tesla leaned over.

"Not the vertical airplane," he whispered shiftily. "Anne, be my guinea pig?" Tesla asked.

Intrigued, she nodded.

"I mentioned your magnetic personality," he continued. "Yet way back, I experimented with oscillators, with vibration and how it affects not only its own emission but the resonant harmonics of things. Imagine your voice, dear lady, its vibration and tone influences, can lure someone into your field of resonance or what Toto might describe, your field of attraction."

Anne tried her best to follow Nikola, while Toto absorbed by the reference to attraction, wondered about his growing infatuation towards her.

"Voice vibration is powerful. The hypnotist plays with it, yet probably is neither aware of nor cares for its deeper meaning. Imagine this. Using the power of acoustic resonance it's possible to generate standing waves. At the right level they create a precise relationship, producing harmonics and sub harmonics. Fibonacci discovered that."

"You've lost me at standing waves," interrupted Toto. "That really makes little sense to ears not on your level. Can you simplify it and explain who this Fibonacci was."

Anne nodded in agreement.

"Anne," Tesla replied, "young Toto's always hungry for new science, where most could give not a jot. We go back a long way so normal impatience with ignorance I'll lay to one side."

Anne felt Nikola's soft side though he came across brusque. She appreciated that.

"Fibonacci was one of the great mathematicians way back in the twelfth century. He learned his arithmetic in North Africa and the Mediterranean. Was responsible for giving us in the West so much we use today. Learned at the feet of his Moorish mentors, a lesson we'd do well to remember, with our disdain for the Arab. His work broke open the pathway to the golden ratio, the bedrock of all existence, a core template for creation. This's what we call Fibonacci numbers."

"Sounds vast," admitted Toto.

"It most certainly is, as vast as the universe itself. Just look at the branches of the tree over there. Now the leaves are covering what in winter makes plain sight, the branches naturally form themselves into shapes and forms predetermined. This shape, no matter what form nature may create, is precise forming out of nothing every time. It follows an unseen memory, a pattern Nature breathes into existence at every twist and turn. There are an infinite number of differences in nature, yet never a mistake, never an absolute identical sameness. Even the leaves hold this pattern just as those small ferns at the base of the tree uncurl and constantly illustrate the same creative patterning. Fibonacci managed to illustrate through numbers this illimitable perfection. I discovered the alignment in this perfection when the interaction of acoustic waves offer no energy loss at specific harmonics. This creates a means of producing power, energy and fuel at little or no cost."

"Free energy then?" asked Anne.

"Precisely," Nikola confirmed. "Those investing in me had no idea or desire what this could do for humanity. All they saw was free meant no return. They understood nothing, nothing at all. How arrogant and small-minded these philistines are."

Toto was eager to clear up a question.

"Is that why Morgan pulled out of funding Wardenclyffe?"

Tesla's face visibly reddened and his audience felt the anger rise. Unsure of what might follow they edged back on the bench, Toto wondered if he might regret asking.

Tesla stood up abruptly, making the dove fly off. Tesla's gaze followed her.

"That selfish, evil bastard had no idea how we can change the world. How what I did at Wardenclyffe would have transformed the way we communicate, industrial power, houses and life. All he saw were profits disappearing, investors pulling out from a project reaping no reward. They understood nothing. They called me a con merchant, a thief. By God, they are the thieves, they knew *nothing*."

As he spat out the word nothing, he turned his back to the others and continued, spewing his anger at the bench and park beyond.

"Nothing, you hear, nothing. My genius ignored. They used me, as did Marconi abusing his apprenticeship, and Edison puffing his breast with all I gave him. These corporate cockroaches walked all over me, stole from me, tricked me until they had bled everything. Yet they never take my mind where I keep locked my best secrets and inventions. They know nothing, these imbeciles," he repeated.

Toto felt the anger and injustice. He rose to contain Tesla's rage but as quickly as the inventor had blown his fuse, he returned to the bench and quietly sat down again, his shoulders sagging under the memory of ill treatment. Anne placed a concerned hand on his shoulder and Nikola allowed it to remain there.

After a few moments he raised his head looking to the trees for sight of his beloved dove. She flew back and settled on the other shoulder, returning a calm to Nikola's tone. Anne released her contact.

He wistfully gazed over across the park to the city beyond. Tiredness descended, comforted only by the company.

"Can we help temper the hardship?" Toto asked.

"Thoughtful man you are. There are better ways to open people's minds than inured slavery to money. Tap into, observe and learn from Nature. Her riches dwarf the temples of the godless. The secrets of the universe are within energy, frequency and vibration."

His words held weariness and a spirit near breaking point.

"Remind those newspapers of yours to be more generous to my work. Stop feeding from the pockets of oligarchs," Nikola suggested, bringing the meeting to an end as he rose from the bench.

Their time was up. Wishing them goodbye the scientist made a hasty retreat towards Sixth Avenue.

"What a character," said Anne as they moved towards the library. "An incredible mind. Notice how tired he became as his anger passed?"

"So inspirational, so misunderstood and they label him crazy. The relationship with the dove; most see a man who's lost his mind. Yet his work reveals the opposite," Toto mused. "Powerful what he said at the end about the secrets of the universe."

"Very," she agreed. "When you see the love he obviously has for that bird, as crazy as it seems, there's no denying his belief. Look how he changed as the dove returned. If that's love acting then does it really matter where it comes from?"

"You're right, who knows when love drops by changing everything," he answered, gently locking arms as they walked absorbed in the silence of reflection.

The sun broke through a cloud and both laughed at its synchronicity and the joy it wrapped them in.

CHAPTER SIXTEEN

Anne Gregorie slipped into big city life with seamless precision. New York, a huge change, did not deter her adept and confident approach. She was comfortable meeting Toto's connections, visiting the library and their continuing work together.

Her unearthing the discovery of a minor indent cashed in, following the Civil War helped the journey towards Congress. The media were fired up, film script prepared and influential support looked positive.

It was with a spring in his step he knocked boldly on the door to the suite Anne occupied. A voice from within wafted through the unlocked door swinging open to his vigorous knock.

"Come in, make yourself comfortable," she invited. "I'm still getting ready."

Toto entered to find a magnificent display of flowers, fresh fruits and canapés decorating a large round table. On the sideboard was an opened bottle of chilled champagne, two glasses and olives in a delicate decorated Chinese porcelain bowl. Toto blinked with astonishment.

Were they not in the heart of prohibition? he wondered.

"You're the sweetest, most romantic, thoughtful and considerate criminal I've ever met," she called out.

Toto perplexed, knew none of this was his doing. The effect it registered, he decided to spill no beans.

"Criminal?," he protested.

He lent over, poured champagne into both flutes and turning towards her dressing room. Anne entered and cruised up to Toto, standing open mouthed, glass in each hand. Her smile was electric.

"D'ya like my blue and pink negligee, Captain? Meets your approval?" she quizzed sliding a deft hand towards one of the glasses.

"So wicked. I could become very fond of a criminal mind conjuring up the prohibited."

She drew close, Toto finding it hard to reconcile the researcher sitting across the library desk earlier and the purring kitten he confronted now.

"Certain things this hostelry keeps *en famille*. A word in an ear holds a powerful resonance, you know," he lied, as she drew closer.

"Willy has close friends we can be grateful to," he guessed.

"That doesn't stop you, my love, from touching a girl where she most secretly desires," she encouraged pressing herself to him.

Her warm sweetly scented body beneath the satin peignoir wrapped around her ached for his attention. He offered one hand caress her back. She brought hers round and gently squeezed his backside. He twitched involuntarily.

"Is my military man afraid?"

"Not at all," he replied in an emotionally squeezed response. "All a bit of a surprise this."

"This what? Intimacy?" Anne helped him.

"Yes, I mean I really thought…"

"You really thought too much, sweet Toto. Now is not the time for thinking. It's time for action and seduction," she encouraged him.

"I'm taking on both at present, so do me the honor of reciprocating," she teased, as she brought her whole body into his already crumpling tuxedo.

"Way time you dispensed with the tux," she continued, as her hand left his buttock and deftly undid its buttons.

The scent of flowers, his own arousal relaxed him to accept her magic.

"Wasn't it you who said who knows when love drops by and changes everything?"

She kissed him gently on the cheek.

"You're right. Trouble is I didn't see it changing me."

Anne stepped back enough to raise her glass and said.

" Let's drink to change."

"To change," agreed Toto and downed his glass in one.

Anne did the same, throwing her glass onto the divan as he placed his on the table. She deftly relieved him of his tux. He offered no resistance. They held each other and kissed passionately.

Anne tasted the champagne on his lips and caressed them with her tongue then sent it on its own journey of discovery. He groaned lightly and reciprocated. To silent music they twirled round the room until falling onto the vast round eggshell-patterned silk spread covering the bed. Toto's hair flopped lasciviously across Anne's face. She giggled like a teenager and ruffled his whole head in both hands.

He let his caress her breasts and upper body. Her nipples hardened. She gave a whimper of pleasure. He drank it in like delicate elixir.

Bursting to tell her he loved her, he smothered her in kisses. Her nipples silenced him as he buried into each breast, targeting each nipple with passion. Their sweet softness overcame him. Her moaning in his ear encouraged his efforts, in turn increasing her pleasure.

His pleasure hardened. She felt it stronger as her gown slipped from her thighs revealing a widening valley of acceptance her opened legs defined.

80

He struggled manfully to undo his trousers. Her assistance soon had them locked in ecstatic lovemaking both had imagined and now realized. Her generous lubrication urged him fracture an unbroken seal.

Christ, he thought, *a virgin.*

He hesitated. She felt it and whispered.

"Yes it must be you. Take me, please take me."

For an instant he wanted to stop, yet her desire to have him, her passion thrusting his body further into her overrode everything. They rose together, his shirt cast off and her body free from the silk confines of the gown. Both moaned in unison, kissed harder as they rocked back and forth. He rose to his knees, clasping her waist between them and drew back and forth, as a tear of pleasured pain dropped from her cheek. Concern brought him close.

"Are you," he began, as she brought her finger to his lips.

A blissful smile replied.

He continued gently to pleasure her. She closed her eyes and felt the heat of his manhood penetrate a whole new life within. No one had told her the pain and pleasure she experienced would lead so willingly to the rising orgasm and exhilarating climax she approached with rapture. Her desire to have this man totally and embrace all the adventure with it, was something she held deep within, ready and waiting. Probing hands, fingers making tactile discoveries through each and every orifice created a symphony of tenderness she surrendered to. The strength and power of delivery as he penetrated deeply, back and forth within, brought shivers of pleasure throughout her body. Her head was on fire. Every molecule of her being whispered a language of love all of its own. Toto experienced a charge unlike anything he had known. She begged it lift her higher. It did and they climaxed together, collapsing into each other's embrace, refusing to part.

Toto rolled over, eventually.

"What just happened?" he asked, as Anne lay in bliss.

"I've an idea," she murmured.

"I'm glad, because I don't; something major certainly did."

"We won the campaign my love," Anne smiled, deeply satisfied.

She turned to face Toto. He gazed in amazement at her and then to the ceiling.

"You never cease to surprise me. When I arrived I would never have guessed what you had in mind. To cap it all it, Willy must have been in on your plan and this honeytrap."

Anne turned and with the full force of her feet pushed him over the side of the bed.

"Honeytrap? Can't you recognize when a woman truly wants you?" she reprimanded, bursting into laughter.

Toto dragged himself off the carpet and lifted his face sheepishly above the side of the bed. She rolled over, placing herself nose to nose with him, took his ruffled hair in both hands and placed a kiss smack centre on his lips.

"You're incorrigible, but you know, I think that's why I'm so fond of you."

Toto felt like a youngster found out, yet favored. Leaping up he shouted.

"Well that calls for another celebration."

He rescued her glass from the divan and his from the table, filled them both and returned to the bed. Catching sight of an envelope on the table, marked *For an occasion*, he handed Anne her glass and opened it. He read it aloud.

Once you've enjoyed the canapés and bootleg, hightail it over to 640 Fifth Avenue where Grace is dying to meet you both – and I need a trusted friend to cheer me up.

"I think we've just solved the mystery of the table," he said, gesturing to the canapés.

"You mean it wasn't you who whistled this all up?" Anne feigned disappointment.

" Precisely as I would have, were I as well heeled as he who is!"

"Was it Willy?" Anne queried.

Toto leaned over, kissed her moist lips.

"Wrong again. This is Neily's naughtiness. He's also bored out of his mind and needs rescuing!"

"Cornelius Vanderbilt?"

 She looked aghast.

"How did he know we were here, let alone together?"

"You don't get rich being out of the loop and Neily is very rich. Willy would have disclosed my assistant and where to find us."

"That doesn't explain why he'd assume us being in the same room, doing this."

"You're right, yet to know Neily is to know how his mind works. In spite of his wealth, relationship and social standing he's become extremely bored with all the parties and extravagant life style Grace throws week in week out. His search for other distractions, usually on his yacht, is the stuff of party gossip. As for knowing our own little distraction, in short, he doesn't. He merely guesses from experience." Toto explained.

"So this distraction, as you so charmingly put it, is what for you then?"

Anne demanded of Toto.

Toto hoped she jested.

"The most worthwhile I've encountered since discovering the Moore Millions," he replied, bouncing right down next to her and onto his back, pouring bootleg bubbles down her throat.

In her surprise she jettisoned her glass to the ceiling covering them both in Bollinger. Discarding the bottle and glass, he rolled across the huge bed, in her embrace as her glass fell back, unbroken, onto the bed beside them.

"Let's continue celebrating on Fifth Avenue. I can officially introduce you to Grace, Neily and the cream of New York's aristocracy." Toto suggested as he broke their embrace.

"As long as we treat it as an interlude," she ordered.

"An interlude it is," Toto assured her.

Arrival at a Vanderbilt party was never judged on punctuality, so their arriving an hour into proceedings went unnoticed. Most guests hustled to be the first, the social set never tiring the desire to be seen by one and all. It was precisely this habitual partying Cornelius Vanderbilt had become sick of, to say nothing of the annual quarter million it cost him to keep Grace happy.

Neily spotted them enter, with a refreshing lack of ostentation.

"Thank God, old man you found my suggestion. What a delight to meet your ravishing assistant," he acknowledged.

Taking Anne by the hand, he placed a chivalrous kiss and introduced himself.

"I'm Neily, host of this bunfight and it's my pleasure."

"The pleasure's mine, Mister Vanderbilt," Anne replied with a courteous smile.

Her southern upbringing had taught politeness works on all occasions, so subsequent relaxation of etiquette could be observed not assumed.

"Call me Neily, " her host suggested. "I'm sure Toto's told you a bit of our relationship and how far we go back. Let me whip you through the maelstrom of social one-upmanship and see how they cope with you."

Anne instinctively felt Neily cared little for social graces. In spite of the opulence around her, she threw caution to the wind, released etiquette and addressed her host, as they mounted the grand staircase to the ballroom.

"Neily, you're aware of my roots, no doubt having spies in all camps. The Southern circuit may not be as rarefied as here, nor as wealthy, but training in those backwaters certainly honed resilience to the daughters of the American

Revolution and the glitterati of the backbiting set there."

"Of that I have no doubt," he responded.

He turned to Toto and continued.

"Toto, dear fellow, you have one most attractive and credible partner in crime in Anne. I feel she'll hold her own amongst the bankers' banshees tonight."

Toto squeezed Anne's arm gently by way of acknowledging Neily's perception.

"Talk of American Revolution is most appropriate as we have one such daughter amongst us who I'd be delighted to introduce. Toto – for you I've an excellent contact rolled into town from the emporium of entertainment."

"There's a proposition!" Toto agreed.

Curious as he was to meet Neily's choices he could not stop wondering how deep his inside information penetrated.

Vanderbilt guided them through a milling guest roster. Heads turned, ingratiatingly insincere smiles spread across heavily made up faces, oozing superficial pleasure. Social mountaineering required more theatre than authenticity. The grandstanding performed by female counterparts was as obvious as it was hilarious. Anne did well to hold back her chuckles and just smiled sweetly.

Toto leaned towards Neily.

"Never expected such an abundance of talent at one sitting, you've outdone yourself."

"When I heard you were in town eager to get the project moving, it would have been remiss not to message the grapevine. You know how rabid these bloodhounds are to the scent of fame and fortune. Grace's invites are mere gilded signposts."

Their progress stopped abruptly.

"Darling Neily, you navigate through these glittering stars without first acknowledging the center of your firmament," the unmistakable voice of Grace Vanderbilt rang out.

As she crossed their path alongside a cluster of acolytes each claiming her trail as their own, she continued.

"Toto dearest, you're the picture of the adventurer. How gracious of you to pop by."

"Grace, my pleasure sharing this fabled, fabulous function."

By the time he finished his sentence Grace had wrapped her jewel-encrusted form around him, landing a magnificent kiss on both his cheeks, to the amazement of one and all, not least Anne.

She spun round to face her audience, knowing full well all eyes would be on her, and announced.

"My Captain Trapman, a most noble European and favorite Prussian exotic adventurer, entirely deserves the greeting I delivered."

She planted a third to confirm her statement.

Toto visibly blushed, making him even more interesting to the gathered admirers. Somewhat stunned, he replied to feed the scandal.

"Humbled and somewhat overcome, Grace, but then we do have history in extravagant embraces."

"That we do," Grace replied, to the now hushed twitters of an expectant audience.

"Something Neily always supported," she added, to a horrified intake of breath around her husband.

She continued to feed the room more outrageous behavior, beloved of the gossip columns and social set telegraph. They drank it in as eagerly as some partook the hidden alcohol in the juices served.

Grace adored attention and reveled in maintaining her guests spellbound. She was never so attractive to her guests as when in full flow.

Anne's interest became caught in this web, as Grace continued.

"Ah, yes, let him tell you himself about how I had him rush into my arms on the high seas to avoid a diplomatic incident."

Another intake of collective breath encouraged her.

"Indeed, when the whole world on that vast vessel knew me to be Neily's betrothed, they were scandalized to see such an overt tryst develop."

Turning to Neily, placing a hand on his right cheek, she reassured.

"But my diamond, you were in on it from the start."

Toto looked to him for assistance. He reciprocated.

"We made a great team in the games we played and Grace as bait made it game, set and match every time."

His response created more questions than answers. It also increased Toto's social coinage. He, aware Anne had not yet been introduced, did just that. Grace poured out more superlatives.

"How simply charming to meet you and with a more gallant, honorable gentleman, I could not hope for. Neily – take our adorable couple to meet the guests."

On her cue a voice from the crowd broke the silence of the onlookers.

"So it looks as if there could be an exciting new script for my next production."

Through the circle appeared the figure of Edwin Carewe. He marched towards them.

"A splendid tale sir and may I have the pleasure of introducing myself, Edwin Carewe, film director and seeker after scripts," he announced with a magnificent flourish of self assurance and desire to be front of house.

Grace took the cue and backed off; confident her usual effulgence had sparked the appropriate excuse for the chattering buzz these socialite aficionados loved to cruise on for the remainder of the evening.

"Edwin, Captain Albert Trapman," Neily hurriedly interjected.

"Captain, a pleasure and quite an honor to meet a war hero amongst our great and good. They've probably, none of them with exception of Neily, ever raised arms in anger except across the bedroom boudoir," the director laughed expansively.

"Well I wouldn't call myself a hero," Toto swiftly corrected him, as Anne came to his defense.

"Now that's not quite true. Remember the time Churchill was captured after your secret service bikers made a dash for freedom from ambush in the Transvaal."

Toto raised his eyebrows, having completely forgotten telling her of the incident and also surprised again at her sharp memory.

"Well that was a long time ago."

"You see," confirmed Edwin, "I can spot talent even when hidden deep in the shade of modesty. So you really have a story to tell and I see a most attractive sidekick to help you tell it."

Carewe turned to Anne, took her hand and over zealously kissed it. "Charmed I'm sure, my dear. Have you done any acting before?"

"Steady on Edwin, your schmoozing just confirms Hollywood's reputation," mocked Neily. "You're talking to one of the great historical researchers from our magnificent South, not some two bit flapper, desperate to get into movies."

"Captain, as you're more than aware the relaxed atmosphere at these thrashes are known for their frizzle and fun, so please take no insult at my admiration of your partner's beauty."

"None taken and I don't have to speak for her. If Anne had taken it as brash and boorish you'd have been the first to know, would he not?" Toto turned to Anne.

"I am, Mister Carewe, my own woman," Anne corroborated. "Your reputation as a director goes before you, so take what you said in its best light. As for my acting abilities as any good Southern girl knows, act straight, tell it as it is, then you'll have no problems to deal with. Your interpretation of Tolstoy's Resurrection speaks volumes for your talent."

"Well, I'm happy you appreciate my work," Carewe responded, respecting and admiring her research capabilities of his work.

Neily whispered in Toto's ear.

"A fine filly you've got there. Able to hold her own and knows her facts."

Neily allowed Carewe to continue, as the rest of the room settled back into animated chatter.

"Captain Trapman, you seem to have lived a most adventurous and swashbuckling life, could we see a script coming out of all this?"

"Funny you mention that, perhaps I do," replied Toto, recognizing a good segue.

Anne saw where he was going and took up the conversation.

"As you may have heard, Mister Carewe, I've been researching with the Captain on something we both feel would make a superb follow up to your extensive body of work."

"Sounds promising," the director agreed, tossing back the remainder of his glass.

Toto took over the tale.

"My forebear's family settled in Charleston and he was a great supporter of the Independence movement. When things became dicey for Washington, he donated a considerable sum in gold to improve their plight at Valley Forge. In the nick of time as our King was about to thrash the living daylights out of his unruly rebels. It allowed us to find ourselves here today with Neily and Grace, king and queen of American aristocracy, untroubled or ruled over by London. The fact it's an outstanding loan worth a heck of a lot makes for a great celluloid adventure."

"Sounds like it would pluck the heartstrings of national pride when needed most. My brothers and I would be happy to see a treatment. Send it to us."

"You're in partnership then?" Toto asked.

"Well I suppose you could call it that, since between brothers Finis, Wallace Fox and myself we practically own Hollywood."

Toto felt an absolute chump. He had completely overlooked the bloody obvious that Edwin was of course Jay Fox, one of the illustrious Fox brothers who seemed to produce most of the fare coming out of Hollywood. Covering his embarrassment he replied.

"Where better could this gem have fallen. I'll get something over. You staying?"

"Going back at the weekend, we've a full schedule to plough through. Time we looked to developing the Talkies. Perhaps this could be the one to launch that," Carewe suggested. "I'll get Finis, he deals with scripts, look it over and have you fellows connect."

Anne could see in Carewe's fine bone structure his Chickasaw inheritance and inability to stand still for more than a few moments. That she put down to genetic alertness and the frenetic pace of Hollywood.

"You'll find the slant Albert's treatment has with the Chickasaw to be more than a little fascinating," suggested Anne.

"Is that so and how perceptive of you to be aware of my roots," Carewe complimented her.

"Historical heritage is my expertise and subject of my master's, if I can get past all the men who tell me women don't do that sort of thing," she shared.

"Master's degree, well that's quite something for a woman in these times. I somehow feel you're going to prove them wrong. You and I have more than a little in common."

"What would that be?" Toto asked.

"Both Anne and I seem to be challenging the status quo in this country of so-called equality. That always lends a frisson of potency."

"Edwin, you'll find more than enough to get excited about in what I shall send, and as for challenging the status quo who knows: this could be a great vehicle," Toto offered, excited at the opportunity to pitch his ideas and help the journey forward.

"Edwin, return to persuade Miss Gish over there to perform for you. I need to move our two guests on."

Edwin laughed and turned back to accomplish precisely that after throwing an invite to Anne.

"When you're through come and meet Miss Gish, as fine an example of a daughter of the Revolution as you'll ever find."

Anne acknowledged his invitation with a smile and a nod.

Neily wrapped his arms around both of them and led them to the other side of the room.

They weaved their way through the multitude of New York's aristocracy, some nodding acknowledgment at Neily while others threw gratitude, like confetti onto their host and his generosity, each one far more interested giving Toto and his partner the once over. Toto felt events were laying support for what lay ahead.

"Neily, I've mentioned her before but you really ought to meet sister Leila when you're next over in Europe, she's on first name terms with Kaiser Wilhelm."

"Already have, in the days he was still the Kaiser, we spent good times with him in Europe on the yacht. Met your sister and husband Wilhelm when they were here. You were still in South America then, as I remember."

" Playing around with glass bottom boats on the Amazon. Seems a million years away."

"Boats?" Anne asked.

"Yes, he had this brainwave to launch a tourist industry for those visiting the Amazon, Manaus and its opera, sending excited visitors down river in glass bottomed boats with the river life below," Neily explained.

"We all now know why the Rio Negro got its name. Clarity was negligible." Toto laughed.

"Oops," Anne said, with sympathy for a basic error. "A fundamental business flaw?"

"Darned right it was, and good reason to retreat to the world of the buzzing and living in the backwaters of Wall Street and Fifth Avenue," replied Toto.

They arrived opposite a highly decorated and pompously dressed gentleman who held out his hand to his host with an eagerness befitting the attire. Neily shook hands.

"Your Excellency, may I introduce you to my good friend and writer Captain Trapman and his partner Miss Gregorie," he said, gently ushering the two forward.

"This gentleman is not only the Brazilian consul to New York but also another journalist like you, Captain, who from his reputation was always ahead of the pack with a scoop."

"Capitão Trapman, Gustavo Barosso, my pleasure and an honor to meet you and your most delightful friend."

"Likewise," mouthed Toto, as familiarity with the man's face in the attire bothered him. He tried to remember. Something urged him remember. He decided to test the pester.

"There's something familiar about you begging me ask, have we met before?"

"Captain Trapman arrived back some years ago from South America, in fact from Brazil," Neily assisted helpfully.

"You're most correct Senhõr Vanderbilt. Capitão Trapman is also correct;

we have met before, some several years ago, before my role here as consul. When I too lived and worked in Manaus. I'm sure the Capitão's memory is flooding back, not unlike the tidal floods putting paid to his tourist ambitions," he confirmed with a twisted smile.

They flooded back alright like the Rio Negro on surge, reminding him again of dismal failures with boats. He remembered with a vengeance the bitterness he felt towards this overdressed example of priggish pomposity before him. He could have willingly laid him out there and then had it been another place, but manners restrained him. He was in no mood to give the man the pleasure of destroying yet another project. Toto smiled courteously and responded.

"Ah, yes, your pen persuaded the great and good the tide had yet to turn for tourists to the area. How's the Amazonas Opera House developing these days?" he added, deflecting attention away from their relationship.

"It thrives despite a disappearing spiral of revenue from the rubber industry. Shame your schemes were not the success you trumpeted. Our economy needed it."

Toto ignored the remark.

"Success seems to have smiled on your career, bringing you to New York. Are you enjoying your new role as ambassador?" Toto asked, deciding to be as diplomatic as possible.

Whilst the ambassador endeavored to sort the various deflections Toto threw, Anne stepped in.

"Do you find it different here your Excellency? I expect the pace is more frenetic?"

"I fear dear lady you've not encountered the Samba. It is the way we've always expressed frenetic *passion*," he retorted, with a crude emphasis on the word passion.

"I cannot say I know much about this, Samba thing. Sounds wonderfully exotic. Perhaps we might get a demonstration one of these days," suggested Anne.

Toto had witnessed the Rio-based sensation leak upwards into Amazonia and the Opera House on occasion.

Neily returned just in time to catch Anne's remark.

"How about we organize something down at the Three Hundred Club, there are plenty of people interested to experience passion."

They all turned to him, perplexed.

"You're right, this place does have a reputation and following. I bet Texas would be up for it," Toto mischievously goaded Barosso.

The consul could not believe his ears as he listened to Toto's suggestion. He knew the club to be one of the most notorious speakeasies in the city and Texas Guinan, its outrageous owner, known for her run-ins with the police department refusing to acknowledge prohibition, made it even more risqué. His own visits he wished kept well under wraps.

Neily chimed in.

"Seems like a plan. So you'll arrange something for us there?"

Squirming awkwardly, the consul backed off. The last thing he wanted was exposure to a weaknesses for drink, women and dance. He would have been far happier if the Englishman was the one feeling discomfort. He recognized present circumstances were not on his side and quickly made an excuse to leave, making sure the right time and place, on his terms, would appear. He hated with a vengeance these aristocrats, littering the New York ladder upon which he had engineered his own climb. His purpose was never to ingratiate himself into this frivolous society; his goal lay in Brazil, on a far greater project.

"Oh dear," sighed Toto, with false sorrow, as his Brazilian nemesis disappeared from view. "Looks like we said something uncomfortably close to truth and exposed our guest. Can't imagine him ever having danced a samba in his life, let alone letting his hair down."

Anne looked across at Toto and made a scolding sound nannies delivered to their out of order charges.

"A bit harsh on the poor man. He probably felt out of his depth among this lot, but far too forward towards me with his body language."

"Spot on."

Realizing where he was, Toto apologized.

"No apology needed, they're here for Grace, not me or anyone pretending to be anything other than themselves. I fund the functions, keep her happy, them chattering and bitching and you and I amused at the shallowness of New York high society, so a visit to the Three Hundred will be just the ticket."

Toto was pleased the project was running smoothly and, beyond expectations, how things were developing with Anne.

He had shown her a repertoire of abilities. That their relationship had, quite unexpectedly, burst into a passion he would never have gambled on twenty four hours earlier, made the whole time they spent together sweet as juniper.

CHAPTER SEVENTEEN

Randolph Mason's employment as General Counsel of the Federal Reserve Bank of New York had been, even on his own estimation, an unqualified success. Having given up his position as attorney to join the bank's New York offices on its inception in 1920, he felt the nature of the job, his ability to move within the fraternity of banking circles and his adept legal ear and eye for procedural matters, had made him some good and influential friends. Certainly his structural approach had not gone unnoticed by the board and governors. For Mason this corporation, founded fifteen years earlier held no problems for him by way of legitimacy and purpose, in fact it suited him down to the ground.

It was Benjamin Strong himself who had earmarked Mason for the eventual post of General Counsel. Strong having headed up, since 1904, Banker's Trust, an entity set up by the eight families, was accustomed to recognize and encourage all those who were warm to the party line the bankers laid out across the Federal Reserve domain. The originating families consisted of centuries-old lineage in European banking that included the Rothschilds, Goldman Sachs, Kuhn Loebs and Warburgs. In 1923 Mason found himself at the helm of a post wielding power and influence. This he enjoyed, garnering support and praise from Strong. In his dealings with the multiplicity of clients, associates and fraternity of the rich and plutocratic he came into contact with many of their attorneys. It was to one establishment, Curtis Fosdick and Belknap whose Broadway offices he had visited many times, that Raymond Fosdick, attorney to John D. Rockefeller arrived as usual early one morning. The same morning Toto found himself in front of another office on Broadway, for a meeting with John Rockefeller Prentice.

Having been contacted some days previously by Prentice, he had arranged they meet at the Alpha Delta Club. Rockefeller, for reasons he did not divulge, persuaded Toto to meet early at offices he designated on Broadway not a stone's throw from Fosdick's enterprise. Toto, oblivious to any implications of proximity, met him there.

"Glad you could come, Captain, or may I call you Albert?"

"Albert's fine," acknowledged Toto, settling himself down into one of two seats in the otherwise spartan office.

"Sounds like you've some leads helping investigations on the War Loans trail?"

"Since our last meeting," Prentice began, "I've managed to connect with the family attorneys and gave them a brief overview of your needs and seems they may be able to help."

"I've come up with information," replied Toto, "confirming the legitimacy of the claim, so with assistance from your contacts we can move forward."

Prentice was keen Toto recognized the worth of his introductory hand. Edging forward in his chair he looked across the desk at the Englishman and spoke in a guarded voice. Toto found that behavior strange, since no one else was present.

"As you're aware the attorneys my father uses are several and various. Each sector requires specialist knowledge and expertise."

Toto nodded.

"Fosdick and his group do not involve themselves in business not guaranteeing considerable remuneration. So you appreciate my connecting would be an inside job. They'd take your case in spite of its lack of worth. Do you follow me?"

Toto felt such a derogatory opinion to be insulting. He personally felt the venture to be worth several millions. Prentice's views he took as immature. Laying his gut feeling aside he answered.

"I hear where you're coming from and am grateful you've been able to use your influence on these people."

Prentice sat up.

"I was hoping we'd consider something more financially rewarding than gratitude."

He shifted noticeably as he awaited a response from the researcher. Toto sat upright in silence knowing his intuition to be correct. He waited for Prentice to become uncomfortable enough with the silence to proceed. He wanted the go between to call himself out, then he would respond.

"Well," continued Prentice uneasily, "we really don't know where this thing could go, how long it may take, but as you can appreciate Rockefellers make sure they maximize both time and energy in the pursuit of good business."

That they probably do, thought Toto as he witnessed Prentice's behavior becoming more uncouth.

One question he could not figure out.

Why is he pressing so early for a deal?

Toto assumed the man, still in his twenties, would have carried more acumen. He began to doubt this assumption. In spite of this he maintained composure and continued listening.

"So in the eventuality my introductions are found useful and if I'm in any way able to steer your ship further to the port of intentions, what would you say to a consideration of one percent of the final settlement in our partnership?"

"Too early in the process to ascertain percentages as, for all I know we may be talking just a few thousand and one percent would be no way commensurate with the assistance you've offered thus far," he flattered the youth. "We could agree in principle some sort of consideration, and leave the fine detail till we know better the sort of sums we're dealing with."

Toto could tell it was not the sort of reply he had expected. However Prentice did not want Toto to know there were far more pressing matters than wait and see could deal with. He certainly did not want to lose what could be a potential face-saver, and restoration back into the family, on offer. His gambling losses ostracized him from any financial benefit the Rockefeller name carried. He was desperate for any resources, so made a suggestion.

"I understand you've got my best interests at heart, let's suggest we look at an introductory fee then any percentage considerations can be ironed out later."

Toto smelt desperation; the sort of desperation coming from being strapped for even ten dollars. He had been down that road too many times to be a stranger to its face. Yet here was a Rockefeller on his uppers. It made little sense. Another thing he was conscious of was his own position. No way would he dole out hundreds of dollars up front. He thought about best to gain details of the attorneys without being stingy or ungrateful. Prentice hung on his silence.

"Tell you what," replied Toto breaking the pause. "I'll give you twenty dollars today then when the time comes for better clarification, we can look at more meaningful figures."

Toto knew it was a pittance but was more interested in Rockefeller's reaction.

"Yes, that sounds fine by me – happy to negotiate later on," Prentice agreed, trying hard to hide desperation.

Leaning over into a draw in the desk in front of him he pulled a pen and paper from it.

"I'll give you the details here for Fosdick and tell him to expect a visit from you shortly."

Toto wondered why the fellow did not have a business card for these attorneys but let it pass. Prentice stood up, eager the two left swiftly. Toto obliged, as he was somewhat brusquely shepherded out of the office, down the stairs and onto the street.

He missed Prentice swiftly turn the lock in the door behind them and pocket the key. He felt it very odd the meeting came to such an abrupt end. At least he had a contact. Prentice hurriedly bid his farewell, speeding off in the opposite direction.

Had Toto not had his back to the office they had just vacated, he would have witnessed the rightful owners arrive for another day's work, oblivious to the fact they had hosted, minutes earlier, a cuckoo in their nest.

CHAPTER EIGHTEEN

In his mailbox at the Alpha Delta Club, several envelopes awaited him. One carried a German postmark. He ignored the others.

Sitting down at a mahogany table lit warmly by an art deco lamp, he proceeded to open the stuffed envelope, while the others lay scattered across the table top. It was from sister Leila. Reading the lengthy epistle told him all he needed to know. Both Louis and Leila were glad to receive the memorandum, they supported further research and had remitted one hundred and seventy five pounds to the nominated bank. Toto lent back much relieved. A quick mental calculation assured a good reserve.

As he considered next options, as Willy entered.

"Thought I'd find you here," his nephew greeted cheerily, "Having visited the attorneys on Broadway, thought I'd check out a hunch."

"Your timing's perfect, as I've just read Leila's reply."

Willy looked apprehensive.

"No need," encouraged Toto, "all's good, though Louis was keen for me to get professional advice as soon as possible."

"Eminently sensible and news is the attorneys are happy to have a meeting with you when you're ready," Willy shared.

"So who are these guys you've set me up with?" asked Toto.

"A good company Curtis Fosdick..."

"and Belknap," completed Toto.

"How did you know?" Willy asked, surprised at his uncle's insight.

Toto realized he had not told him about the meeting with Prentice.

"That's because it's the second time I've heard that name. Had a strange meeting with Prentice who suggested the same people, informing me they were family attorneys."

"They are," confirmed Willy. "Working with us for some time now. Why strange?"

"He became awfully pushy on commissions for his part in all this. Felt too sudden, hardly meriting his background, really odd."

"Word on the grapevine," Willy informed him, "is the young man's not too hot at holding onto money. At Yale he frittered away a small fortune on the gaming tables and old Prentice royally pissed with his son, last heard, cut him from the family coffers."

"That makes a lot of sense, from his behavior with me. Thankfully I was loathe to move that conversation on at all," Toto shared with evident relief.

97

"Thanks for clearing that one up, now I'm decided," he added.

"On what?"

"Before you arrived I was wondering in which order I tackle the tasks ahead. Charleston needs clearing up."

"Unfinished personal business?" Willy asked. "By all accounts you two made a huge impact on the chattering champagne set at Neily's, and before you mention it, yes, news travels like wildfire with that lot. The more the rich and famous come on board, the easier it is to muster press, bankers and public."

Toto was happy.

"So see Fosdick, visit Anne, what next?"

"Europe, Leila and Louis, then back here early next year. "

"Attorneys need detail to work on before rushing back to Europe." Willy suggested anxiously.

They agreed and Willy left assured by Toto he'd meet after Fosdick.

A letter with a Charleston postmark lay in front of him. Opening it he read Anne's message. He missed her terribly. This relationship felt different from the others.

Isabella, his wife, Adrian's mother, had come at a time when he desperately wanted a marriage matching what Leila and Rose had found - aristocracy, moneyed families, a swirling social scene and reciprocal wealth. Louis married for love. His path felt like abject failure compared to theirs.

Yet here in New York, following a failed marriage, desertion of his son, failure in Brazil, he began to view Anne as heralding new beginnings in work and relationship. He reread her words. Strange days. Still no tangible reference point. Where would the dog turn? What nudge would he give his master? He laid it out so succinctly in a book, yet he was human. He thought of Baum. That dog never gave Dorothy an answer. It bugged him. He thought about that.

He asked himself, who is Toto? The question went round and round. Then it hit him. He was, quite simply, himself. His mind wandered back to the bedroom at Cavendish.

His Toto understood. His inner self knew and guided him. As he remembered how important it had been to listen, he realized Baum created Toto to reflect Dorothy's own Self. Baum's intention gradually dawned on Toto and recognized that message was far more than whirlwinds, tin men, and scarecrows travelling the yellow brick road. Hijacking his nickname, interpreting it, as theft was really a gift in disguise. He finally got it.

Yes, listening to inner guidance all is well. Failures were times he did not. He remembered Tesla's words, so familiar. The table lamp, casting its light beam across his letters, like a switch, opened his mind. Realization dawned, it all became clear.

He picked up her letter, kissed it, thanking Anne for words whose magic had performed such service.

"Yes! Yes! Yes!" he exclaimed, punching the erudite air of the common room.

Members littered in chairs around the room looked up from their newspapers with expressions reserved for irritating flies. Before Toto came into swatting distance, he had made the call for an appointment that afternoon with Fosdick.

CHAPTER NINETEEN

The economic boom defining the twenties in America could be described simply as the bedrock strength of a country intent on establishing its greater, more powerful influence on a world keen to move forward from the ravages of conflict and deprivation. Toto's experiences in the trenches in Europe had shocked and disillusioned him enough to realize wars merely served those that never went over the top nor suffered, shell shocked from munitions others made fortunes from. The catastrophe of senseless slaughter led him to resign his commission. His pen became his sword. Sister Leila, having spent the war years in Germany around the Kaiser, shared her perspective within the family; a viewpoint starkly illustrating how propaganda and desire to cast the enemy as prime motivator of terrible, self serving actions became essential tools justifying, to the ill educated, the rightness of war. In short Toto gained first-hand life lessons in the art of propaganda and manipulation. It sickened and disillusioned him in equal measure.

Willy also experienced both sides of the coin. It colored his approach and motivation in his present position. Meeting his uncle, following the attorney's appointment, he noticed Toto to be far brighter and eager to share.

"During the meeting Fosdick confirmed, in no uncertain terms, Prentice's relation to the firm. He also, credit to him, went beyond client confidentiality and explained the situation between Rockefeller and his son. It included the gambling you referred to, indicating a level of regard and trust for both the project and myself."

"Not wishing to usurp youth over years, but everyone in this business, from my experience, has an agenda either personal or prompted by ulterior motive. Inevitably that fulfils someone higher up the chain."

"Fosdick is absolute in his allegiance to his major clients, so take it from me it was merely to initiate, soften up and gain your confidence he shared the information. As much as our company has dealings with them, it's obvious when push comes to shove, we're minnows compared with the Rockefeller whale," Willy clarified.

"He gave me the name of a Mister Mason over at the Federal Reserve, are you saying that was with an ulterior motive as well?"

"Perhaps not, Toto, it's often hard to decipher rings within rings these people spin. Always good to be aware a stranger's interest or kindness, especially when it revolves around money – and in this case a lot of money potentially

– will always carry motive and self interest, even if it is as innocent as to look like helpful. I'd add, coming from an attorney, it's twice as likely to be self-serving. They do love accruing business directly or through favor."

Toto respected his nephew enough to take the advice he shared.

"So this Mason fellow, how did Fosdick paint him?" Willy asked, eager to find out more.

"Just that he was well positioned in the Federal Reserve, had a good ear and eye on what may or may not be going on in respect of the Government's War Loans commitments. He also added Mason had a background in law and therefore could be instructive in the legality and approach necessary. I can quite see how that could be a plus. He said the position of General Counsel was a powerful one."

"Quite right, it is. Attorneys, even with the sort of clientele Fosdick can boast, enjoy feasting on a good case if it looks like the end result means accrued fees. It's why I use the firm with deliberate restraint," his nephew confided.

"I think you'll find Mason useful and worth your while hashing up on the Fed; see how they're positioned in respect of Government commitments. The war loans issue has been a hot potato with no one willing to step up to the plate and put a signature to it. Since the Fed tends to open and close the sluice gate of funds, their role is crucial for a positive outcome. When are you meeting with Mason?"

"The sooner the better, I can then plan Europe." Toto concluded, feeling the urgency of things.

"Worth thinking why Fosdick, an attorney, suggested Mason, also an attorney. Of course he's in the Fed, but Mason and Fosdick are not exactly business partners. So ask yourself, why would you give away a good prospect?" Willy suggested as a parting thought.

Toto promised to look at that detail. He did not inform his nephew of added funds, whose telegraphed notice he had received and drawn down.

Several days later the meeting with Mason arrived. In front of an impressive glass-doored entrance to the Federal Reserve on Liberty Street, he was ushered into the Bank by two heavily armed guards. Others around the entrance carried Winchester repeaters. A bank heist would not have been a prudent way to riches here, he mused recognizing the wisdom in an appointment.

The imposing interior sent a shiver of respect down Toto's spine, as the side-armed usher led him down a long corridor, up some stairs and towards the office of Randolph Mason.

Entering his attention was drawn to the deep pile carpet underfoot. To his left floor to ceiling bookcases along one wall, were loaded with heavy tomes and accounting ledgers. One whole shelf had burgundy, leather-bound sets of books with indecipherable titles - legal volumes for sure. Nothing passed this man unless it contained his signature of approval. In front of him he was guided to one of two oak chairs expensively plumped in leather upholstery. These faced a heavy oak office table whose top held three sections covered in expensive Italian leather inlay. Sitting there, confronted by three highly decorated panels on the desk facing him, its Italian style motifs demonstrated respect for European taste. It also carried the gravitas an institution wishing to be conveyed to anyone on his side. He pondered this showcasing as Mason entered.

"Captain Trapman, thank you for coming, and I beg your pardon for keeping you waiting."

"Not at all," Toto responded, getting up to shake the General Counsel's hand. "Kind of you to see me at such short notice."

They both sat down and Mason opened the discussion.

"I understand from Mister Fosdick you've a project that could benefit from our assistance here at the Federal Reserve. Perhaps it's best you give me an overview."

Toto proceeded to give Mason an account of his research and discovery of the outstanding Revolutionary War Loan. Mason listened intently and as Toto finished, he sat back in his chair behind the massive desk.

Bringing his hands together, fingers touching and elbows resting on the arms of the chair, he pondered a moment before responding, tapping his fingers together. Mason was a considered man. Easy to see how any legal argument would journey within the recesses of such a mind. His stocky five foot eight build, shortened neck and lean features reminded Toto of some of those East End boxers who had the temerity to saunter over to the Chelsea barracks in London and challenge the Royal Engineers to a boxing tournament. Mason had no broken nose, so his looks reflected the studious rather than the sporty.

"That, Captain is an impressive tale. It highlights an equally impressive debt the country owes your forebear. Although I'm merely the legal arm of this institution, at six percent compound that would create a sizeable sum outstanding."

Toto was glad the man recognized its substance.

"So how do you feel we at the Fed could aid you in your quest for reparation?"

"I believe your legal background can assist in guiding this case through the appropriate channels to repayment. Since you're within the confines of what I assume would be those funding such repayments, inside assistance would help," Toto remarked.

Mason shifted his position, pulled a pad towards him he had been jotting points on and made more notes.

"I admit I'm intrigued with this case and happy to be of whatever help I can be to aid your progress. Certainly it might involve inside knowledge, as you rightly point out."

Toto looked cheered.

"However the nature of such a claim does rather make one thing apparent. At the Federal Reserve our natural inclination and position are, let's say, on the opposite side of the fence, if you will."

Toto looked perplexed. It had never occurred to him there may be conflict of interests.

"Does that rule out your being able to help me?"

"On the contrary, Captain. Luckily having been here for some years I've decided to move back into my former capacity as an attorney enabling me to help you with, let's say, fewer hands tied behind my back. My contacts within the Federal Reserve become an asset."

"Sounds useful," agreed Toto.

Mason grimaced. His features gaunt, yet retaining signs of a life well fed and watered, offered no real warmth as he proffered his best attempt at a smile. For Toto it appeared more condescending than honest. Mason's black-rimmed spectacles struggled to remain in place as he attempted this facial maneuver.

How strangely a face can change in moments, thought Toto.

Before he was tempted to ask what was on the Council's mind, Mason spoke.

"From what you've told me I suggest public backing for this venture, interest and support. I can sort legal formats you'll need for the case. Getting backing from prominent members of Congress is a must. Have you thought about public perception?"

Toto aware marketing on the public consciousness was crucial including his moves towards Hollywood,was cautious divulging his steps to Mason. Something bugged him. He felt the man was reading the script he, Toto, was writing.

"With a friendly press and as a correspondent with my London newspaper, that's easy to mobilize."

Mason raised his eyebrows.

"Journalist? No wonder your facts and figures are rigorous, I can assure you it'll serve you well when it comes to the legal case. You'll need all the figures and facts you can lay your hands on," warned Mason.

"The Federal Reserve is minded to make sure all government commitments are honorably met as long as the legal entitlement runs to your door. I cannot see we'll encounter problems. From what you say our nation might not have been created, Washington ending up at the end of a rope, one more troublemaker on the gallows of Empire. Without your ancestor Moore, we might never have met. If nothing else I thank the family for making all this possible," Mason said, genially gesticulating with both arms an imaginary landscape of continent to his left and right.

"It's good to be part of a magnanimous gesture, yet I can't take more credit than rediscovering the generous gift," Toto replied humbly.

"One discovery, Captain Trapman, that could see you the recipient of a considerable windfall. Let's hope that's the case, not forgetting it may very well be an irritant in the side of the Government's financial well-being, stranger things have happened."

Mason again offered an ingratiating smile. It failed miserably. Toto realized the man would be a useless poker player. He might though, turn out to be the person in the right place at the right time with the right connections. That looked to be four useful aces for Toto to play with.

"Prepare a report on your findings, along with some of the main leads you've made with supporting documents and send it to me."

"Sounds a sensible plan. I'll get them sent over," Toto confidently assured Mason.

The Council rose from his seat, signaling the end of their meeting. Toto obliged by doing the same. They shook hands over the table and he was escorted to the front door of the building. As Toto exited onto Liberty Street Mason turned round and placed a call to his contact at Curtis Fosdick and Belknap.

Back at the club, Toto gathered notes, checked the status of where he was with the whole business and answered a newly arrived letter from Anne.

How easy she's made it for me, he thought.

Their time together made him yearn to see her again. He decided on a letter of thanks. A visit to Charleston would delay Europe, an imperative. It was Nikola Tesla who was long overdue a visit. Opening the travel case, prepared for his trip, a small box dropped from a pocket in the lid. It was from the triquetra heirloom.

Now if that's not a sign to meet up with Nikola he thought, *nothing is.*

Toto remembered the last conversation they had, where Nikola talked of gold not being the glory of power and progress starting in the mind. Donning his bicycle clips, he set off for West 40th on two wheels.

CHAPTER TWENTY

The case for the repayment of war loans by the government, revolutionary or otherwise had been a constant thorn in the side of subsequent administrations. Calvin Coolidge looked favorably on claims presented to the administration. This support encouraged Toto as he gathered more evidence on the legality of the claim.

In the offices of Curtis Fosdick and Belknap, a call from the Federal Reserve looked like strengthening his case. James Curtis lifted the receiver. His long acquaintance with the Bank and direct responsibility leading up to its establishment in 1913 meant strong relationships existed not only between himself and the Fed but for the whole firm of attorneys at law. It was the firm's intimate dealings with Rockefeller that allowed a seamless contact between the financial repository and one of the country's major corporate players and their important client.

"I had a meeting with your Captain Trapman and as you suggested I showed interest towards his enquiries. It would be best to lay out the procedural steps needed to advance this case."

Curtis made some notes as he listened.

"Certainly, I will speak with him when we next meet and let you know the outcome."

"Good," replied Mason. "If this claim looks like going the distance, because of its relative size, we need to make sure it does not become an embarrassment to the government. I'd therefore advise you make him aware of steps needed which could turn out to be lengthy."

"Understood," Curtis replied, knowing full well his role would be to temper or accelerate any progress.

Toto meanwhile arrived on West 40th making his way into number eight. Scanning the nameplates it was easy to spot Tesla's whereabouts. He hastened to his door. Kneeling to unfasten his bicycle clips, he knocked on the door. The right hand clip refused to extricate itself from round his ankle so he gave it a few firm tugs. The door opened.

"Doesn't seem to be anyone here," a voice shouted back into the room.

Toto looked up at a tall well dressed individual he knew immediately not to be Nikola.

"I am," he replied to the waist of the doorman, as he rose to his feet.

The man immediately leapt back in surprise at Toto's sudden appearance.

"Where did you come from?" he queried in astonishment.

"There," responded Toto pointing to the ground beneath him.

"The cellar?" replied the baffled gentleman at the door.

"Cellar, what cellar?" an equally perplexed Toto answered.

"Who's at the door, George?" Tesla's voice boomed across the room. "Come in whoever you are and close that door, the draught's disturbing the experiment," he commanded with impatience.

As Toto entered he witnessed the confused order Tesla was renowned for, all over the large office. Desks along the wall to his right contained files, papers and some impressive measuring instruments. In the center of the room a large long table set out with various measuring vessels, a carriage clock and several cups alongside an elegant pot he assumed was for Nikola's herb tea. He scanned to his left and met the scientist full on as he had turned to see who dropped by. A look of concern melted as Tesla recognized Toto.

"You dropped by," he proclaimed, as if the invitation had been made yesterday. Turning to George, he introduced him.

"You remember George, Captain, he looks after my affairs."

George stood up and moved towards Toto.

"We've not had the pleasure, George Scherff."

Toto reciprocated, making no issue of Tesla's memory lapse.

"George looks after the accounts, sees to my diary, deals with the patents and overall is my general manager. As a scientist I'm in need of order. George here is an invaluable asset and we've been a team for what...?"

"Thirty three years, Nikola," Scherff assisted Tesla.

Nikola leapt up.

"All the threes, very special number three. Very special indeed."

"Why's that?"

Nikola moved over to the table in the center of the room and beckoned Toto sit. He obliged and awaited an answer. Tesla paced up and down in front of him.

"It's the trilogy of energy, frequency and vibration. Holds the template of the master creator, the secrets of the universe, the controlling element of force, matter and consciousness. Without these vital elements I'd never have sensed the pathways to my inventions," Tesla explained.

"Interesting you use the word sense, Nikola. I've always been convinced science is a nuts and bolts development," Toto remarked.

Nikola shot back.

"Nuts and bolts as you call them only appear once the labyrinth of mental discovery has been negotiated. Your classical education showed you a labyrinth's a place to get easily lost without the slim silk cord of consciousness connecting the start. Having suffered egos flexing in their own research, attempting to cut my silken connection, consciousness is the single most important factor in our development. Without it we remain mere parrots of what others tell us reality is. That's the damnation afflicting so many in the world."

Toto sat spellbound. He appreciated how someone with Tesla's intellect and vision fed different canyons of the mind, those offering larger more meaningful creation than mere dollars and gold. He also recognized his present quest was precisely constructed to accrue dollars and gold yet felt no conflict of interest, merely healthy distraction.

"So what's reality for you, Nikola?" Toto eagerly asked.

Tesla stopped pacing and turned directly to his visitor.

"Life is and will ever remain an equation incapable of solution, but it contains certain known factors. A realization I came to some time back. Our virtues and failings are inseparable, like force and matter. When they separate, man is no more. Reality is of our own making and that can only be asserted through the age old precepts of science. Experimentation until a satisfactory result is obtained."

"So are you telling me failure is merely an experimental stepping stone on the path to success?"

"Absolutely, it can be nothing other, though fine men have dragged themselves to ruinous thinking allowing failure to define their life and work. This powerful aid to success has been turned into a tyrant and overlord."

"Certainly sheds new light on my escapades in the Amazon. Others chalked it up as yet another failure of vision, planning and enterprise."

"What they forget is the very failure energized you come here to New York, sit, research deeply and create a volume of profound insight into the canine race. That in turn led you to make discoveries previously undiscovered by your consciousness. That led you seek justice for a past good overdue reparation. These things await us, in spite of our present ignorance as to their existence. As researchers and scientists we need an open mind; clear thought processes and a willingness to accept failure as part and parcel of the whole."

"Many scientists think deeply," Toto, suggested.

"Scientists of today think deeply instead of clearly. One must be sane to think clearly, but one can think deeply and be quite insane," Tesla replied, allowing a wry smile to cross his face.

Scherff turned around as Tesla spoke and added.

"Many suffering insanity in our community today, defend that insanity by trashing patents Nikola keeps supplying."

Toto turned in his chair and asked.

"Why is that, George? Does jealousy run so deep as to deafen the exchange of competing views?"

"Competition feeds baser energies of ego and drowns out cooperative ventures leading to progress. Desperation to win, conquer and overcome all opposition, holds a vice-like grip on our world today," Scherff concluded in a considered tone he reserved for such private conversations.

"Is competition outmoded?" Toto asked, unable to grasp the concept.

"Far from it," replied Scherff. "Absolute power requires absolute control. When that control looks like slipping, the mighty struggling for domination show their teeth. Explicitly when Morgan pulled out of Wardenclyffe. It became a threat to his empire of supply. For Nikola it was an opportunity to furnish mankind with free energy."

Nikola looked at the two of them. The passage of time had not lessened pain, etched on his features.

Sighing deeply he answered Scherff.

"I said then and repeat now. Humanity has not yet sufficiently advanced to be willingly led by the discoverer's keen searching sense. But who knows, perhaps it's better in this present world of ours that a revolutionary idea or invention instead of being helped and patted, be hampered and ill-treated in its adolescence – by want of means, by selfish interest, pedantry, stupidity and ignorance. That it be attacked and stifled, pass through bitter trials and tribulations and through the strife of commercial existence. So one day the light of its origins shines for all. All that was great in the past was ridiculed, condemned, combated, suppressed – only to emerge all the more powerfully, all the more triumphantly from the struggle."

All three for a moment bathed in Tesla's profound insight.

"The very nature of three, Toto, force, matter and consciousness at play. That is why I hold the number three as a pivotal axis in everything I do, inspire and create," Tesla continued.

Toto remembered he brought the triquetra and took it from around his neck.

"What have we got there," asked Tesla noticing the heirloom. "You're going to present me with some medal of discovery, then?"

Both chuckled.

"After our last talk on the way home from the Astor, I wanted to show you something. You said then that gold was not in the glory of power but started in the mind."

"Good, yes you have an excellent memory, like mine," the scientist encouraged.

"The reason it reminded me was because of this my father gave me."

"On the boat coming over to meet me years ago, I remember," Tesla recalled, with a friendly impatience to see the object of their discussion.

"Precisely. Here's the piece."

He placed it delicately in the inventor's open palms. Tesla gazed with wonder at the three-pointed interlaced symbol.

The Latin insignia complemented the simple design. Tesla ran a forefinger along the inscription as if decoding a hidden meaning. Toto watched the progress, then looked up at the older man's face. He could have sworn it shone with a luminance blotting out the lines of fatigue yet excused the image as a trick of the light. It lingered, with Toto feeling strange.

Nikola asked Toto to repeat its meaning.

The researcher returned to the present.

"I thought as much," replied the scientist. "Remember what I said on Fifth Avenue. You've not been endowed this token for trivial purpose. Your journey's just beginning. It's imperative you cultivate a mind to cut through dark recesses you'll negotiate. Learn from my experience. Glory as others interpret it is not for the taking. It's for those coming after us. It's the gift fearless souls seed that will break through the mockeries of men."

He paused to let it sink into Toto's consciousness. Toto felt trapped in what felt like steel pincers holding his skull. Had he been in one of those nineteenth century photography studios in Mayfair he might have expected this torture keeping the head and body still for long exposures. Here it riveted attention and movement to the spot. He listened as Tesla continued.

"William had a noble soul to have us meet as we did. Your innocence though will be your undoing, unless you harness it. In this world of knaves your naïveté must be throttled."

"At this moment I feel my head both throttled and harnessed," Toto blurted out inelegantly.

Taking his remark in his stride Tesla merely replied.

"For those experiencing a rapid and precise focus on the present it can feel that way. Rest assured once you have experienced it a few more times, you'll recognize it heralding a call for your fullest attention."

Whatever is he talking about? Toto wondered.

Like a mind-reader Tesla answered.

"I'm talking about that certain space we all can enter. The creative silent place of listening. I call it inner space. You allowed yourself to fold into it. The ease with which you relaxed into our conversation made space for inner reception to become alert. In that space I receive my most profound insights. Just allow it to happen without getting yourself in the way. It acts as conduit for extraordinary insight."

Tesla motioned for George to join them. He was keen to share his insight into the heirloom with both of them.

As weird as what he had just experienced felt, Toto was perfectly able to accept anything could happen in the presence of this extraordinary man and let it settle.

Tesla raised the triquetra so George, who had by now appeared over his right shoulder, could glimpse it better.

"You see George how this is three-pointed. It holds the three dimensions of space, thought, thinker and the thing. It is past, present and future. It is time itself, penetration, procedure and pervasion. You of all people know how sacred the number three is to me. Perhaps this now enlightens you as to why it holds this power."

George Scherff nodded.

Toto listened.

"The day science begins to study non-physical phenomena, it will make more progress in one decade than in all the previous centuries of its existence. So for now I carry on creating through connection to the non-physical and you Toto, with this as talisman, must address the physical head on. This will remind you, help you and be your very own conduit to the answer."

Tesla sat back, closed his eyes and held the heirloom tightly between both hands. Scherff slid silently back to his desk and Toto began processing everything he had heard.

As Tesla opened his eyes, they seemed bright, powerful and at peace. It was the first time Toto had witnessed such serenity in the man. When he spoke his voice was soft, yet powerful.

"When you return to New York, visit me. If I have moved you will know where to find me. I'm here for you."

"As I am for you," Toto heard himself reply instantly.

He had not told the inventor of his plans to return to Europe.

Interesting, he thought.

"You keep yourself and your work safe while I'm gone."

Looking across to George, Toto added.

"Though you have a trusted ally to protect you from the wolves."

"Worry not," replied Tesla. "All my best work is held here."

He tapped his temple with two fingers.

"Everything important is in here, they never leave this safe," he repeated, giving his head another couple of taps.

George Scherff looked over as Toto turned around. He could have sworn Scherff frowned at Tesla's response.

Tesla carefully returned the triquetra and Toto felt its warmth having been in Nikola's hands. Replacing it around his neck, he and Tesla made for the door. They bid each other farewell, promising to meet on his return.

As he pedaled past the Library on his left, Toto remembered with amusement the long hours compiling and completing the book on dogs. A similar impulse felt back with Tesla had been at work during his research into the supernatural attributes of the dog, those moments of clarity and insight. Perhaps as Tesla suggested, there is a space beyond the material where all strands of knowledge, known and unknown, float and have their being. He wished the Gordian knot within his present quest could as easily be cut to release the fortune he so dearly craved.

CHAPTER TWENTY-ONE

Aaron Kersh purposely cultivated ties on the Lower East Side of New York. In spite of accumulated wealth in property speculation and Wall Street, his substantial townhouse on West 15th Street represented meteoric progress up the greasy pole that was opportunity in America.

From the very first days after disembarking the Lucania, he came to realize stepping-stones to riches were people. It meant becoming indispensable to those above, ingratiating to those around you and invaluable to those beneath. Perception was important and to the ambitious young Kersh cultivation of Khazarian roots had been one of his main weapons on his ascent. As poor and victimized as his beginnings had been, these circumstances became fuel to power and merciless endeavor.

His Jewish cloak reminded him of the stench and filth he grew up with. His loathing of European Jews, represented by the likes of the Kuhn Loeb Company had to be hidden. He knew full well these Jewish bankers and traders were despised and respected equally, yet carried his ticket to money and power. It was the House of Morgan, the epitome of Yankee American ruling and operating alongside Kuhn Loeb in Wall Street, that received his greatest contempt. These two giants jousted for ownership atop the financial pyramid.

In the mid twenties Kersh, fortunate enough to catch the coat tails of a whirlwind get rich quick epidemic, emulated the king of schemes, one Charles Ponzi.

His Florida property scams encouraged Kersh to offer property purchasing at ten percent down with sell-on profits as swift as a tropical storm on the Keys. Kersh's ability to sell the dream, turn it round and sell it again before anyone cared or realized its intangibility earned him fortunes. Unlike Ponzi, Kersh sidestepped the inevitable fall and prosecution through timing, reinvestment and shell companies in New York property. He also played the penny share addiction, the precursor to the misery to follow.

His hatred of the Germanic Anglophile penchant riding up and down the Wall had others view him as a slick, get rich quick trader. He employed Jews, Armenians, Turks, German and Italian clerks and brokers to develop business. This marked him as tasteless from the big houses and a champion of the people from small investors.

Those hand-picked from the Lower East Side he found adroit, cheap and swift to learn. Where an unspoken, anti-Semitic attitude towards Jewish influx along the Wall was practiced, since the turn of the century, he went out of his way refuting such snobbery by recognizing their skills. The Morgan company, stamping Yankee American credentials all over their business, could not but cede recognition to their main rivals, the Kuhn Loeb business.

This self-serving acceptance did not prevent Kersh playing one off against the other to his own ends.

Unlike many having made their way up the ranks of the House of Morgan, Kuhn Loeb or Goldman Sachs, he interned under his own rules, his own show and never became answerable to anyone. To be invited into these establishments would have been an anathema.

Kersh intended his presence in the money markets to be far more than an irritation. He envisioned his drive, accrued influence and gratuitous disregard for law to grant third player status eventually swamping all other incumbents.

Disinterested in who and what traded along and around the Wall, Toto prepared for Europe.

To say he was oblivious to money and investment fever taking hold of the national psyche over the summer of 1928 would be factually incorrect.

His personal drive for riches and personal focus happened to rest solely on delivering the outstanding IOU. Others might have seen him as optimistic, an idealist, yet he found strength in the well researched rather than the gamble played out in sectors he knew little about. The never-had-it-so-good epidemic of the country, confirmed his time had arrived.

CHAPTER TWENTY-TWO

Mid October found Toto in Willy's office in New York. Having prepared to take the transatlantic crossing to Southampton, Toto made final plans for departure. As he sat with Willy a wry smile came across his nephew's face.

"What if I told you I'd arranged to get you to Europe in three days?" Willy threw him.

"I'd say you were pranking me, unless you've a rocket."

"Next best thing, old chap."

Toto leaned forward with interest and shot back.

"You been drinking or has Stafford designed you an airship?"

"Close but no potato. In your absence I've had interesting discussions with a Frankfurt based airship company and there could be developments handling their American business. I told them I had this journalist that would help them letting him fly the return leg of the first transatlantic flight." Willy proudly announced.

He sat back in his chair watching Toto's mouth drop.

He could not have been more surprised.

"Seriously?" Toto blurted with a mix of wonder and doubt.

"Deadly, almost inclined to take the ticket myself, but seeing it makes a heck of a story and delivers you post-haste to mother's door, seems only fair to make it out in your name."

Willy handed a one-way ticket for the Graf Zeppelin to Toto who took it and held it as if it were the most precious document.

Willy continued, relishing Toto's fascination.

"She flies in today, you'll be off tomorrow to Friedrichshafen?"

"Amazing. What an opportunity. A great story for a war correspondent with no war in sight."

The telephone rang. Willy picked it up.

As he listened to the caller, his expression changed.

Toto waited.

Placing the phone back on the receiver he looked across the desk at his uncle.

"The airship hit a snag in flight and after a bit of a zigzag journey, landed a few minutes ago at Lakehurst. Red faces but a huge success overflying Washington, Baltimore and Philadelphia and us here in New York. I'm told it's going to have to stay here a couple of weeks to repair the damage for the return. So news of your departure was premature," Willy joked as Toto's enthusiasm paused.

Two weeks later he found himself on the airship settling down to a three day return journey.

As good as their word and relief of a very enthralled Toto, the ship arrived before dawn on the first of November, a little under the three day estimate. On landing he made his way to the rail station, and a relaxing journey to Bad Homburg and a meeting with Leila.

During the journey he mapped each contact point in Europe and Britain.

Back in New York James Warburg, son of a pillar of the Federal Reserve, sat at his regular table at the back of the Three Hundred Club. Around him, several dancers lounged on chairs around his table as his sharpened pencil sketched away. The accomplished artist cut an unlikely figure, yet a high flier in finance, he created his own schedules. Adroit management, insight and an electric mind were the qualities to surpass his father's achievements.

The girls moved aside as another of the city's elite arrived at the table.

Warburg, signalled, pencil in hand, for him to sit.

"Thought a bevy of beauties would entice you."

"Their form's more honest than the bubbles," his guest responded, sitting down.

Warburg lay the pencil down, with a dismissive gesture, shooed his models away.

"Pretty things, but you're here on business, Neily."

Neily Vanderbilt knew perfectly well the young financier's request was anything but social.

"Bored of working the Wall, then?"

"Never. Just needed somewhere Morgan's people weren't littering. You'd have suggested the Yacht Club, crawling with brown-nose Morganites."

"Here's a good second. How can I help?"

"Pools."

Vanderbilt looked quizzical.

"We've several opportunities for investors to cream a lot off pools our people created," the young financier confided.

"You're telling me you need cover?" Neily inquired.

"Nothing as banal. The Englishman you're helping," Warburg clarified.

"I help many people, including the English. Who precisely?"

"That Trapman fellow, we need to know you can fully support him."

Vanderbilt was curious.

"He's on a mission with a claim on the Government."

"We're aware, something close to our heart. He's been asking help for it in several quarters. We're cooperating and wondered whether you'd be happy to continue support."

"You're aware I support him all the way. He's as much right to pursue his goals as any."

Warburg gazed at the results of his sketching, smiled to himself and looked Neily in the eye.

"We appreciate that. As you're aware, you have our complete support and we'll make sure you're taken care of, looking after our interests. The American dream is a most wonderful thing. We need it to be kept front of house for everyone do you understand?"

Neily grunted.

At that moment a young man leapt onto the stage below, sat at the piano and launched into a jazz number, Rhapsody in Blue.

"Now that's music," Neily said.

"Nope, Gershwin," Warburg corrected.

CHAPTER TWENTY-THREE

Toto's sister and brother-in-law celebrated his arrival in Bad Homburg, a spa town a short distance from Germany's financial center in Frankfurt am Main, making him feel part of the family.

Leila held a fond and protective custody over her younger brother, in spite of numerous demonstrations of bad judgment. She, of all the family knew the hardship he suffered following Louise, and the loss of both mother and brother. The man before her, was not the man she remembered.

"You're looking so well," she exclaimed as he walked with them into the villa they had built for themselves.

"Willy arranged traveling on the Graf Zeppelin," Toto replied.

"I heard. So much to catch up on," Leila bubbled over in her joy at his arrival.

"Hans is away at the moment and often talks about joining brother Willy in New York, in spite of good opportunities here. So for a few blissful days we have you to ourselves, which means planning the Moore Millions project," Leila suggested, as they all settled into the large, light and imposing living room gracing the eighteenth century villa.

His arrival was well timed as the maid appeared with full tea and cakes.

"All very familiar," noted Toto, at ease in the presence of his sister.

He enjoyed the company of his brother-in-law and was happy to see Leila so content.

Wilhelm von Meister, a very handsome, charming and imposingly tall Prussian, carried a natural military bearing with confidence. Having spent much of his professional life in the service of government and diplomacy, these qualities were what first attracted attention, early in life, from the Royal Court. Empress Frederick asked Wilhelm to come and serve in Homburg and from that time the family often called upon his judgment and opinion. With Leila's inimitable charm, talents and natural diplomatic manner they procured a unique position within the higher echelons of the Royal Court and German aristocracy. Toto recognized full well this could only become an asset for his own goals. That the Kaiser also demanded to become Willy's godfather carried kudos as he and Willy worked Europe.

"Leila tells me you've discovered a pot of gold," Wilhelm kick-started the conversation.

"Great if it was a done deal but every treasure hunt has its curves and forks," Toto replied realistically.

"Willy, listen to what he has to say. It's not another of his madcap ideas."

"As much as I've ended up on my bum many times," Toto admitted, "we've leads from the Federal Reserve and the legislature, calling this loan in."

"You're implying help from our contacts could influence Congressional interests to close the overdue reparation."

"Precisely," Toto agreed.

"Wouldn't our economic pit carry less weight than, say, the British?" Wilhelm queried.

"Toto's going to England. We're part of a European support initiative," Leila reminded.

"The point is," Toto broke in, "I've got press and Hollywood backing the political clout we can gather this side. Getting the City and the likes of Lady Astor to root for us is icing on the cake. Leila, you're well connected with Haldene, Hardinge and their kind. Been a few years since he was Ambassador to France but they're all favors to call in."

Leila looked to Wilhelm with tender affection.

"I'm sure between Willy and myself we can gather necessary contacts willing to support the cause. As for Hardinge, he's easily flattered. Leave that to your sister." Leila assured her brother.

She turned to Wilhelm.

"What about Ludwig Landmann, can't he connect us with the financial bigwigs in Frankfurt?"

Landmann, renowned as he was respected, was the first Jewish mayor of Frankfurt. What he had done during his time in office to transform the reputation and look of this financial hub was exemplary.

"You're such a strategist. I've no doubt left in a room of squabbling diplomats and politicians she'd bring them to order in minutes," replied Wilhelm, in admiration of his wife's skills.

"Maybe this Landmann chap has contacts with the voracious Kuhn Loeb empire ruling Wall Street," suggested Toto.

"You'll find the Kuhn Loeb family have very good connections. They're married into Warburg here in Hamburg. The banking families maintain a strong hold on US and global financial markets. Worth remembering they're also a law unto themselves. Get on the wrong side of them – you won't enjoy the ride. Ludwig can testify to that," Wilhelm warned Toto, in a tone hiding nothing for his low opinion of moneymen.

"Sounds like you've little time for bankers and speculators," Toto observed.

Wilhelm took the opportunity to expand on the view.

"Frankly these men spend their lives not only lining their own pockets at the expense of everyone else, but have no compunction placing the most onerous pressure on anyone standing in their way. I've seen first hand how, especially here in Frankfurt, they manipulate power and political sway producing vile, if not criminal, outcomes. As for those vultures on Wall Street, I would advise no one cross them or try to beat them."

"The attorneys we're using work for Rockefeller and they partner Kuhn Loeb. From what you're saying I'd best keep an eye our project doesn't cross anyone there," Toto suggested.

"Precisely, always a good idea keeping potential allies sweet. Willy has the measure of these wolves," Wilhelm advised. "We can muster the right noises here for you."

Wilhelm swiftly set up a meeting with friend Ludwig Landmann and as they both crossed Romerberg Square, the mayor cut across to meet them from the city hall. Toto marveled at the medieval architecture as Landmann guided them to a cafe tucked into some of its best features.

They entered, with those recognizing Landmann turning to acknowledge the local figurehead. An eager waiter ushered them to a table, set back from the main group. Toto enjoyed the association of brother-in-law and powerful local dignitary. Although an unknown quantity, Landmann's authority impressed him.

The mayor mischievously leaned towards Toto and in a pronounced yet distinctive accent addressed the researcher.

"Captain Trapman, Wilhelm tells me you're on a mission. I'm most attracted to missions. My present mission is to make Frankfurt the financial centre of the world. Is yours as grand?" he pronounced, rolling back in his chair, chortling quietly.

The shrewd Jew reciprocated the comfortable relationship the others had.

Toto delivered a fluent overview to the mayor. The latter fascinated over the dependence the founding fathers placed on philanthropy to a cause.

"Philanthropy is a magnificent action. Speaks volumes for those whose belief is strong enough to lend it financial support," he observed.

"In the States there are two sorts of philanthropy," Toto responded. "One self-serving and the other coming from selfless service. The former brings out the worst doing it for self glory, the goodwill card a mere gesture."

The others listened intently, neither having a great deal of personal experience of the States.

"True. Here in Germany we have those willing to steal one's birthright as swiftly as offer support, none more so than the bankers," suggested Wilhelm.

Landmann nodded agreement.

"There are very powerful elements controlling the banking system's ebb and flow, hidden behind a facade of legitimacy. As mayor I get glimpses of such things, though my position offers little hope to expose such matters. It's always been a messy mix of political, corporate and financial incest each serving its own interests."

He scanned the cafe, mentally noting influential faces, taking the opportunity to acknowledge anyone he had missed on arrival. Toto noticed the gesture.

"Do you feel you have to watch your back around here as mayor?"

Landmann, surprised at Toto's observation, answered.

"Not so much as feeling I have to be on my guard, careful not to cross anyone by ignoring them. Vanity in this city, as in all centers of high commerce, is a game of competing egos. So in my brief sojourn as mayor I play my part, keep my own counsel and learn everyone's position on a constantly changing ladder."

Landmann, stickler for protocol, was no fool and adept at recognizing this changing landscape. He also chose his close friends with great discrimination. Wilhelm was one such choice.

"Wilhelm asked me to meet you as your mission requires some influence within European financial circles."

"Right," confirmed Toto.

Landmann continued.

"So we need to furnish you with some heavy hitters from the financial sector and aristocrats not already included on your family's roster. I'm happy to be eyes and ears, from within the belly of the financial beast."

"Sounds both intriguing and a little dangerous."

"Captain, as the first Jewish mayor, I've had my share of intimidation to face, confront and overcome."

"If there's a way to bend the Kuhn Loeb ear and direct their influence in Wall Street, I'd appreciate it. Their leverage in the Federal Reserve and Congress is considerable," Toto shared.

"As is their relation with Warburg as I mentioned. I can work on that," assured Landmann.

"What sort of quid pro quo is entailed?" Toto asked.

Landmann appreciated Toto's grasp of back scratching.

"I may not be too familiar with the inside dealings on Wall Street, however money centers are pretty much the same everywhere, be it here, London or New York. Carrot and stick against donkeys and thoroughbreds alike attract the same diet.

"American banks own much of our infrastructure in lieu of loans and security against war reparations. The Versailles Treaty saw to that. I just hope the Weimar's dependence on American financial support does not weaken the cause," Wilhelm added.

"That dependency creates underdogs. Luckily I'm well aware Herr Schacht as president of the Reichsbank is keen to lessen that dependency. His trips recently to New York with your Bank of England head Montagu Norman, have helped lessen reparations. He has influence and contacts. That's my territory," agreed Landmann.

Toto felt energized. He warmed to the wise and empathic mayor. Landmann had the mischievous look of one who enjoyed untangling insuperable problems.

"So now we launch this great mission," Landmann suggested rubbing his hands together. "Let's develop the strongest case for a just outcome. If we can persuade Americans philanthropy leads to greater brotherhood, then the old dogs of Europe can still teach young pups new tricks."

Toto laughed. He immediately knew where a copy of his book on dogs he had with him, needed to be gifted.

"As it happens," he remarked, "I've recently published a book on dogs. Seems appropriate you should get a copy, assuming you like the creatures."

"I most certainly do. My wife and I have a most faithful German Shepherd keeping us safe and sane when mayoral madness tests our limits. He also has a, how do you English say, bark greater than bite frightening unannounced visitors."

Toto handed the volume to the mayor, who received it with the utmost respect. Mission accomplished, all three left the cafe and bid Landmann farewell.

After a hectic round of soirées, teas and lunches Toto headed for the station and boat train to Calais and home.

As he boarded, a hand tugged his elbow. He turned surprised to see Landmann on the platform.

"Glad I caught you before leaving, a quiet word," he urged. " The train is delayed a few minutes so we still have time."

Toto saw concern written all over Landmann's face. He let the porter take his bags and joined the mayor on a bench.

"I've been investigating on your behalf. Seems your case has the big wigs in Frankfurt talking. That's not what I want to tell you."

"What?" Toto asked

"We're dealing on many layers. The bankers, money, who wins, who loses," Landmann confided.

"Dog eat dog," suggested Toto.

"Precisely," agreed the mayor with no hint of humor. "That's why it's so important you realize who you're dealing with."

"I don't understand, they're merely bankers?"

"More than that Captain. There are ruthless parties who control. I know well of what I'm telling you. It's important you're forewarned."

"Forewarned is forearmed," Toto replied.

"Precisely. As a Jew in this country it's becoming a challenge. My position as mayor is celebrated as something of an achievement. I have broken a mould, part of the established order."

"That's good, right?"

"Yes and no. Sometimes these things happen for reasons beyond what appears to be represented. I'm no fool, at the same time I also love this country and recognize it's dragging itself from a dark hell. I see a bright future for us all, like you, where difference is celebrated, not stigmatized. I know your efforts are coming from that place. Some however are hell-bent on cultivating division as a control tool. These people, I'm sad to share have taken on the appearance of being part of the Jewish people. With their craft and wit, they use the veins of finance and banking, which we're so gifted in handling, to run tentacles throughout these corridors and our lives. One aim as mayor is to make Frankfurt a financial capital writ large in the world and ethical."

"From what I've heard you've a very impressive following already," added Toto.

"What you've not heard is there are elements behind the adulation who see me as the enemy, a hindrance to their plans. I wish the reputation I seek to be built on trust, transparency and integrity, qualities some loathe. My advice to you is, never take anyone for who they say they are, who they project to the world. In your book I read about the supernatural qualities you suggest dogs have and utilize. The senses so fine-tuned as to decipher between a threat and a friend. Hone these senses in yourself. Develop fine discrimination around everyone – and I mean everyone. That my dear Captain will be your strength, not your weakness."

Toto was shocked by the mayor's words, yet felt compelled to listen.

"You're destined for great things and because of that you will be sorely tested. It's the way of these things. The best are never handed it on a silver platter, they have to dig and dig deep."

The mayor stood and ushered Toto to his feet.

"Now your train's about to depart and the real journey is beginning. I shall be in contact. Be cautious, careful and treasure your nearest and dearest. That's the real gold."

Toto climbed into the carriage and turned to thank his visitor. The train pulled away and he watched a slight yet powerful figure, hands in pocket, witness his departure, then disappear swiftly into the belching steam from the mighty engine.

CHAPTER TWENTY FOUR

The boat train made good time to London, with Toto making connection to Tunbridge Wells and a stay with brother Louis, nephew John and a healthy retinue making up the Trapman household. Young John, at thirteen, reminded him of Adrian, his own son. He wondered, as the train sped through the English countryside, why his fondness for his nephew felt stronger than for his son.

"Father tells us you've been fighting the bankers and Americans!" John exclaimed excitedly as he attempted to pick up and carry the smaller of two cases dropped onto the platform on Toto's arrival.

Toto smiled, reminded of his own childhood excitement felt on William's returns from foreign excursions.

"It's been one heck of a skirmish but we survived. I seem to recall we never finished that battle of the Dardanelles we got into last time. If we get a chance we'll pick it up, following the rules Mister Wells laid down in Little Wars."

"Oh, yes please Uncle. I love that book you sent me. Can we, father?" John asked, turning to Louis.

His father, a towering, handsome figure of a gentleman, blue eyes sparkling, dressed in a fine mohair coat, sporting a dark trilby and the finest shoes Jermyn Street in London's Piccadilly furnished, nodded approval. Swiftly he ushered the reception committee and his brother to the awaiting car, where Rumens, their chauffeur, waited to drive them all home.

Once settled, Louis turned to Toto.

"Keen to hear how it went in Germany and how dear Leila and Willy are. You must be tired from all the travelling."

"Exciting developments all round over there," replied his brother, not wishing to divulge the overview before they arrived.

"Feels I've been on the move for weeks."

They pulled up alongside a substantial residence on Broadwater Down reminding Toto how well Louis had done, compared to his own life skirmishes. His elder brother's retirement, well earned, and his extended family he willingly had taken responsibility for, flourished around him. Louis's compassion, selflessness and generosity in taking his wife's three children from previous failed marriages added to the distance the two brothers reflected, within the context of long-term relationships.

Tunbridge Wells, its gentile and well heeled atmosphere became a perfect spot for him to reset his native compass and map out a route towards gathering support and financial backing from both the moneyed, politically influential friends and acquaintances the family had in England.

Over the next days he and his brother took time to bond. Louis felt it a perfect time to share his experiences and Toto was keen to learn new tricks.

He chose an afternoon on the garden terrace to confide some thoughts with Toto.

"I'm not a great example of outwardly showing emotions, but always conscious of making sure my nearest and dearest are taken care of."

Toto coughed nervously as he sensed the introduction of hitherto hidden aspects.

"My generosity of spirit with the family is because my life afforded me such gestures. With the potential of something coming from your attempts to retrieve family loans, I'd like to feel you'd be able to look after your own in the same way."

"Your generosity not only towards my project but as I witness with your family, is something I've always wanted to emulate."

"Despite the doubts your sister and I have had on your projects I do sense your desire. It's with that in mind I'm going to share a practice you'd be well advised to emulate when the opportunity presents itself."

Toto listened intently.

"Over all the years I worked I made sure I turned some savings into gold. This I regularly sequestered away, on our trips, in Switzerland. Today it leaves them a security and me, the knowledge they're well catered for when I'm gone."

"Are you telling me you're about to pass away?" Toto asked with concern in his voice.

"Good lord no, many years left in the old dog, however I just wanted you to benefit from an elder brother's advice. Make of it what you will, flow benefits forward."

"I'll remember that all the more, as Adrian has been sorely disregarded of late."

Toto knew a meeting with Adrian to be long overdue. He had written the occasional letter from New York but had never really sat down and had a man-to-man talk about marriage, the boy's mother and how he intended to move on with their relationship, develop any real insight into who his son was becoming or how he could offer financial support. As with so many of his intimate relationships, he found himself completely at sea.

After the fraternal talk, it was his sister-in-law who brought him the boat and paddle the following morning.

"Toto dear, I've taken the liberty of inviting young Adrian down this weekend as I'm sure you have lots to catch up on and John always loves to see his cousin on his rare visits," Hetty suggested over the breakfast table.

"Good idea," Louis added. "Leila, Hetty and I have been concerned as to the boy's well-being. As you know, we've supported him financially these past few years. As much as you've been limited, now you're here, some more brotherly advice – give him your attention. He deserves a father, not just uncles and aunts."

"I appreciate what you're both doing for him and do recognize my paternal neglect. It'll be good to have an opportunity to mend fences."

"Wise idea, though it may be more rebuilding the house from the ground up!" Louis concluded, wryly.

It was arranged Toto would take the car, pick up Adrian from the station and loaded with fishing gear, picnic hamper and cover for the seasonal chill, the two of them would be driven over to Hartfield where the bucolic banks of the Upper Medway, became the location to catch up, bond and somehow close the gap of years bereft of paternal stewardship.

Chauffeur Rumens pulled the car up at the railway station as Toto gingerly stepped out to meet a son neglected from fear, cowardice and an insatiable inability to develop closeness. At least the weather that October morning offered promise of unseasonable warmth. Little else he feared would, though wishing dearly to right wrongs he had been so dismally responsible for.

Reaching the platform he wondered why the camaraderie amongst fellow officers in the army seemed so much easier to develop than his own flesh and blood. Closed emotions held him at a vice like distance, across which he had been unable to traverse. Telltale smoke and a cheery hoot from the engine signaled Adrian's arrival.

As the train came to a halt, a single door opened in front of him and out stepped a young man, confident, well dressed in a fawn and speckled outfit, representing the height of twenties fashion. It had been many years since he had last seen his son and the youngster he had left, like some magical mutation, transformed into what he imagined himself to have looked like at eighteen, without the insecurities. A long-lost feeling of pride coursed through him as he walked towards the young man.

Was this really the outcome of his participation in creation, he pondered, as deep satisfaction having done something well swept over him.

He opened his arms to receive his son who responded with a perfunctory handshake.

Toto struck by awkwardness hurriedly pretended his own gesture to be one of surprise.

"Goodness, a young man already," he blurted still waving his arms around.

Adrian retained his hand to shake. Toto took it and held his son's hand in both of his.

"You've really changed."

"Years do that to you, father, no-one stays a child forever," responded Adrian, with a chill tone.

"Let me take your bag."

"No thanks, I'm perfectly capable of managing myself."

Toto swiveled round, ignoring the rebuttal and they both headed out to the car. As they got in, his son greeted Rumens like an old friend. Rumens acknowledged the gesture and they drove off.

"I thought you'd like to join me fishing on the river. It's such a great day and we've so much to talk about," Toto suggested.

"We have?" Adrian queried.

"It's been a long time since we last met," Toto replied.

"And whose fault is that? Just disappearing off to the jungle, following your wild adventures, leaving mother and myself."

Adrian managed to contain the frustration and anger his father's desertion had festered in him.

Involuntarily, he bit his lip.

"I understand your feelings, but I had to go. I had to follow my dreams," Toto admitted.

"Dreams leaving me with nightmares. Yes, I can see how that must have somehow exonerated you from what you left behind. I was your son and in my world it's no way to treat a son," Adrian vented, turning to look out of the window.

"In your world, and what do you know of your world?" his father cut back.

"I know unless they get cut down on the battlefield or by disease, most fathers are there for their sons. There to support and follow their progress to adulthood."

"What sort of way is that to talk to your father?" Toto replied, feeling both hurt and angry at the cutting remark.

"The sort of way every moment you weren't there for me, every time I succeeded at school, every birthday you missed, every advice I yearned to hear from my father."

Rumens could not help but overhear the altercation in the back seat and purposefully powered the car to hide their conversation.

Adrian continued.

"And you think a day's fishing's going to mend everything and heal wounds?"

"Well," Toto stammered.

"I don't even much like fishing," interrupted his son sharply, "so that shows what a great researcher you must be."

"Look, I admit I've been bloody useless at this. You're right, I know so little about you and accept my fault in it, but can we at least give it our best shot and start over get to know each other like I ought to have done in the first place?" Toto pleaded.

Adrian turned back to face his father and saw a man helpless in his own befuddlement, emotionally unable to match his own awareness. His heart broke for the hopelessness and years of nurturing a hardened heart began to melt.

"I appreciate your effort, I realize we both know little of the other and, in our own way, hold feelings against the other. We can either fight or give ground. Fighting's something you've experienced far more and with deeper intensity than I ever wish to. I vowed never to go that road, whatever the circumstances, so it's foolish for us to start off again like that."

Toto was shocked, yet appreciative of his son's perception and nodded as the young man continued.

"There's lots I want to know about you, loads of questions I determined to put to you. I'm off to university in Edinburgh for a career in the diplomatic service. Why don't we agree to get reacquainted, rather than waste time blaming each other."

"I agree," Toto replied with relief.

Looking his son in the eye, he smiled.

"I also see the Diplomatic Service is going to have an excellent addition to their ranks."

His lightness dissipated a heavy cloud threatening to build between them.

"So you don't like fishing then."

"No, never saw the attraction of sitting for hours waiting for something to happen. Why, do you?"

"It has its attractions, though never seemed to find them either. Best leave the fish in peace," his father replied. 'Since Hettie's organized a delicious hamper with a couple of bottles of decent Chablis, why not take the best bits and see if we can build on them?"

Adrian gasped.

"But I thought Aunt Hettie was a good Christian Scientist."

Toto leaned over to his son.

"Oh, she is, but she's also wise enough to know we're not and Louis is well aware a glass of wine is a great conversation breaker!"

Adrian felt for the first time something akin to bonding with a father, previously something he had only ever dreamed of. Rumens, unable to prevent overhearing the change of mood in spite of his acceleration, called back to his passengers.

"So will it be the banks of the Medway, gentlemen?"

"Yes Rumens," they answered in unison.

The banks of that particular part of the Medway were as archetypical as a quiet Kentish Sussex river idyll gets. The autumn meadow plants stretching their stems in a last push honored overhanging willows, whose branch tips teased trout in deep pools imitating tasty gnats. Father and son sat beside the flowing waters on a rug supplied by Rumens with a fulsome hamper open between them. Rods had been engineered to rest on long sticks of willow, each bearing a y fork, giving the semblance of fishing in action. Lines cast with suitable grubs floated aimlessly locking themselves into constant eddy spirals of a nearby pool. A bottle of Chablis netted in the cool water held expectations of a long, languishing sojourn. Another open bottle quenched their thirst and opened a corridor to sharing.

"Edinburgh it is. What will you study?" Toto asked.

"Amharic mainly. It's why I chose it. A diplomatic post in Ethiopia not only demands it but helps enormously."

"Following in the family vein. Grandfather was in the diplomatic service for Prussia, in South Carolina. He'd be proud of you," Toto suggested admiringly.

"So all this stuff you're doing in the States, is that to do with Grandpa?"

"Sort of," his father replied, "though more to do with the larger family history and the legacy they left the independence-seeking Revolutionaries."

"Uncle Louis says there could be a fair payback coming if your efforts gain momentum, but mother says you're just chasing more rainbows."

"She never really grasped the bigger picture, did she?" his father replied.

"As much as I may not agree with her, what is the bigger picture? From what I've heard few if any of your projects ever came to anything."

"Maybe it's well overdue to fill you in who I am, where I'm going and what I believe are the essentials of creating a useful life."

"That'd be a first!" Adrian chipped in.

"You deserve to hear it from the horse's mouth rather than the Chinese whispers from all and sundry."

His father then settled down and gave a full account of his absent times. He was also glad the wine shared went down well and the day was theirs together. Adrian listened intently, questioning and clarifying as they progressed. Time passed, yet seemed irrelevant.

The trout respected their absorption by absenting themselves from the sodden lures now utterly exposed for the fakes they were. Adrian began to respect someone he had begun to consider a fraud.

"So your time in the Army involved helping form The Bicycle Corps, being sent on mysterious missions against Boers and surviving the mass slaughter of the war. Was your writing merely frustration at the idiots in the War Office?"

"Yes and no," replied Toto. "The bloody Balkan war in twelve, and treatment of the Greeks showed me war's a con. How could I bring the treatment of the Greeks to the public psyche; that was the conundrum. Thanks to Viscount Burnham, he offered me the post of war correspondent at the Telegraph. The pen became formidable against the sword."

"Did that exposure help?"

"Unfortunately newspapers have become mouthpieces for the political class, so getting the real facts across is an uphill struggle, if it's not in their interest. Somewhat blunted my pen, but I slipped enough through the net and who you know also helps."

"Even if the message is not to their liking?" Adrian queried.

"That's where cunning – and knowing who exactly to speak to – comes in."

"A bit like diplomacy, then."

"A lot like diplomacy but with a healthy load of cloak and dagger."

"Like your spying sorties in South Africa?"

"Yes, and remembering who you told what to and why they needed to know. That's where research is so valuable connecting the dots."

"Connecting dots?" his son asked.

"Adrian, if nothing else I can impart as a father and hopefully a friend, seeing the greater picture, piecing the bits of the puzzle together and then deducing the likely outcomes is a strategy as old as the ancient Chinese. Sun Tzu, that great strategist said; *Keep your friends close and your enemies closer.*"

"He also said, *Appear weak when strong, and strong when weak*, replied his son.

"You've done your homework. Edinburgh looks like welcoming a great asset to its halls," his father answered, with pride in the boy swelling his breast.

"When are you off?"

"I take the train from Euston Tuesday afternoon."

"Well you can bank on me being there to see you off."

"You don't have to," his son said.

"I want to, and having spent this time together it's only be right to start off a new chapter in our relationship being there for you."

"Agreed, then," Adrian beamed, happy to witness the return of a father he had given up as lost.

The chill the water attracted began to creep in as they packed away the remnants of an excellent day together and headed for the car magically reappearing with Rumens at the wheel for their return to the house.

"So you'll be at Euston then, five thirty is the night train?"

"Of course, five in the tea room. Handy as I've a meeting with Burnham for lunch, for old times sake and to gear up more press interest."

Adrian settled back in his seat next to a father he began feeling more connected to. He smiled to himself.

"What's that for?" Toto queried, seeing the smile break.

"I'm beginning to appreciate the art of fishing," replied his son.

"But we did none."

"Men go fishing all of their lives without knowing it's not fish they're after," his son replied.

Toto turned and looked his son in the eye.

"That's profound!"

"No Dad, it's Thoreau!"

Toto relished the *Dad* part thoroughly and secretly conceded he had been utterly outwitted by his son.

CHAPTER TWENTY-FIVE

The Carlton Club in London's Pall Mall reeked of privilege and ancestral power, the sort of power oozing from fat cigars, port and an elite secure in its tenure holding the reins of control and progress. Aristocracy and overtly Tory political members etched an almost granite-like foundation to the establishment's fabric whilst its bricks and mortar found themselves sadly wanting against the persistence of London rain. If symbolism of the power of wealth against temporal impermanence held an image, this would certainly rank as a contender. Blaming the Caen stone, used in its third rebuild, could be blamed as a French conspiracy.

Yet for Toto, arriving at its doors, it heralded yet one more hub of connectivity on a journey to etch a solid fortune from an indebted American ruling class.

As he briskly walked through the front doors of the club, an attentive coat check took his drenched overcoat and umbrella, silently making it disappear into a vault of hidden cloakrooms. Another more senior employee with a memory to stun the most infrequent visitor greeted him.

"Viscount Burnham is expecting you Captain Trapman, in the Smoking Room."

Where else? thought Toto, as he remembered the cigar-loving press magnate and his addiction to the very best in South American leaf.

He strode commandingly up the stairs to where his lunch appointment waited. Burnham, long-time friend of the family, made this meeting as much personal as business.

The magnate, from a quiet corner of the room, spied his protégé enter and imperiously waved a swift hand movement towards him. In spite of family, his conditioning to make the world come to him rather than stand and greet one as equal reminded Toto of his own position in this relationship.

"So they let young Odysseus through the gates of Elysium, then?"

"The Fortunate Isles must be less discriminating than I remember," replied Toto. "Though the club's memory of one who last stepped through these doors an eternity ago is almost elephantine."

"Yes, Jackson does have an inordinate photographic memory. Pity we can't use it on the printed page. But thankfully my responsibility in that direction is, as you probably heard from Louis, a thing of the past since selling on," Burnham reminded.

"All things change."

"Rest assured Albert, I made sure the new proprietors continue with one of my most professional journalists in war correspondence; even though you often diverge from the party line, your independence is frankly, a breath of fresh air amongst the old fogies of the establishment."

Toto smiled.

"So you're now etching out a rebellious card to play, free from the shackles of the title?"

"Absolutely. That's the privilege of the stinking rich and influential. Create mayhem in the midst of their own. That, dear fellow is why I'm backing your quest for restitution of your ancestors' donations."

Inasmuch as Burnham had been instrumental in helping secure an ongoing position with the Telegraph after Toto's military adventures, it was adoration of his sister Leila that encouraged the Viscount to persevere with aiding the Trapman quest. Such contacts were invaluable in getting on board as many of the influential, political and powerful.

Over a substantial lunch and an excellent nineteen hundred Bordeaux the like Toto had not recently experienced, the two of them discussed who to approach, persuade and were in a position to act as arrows of influence. The researcher relaxed, reminded of his sister's influence within the corridors of power. As the port and inevitable cigars made their appearance, he realized the alcoholic intake was taking effect allowing nervousness around his later meeting with Adrian at Euston to dissipate.

Burnham leaned over, idly holding a glass of port in one hand.

"I would add, not all my friends feel the same way as I do concerning pressure on our American leaders to be favorable of War Loan reparation but then some, candidly, would change their tune if financial gain was on the cards."

"That seems to be the consensus amongst so many. Scratch my back and I'll scratch yours," reflected Toto.

"The wheels of power never rusted on being oiled by the same juices working in perpetuity, there you're right. If oiling were needed, persuasion nudged, I'm sure we can come up with ways and means."

Although obvious to any student of power, it still came as a shock Burnham openly admitting such ways and means. The drink allowed truth to flow, as Toto answered.

"I appreciate the gesture, but do we need to go these lengths; its value stands on merit".

"Ah, the innocence of belief in best outcome. All is for the best in the best of all possible worlds. Be aware, it is wise to cultivate your own garden of needs before placing any faith in humanity as a whole, who waste their dreams on collective market gardens!"

"Without being rude, seems blindingly obvious it's precisely what the rich and powerful are working towards."

"Hole in one, dear fellow. Remember, it's definitive bad form to voice obvious truth, especially in these hallowed halls. Good you're among close friends. Remember the rich loathe being reminded of their subjugation of the working class. Sort of grates a conscience barely ticking, don't you know."

Toto appreciated the Viscount's candor. The skill and wit of his lineage, as outsiders, played its hand again. It gave him hope, not only for the project but for a chance to make a difference for everyone, rich and poor.

One of the many club clocks reminded both men time passes swiftly, the one over the fireplace striking a genteel and sonorous four strokes.

"Good Lord, sorry to rush but those strikes remind me I promised to meet Adrian at Euston. He's off to Edinburgh tonight in pursuit of diplomatic honors. Told him I'd make amends for past negligence."

"Quite right, quite right. Family first. I'll get Jackson to rustle up a cab. The Club will take care of it so you can get there directly."

"That's most thoughtful."

"Think nothing of it," Burnham assured him.

Both parties stood up. Burnham caught an appropriate eye. Shaking hands, Toto made his way carefully through the room down the stairs and to the exit.

Jackson stood waiting himself with the journalist's coat and umbrella.

"No need to worry yourself sir," Jackson preempted. "The Viscount has taken care of everything."

Toto stepped into the cab, amazed as to how the mix of sign language, understood protocol and privilege seemed to flow like some uninterrupted stream. That thought reminded him of Adrian's comment about fishing: it's not the fish they are after. So was he a fish in that stream or a fisherman on the bank? He felt Burnham could not have cared less as to how others viewed him. His power and influence etched the feeling he liked to be viewed as one of the gods atop Olympus.

The cab turned into Charing Cross Road, heading with good time to spare, towards the promised rendezvous with his son. Traffic hindered the cab's progress. Toto gazed out of the window, scanned the multiplicity of bookshops and made a mental note to visit a few to promote his own volume. The cabbie mumbled something about rain and queues being the bane of his life as the street side door burst open and in leapt a figure in dark overcoat, high collar and a smell of rain soaked wool. Toto turned, shocked at the intrusion. The cabbie turned, annoyed at being hijacked. The visitor plumped himself into the seat next to Toto and spoke.

"Trappers, thought I'd catch you here. How goes it old man?"

Toto looked aghast as he surveyed the face of the interloper. The cab driver, still stationary, wildly gesticulated the invasion. Toto turned swiftly to the enraged driver.

"It's OK, he's a friend," he reassured.

He may have known the man but the last thing he expected was him crashing into his life today.

"What the hell are you doing here barging in like this? How the devil did you know I was in London, let alone this cab?" Toto demanded furiously.

"Keep your hat on old chap. We in the service try and make sure no one expects us, least of all those we hunt."

"Doesn't explain the bollocking way you dive into my cab, as if the most natural thing in the world. Again, what the hell are you doing here? I thought we'd tied up business in South Africa."

The cab pulled away as congestion eased. The stranger tapped the dividing glass and shouted for the man to stop again. He did. Toto was bundled out with his uninvited guest following close behind. The stranger slipped a shilling into the open window of the driver. His swiftly raised hand met the coin gratefully. No need to inform a fool with his money he had already been reimbursed for the journey. The window closed swiftly and the cab pulled away.

Toto, confused, struggled to make head or tail of what was going on. The stranger took his arm and led him quickly into an alleyway, filled with small retailers and specialist bookshops. Toto mentally noted the shops. He was guided forcibly into a small tea room where, out of the rain, the heat from the continuing flow of customers' bodies misted up the windows on the street. Shown a table, sitting down he stared incredulously at his guide.

"What the dickens are you raising your uncalled for head, Claude," Toto asked impatiently.

"It's Uncle Claude now, I've moved ahead since our last encounter. You remember?"

"How could I bloody forget, you nearly got me shot."

"Damned Turks, couldn't hit a jackrabbit at close quarters, let alone a group of Greeks on the forage. Seemed you preferred the Greek myth in that little excursion?"

"At least I told the truth about the British and their treachery with the murderous Ottoman bastards."

"You got a gong from the Greeks, whereas the boys upstairs promoted me to some pretty good capers in all sorts of covert places," Claude Dansey admitted.

He smiled at the thought of the rapid rise through the ranks of the Special Intelligence Services, within which both he and Toto had briefly shared time.

Born a week before Toto in Kensington, a burgeoning suburb of London, both shared this youthful stomping ground, equally fascinated with all things military, though for markedly very different reasons. Unlike Toto's family, Dansey's consisted of a hive of nine dysfunctional children beaten and reprimanded at the slightest whim by their military father. He had no choice other than the military option. Toto's love of the armed services brought them together for their separate skills in intelligence against the Boers.

"Remember how we took those Crunchies by surprise on your two-wheeled fliers. Thought the bastards and Kruger would never survive the sorties. Uncle Claude seemed doomed."

"Just shows you how wrong and arrogant the Brits were in their adventures." Toto replied disdainfully.

The waitress brought two steaming mugs of tea to the table, along with a plate of biscuits.

"Did you order this?" he demanded, glaring at his opposite number.

"Thought we could chat better with something to wet the lips."

Toto felt his lunchtime high dramatically plummet. The tea room, quaint enough and certainly more a place he felt accustomed to, carried the sort of culture shock a traveler might experience transported instantaneously from riverside meadow to teeming city center. Too many questions flooded his mind.

"I'm on my way…"

"To meet your son at Euston, yes I know," broke in Dansey.

"How the..."

"We are the Secret Service old chap, our business to know our operatives' movements," Dansey whispered, grinning from cheek to cheek.

"Operatives, since when?" Toto asked vaguely.

Dansey's inane and maniacal smile sickened him. He remembered it the time Dansey calmly shot his Greek chauffeur, for no better reason than the poor fellow overheard their conversation.

"You bastard Dansey," Toto cursed. "I have to get to my son, that's

141

important. What's so important for your sudden appearance to hijack me?"

"Look old fellow, it'll only take a few minutes, please humor me."

"The last thing I feel like doing. A stuffed pig couldn't raise a smile from your tight features. What is it, make it quick?"

Toto, really agitated now, saw something far more precious than a meeting with this emotionless killer slip away. He felt less like taking a sip of the tea than entering the gates of hell. Involuntarily, he began to tap his fingers on the table.

"Quex wanted me to connect with you. We knew you were over here drumming up interest for your capers in New York. Happy for you, hope all goes to plan. Your service record, what you and Bertie brought to the table, always good."

Toto pieced the puzzle together. Bertie Stewart, a captain like himself, had been a passionate comrade in building and energizing the London Bicycle Brigade. Commissioned into the West Kent Yeomanry, Bertram Stewart had always confided in Toto his passion to make his mark on history, do something for King and country. Something spectacular. He was a natural spy. They both knew that. His own fascination with Stewart's passions drew him to the attention of those familiar with his bicycle exploits, behind enemy lines. C, code name for Mansfield Cummings, initiate head of the Service, recognized his talent. Toto remembered Bertie's joy when commissioned to investigate German intentions before the war. His subsequent capture and release through a suspect amnesty enabled Bertie to leap into the war effort.

"Bloody tragedy he became one of the first casualties. You would have made a great team," Dansey broke into Toto's reminiscences.

Toto felt the pain of his friend's untimely end.

"Another reason I got so bloody disillusioned with war," he replied.

"Death comes to us all, the strange thing is we never know when it'll rob us. Like me popping into your cab."

"You never lost your insensitivity, you bastard."

"Now, now. Can't afford those luxuries faced with pistol or booby trap. Still, be comforted, I'm not here to steal your life. Just a few moments!"

Toto again wished the meeting would end, to keep his appointment.

"Cut to the chase, Dansey. What do you want?"

The operative leaned forward. Toto caught his foul breath, winced and involuntarily pulled back, dragging the tea cup to his lips, to cover retreat.

"Quex wants to see you. Following some contraband racket, roots in Colombia. Seems your stay there and the Manaus operation, he feels you know the place and people and can pull local knowledge to prize open leads."

"What the hell does South America have to do with the Service ?"

"Everything!"

"Then you know Brazilian and Spanish are totally different languages, let alone countries. Do you people ever do real research?" Toto reminded his visitor.

"You know the office, everyone with a straw hat speaks the same lingo," Dansey replied.

"Lucky for you lot I speak enough of both. Proves my point at how little intelligence the department exhibits at times," Toto fired back.

"We're somewhat underfunded. More to the point, it seems some very in-fluential heads are rolling with the cartels there to augment their lousy rich lives. Since we need pressure points squeezed, when push comes to nudge, leverage needed, your insights, research and ear to the ground would be much appreciated."

"Knowing the poverty of your department, it'd be foolish of me to believe there's anything in it for me financially," Toto asked almost rhetorically.

"King and country old chap, reward enough?"

"God save us, not that chestnut, please. We're not all stuck to the flag like flies to shit. How am I expected to look after body and soul? What's the deal?"

Toto suddenly realized getting down to South America again, tidying up loose ends, opening up future business might, after all, benefit some financial assistance. If the passage was met, some expenses and whatever else he could draw out of them, it might be opportune.

"Come see Quex, in spite of our drained coffers he's got a deal you'll ap-preciate," suggested Dansey.

"Damn," exclaimed Toto as he caught the time on the clock above the counter.

He leaped up and rushed for the door.

"Well?"

"Friday!" Toto shouted, as he bolted through the door and down the alley to the main road.

He tried hailing a cab. None stopped. He bolted along Holborn at a sprint. Cutting through the back streets he headed to the terminus. The rain thank-fully had stopped. His fitness stayed with him as his legs responded to the push forward. How he wished he had two wheels now.

In the room twinned as meeting place and tea lounge, Adrian waited. He looked up at the clock. Ten minutes past five. Holding his ticket in hand, he continued waiting, two large suitcases beside the table. He so hoped his father had not forgotten once again. The minutes ticked by.

The Georgian houses lining the square Toto tore across began to light up as early dusk approached. He tripped over a badly laid pavement, swore and briskly walked on. Running had expired. Fitness and age caught him like treacle round the ankles. He could no way miss this appointment. He had promised. Why the hell did these people have such bad timing. Another nest of streets weaved before him.

A railway clerk poked his head round the waiting room door.

"Anyone still for the Highland Express. Leaves in seven minutes."

Adrian felt sick to his stomach. The disappointment welled within. He knew tears were not far behind but then, he thought, *when has that man ever been here for me. What should I expect except the inevitable?*

He looked at the two cases, looked back at the clock, his sole wish shattered. Standing up, a porter approached.

"The Scottish train, sir?"

"Yes," he replied, absent-minded.

Then he snapped to.

"It's OK, I can manage myself."

"Not to worry sir, see you need a hand. I have to wave the train off, so you're best with me," he chuckled.

Adrian appreciated the humanity of the man and smiled. They walked at a good pace towards the platform.

Toto hurled himself across Euston Road dodging cars, horses, trades vehicles and fellow pedestrians ambling, everyone else in no hurry to catch anything. Barging past dawdlers bumping into some, avoiding others. Each contact eliciting an apology. Some returned an angry cuss. Too concerned in reaching the station, missed them all.

The smoke from the engine rose in great bursts of acrid clouds and grime into the rafters of the vaulted roof. Latecomers rushed to their carriage. In the charge of the one man who gave the signal to go, Adrian knew he would not miss the train.

As for his father, he was far less confident. Bundling into the station, he ran full pelt towards the platform holding the Scottish Express. A whistle blasted. A powerful jet of steam expelled from the engine as the railwayman lowered and raised his green flag, marking a journey beginning for many and ending for another.

Toto raced along the platform keeping ahead of the carriages as they inched slowly forward.

The railman guessed this might be the man the young lad told him he had waited for and shouted to Toto.

"Next carriage, next carriage!"

Toto heard, registered and ran forward.

Adrian stood up in the carriage, lifting a case onto the luggage rack. Out of the corner of his eye, streaming with tears he caught sight of a familiar figure waving hysterically with equal enthusiasm and futility. As his father made one last attempt to come alongside, he caught his son at the carriage window mouthing the same word over and over.

"Why? Why? Why?"

Another sharp hoot drowned communication as the train picked up momentum and the carriage disappeared into its engine's smoke.

CHAPTER TWENTY-SIX

Admiral Sir Hugh "Quex" Sinclair took over the reins of the Secret Intelligence Service in 1923, on C's death. The SIS, mainly tasked with the rise of Soviet activities, had Sinclair create specific divisions dealing with counter espionage, economic intelligence, watch on diplomatic activities and covert political actions in time of war. It was in the division dealing with contraband Sinclair saw opportunity for Captain Trapman, as his historical usefulness remained on file. What Toto was not aware of was what they held on family history. British Intelligence noted both father and grandfather as important cogs in European intelligence operations under guise of diplomatic status. His father, the file revealed, had been targeted to bring intelligence from the United States when British interests were considered susceptible to infiltration and deception. Also noted on his file, albeit unsubstantiated, was that certain members of the family had held double agent status. With this information at his fingertips, Quex had summoned Toto.

Toto meeting Quex saw potential for free passage and expenses to further Colombian ventures. The import export coffee business he and Willy had discussed was one such venture.

A small group of faceless office doors, sporting an anteroom and female secretary directing movements in and out, was all there was marking the presence of the SIS. In an anonymous backwater of Whitehall, such locations were ten a penny. Only through sharp study of unremarkable sign-posts was Toto able to find his destination.

The receptionist knew him to be Quex's morning appointment and offered tea and a seat. Toto obliged, sitting to contemplate what sort of figure this Quex character might be. A matter of minutes passed before he was confronted by an imposing figure, several years his senior, striding out in as friendly a manner as anyone could muster in the civil service. He carried the confidence of the admiral he had been, yet admirably adept at portraying the air of a friendly bank manager. A wry twinkle in his eye and warm handshake belied his power and influence. Toto stood, reciprocated and was led into his office.

"I really must apologize for my man Dansey springing that surprise on you the other day. You know what it's like they get overexcited, take every target as a challenge. Hope you weren't too upset and managed your appointment."

Toto was unsure what Quex meant when referring to him as a target but played the dumb card.

"Missed meeting my son thanks to Dansey's interference. As for his message I agreed to meet you purely for mutual goals. More than that I'd hoped past activities were just that – past."

"Apologies and sorry your boy missed his father but know from personal experience these things make a man of us eventually, I'm sure you'll explain later. You're right, we do have mutually advantageous goals," Quex replied, brushing over any hint of empathy.

Toto resented Sinclair's remark over his son, yet shrugged it off as emotional frigidity covering contrived warmth. Came with the territory where emotions had been shot to bits through the horrors of war.

Quex continued.

"Understand you're set on a course recovering a debt owed your people from way back. Seeking support amongst the rich and influential is noted. We have, as you can appreciate, eyes and ears in many of these selfsame quarters, since money, influence and power tend to go hand in hand. No secret if I told you with power comes responsibility and with responsibility comes denial of the same under guise of selfless interest. The reality is, it's all nonsense. No self-respecting power broker affords himself the luxury of selflessness, quite the opposite. It's like asking the captain to be gentle on the oncoming iceberg."

Toto listened. Sinclair continued.

"You're probably asking yourself where this is going."

Toto nodded.

"For some time we've been aware certain financial associations in South America, specifically for our purposes, Colombia, have taken root. Some as yet undisclosed names have struck up with unsavory criminal types who are jumping on the coca market. Feeds the prohibition-hit States, not in itself illegal. However funds channeled through British and European entities, land up in organizations, fronts for criminal activity here and on the continent. That this funds the Bolsheviks is of interest, yet not what you're here for."

"So you think I've contacts with drug lords in Colombia persuaded to grass on their connections?" Toto asked incredulously.

"Good heavens no. Not at all," Sinclair refrained from further insight.

"That's a relief; these people are dangerous and ruthless," Toto responded, laughing nervously.

"No Captain, the point is, we're hoping you could go about your business, act as if merely setting up your commerce. Keep an eye on who's meeting who. Gain insight, send information and try find who the main dealers are and their gold traffic. We know gold's involved with coca, just need to know who's passing it, how and to whom. That's really all it'll be."

"Just that! Apart from King and country..."

"Of course as having served well, we can assure influence both in the States and here will help ongoing attempts in your project are honored. We do have influence outside these walls, yet a low profile serves best. As for expenses, Evelyn has your boat tickets and some expenses the department felt would help."

Toto was relieved he had got what he wanted without asking.

"Thank you Admiral."

"No, thank you Captain and have a good trip."

Toto was handed tickets and funds by Evelyn, his assistant who smiled graciously, showing him the door.

He crossed St. James's Park, walked past the duck pond where each fought the other for crumbs thrown by passers by and nanny-supervised children.

Had he just won a crumb or two from the Crown to prosecute their work? he asked himself.

Continuing across the park, he reached Buckingham Palace, crossed the road glancing up at the gilded representation of Empire.

What had all the conquests, bloodshed, pillage of resources and people really achieved? Servitude to power was as rampant as it ever had been. The ocean separating wealth from poverty, an inured acceptance by the masses, and a whole generation of young men wiped from the face of the earth. Was this all we've achieved? he wondered.

A policeman on point tipped his helmet as Toto passed. He walked up Constitution Hill, thoughts of riches sought, scores settled and fame gained further from his mind than ever. He had disappointed, once again, the son to whom he promised new beginnings. His best-laid plans hijacked. No matter how much pomp and circumstance oozed through this capital, family came first and priority to rebuild what had become ruins within his particular empire were his utmost priority.

One more meeting was essential, before heading down to Southampton and the boat to Colombia. It was reconnecting with Smokey.

Smokey Greene, distant cousin of family friends, had met Toto on his return from his South African assignment. The fifteen year old attached himself limpet-like to Toto, fascinated with stories and adventures the researcher spun. For Toto this young lad inspired a paternal attraction to a youthful ear. Over the next few years, between his Army and Bicycle Battalion commitments, he developed a fascination and bond for the lad, whose wisdom exceeded his years. When some years later Toto married Adrian's mother, Smokey attended the ceremony as one of the family. Throughout the stormy and misguided pairing with Isabella, his ex wife, Toto had access to Smokey's support and insight that displayed extraordinary awareness. It helped him understand the relationship. During these times he found it impossible to relate to Adrian. From his birth, the child had been smothered under his mother's overpowering wings and their relationship used as both wedge and weapon between husband and wife. Toto naturally, outside of his army comrades, found solace and camaraderie in Smokey's guidance. Smokey's increased fascination with all things mystical and magical helped Toto draw deeper into his friend's inner and worldly development.

It was no surprise therefore when Smokey suggested they join mutual friends in Wiltshire. Toto's discovery of Smokey's ability to move in and out of social circles, artistic and aristocratic, drew a comparative similarity to the Trapman family, past masters at that art. Nora, the wife of their host at Avebury Manor, Lt. Colonel Leopold Jenner, was an active supporter of the suffragette movement.

Smokey encouraged her to use her ample creative skills to push forward the feminist rebellion. Avebury, with its ancient earth temple to older orders and knowledge, far preceding the modern belligerence of empire, seemed a fitting place from whence to encourage these movements. For the two men it acted as a retreat where they could reflect on the past and plan the future.

Arriving at the Manor, they were greeted with open arms and hearts. A lot of shared history made for a comfortable and relaxing atmosphere. After a morning catching up, Jenner went hunting as Toto and Smokey took a long, easy walk along the Henge towards West Kennet and Silbury Hill. As they reached the mysterious Silbury mound, a short climb to its summit afforded them a spectacular view over the Wiltshire countryside. Sitting down on the edge looking across to the Longbarrow at West Kennet, Toto sighed deeply.

"This is something I never get bored of."

"What's that?" Smokey asked.

"This countryside. Nothing comes close to it."

"The shoreline of Connemara must be a close contender," Smokey chipped in.

"OK I'll give you that, yet coming home you realize just how beautiful this land is," Toto replied. "The Amazon's vast, its rivers mind-boggling, even the Rockies shed superhuman beauty across magical expanses of sky, yet here, the pastoral beauty, the stillness. It nudges you into silence and contemplation. Too beautiful to express any other way."

"So the question is." Smokey remarked, "why go away, why travel, why seek fortunes elsewhere?"

"No, the question is, where do we go from here?"

"As always," Smokey mused, "You've choices."

He knew Toto referred to his own future, yet he knew him well enough to recognize the inclusivity with which his friend always punctuated his words.

"You've achieved good groundwork and an array of support for the project like no other. The question is, which of the elements are important. Is it money, fame or some other higher purpose?"

"I've never really known what that means – some higher purpose. Maybe that's the problem. Why I'm sitting here faced with all this, feeling so lost. Well, lost enough to ask you, probably my closest friend – what's the purpose of all this?"

Smokey recognized Toto faced a crucial crossroads in his life. He also knew these moments were as delicate as gossamer. He could only help if Toto's desire to seek the right question was strong enough to field the correct answer.

The aroma of the dew dampened grass injected with the sun's warmth, created an intoxicating mixture of earth, breeze and fire. It planted memories of distant meadows on the senses complimenting a pervasive silence. Synapses of awareness in Toto connected. A switch thrown, unleashed the flight of ideas, feelings, of something new alongside release of old feelings chained deep. Had he been back in Colombia he would have sworn he had been infected by coca chemistry. Sitting here amidst magic and beauty, he knew something utterly different had its being within. Snakelike, it curled around and up his spine and into his consciousness. He felt himself open and expand. Turning towards his friend, Smokey was looking at him.

"Are you feeling the same?"

Smokey silently raised a finger to his lips indicating Toto remain silent. They both gazed ahead for several minutes. Then in unison, came back.

"It's a feeling I've touched before, yet I'd wager your first time," Smokey suggested.

"What just happened?"

"Strange new things," replied the younger man.

"You can say that again, but the peace, the insight. I felt the answers all dropping into place yet can't verbalize them."

"That's okay. It's as it is, where remembering it, needs no jolt. What you've just experienced is locked into your being, accessible anytime. That is, as long as you allow yourself to open and observe the bigger picture. Let the 'you' part get out of the way."

"God, I just remember the same conversations I had as a kid with my invisible Self. Remember?"

"Of course, that's what made me realize we had so much in common. It's just that you've been so busy doing, trying, pushing you forgot the essential part of you," Smokey reminded him gently.

"So bloody true. How can that impact my decision making, from here on in?" Toto asked.

"First of all, everything remains fluid. Change is not only inevitable it's always within your command. In order to act appropriately you need to comprehend the question. Every question has several answers, which answer's appropriate is your choice. Research throws up many pieces of information offering a variety of outcomes. Intuition will spot the correct one. So why are you going back to the Americas?

"To prove I'm a success," Toto blurted out.

"Therein lies truth," Smokey replied. "What if you already are successful, have you ever wondered?"

"Through the eyes of my brother, sisters, ex wife, son and others, I'm not" admitted Toto, lowering his head.

"So who lives your life; them or you? You've achieved great things. You've gone places few others have. You've conversed, reported, written like no other. In my eyes that's success. Perhaps not the success you crave, merely fear of the success you judge others' experience."

"What if I believed I really was successful?"

"Now that's the right question. How do you answer that?

"I wouldn't struggle so."

"What would that open up for you, putting struggle aside?"

Toto pondered a moment.

"It would help me take dynamic action. See others as my equal, not holding me back."

"How important is the money? Still the be all and end all of your ambitions?"

"Obviously not," replied Toto. "It'd have its uses, but my vision of where I see myself would no longer be restrained by lack of resources. I'd have wings."

"Now you're seeing things in a wholly different light, yet, unless clipped of the old enthusiasm and blind dreams, those wings take you dangerously close to the sun and we all know what that meant for Icarus."

"Are you suggesting dropping dreams for reality?"

"I'm saying be very aware: the world you see and interpret has many layers idealism and dreams can blind you to. Dreams are important they contain the alchemist's base metal from which he fashions gold. When dreams are interpreted as the gold itself, the illusion has already hardened and lost reality's ability to be burnished."

Toto was transfixed. Everything Smokey shared made absolute sense. Words opened up door after door of insight. The power of each syllable ignited an inner torch. Clarity caressed his being.

"Such a power in this place, difficult to believe I hadn't felt it," Toto admitted.

"It's everywhere. Up to us to connect. At Avebury it's especially powerful. Most are utterly unaware of these dimensions. Our hosts recognize it, that's why they put so much energy and love into caring and restoring the landscape they steward. Leopold, dear fellow, is dyed in the wool Empire, King and country, up the ruling class, unable to extricate ancestral chains. Yet, in his own way his money and position, with a caring heart and a liberated wife, make them both well-chosen stewards for this temple. We each participate in our own way; equally it would be impossible to have these conversations with them. Their references are something quite different."

"So where does this all fit with me?" Toto asked.

"Your family is extremely gifted, moving with ease between levels of society. No wonder your common heritage is diplomacy. Your own adept nature at connecting with great magnates such as Vanderbilt, Rockefeller, scientists like Tesla, bankers, political influences as well as the ordinary man, is an art, a skill."

"They each bring something to the investigation."

"Precisely. Working out what that something is can be as important as what you feel it is and what they know it is, the two not necessarily being mutual. That, Toto, can be the difference between success and failure. Sometimes a visible thread, at other times an invisible one until recognized for what it is. Just like the power underneath us here. Invisible to those having no connection, yet potently tangible to those who create the space for it to reveal itself."

"That sounds suspiciously like a word of caution," Toto conjectured.

"Should I be afraid?"

"Yes to the first and absolutely no to the second. Fear is your sharpest most virulent enemy. It'll lay bare your every defense in a second. Fearless and aware you will reach your goal," Smokey assured him.

Their time on the hill was up. Making their way down back to the house, they passed a huge stone within the circle of stones that lay inside the ditch running around the village. Smokey stopped.

"See this stone. Notice the seat within. All those who sit there hold the power of this temple in their being. Take a seat."

Toto laughed nervously. "Is this one of your Irish tales?"

Smokey insisted.

"Sit."

For anyone else he would have rather died than make a fool of himself, but Smokey was not anyone else. He gingerly moved towards the impressive menhir and settled into its opening.

"Nothing!" he cried triumphantly.

"Still!" Smokey commanded.

Toto assumed stillness. He leapt up immediately, brushing himself down as he unceremoniously put distance between him and the stone.

"What the hell was that?"

"What?"

"That," insisted Toto, pointing towards the Sarsen stone. "What just happened?"

"What did just happen? Tell me, what did you experience?"

"It was just a feeling of cold, dread, something unutterably dark."

"Interesting," his young magus friend trilled. "Do you know what they call this stone around here?

"No doubt you're about to tell me!"

"They call it the Devil's Chair. On Beltane, tradition sees women sit and make a wish. It's the entrance stone from the avenue of stones leading up to the inner circle, acting as transformer to the energy we felt on the hill. As with all power, it can be used for good or evil. I'd wager the cold and dread offers insight into the importance of discrimination when dealing with power or dare I say, power brokers!"

"Gives a whole new meaning to hot seat," answered Toto.

They both laughed, with Toto betraying nervousness to Smokey's deep, resonant belly laugh.

CHAPTER TWENTY-SEVEN

O nly on their return to London did Toto and Smokey check the ticket Quex had issued. A typically tight fisted civil service had booked Toto on a banana boat heading direct to Santa Marta from Avonmouth. The only cheer was Smokey volunteering to accompany him to the boat.

As they made their way onto the dock, Smokey carried one bag, his other hand placed on Toto's shoulder.

"Look at it as going under cover from the outset. You're going to need to keep a low profile. Steaming into Colombia on a great liner rather blows your cover out of the water."

"It's just their whole approach is: use the buggers, get the info and dispose."

"That's what the rich and powerful do all the time. Trick is to make it a win-win. They funded you, right?"

"Enough to get around," replied Toto.

"Just watch your back, make sure you don't get on the wrong side of the cartels."

Having already spent some time in Colombia, following the unsuccessful Brazil caper on a muddy Amazon, Toto knew the sort of ruthless types protecting their interests against any elbowing in from indigenous or foreign interest. Thus far that insight enabled him to keep his nose clean. He bid Smokey farewell and promised to keep him updated, assuring him they would get back together on his return.

The next fourteen days took him, a boatload of general cargo and several other passengers through storm, rain and wind to arrive in Santa Marta, Colombia on a steamy, bright and overbearingly hot November morning. Toto was glad to leave the confines of a boat whose quarters afforded him time to catch up on his notes on the War Loan quest.

As he made his way through the bustling port entry, customs and frenetic touting for ongoing travel, a hand grabbed his arm from behind. He spun round, ready to clout the culprit with his suitcase.

"Wow, not so fast," cried a voice as plum as the fruit and straight out of Eton. Toto came face to face with a sunburnt fellow reminding him of so many of the wannabe officers from the Royal Fusiliers, his regiment.

"Drayton Buffett, pleasure to meet you Captain Trapman."

Toto took a moment to settle.

"Have we met?"

"We have now," replied the stranger with a laugh. "Actually the boys in

Whitehall telegraphed me suggesting I meet you off the boat. Thought it would help you get your bearings."

"I'm no stranger to this place," Toto mentioned with some annoyance.

"Of course, come with me and I can fill you in on things, less publicly," insisted Buffett, as he escorted Toto to a waiting car.

Bundled in, luggage in the back seat, the car sped off, hooter blasting through the chaos of the Santa Marta port.

"Quex was keen I touched base with you as soon as you got here. Things are pretty active at the moment. Something seems to be going down London wants us to follow."

Toto was going to get no time to quietly settle in and was equally concerned to be roped into top gear immediately.

"I was told to keep a low profile, go about my business before deeper investigation. Seems orders have changed," Toto shouted as Buffett drove like a demon possessed, narrowly missing all in his way.

Cursing traders and shoppers alike swore at the car as it tore through their otherwise laid back morning. The dusty rain parched road merely left all and sundry covered in foul red dust as the vehicle sped by.

"Do you normally drive so crazily or are you trying to impress? Toto asked.

"Better travel hopefully than arrive."

"Well I would prefer to arrive, in one piece," Toto confirmed.

"That you will old chap, that you will, as we're here."

The car screeched to a halt outside a typical white Spanish looking town house, leaving the two of them and the vehicle enveloped in a tailing dust cloud. Both made a quick exit.

"What about the luggage?"

"Taken care of," replied Buffett.

As he clicked his fingers, two young lads scurried out, rummaged out Toto's luggage, and disappeared into the side of the house. The two men walked through the front gate into a large entrance hall ventilated by two vast ceiling fans. Toto was ushered into an equally cooling courtyard sporting a fountain and pool at its center. Colorful tropical fish swam lazily around, appearing from time to time from under a profusion of lilies. Two wicker seats and a table appeared. They sat down, Buffett making use of a footstool in front of his. Toto dangled his hand in the pool.

"Wouldn't do that, some pretty hungry piranha in there amongst the color," suggested his contact.

Toto whipped his hand to the safety of his lap.

"Worth remembering there's danger round every corner," Buffett added. "Fancy a cuppa?"

"Coffee's fine," Toto answered.

"Ah, yes, an old hand not typically English," Buffett noted. "Loathe Brits who come here expecting tea and scones. Damn it, South America is the capital of the coffee bean."

From out of a back room appeared a young girl carrying a silver tray, silver coffee dispenser and two bone china cups. A small silver bowl contained four sugar lumps with accompanying pincers.

"See you brought the family silver with you," Toto noted sarcastically.

"Old habits, you know. Now down to business. Just to get you up to speed, Quex probably told you I was to be your eyes and ears here and we'd be working together."

"No, he did not!"

"Oh, dear the Service does seem to leave out the important details on hurriedly concocted plans. Still, that's it and as long as you're happy then we can get to know each other, get down to work and track the money."

The self styled aide did not even wait for any confirmation and carried on.

Toto retained composure and heard the fellow out.

"I've been retained by London for six months, recruited some eighteen months ago to cover various European theatres, first time over here. Understand you did some work before the war with them in South Africa."

"Something like that," Toto answered vaguely, not having a good feeling about this new introduction on the scene.

All he saw was a cocky upper class chancer, playing spy. The sort of operative littering the service and the type he had sworn to avoid like the plague. Bertie's death spurned Toto to make a fresh start and South America offered creative attractions.

"When I was asked to monitor the coca production and its routes out of here to the States and Europe, they were keen to track where the money crossed," continued Buffett. "London wants to know who, how much and when."

Toto put down his coffee.

"That much I was briefed. So when can I get on and do what I've come here to do. They don't expect me to hang around with you for months on end, do they?"

"Steady on old fellow, don't get so tetchy, I'm here for contact only, not to nanny you. By the way, understand you're developing coffee interests here as

157

well. London intimated"

Toto wondered who, realizing need to know had fallen out of the window.

"Here's a couple of useful contacts, you might find helpful," Buffett offered passing Toto a list of several names and whereabouts.

Any new potential prospect helps he thought, and took it from Buffett.

"Now we're clear, I'll take my stuff, go settle into what I have come to do and see you as and when."

He reached into his pocket, took a card and handed it to Buffett.

"Contact me here, though I'd advise forewarning if you're popping round. Spending a lot of time in the field."

Toto stood, indicating an immediate departure.

"Don't you want to know about the cartels?" Buffett stammered, flummoxed at the researcher's change of mood.

"Not presently, looks like I'll be here for several months. Plenty of time to get details. I'll see myself out and appreciate your fellow driving me."

Toto marched out to the street, placed himself in the car and awaited the driver. He was very pleased his newly developed firmness in the face of uncertainty had the desired effect, neutralizing any control the other man may have wished to exert. The driver appeared with the suitcases and they drove off leaving Buffett dusty and silent on the sidewalk.

The next few weeks had Toto setting up the business plan arranged with Willy, finding small coffee planters willing to grow and export to the States. Since the market was good and the area chosen in the Antioquia region turned out to be ideal, he reached it via boat to Turbo, on the Caribbean coast then overland to Medellín. One trip across the region had him arrive at a vibrant plantation a few miles north of Santa Fe di Antioquia. The area had retained its rich resources on the back of both gold mining and a solid coffee cultivation. The Cauca River, apart from its gold deposits, fed the slopes from the highlands with superb irrigation. As he made his way up what passed for a road towards the main house on the estate, a couple of cowboys overtook the vehicle coming to a halt in the courtyard of the house. Toto stepped out of the car and approached one rider.

"*Hola!* I'm looking for the owner," he announced in his best Spanish.

The rider nearest him twisted round in the saddle atop a strong black stallion. A large black Cordovan sombrero hid the features, yet Toto caught the long black ponytail flowing from it, as it swished out of sight as the head turned.

"That would be me," replied the rider.

At that moment the head raised revealing a face. Toto gasped and stepped back.

"Is that really you?"

"Capitão, your memory sharp as ever. Welcome to Casa Cauca," Faviola Isidoro announced proudly as she dismounted, gave the horse to a stable boy and slapped its rear quarters.

"Whatever brings you here?"

Toto, still in shock at finding his raven-haired beauty in the depths of the Colombian countryside, replied.

"I might ask you the same question."

"Come in, let's have a cool drink and I can tell you everything since you deserted me in Brazil."

Toto blushed.

They walked into a sumptuous house reflecting well-heeled owners of past years. As with many houses of wealth and substance, a fountain courtyard led off to large open rooms set aside for different functions. Faviola ushered Toto into one looking out to the sloping plantation beyond.

"We have a thriving business here and after the chaos of the last few years, growing into a very self sufficient hacienda."

A glass of ice cool lemonade was presented to Toto.

"I'm astonished to find you here of all places, when I left Manaus you were not only younger but had ideas of the stage in Rio."

"I changed my mind, I needed to establish my own identity. Our relationship allowed me grow wings of hope and two years after you fled a friend of the family invited me to Santa Fe to work on his plantation."

"You know about coffee?"

"What I did not, he taught me."

Faviola lent towards him, playfully tickling his chin. He enjoyed it and the scent of remembrance reminded him of their former intimacy.

"I missed your English humor but learned it. Remember, I'm Brazilian and coffee?"

He laughed long enough to be distracted from catching her rise swiftly from her chair and in full riding gear launch herself at his chair, grasping both wings and leaned into him. He stopped laughing.

"Yet in spite of that you left without even a goodbye," she pronounced, emphasizing each word deliberately, making the final word cut into him like a dagger.

Toto remembered his cowardice, avoiding her that last time.

She continued.

"You think that's the way to leave a woman you profess to love. Just sail away like some pirate having raped, pillaged and stolen treasure?"

Toto, trapped in his seat, looked into the smoking eyes of his downfall. He felt powerless, yet managed to reply.

"Steady on, rape, pillage and treasure?"

"So what do you call virginity?" Faviola demanded. "A gift to the great conquistador?"

"Of course not. I loved you."

"Does a lover walk away, leave without a word, without a thought for his love?"

" It was wrong of me."

"Wrong? You treated me like..."

Faviola tossed her head, looked around for a reference and stared back at him.

"Like a bitch with rabies."

Toto now felt the full force of her anger.

God, these Latins, he thought, *how do you get out with honor, let alone alive?*

He mustered all the humility he could.

"I was a coward. Couldn't face my own failure. Took it out on the woman I loved."

"So this is what a true English gentleman is?"

"You've every right to not forgive me." Toto pleaded.

Faviola stepped back as suddenly as she had launched towards him, swiveled round and paced towards the open window. Toto was left confronted by her silhouette. Still the best figure he had ever set eyes on. The cicada outside filled a long and painful pause until Faviola broke it.

"Forgive you? Like that, forgive you for making me look a *putana* in front of everyone."

She slowly turned towards him and despite the backlight he felt the piercing fire of revenge in her stare. She took precise strides to arrive in front of him. He shivered involuntarily. Suddenly she dropped to her knees, placed her arms around his neck and said in the softest of voices.

"How could I not?"

Her change of tone caught him utterly off guard. She was the soft, slinky lover of years ago. His eyes met hers and saw passion. He could not believe the transformation, yet before he could reply she leaned forward and kissed him hard, holding an embrace melting an eternity.

"What was that for?" he managed, coming up for air.

"For all the years I've waited to do that to you, my cowardly Capitão," she replied, emphasizing the word *that* whilst stroking his cheeks with both hands.

He could not get round the three hundred and sixty degree treatment she dealt him.

"Your years away have dulled you to the Latin temperament. By law, we change instantly."

"What law?"

"The Law of Love, my little English gentleman."

She then corrected him.

"You were no coward running from failure. You just failed to recognize your priorities. Like all men!" she announced triumphantly.

Toto took the reprimand fully then tried changing the subject.

"So what happened to your friend who taught you your coffee ways?"

"Like all too-misdirected over-passionate men, he taught me what I needed, then died of a heart attack trying to impose himself on me."

"He was your lover?" Toto asked.

Faviola laughed uproariously.

"Lover, at seventy? A dead bird never fell out of that nest. He just had a vision of youth returning, enough to kill him instantly. Faviola chooses her lovers, no one else."

He could believe that.

"That's why I chose you and still do," she stated with absolute authority. "I'm going to wipe off the dust, we shall sit down to lunch and find out why you're really here."

Faviola got to her feet and walked, like a champion prizefighter, out of the room. Toto was left accepting another cool drink and retreated to the verandah to ponder her strength and the richness of her plantation ahead of him.

The cascade of a waterfall beyond confirmed the verdant view.

Over lunch Toto told of his search for coffee growers who could supply the new stateside import market Willy and he set up. He already knew he had found one and waited to hear if she felt the same.

"Not only can we supply, we have several other growers happy to increase their share of the market. We act as a small cooperative. I know them all well. They're hard working and produce excellent beans."

"That makes my job a lot easier, especially with you as leading expert on the ground."

"It may have taken you years but finally you're backed by a winner who supplies a winning team. Stay around savor the bonuses that come with it," Faviola suggested, placing a succulent slice of watermelon between her lips and letting the juice tease its way over her bottom lip and down her chin.

"I think I may very well do that!" Toto replied.

CHAPTER TWENTY-EIGHT

G uy Fawkes Night in England was a handed-down tradition celebrating the burning of treason against government. The tale told implicated a figurehead of the same name ending up being immolated annually, as a national family ritual. Tradition burned brightly in this part of the country as Louis Trapman, accompanied by wife Hettie and son John, arrived at the boy's school celebration of the rite. High spirits crackled in competition with the odd illicit firecracker set off by an unruly student.

His mother handed John a generously caramelized apple whilst his father looked on disapprovingly.

"The boy's got a sweet enough tooth as it is, without encouraging him."

"Don't spoil a night out with your ways. He deserves it with the results he got this term."

John moved closer to his mother's approval.

"Never happened in my day," replied her husband.

"What you mean is the favored eye always fell on Toto. As the eldest your father expected you to have grown out of expectation."

Louis knew it was hopeless going up against his wife. She always held her corner and annoyingly was more often right. A proven solution was always to defer.

"If you say so."

"Indeed I do," she replied, squeezing her son close and smiling triumphantly. At that moment a thunderous explosion ripped through the gathering as a giant firework marked the opening of celebrations. John's eyes widened, his jaw dropped and a life long love of big bangs was born. The family, having enjoyed the display, moved closer to the huge bonfire sparking into life. As Louis stood, dressed in a heavy camel-hair coat against the November chill, he quietly removed one glove and opened a sleek cigarette case held in the other. Placing a Gitane, his favorite brand, to his lips he closed the case returning it back into his coat. Drawing out a silver lighter, he lit the cigarette and took satisfaction from a first deep inhalation.

"Louis Trapman, I presume," a voice crowed from beside him.

He turned to confront one of the other boy's mothers whom he vaguely recognized as Lady Astor. Being a very polite and respectful man he replied.

"Indeed madam and who might I have the pleasure of meeting?"

"Lady Astor of course," she blasted.

To compliment her brusque introduction and noticing the cigarette he held in his gloved hand, she immediately chastised him.

"Only a filthy worm smokes tobacco."

Shocked, he recoiled, retaining enough composure to reply.

"I would hardly expect such an observation from anyone, let alone a Lady, madam."

"That's as may be but to cap it all, it's hardly an accepted Christian Science trait."

The bonfire warmed his defense and recharged his valor.

"Madam, nor is drink but some overly indulge in that activity."

His observation halted Her Ladyship, who carried a reputation for liking the liquor. He relished the bullseye and continued.

"So apart from your boys attending this place, what do I owe the pleasure of this encounter?"

"I hear from my people your brother is trying to persuade our people in Washington to change the position on War Loans."

"He's presently engaged in a project towards that end," Louis admitted with caution.

"Well he's not going to get very far," the aristocrat pronounced firmly, with the roaring bonfire unable to cover her rising volume.

Hetty caught the booming reply, looked round to investigate who Louis was talking to and simultaneously covered her son's ears.

"Pray why?" Louis asked Astor.

"Without our support you can kiss his chances goodbye."

"I see," he answered politely refusing to engage her rudeness, although patently unable to understand her observation.

"My people tell me his efforts are worthy of support and since they're in the know and rarely wrong, I merely wish to convey, we'll assist his cause."

Louis, taken aback, was no stranger to people of position being abrupt, though he always expected a certain amount of social decorum. However Lady Astor's reputation went before her. He was also intrigued as to her reference to *my people*.

He attempted to respond, however she had turned tail in her vast fur coat and swung out of sight cutting through the advancing crowd to the bonfire, like a hot blade through butter.

"Who was that dear?

"Lady Astor, evidently," he replied, retrieving his composure.

"That trout has two of hers here and certainly not because she's devoted to the doctrine."

Hetty confirmed with a candor Louis had come to adore from his wife. It helped him contain the anger he felt rising by her rudeness.

"Trout she may be but if she's behind Toto's efforts, well, we can suffer arrogance in exchange for means and clout," she stated definitively, closing the affair and drawing her man back to the entertainment.

Several months later while the wealthy withdrew to lavish Christmas and New Year celebrations in their country retreats and the population in their turn recovered from overindulgence and drunken stupors, bequeathed them by New Year celebrations, Montagu Norman, governor of the Bank of England sat in a private room of a very closed London club, alongside Sir Hugh Sinclair, head of the Secret Intelligence Service. Norman had requested Sinclair be present, in relation to their mutual ongoing campaign on money laundering. Both men considered personal time secondary to their respective duty and service to the state.

"These funds from Colombian gold and coca can be traced into several accounts held in Europe and Central America; however we're far more interested in the destination of the gold itself," Norman offered his Secret Service counterpart.

"Understand you've got feet on the ground out there presently."

"Correct, latest is that our man has traced shipping routes for the gold and paper trails for coca. Do you require more in depth?" Sinclair asked.

"Not presently, however I've learned from my contacts in the Fed, one of your fellows happens to be engaged in extracting an overdue War Loan," assured the banker.

"You got a problem with that?" Sinclair asked, not seeing the connection.

"Not in respect of the loan, looks kosher enough. His people are demanding the loan be repaid in gold, as initially given. Creates a problem for our friends in the States. We're looking for as much gold to come back here. Any siphoning off is unhelpful. Normally the odd bar would be fine but the amount of the debt with interest goes way beyond a few bars."

"So what are you suggesting, we persuade him to deposit it over here?" Sinclair asked.

Norman leaned forward purposefully in the ample Chesterfield he occupied. Stroking his perfectly trimmed moustache and caressing an equally coiffed beard, answered.

"I'm intending to raise rates here to counter the U.S. position currently causing gold to hemorrhage to Manhattan. This will put pressure on gold to return to the City, benefiting the rate. Whether his gold arrives here or not is neither here nor there."

"So I still don't understand how this affects our man in Colombia?"

"His venture in seeking reparation is useful for us, a diversion, let's say, within our planning. Keeps the speculative bubble growing in spite of the hit our move will initiate. The public there need to feel the good times in every deal. When have Americans ever shied away from good old rags to riches stories to support their dreams? It ultimately encourages more and more speculation."

"So you're suggesting we pull him from South America and get him back into the States to work on whatever plans he has going?"

Norman's hawk like eyes shone, as his features hardened. His empathy for the general public had never risen above zero, nor sought a scale on which to register. His sole purpose was to become commander in chief of a personal war maintaining British supremacy over a financial global stage. If that meant creating poverty, unemployment and suffering, so be it.

"As long as his efforts help our goal, he remains fit for purpose. You know better than anyone, the fleet with the bigger guns and greater firepower will always beat the enemy, especially if their decoys are believed on all sides to be verifiable," the banker admitted with cold joy exuding from an even colder delivery.

"Leave that detail to us," confirmed the Admiral.

"Excellent, then we're done here."

The two got up to go their separate ways and as they stood outside the Mayfair club, with the London streets displaying only the occasional vagrant, lost from the previous night's excesses, Sinclair turned to Norman.

"A few names turning up on the coca profits dangerously close to your people in the City. Would this be useful fuel for your fire?"

"No, keep the files. Already know much of what needs to be culled. Seems some of your fellows have loose mouths in the wrong places. Suggest you tighten up on that," Norman responded as he closed the conversation and walked briskly to a waiting limousine, having delivered his full hand of aces.

Sinclair was livid his agency had been so transparently infiltrated and swore to tighten up on field operatives' behavior. All information gathered was strictly internal, specific eyes and ears only. As much as Norman may have been part of the establishment, entitling him to some information, it was solely at his discretion, as head of the service to impart any, if at all.

166

He would not be held hostage through loose talk from his own people. Sinclair refused also to be patsy to Norman's or anyone's private goals. The influence and control of the Secret Service was his and his alone. That is how he wished it remain.

CHAPTER TWENTY NINE

Casa Cauca had been a refreshing and invigorating space for Toto to redesign a much vacated perspective on his own world and on plans he wished to develop beyond the confines of past tribulations. Faviola's youthful presence and physical willingness to share both body and soul had been the surprise and ignition encouraging a renewed vigor to course through his being. As he lay under a huge mosquito net, atop cotton sheets still impregnated with the impression of the previous night's activity, his gratitude for this turn of fortunes brought a smile to his face.

These past few months had seen his coffee project develop into a business both he and Willy could develop profitably. Faviola's plantation, along with a very impressive and willing cooperative, seemed destined to supply their ongoing needs. Several trips to Medellín, contacts with producers in coca, keen to augment their returns in exchange for sight of shady paperwork, had rewarded him with trails pleasing his masters in London. In spite of the annoyance of having to meet and communicate with his shadow in Santa Marta, his present situation here made even that bearable.

The terrace door opened as he lay luxuriating. In walked Faviola without a stitch of clothing on, save a loose translucent length of silk draped over her shoulder, cascading down across pert breasts and offering scant deference to a neatly trimmed triangle pointing to the pleasure gates he entered regularly. His body language gave him away, as it had done every time he cast eyes on this treasure. The mosquito net hid nothing.

"You never stop being thrilled to see me," she cooed as she slipped her soft brown body through a gap in the net.

Toto rolled over to allow her knees to straddle him. He could understand her black stallion's total acceptance of her in the saddle on its back daily.

"I can't get enough of you mounting me," he replied, justifying his erection.

"I never have need of a whip, like the horse. Are you that obedient?"

"Why even resist when temptation falls so easily from the tree?"

"Temptation, not lover?"

"Both and more."

"More?"

"Business partner as well."

"No time lost penetrating this one" Faviola purred, positioning herself to receive him.

"Lost in Brazilian beauty," he replied.

"Let me lose myself in you," she replied bringing herself down on his hardened expectation.

She allowed it to slip between her thighs, through moistened lips. Toto gently thrust himself deeper into her as she brought her body into his and back in a rhythm he enjoyed more each time. A cool breeze entering from outside was no match for the heat transmuting and growing between them.

In the distance a peregrine falcon screeched its success at catching unsuspecting prey from above the waterfall, as Faviola rolled over satiated from their lovemaking. It had become a ritual starting most days and Toto was never one to pass up an excellent program. Then quick as a flash she changed gear, rolled off the bed and slinkily made her way to the natural shower created off the bedroom. Toto joined her and soon they were dressed and ready to ride into town.

His months based at the plantation afforded him excellent opportunity to become an adept rider. The journey had him savor what they shared intimately, making each trip memorable and pass swiftly.

As they dismounted in town, he secured the reins round a wooden stump and both retired to the local meeting place, serving as bar, post office, community spot and newsroom. The unofficial telegraph officer raced over to the couple as they sat down at a table with their coffee.

He looked wide-eyed at Faviola and blurted.

"Signora, a message for the gringo, excuse, excuse, Capitano Trapman, just came in."

"Well hand it to him yourself, Pedro," she snapped back.

Flustered, the clerk rushed back to retrieve the forgotten missive.

As he handed it to Toto, the captain smiled graciously. He had got used to local rudeness towards foreigners and was accustomed to Faviola giving them short shrift whenever they lost their manners. What surprised him was how inept they were at learning to stop, which, in short, they never did.

He opened the telegram.

MISSION ACCOMPLISHED STOP ALL GOOD STOP TICKET FOR NYC AT SANTA MARTA.

His face dropped.

"Sod it. I've got my marching orders," he informed her despondently.

"What do you mean?" inquired his lover.

"The research for the English is finished, they want me to go back to New York."

"Do you want to?"

"It's the hardest decision I thought I'd never have to make."

"But your claim against the government in Washington, that must be important."

"It was and still is but my heart's here, with you."

Toto admitted knowing part of him would have stayed forever. Another part had to complete the War Loan business.

"I left you once badly, a huge mistake, whatever the excuses. Consolation of leaving you now is, I'll not be running away, I'll finish business and return."

Faviola looked deep into his eyes. He could not stand the pain of missing those orbs drawing him in so sensually. He wished he could drown in them.

"I know I'll see you again. Here, England or America," she assured him.

The certainty of her tone cheered him enough to realize he had to finish the job he had spent such energy on.

"In England having such profound experiences with Smokey, I feel my life has changed just so much. I'm stronger, more focused, more of a man than ever."

"You're not the man I knew in Manaus, that's certain," she agreed.

"After years of cock-ups, I now have a life of purpose, meaning and direction. These last few months have felt as different as if I'd been reborn."

Faviola took his hands in hers, ignoring local relish at romantic drama.

"We'll meet again. You must complete and whatever life holds, we'll embrace it."

Toto knew he had never been happier. Everything revolved a million miles away from this spot here and now, in Colombia, in Santa Fe di Antioquia, in this taverna, at this table, between their two bodies.

The rest of the morning was spent tidying up business. As they set out one final time for Casa Cauca, they passed the West Bridge, a totem of the modern world in the depths of Colombia. Toto drew to a halt.

"When I cross the Brooklyn Bridge in New York, I shall remind myself the many crossings we made here. Like Villa, who lent his genius to both bridges, I see our time together as a bridge bringing two worlds together."

"We'll walk in step, in time."

Faviola added, then, as if another world called, dug her stirrups into the steed's flank and bolted off, with Toto hard-pressed to catch her, in pursuit.

He found it difficult leaving. He delayed as long as possible, but time was against him. After a long and emotionally tiring journey, he arrived back in Santa Marta. Connecting with Buffet, he parried all attempts at having any details extracted of his time in Antioquia and left. A late spring arrival back in New York threw him headlong into an atmosphere of frenetic moneymaking madness and a world away from where he had come from.

First port of call was Willy. The von Meister backyard in New Jersey resembled nothing of the jungle he had left. Its borders and plants were as European as they could be; however the welcome was as warm as the Colombian heat, without the sweat.

"Seems you hit pay dirt coming across Faviola again, timed and placed to perfection."

"A real turn up for the book. I don't know who was more surprised, me or her. Bodes well for the future."

"So what news from our friends in the Fed, the attorneys and…"

Willy picked up a bunch of mail and files and threw them into his uncle's lap.

"Spend as much time as you want catching up with that lot, while I wash off Manhattan madness tending the garden."

Toto went through each thoroughly as Willy enjoyed horticultural therapy.

"Looks like they're ready to roll in Hollywood with the screenplay, Mason's new post with our attorneys has managed to get a move on the request for a Congressional hearing on war loans. Also a comprehensive file from Anne in Charleston filling gaps."

Willy raised himself from tending a border and walked back to his uncle. He placed a neat bunch of lily of the valley in a vase on the table.

"Nothing like their fragrance to bring one back to earth," he said as he bent over to catch another whiff of their potent scent.

"The smell of money, gambling and lunatic trading in the market is far from pleasant. It infects so many with the lie of infinite joy. Concerns me how manic people are getting."

"All signs point to it getting even better," Toto suggested.

"That's exactly my worry. Warburg warned the orgy of unrestrained speculation could lead to a mighty crash followed by depression. Anything like that would scuttle or at best delay your claim interminably."

"Landmann suggested Warburg and the Kuhn Loebs were family, so if speculation is driven by Wall Street, then why would Warburg make such a statement, if he thought it might frighten the market, slow down and staunch money coming through the Wall?"

"I'm no broker nor banker but my business head tells me it was a diversion sown to test the water. The higher profile the diversion, the more credible."

"Well it didn't seem to take the steam out of the market," observed Toto.

"Which makes it even more important we get the claim rolling. Suggest you contact Ochs, push the Fox Brothers and get Neily and Grace to spread the word Congress is about to reconsider war loans."

It was not long before Toto was sitting across the table from Mason at the attorney's office, keen to hear what the firm's new partner had to say, having had time to work through the files.

"While you were abroad we had a chance to correlate papers and research and it only remains for us to present our case to Congress," the attorney advised, having completed the summary of his own work.

"That's good news then?" Toto asked.

"Moving smoothly on," responded Mason. "My only concern, Captain, is the stipulation for repayments to be made in gold. It creates an obstacle but we're working on it."

Toto looked surprised.

"I presumed having been initially paid in gold it would automatically be repaid in kind."

"There is precedence for such repayments, however repayment of gold is something of a touchy subject currently," replied Mason.

"From what I've heard," Toto cut in, "gold's flooding into Manhattan from London with the competitive rates on offer. Why the problem?"

Mason shifted uncomfortably.

"Gold is not readily available for use by the Treasury."

"Which gold is?" joked Toto.

"That's our sticking point. The Treasury feels at this time it's inappropriate to repay gold on Revolutionary debts."

"Well they were perfectly happy to accept it when they needed it."

"That, sir, was a long time ago."

"So is the overdue repayment."

"Look, to be frank, getting this project to the stage we have is a minor miracle in itself."

"Excuse me? Precisely why we instruct you to do what you're doing. It's no good telling us it's a miracle you're doing what you're paid to do. Coming from the Fed surely you can do better than that."

"My credentials afford excellent contacts Captain, however even for the most demanding of our clients we cannot guarantee results where national security interests are at stake."

"Are you telling me our loan repayment is now involved in national security interests?"

"It's just that..." Mason was cut short.

"We're calling in our debt, Mister Mason. One the government and this country have benefited from for far too long. The interest we have on this is getting larger by the day. Therefore use your connections, put pressure on the corridors of power. I'll be instructing my elements to bring this overdue account to the attention of the people and to the world."

Toto impressed even himself on the strength of his command over the meeting.

"Please bear with us and I'll see how we can make this happen," Mason conceded, resisting his annoyance at the Englishman's tone.

"I expect nothing less," Toto concluded.

He got up, turned to leave Mason's office. As he got to the door Mason stood up.

"As my client, I must advise your caution on bringing this forward too hastily."

Toto, furious and impatient, turned midway between office and exit.

"One hundred and fifty years on my watch comes nowhere close to hasty. If it does for you then I suggest you invest in a new watch, sir."

He closed the door, marched through the waiting area and out onto Broadway.

CHAPTER-THIRTY

George L. Harrison had been a close partner and associate at the Federal Reserve Bank since its inception. Having served as both assistant and then General Counsel to the Bank, the appointment of Randolph Mason in 1922 to that same top post enabled Harrison to focus on his deputy governorship within the Federal Reserve at the same time as having a strong, dependable ally as Counsel. Governor Benjamin Strong's death in 1928 allowed the seamless transition for Harrison to take over the reins of governorship.

For his part, Montagu Norman's close partnership with Strong merely allowed an equally smooth transition for the mantle to pass, offering no disturbance to Norman's long-term plans. It merely secured links in a chain of control he held firm. Whatever Norman transmitted to Harrison and the Federal Reserve was based always on self-benefit. Where trade was needed, he made sure it was at as near zero loss to his own account.

With the Fed now under Harrison's guidance, and Paul Warburg's advisory position replacement with William Potter as President of the Guaranty Trust Company, Raymond Mason was assured steel-clad connections for not only himself but the whole legal team within which he was an active partner. The Guaranty Trust Company, a lucrative offspring of a Vanderbilt, Rockefeller and Harriman investment, was strengthened through Harriman's share sale to JP Morgan in 1912. It became a useful filter, eyes and ears for all activity within and around the Federal Reserve. Mason was cognizant of this oversight that ran deeply into what control was manipulated from England and Europe.

Nor was it flippant happenstance that the Rockefeller empire chose Curtis Fosdick and Belknap as a major arm of their legal team. Mason's move from the Fed to these attorneys was as natural as night follows day. He understood the intricate revolving doors operating within control center steering global finance. His signature at the Fed finalized a multiplicity of decisions made within the Bank. Equally, he never questioned any request emanating to or from Norman, the Fed, Rockefeller and their contacts on the Wall and beyond. When alerted, Norman was prepared to supply gold needed in the case of a positive resolution to the Revolutionary debt; thus Mason prepared merely to be its messenger.

The summer of twenty-nine saw a roller coaster of activity in trading stocks and shares settle. Along Wall, Broad and Nassau brokerage houses were busier than ever. In the relative calm, paper fortunes were being created for both those on top of the ladder as well as those just starting the climb. Toto sensed going public with his gold recovery project to be imminent. To that end, he found himself in the news desk department of the New York Times.

Jerry Graves, having handled Toto's submissions over the years, was a sub editor on the Times who had, like so many on the title, much respect for the war correspondent and his work. His present quest, outside of his journalistic remit, caught the imagination of the readers and on Ochs' instruction the Times decided to cover the story from start to finish.

"Captain, I'm ready to file whatever you have there," Graves greeted the journalist, expecting to receive the journalist's latest.

"Breaking news," Toto announced. "We're launching the full campaign getting Congress to throw its weight behind the Supporters for Independence Repayment. All relevant details, when and where are in there. Appreciate your help on this."

He dropped an envelope on the desk.

As he turned to leave, Graves spoke.

"How's that film coming with the Fox brothers?"

Toto turned and smiled.

"About to meet Carewe. He's just hit town. Will file our meeting later with a photo. Get one of your guys to follow me over to the Plaza."

"Will do," Graves replied as the reporter fell out of earshot.

Although the summer had begun to tarnish the verdant growth of Central Park, the exact opposite was true within the Plaza Hotel where palms and imported greenery lent lushness and abundance to an otherwise barren reception area. All that making it a fitting place for the master of illusion, Edwin Carewe, to choose its renaissance splendor and floral decor as his New York home. Toto for his part loved floating around its wealth and opulence. A fitting compliment to what processed across city and country – the illusion of growing collective wealth.

"Albert, good to see the Colombian sun turned you even more Californian," the film director remarked.

His efforts to handle the tea cup in hand failed miserably. Toto smiled at the clueless way foreigners so hopelessly attempted to emulate the English tea ceremony.

"I thought you chaps were all coffee and left the tea to the Brits," Toto jibed.

"I love my tea unlike my brothers but this dainty china makes me look an idiot."

"I'll forgive you; now tell me how's the schedule rolling?"

"Script's as close to the screenplay as we could make it," confirmed Carewe. "The good news is both Clara Bow and Ronald Coleman are signed for the main roles and we're ready to roll as soon as you go public."

"It'll be at the end of the month. Can I feed names to the press at this stage?"

"Why not, contracts are almost signed."

Toto smiled as he leaned back, having delivered his own cup in the precise English manner, enlightening the American on each detail. The two discussed the script and Carewe cleared up details the studio had instructed him on.

"A personal question on this gift of your forebears: it was given in gold then?"

"Yes, according to our records."

"So you're demanding repayment be made in gold, is that correct?"

"Yes," Toto replied.

"Any reason?"

The journalist leaned forward, placed his cup on the table in front of him and rested his elbows on his knees, interlocked his fingers.

"As you can't fail to notice, this country is presently consumed in a rising mania for everything wealth centered, the likes of which we've rarely witnessed; one thing is obvious, paper money is transient. Today's wealthy is tomorrow's pauper, and speaking from past pauper experience, here's an opportunity to hold longevity in wealth. Advice my brother recently shared, influencing my opinion."

"That's a novel take on the times."

"Novel it may appear, but dressing appearance is your stock in trade. Your industry is built on persuading the public to believe illusion as reality. So also, I believe this madness on the streets outside and through every home in this country is a chimera."

"Heck, this is America, dreams come true and wealth's created by anyone, no matter who or where they come from," Carewe insisted.

"Some time ago I might have agreed with you, yet what passes for wealth today seems more like a three card trick writ large," explained Toto.

"Many would dismiss that as heresy, for what they hold."

Toto felt the power of his intuitive punch, looked the film director in the eye and continued.

177

"Or what they may not hold, at their peril. Gold, on the other hand, holds permanence and value."

"You'll have a hard time selling that to each man and woman holding stock."

"Thankfully that's neither my problem nor goal, Edwin. Reparation of an original gift will do it for me! You, my good man, are going to help with the film and be selling that to the American people, bringing success to both of us."

CHAPTER THIRTY-ONE

Ever since John Rockefeller Prentice ostracized himself from the family and fortune through his addiction to gambling, he had sought ways to restore that position. A relationship with Aaron Kersh, he concluded to be an excellent pathway back. The broker's exploitation of the fanatical pursuit by both rich and poor in the bond and share markets, had made Kersh some very useful friends, himself rich and earned a place on the Stock Exchange floor. His ambitious climb to the top was made easier by the day. Prentice saw the broker's success as the leg-up he craved. He thus made sure the family name worked hard for him.

As Kersh walked up Wall Street, completing another successful day on the floor, Prentice approached as the broker climbed into the back of a waiting car. He leaned in.

"There's a lot of gold in the Englishman."

"Get in before you let the world know," hissed Kersh.

He pulled Prentice in who slumped onto the seat beside him.

"Rumor has it that the man's claim looks good and he'll be looking to invest it in profitable ventures," confided Prentice.

"Firstly, let me remind you nothing is certain. Secondly, your family never made money on wild guesses and thirdly, what makes you think I'm not already in possession of these facts?" Kersh spat in response.

Prentice felt he had been dealt four aces and vainly endeavored to recoup.

"What if I told you Trapman is launching a major campaign on Friday announcing the appeal to Congress for repayment?"

Kersh grunted, indicating his total lack of impression. He turned to Prentice as he opened a briefcase on his lap.

"Then it looks like you're going to represent us at that meeting."

Prentice looked surprised.

"Me?"

"Yes, since he already knows you, it's appropriate."

"Why would I be there?"

"To report back to me how he reacts," answered Kersh.

"To what?" Prentice asked.

"To you giving him these," Kersh replied as he handed Prentice a sheaf of certificates pulled from the briefcase. "Inform him they're a small gift from you from a very successful acquisition you made in a recent pool."

"What pool?" Prentice asked, knowing no such thing happened.

Kersh handed him another sheaf of certificates.

"This pool – and these are your shares in it."

"What pool?" the mystified Rockefeller repeated.

"We recently invested in a small venture in Pennsylvania, a metal works turning its hand to getting America onto two wheels. Bicycles. On the floor today their shares showed very healthy growth. While we've sat here yours have added an extra hundred dollars," Kersh explained.

Prentice gasped.

"So what's the name of this new upstart?"

Kersh was curt.

"New it's not, upstart yes. The company and profits set to soar."

"A bicycle enterprise, sounds ideal for the Englishman."

"Precisely why your job of delivering those certificates to him will be easy, now get your butt out of my car and earn your keep."

The vehicle stopped and Prentice was abruptly disgorged.

Kersh sped off before the new stockholder could collect himself and ask more. He looked down at the bunch of certificates.

The light at the end of the tunnel gets brighter, he reassured himself.

At the Alpha Delta Club Toto read the letter Anne sent from Charleston confirming her arrival in New York for the big disclosure that Friday. Forty-eight hours before the great reveal, he had much to do. Willy and his team were organizing the names hitting town and visiting European dignitaries, local diplomats and political affiliates. Neily had asked to meet in his favorite speakeasy.

For almost four years, Mary Louise Guinan had run her collection of well-frequented clubs. Known by all as Texas, she bludgeoned her patrons with insults and scorn, only making them love her the more. Her haunts buzzed with famous names and infamous faces. The more the decade spiraled into pool rush, buying and selling shares and frantic moneymaking, the more sought after became the magnetic speakeasy. It was amongst the glitterati midweek that Neily welcomed Toto as he weaved his way through the smoke-filled, noisy club.

"Welcome to Pandemonia. Brush the showgirl off your chair, sit yourself down and take a glass," Neily roared above the music.

Toto took it, astonished at so much abandon and conscious decadence. From every angle people came up, slapping him on the shoulder and showering congratulations for he knew not what.

"What's with the congratulations?"

"News is the new virus, your venture's common knowledge."

Toto began to appreciate the power of broadcast.

"Have some real bubbles."

Neily insisted as he thrust a bottle of Krug into Toto's hands.

"Here Prohibition's a bad dream."

From all directions glasses appeared for refill. Toto became confused.

"Look after number one, dear fellow," Neily cried, seeing the thirsty vultures zeroing in on the real deal.

"First law of moneymaking; serve yourself first!"

Toto poured himself a good glass.

"So ya think you can drink your own juice."

A voice caught him as he finished. Toto turned to be confronted with a fur-wrapped ermine, draped around Texas, blond, forty-something and charismatic as ever.

"Honey, no one flaunts the house rules without paying dearly."

She whipped Toto across his embarrassed face with the tail of her wrap.

"Our Neily is such a wicked boy," she pronounced to cheers all around.

Neily raised his glass in acknowledgment, whilst pressing a hundred dollar bill into her stole. She openly acknowledged the gift by pirouetting away to another well-heeled customer.

"You think this is just for you?"

Neily nudged Toto.

"It's like this every night, your breaking news is one in a long line of headlines."

The beat of the orchestra increased in volume by way of confirmation.

"Seems like no one has a care in the world," Toto leaned over, so Vanderbilt could catch his words.

"The point is they're all riding euphoria and Friday will just place a cherry on top of it," Neily shouted back.

"The Astor confirmed the roof garden's available," Toto remarked. "End of July is a great time for all to take away a thrilling get rich story line to follow during the recess," Toto added.

"Precisely, dealings tail off, papers feed the golden tale on to yachts, beaches and mansions – you could not have timed it better," encouraged Neily. "Congress looks primed to vote in your favor on their return, and those of them here will now be on side."

Toto soaked up the atmosphere and flattered himself with the attentions

181

of a couple of the resident girls, hovering round the Vanderbilt table. A crescendo of clapping followed as a small group made way to their table, all eyes following.

"Here comes the star of the moment," cried Neily. "Clara Bow herself."

The starlet, Edwin Carewe in tow, burst through the throng.

"Did you think we'd miss this sort of publicity?" Carewe crowed.

"Delightfully unexpected you and..." Neily turned to the film star, "our most delightful Miss Bow."

Toto bowed gallantly, took Clara's hand and kissed it with panache.

"Edwin, your Captain's a real gentleman. Honored to meet you, gallant sir."

She flashed her penetrating eyes, using all her Hollywood skills in Toto's direction, flattering his innocence.

"Well, thank you," Toto reciprocated.

"Clara was in town, we decided your launch would fail without star quality," Carewe pronounced.

"Star quality traps the press in the Big Apple, Edwin, indebted to you. Plenty of pools, plenty of money but stars, well only you can pull those out of the hat."

An even bigger cheer went up as more and more focused on the table of attention.

Texas, not missing the moment, with an athletic bound was lifted onto the table. She gathered her dress, like a well endowed saloon girl about to break into song and addressed the whole club.

"Ladies and gentlemen, roughnecks, vagrants and anyone remembering who they are, I invite you all to celebrate the next big gold rush starting right here by a most distinguished live one from across the lil' ol' pond, Captain Trapman, accompanied by his butter and egg man Mister Vanderbilt."

A roar went up and Toto blushed deeply.

"Cute as he is, this nugget is the epitome of everything we in the US of A hold dear," Texas continued. "Gold his forebears gave, made us all what we are today!"

"Boozers and womanizers?" a drunken voice blurted from the crowd.

"For you, Senator, yes," shot back Guinan. "For the rest of us the road to riches, so hello suckers and enjoy our gals."

She leapt off the table, navigated through her adoring guests, to reap another verbal onslaught.

"Far better live than on screen, gentlemen," Carewe quipped, as she vanished into in the crowd. "But darn it, she still exudes star quality."

"With her stamp of approval and government guests here, you've got it wrapped," Neily encouraged Toto.

A continent away, a midweek luncheon party convened in a villa in a leafy upmarket suburb of Frankfurt. Carriages delivered the cream of the banking fraternity for a quiet confidential conference. Montagu Norman, Bank of England head, descended his vehicle and was greeted by counterpart Hjalmar Schacht, head of the Reichsbank. The German led him up the steps to a meeting consisting of representatives of the financial heads. They were the eight powerful families including Rothschilds, Kuhn Loebs, Warburgs, Lehmans, Lazards, Israel Moses Seif and Goldman Sachs.

Norman relished this meeting, looking forward to presenting his desired implementations to the assembled bankers. Seif's presence was particularly appreciated as it helped consolidate the power of the City of London and its position held in a tripartite control on global finance.

In New York Toto arrived back at the Alpha Club, to be confronted by the desk clerk keen to deliver a note. The journalist opened it and read

Need to see you soonest, Nikola.

"When did this arrive?" Toto asked.

"A half hour ago, Captain."

Toto retrieved his bicycle, leapt on it and peddled furiously towards Tesla's office. As he turned a corner the familiar figure of the scientist stepped out, nearly knocking him off his wheels.

"Park up and walk with me," the inventor ordered.

Toto did so and walked with him.

"Three is important, you need to be very aware," Tesla pronounced. "We are entering the time where force and matter face great challenges. The evil men impose on others comes dressed as a harlot, seducing the feeble consciousness of those too weak to find the true strength of force. Greed around us, the grabbing of nonexistent wealth will see many suffering. This was planned trust me. It's you that must seek the truth behind this cancer."

Tesla's face carried the pallor of a ghost, yet there was nothing ghostly in the strength and urgency his voice projected.

"The momentum for change certainly looks like coming to fruition where my work is concerned," Toto countered.

"I've urged you before, those money barons supporting your cause are only looking after their own interests. Pay attention to why they support you and prepare yourself for every eventuality. My own case is proof of that," Tesla reminded him.

"So why the urgency?"

Tesla stopped abruptly, took strong hold of Toto's arm and led him into an adjoining alley. He looked him directly in the eye.

"I see dark energies descending on this city. Forces long controlling the ways of men injecting the natural flow with all that is base in man. I recognize how universal force moves and has its being and right now it's being poisoned by arrogant forces assuming ill-gotten control. You're not only a true friend but I see in you the quality and sharpness demanded of the surgeon when asked to cut out the cancerous growth. Everything has its equal and opposite in the universe. Be vigilant, dig deep and trust no one. I mean no one."

The late afternoon was not chilly, nor was it particularly cool in the shade of the alley, yet Toto felt a chill pass through him as Tesla spoke. He felt the truth of the inventor's words penetrate and shuddered involuntarily.

"Although I can't grasp the whole picture, I trust your assessment and will use all my resources to dig deeper," Toto replied, with more faith than knowledge.

"A clear mind cannot cloud consciousness, temptation can."

Tesla responded enigmatically. Then as if he had seen a ghost pass he turned and walked quickly into the main avenue. Toto followed him, dragging his bicycle with him.

Tesla turned. The sun struck his gaunt features.

"Their eyes are everywhere. Your defense is intuition and again trust no one."

He turned and, as Toto digested his parting words, disappeared into thin air. The journalist stood, bicycle at his side, staring into a long sparsely populated sidewalk unable to track his friend.

CHAPTER THIRTY-TWO

The lobby of the Astor Hotel buzzed with activity. Several notable figures, celebrity faces and assorted people of interest attending the evening's upcoming presentation were checking in, on their arrival from out of town. One assigned a special booking was Anne Gregorie. Toto noticed her sitting alone and approached.

"You've found your room and settled in," he asked as Anne turned towards him. He leaned down and gave her a kiss on each cheek.

"Yes, I've everything I need. Ready for the big event?"

Toto took a seat beside her, placing a sheaf of papers to one side.

"Ready as can be, seems we already have a press entourage milling about, luckily there are well known faces to make it newsworthy."

Anne looked distracted. Toto caught it.

"Anything the matter, you look a little on edge."

"It's just I wonder whether I should really be here. My input has been minimal and with all the really important faces here, I just feel…"

Toto cut in.

"Not a word of that nonsense. Frankly without your input and expertise I could very well still be drowning in paperwork and research," he assured her.

"Yes, but I just feel like a small cog in a much larger wheel," she confessed.

"Who was it that told me she was as good as any man, not giving a toss what men believed constituted appropriate academia? The strength of commitment of that woman was something I really love and appreciate. Outside of how I feel towards you personally your professional input has been essential," Toto insisted.

Anne looked at him tenderly.

"I missed you on your travels. Good to have you back."

Toto avoided any mention of his South American exploits. He had in all honesty not missed her, within the rekindled passion he found in Colombia. To explain any of that now would entail dragging out all sorts of feelings he felt incapable of sharing.

He chose to lie.

"Missed you too."

Anne smiled and, about to share more intimate feelings she wanted to express, was interrupted by the arrival of a member of the hotel staff.

"Captain Trapman, could I ask you to meet the head of functions. He's some last minute questions for you."

185

Toto, relieved at the timely distraction, apologized to Anne and left.

Anne for her part decided to take the opportunity later, to share her feelings.

As Toto descended, having ironed out last minute arrangements alone in the lift apart from the lift boy, he looked forward to the following weeks producing a timely hearing in Congress, a film premiere of the Moore Millions and a turn in fortune long overdue.

The lift stopped on the seventh floor. The doors opened and in walked John Rockefeller Prentice. Toto could not have been more surprised had he seen a ghost.

"Just the man I wanted," Prentice exclaimed.

"Whatever are you doing," asked an incredulous Toto. "Surely not staying here?"

"The way things are going, I could well camp out here, old man," the young socialite boasted.

"Fortunes changed, have they?"

"Quite how much I can't tell you, but what I can do is why I came."

Toto, taken completely off guard, replied limply.

"What's that?"

"Well, it's pretty clear most people know you're here today, so taking the punt I came to share a little of my good fortune, since you've been kind enough to help me when I needed it."

The lift took off to the mezzanine floor, the destination Prentice had asked for.

"As you know things are going crazy out there, everyone making more than a buck or two riding the stallion."

Prentice winked at the operator who returned a knowing nod, indicating he also had joined the ranks of the new stockholding elite. A gloved hand came up to cover a knowing cough to the other two passengers. Prentice looked at him.

"There you go, Captain. Everyone's on the train to riches and your little presentation tonight will merely add a plush carriage to the rolling stock."

Toto was none the wiser as to what Prentice wanted with him. The lift jolted to a halt at the mezzanine and the doors opened. Prentice took Toto's arm.

"Your stop as well. Come on. I'll explain all."

Toto keen to find out the young man's purpose followed, as the lift doors closed behind them.

"Got into a no-brainer pool, a little while back and for the last few weeks the stock's made excellent progress, with its performance showing every sign it'll go through the roof."

"What's that got to do with me?'"

"I remember friends who helped me and the name of the stock, reminded me of our conversations, so I asked, who would benefit more and at the same time love the coincidence?'"

Toto studied Prentice's enthusiasm.

"That's when I thought of you."

Prentice drew a sheaf of certificates from his inside coat pocket, wrapped neatly with a crimson ribbon around the bundle.

"So my friend, I felt it only appropriate you share in my fortune so I gift you these shares of the company forging their way to new heights and offering both of us riches we richly deserve."

"I can't possibly accept this," Toto spluttered, taken completely by surprise.

"They're worth a small fortune, it'd be criminal not to," replied Prentice. "Several thousand dollars, last I read the ticker."

Toto was lost for words.

"Come on, the land of infinite opportunity is knocking on your door today."

Prentice thrust the sheaf into Toto's hands.

"So what d'ya think of the company's name?"

Toto unwrapped the roll and read the name of the company.

"Freedom Cycles," he muttered.

"It's a joke."

"No joke and all yours. I just love the name of your successful investment. Have to dash, date and dinner, wouldn't you know."

As they both reached the stairs, Prentice hopped away down them. He turned half way down and called out.

"Good luck tonight, my man."

Toto stood at the top of the flight of stairs, wondering whether this was all a dream. He had no time to resolve the conundrum before a band of journalists ran up the stairs to fire questions at him.

He parried them, inviting them all to the roof garden presentation later.

The Astor's Roof Terrace was a legendary luxury adorning one of the most sought after hotels of the city. A retreat for the well heeled, a playground for those wishing to impress and a challenge for anyone making it in stock or pool with a pretence to solid riches, to be allowed onto its hallowed ground. The terrace played host to them all.

It was part of this lavish landscape Toto and his assistants had reserved for the big reveal and challenge to the country's lawmakers to repay a long over-due debt. Months of persuasion, enticement and passion had gone into gathering a diverse cross-section of public and private lives to this presentation.

The Vanderbilts bent ears and twisted arms. Adolph Ochs mustered the New York Times to spearhead press interest, creating an inevitable following from main rivals not wishing to miss a scoop. In the way only Hollywood could, Edwin Carewe excelled himself bringing forth the expectation of the film to the original story. Toto's visits to Europe and England, with the help of sister Leila, procured the attendance of diplomatic and aristocratic support. It billed as a social event to match the most outrageously lavish displays of overt success New York offered.

Arches draped in vine-covered profusion created a colonnade along which the invited passed. A multi tiered fountain cascaded watery abundance, while in the background a miniature Niagara Falls gave the impression of the existence of the impossible. Carewe invested much time and effort in employing his specialist teams of lighting technicians, set builders and studio expertise to adorn this already sumptuous setting to dream like proportions. Chinese lanterns, magically floating lights above in the sky and a firework display to mirror titanic battles in the struggle for independence would comprise the layout for what followed.

Willy, Toto and Neily all mingled giving time to each and every guest. A stunning sunset melted into twilight offsetting the whole scene. The press was having a field day. The entrance of Carewe with Clara Bow on his arm raised collective applause and synchronized flash bulbs from the photographers. The two made their way to the front of proceedings, joining Toto and the others. The swell of money, self-interest and genuine intrigue at what was to be announced, brought silence to the hundreds gathered. Neily took the platform.

"Lords, ladies, Highnesses, noble architects of this country, fellow beneficiaries, celebrities and press. It is with great honor and a genuine degree of thanks to his forebears I introduce to you a man who single-handed discovered the true indebtedness we all owe to those enabling our founding fathers to so successfully birth this great nation of ours." Neily paused theatrically as a ripple of applause took hold.

"Such generosity and belief endowed the cause of Independence to take root, grow and finally flourish into the magnificence we all witness today. An America whose bounds are endless, potential unfathomable and whose sons and daughters continue to forge the cause of freedom, liberty and commerce into the veins of all people round the world. Such a gift given deserves the recognition earned from our founding President, George Washington. So without usurping my dear friend's rightful introduction, I give you Captain Albert William Trapman."

A roar of applause and cheering broke out, bulbs flashed and Toto beaming from ear to ear took the stage. Anne, standing next to Neily gave him an enthusiastic applause of her own as she turned to Willy, laughing joyfully. A couple of representatives from Toto's attorneys endeavored to be seen catching the spirit of the night. Mason was conspicuously absent. The applause took a moment or two to subside.

"I'm truly overcome at the reception you all give us and humbly thank you for turning out this evening. It's an honor to look out and see so many of you who benefited and made the very most of what this great country has to offer. I certainly came to these shores, as many before me, to relish the opportunities we all have in such abundance. The subsequent discovery my forebear had been instrumental in turning the independence movement into reality at a time when it looked anything but, was fortuitous. Without the help and assistance of so many here tonight, during research and discovery, it would have remained a point of historical interest. Yet the fact we're now able to present Congress with the opportunity to recognize the debt we all owe those funding the reality of life, liberty and the pursuit of happiness, is marvelous."

Toto looked towards Carewe.

"This most creative man is about to set down on celluloid the story my forebear created through gifting a king's ransom to a holy cause."

Toto turned to the press corps in front of him and continued.

"These journalists, like myself, have and will continue to excite and inform the nation towards demanding this government makes good the repayment of war loans, initiating the wonders and opportunity we all enjoy today. My own family's gift was the much-needed spark resetting the tinderbox resulting in the explosion that became independence.

A cheer went up as Carewe nodded assent to an aide whose task it was to start the fireworks. Everyone looked skyward as several explosions lit up the now darkened sky. Applause followed the short display, amidst guests' tables being recharged with food and drink.

"I humbly ask you all to press every contact you have so this honor of life we enjoy be recognized in the bill presented to Congress. The irony of an

Englishman leading this charge is not lost on one and all, I'm sure. Yet, I admit it was another such Englishman who gifted not only his money, but his belief in the dream your founding fathers held for us all."

Another round of applause rolled across the assembled gathering.

The press hacks scribbled frantically, as photographers created more fireworks with their flashes. They all clambered to ask questions. Toto managed them, directing the more specific enquiries to his attorneys.

"Is it true you're demanding repayment in gold?"

Toto and everyone looked towards the questioner standing underneath the colonnade. The journalist unfamiliar to Toto got a reply.

"Yes, correct, we've insisted the repayment of this loan be returned in the same manner it was given."

The journalist moved towards the front as he asked.

"Are you aware the size this outstanding loan amounts to?"

Toto looked quizzical, trying to figure out where this might be going.

"Yes I am. As far as figures go, it's substantial."

The questioner moved through the audience.

"So you would agree the amount of gold involved would, with the interest accrued, be veering way beyond the million mark?"

"I cannot place an exact figure on it but certainly it would be considerable. May I ask the relevance of this amount to you, sir?"

The audience went quiet and was riveted at both the progress of the questioner and the answers Toto had to come up with.

The representative from the attorneys broke the focus on the two men.

"If I may, sir, the amount to be agreed..."

The interrogator cut him off.

"So would you say your interest in this repayment was more about furnishing your own desire for reward than patriotic partnership for us all?

Toto felt the pressure to respond from the gathered crowd bear down on him.

"Not at all, sir, apart from the obvious family interest, there's a matter of principle here that many would agree, I am sure, the government owes to the people of this country. That is honoring the support so many made from inception through to defending this nation's founding principles and today's flourishing wealth distributed across states and country."

Several cries of 'Here, here' rang out across the terrace.

The questioner continued his way towards the front, where he turned to face the guests.

Neily became concerned the focus was being hijacked and made a move to intervene.

"Please sir, I have yet one more question for Captain Trapman, if you will," the stranger insisted.

Irritated, Neily demanded.

"Then ask it sir that we may continue."

"Is it correct, Captain that you were holding some considerable stock in a bicycle company whose worth today shot up by a factor of ten, making you and several others a small fortune?

Toto looked confused. Willy, Neily, Anne and others looked at each other and back to Toto.

"I have no idea what you're getting at or what relevance this might have to what we are here for," Toto retorted.

The man turned to the audience.

"The relevance sir is this. Shortly before the bell, this stock plummeted. You and those you work with, as a pool had already sold at the top, leaving many, who over past weeks, have been led to believe the investment to be watertight lost all. Would you say this was the sign of a gentleman, someone who honored the founding principles of this land?"

"I have no idea what you're talking about. I've never invested in any stock, let alone bicycles."

Toto suddenly remembered what transpired earlier in the day with Prentice. He felt sick.

Willy looked at him and mouthed.

"What the hell's going on?"

Chatter began to rumble around the space. One after another several guests began to heckle the reporter.

"Keep to the point!"

"Let's get back to what we came for!"

"Get that man out of here," another cried.

Fellow journalists crowded the questioner and demanded validation of his remarks. Toto was fast losing it but maintained composure.

"Perhaps the Captain can explain the certificates he has in his coat pocket, then and explain why they are the same he sold today for a small fortune."

The terrace went silent. All eyes were upon Toto.

So many thoughts crashed around his mind. He became aware he still carried the certificates he was handed earlier.

Neily turned to him.

"Have you got them?"

"No, I mean yes but what he's saying makes no sense," Toto stuttered.

"Then show them man, prove you have. Then we'll shut this guy up."

Toto put his hand in his jacket pocket and pulled out the sheaf of certificates.

"Here are the ones I was given today."

The collective intake of breath was like a dagger to Toto's heart. He staggered slightly as every flash from each photographer popped.

"Fuck," he cursed silently, "this will be their bloody scoop."

"I had nothing to do with this pool," he professed to a sea of noise and disbelief at what was taking place. Willy rushed forward to protect his uncle from the barrage of questions. Neily recognized the wolf pack in full chase and offered his weight, shielding Toto.

What was to have been a celebration turned into a rout and the crushing of any credibility Toto might have developed during his search for reparations. Carewe stood open mouthed, unable to take in what had just happened. Anne shocked, moved towards Toto.

The press was in uproar, demanding when he bought into the pool, who were the partners and pressing for a printable quote.

Willy cried "No comment," to them all as the attorneys, forsaking their protective assignment, fled.

As disbelief at the sudden turn of events flooded through the gathering, most of the known faces made themselves scarce. It was more than reputations were worth to be associated with whatever scandal might have just been exposed.

Both Willy and Neily grabbed Toto.

"We've to get out of here, *now!* "Willy commanded.

"This is all rubbish, we must explain."

"There's no time for that. The bomb's dropped. We need to exit pronto."

"You've been targeted, Toto," shouted Neily, as he and the others found a way to the stairs and escape.

Toto was literally shell-shocked.

"Where's Anne?" he asked as they sped down the emergency stairs.

"I'm behind you, trying to keep up," she replied.

Relief that he had at least some friends around him was mixed with confusing thoughts tearing at his mind.

Anne caught up and told the others to exit at the next floor.

"My room's on this level, let's get him in there away from the storm waiting in the lobby," she suggested.

"Good thinking," agreed Willy.

They made way for Anne to unlock the door and bundled in with Toto collapsing on the bed. Neily, Willy and Anne stood round him.

They all caught their breath as a knock on the door made all three jump.

"Who the hell's that?" Willy asked.

"I'll go, it's my room," suggested Anne.

She went to the door opened it and Carewe stood there.

"I followed you down. What's going on, for God's sake?"

Neily came over to the door.

"Edwin, we've no idea. Best you go back retrieve Clara and wait downstairs. I'll be down shortly. OK?"

"Of course, will do."

With that Carewe headed back to the roof terrace.

"Bloody hell, I just didn't see it," Toto swore at his own stupidity.

"What?" Neily asked.

"This morning, on the mezzanine bumping into Prentice."

"Prentice?" The two men repeated in unison.

"I was coming down from finalizing stuff for tonight and Prentice steps into the lift, starts talking about giving me something. Bundles me off the lift on the mezzanine and proceeds to give me these."

Toto handed the certificates over. Willy and Neily looked at the incriminating evidence.

"You mean you hadn't invested in these before today," asked Anne.

"Never knew anything about it till that smarmy Rockefeller palmed me off with them."

"Know anything about these Neily?" Willy asked Vanderbilt.

Vanderbilt looked at the certificates closely.

"Freedom Cycles? Now there was something a month or two back where a small pool started to hype this metal company in Pennsylvania. Freedom Steel or something."

"Why would he give you these, then?" Anne asked.

"I've no idea Anne, Willy knows he's a chancer."

"You've previous with him then?" Neily queried.

"Yes, goes back to when I started investigating who best to represent my case. This guy Prentice suddenly appears at the club, starts chatting to me. Then somehow I mentioned the Moore Millions and he was all over me. I suggested, with his family connections he might know good legal."

"Then we found he suggested the same guys who work for us," Willy chipped in.

"When I first met Fosdick, he did allude to Prentice being the black sheep of the family. I should have paid more attention."

Toto looked at all three in front of him.

"What a bloody cock-up. What a waste of so much time."

He looked at Anne.

"God, I'm so sorry to have wasted so much of your time, bringing you here, witnessing me as a bloody lamb to the slaughter."

"I wouldn't have missed it for the world," Anne comforted him. "Something doesn't smell right here. Put it down to feminine intuition or whatever. These things don't happen without reason."

The men looked at her, impressed.

"Now is not the time to be impressed at what we women are capable of, we've a mystery to solve and honor to restore," she stated with a commanding tone.

"All right," Willy said. "Let's reassess. We've made the front pages for all the wrong reasons. Made a lot of important nobs very unhappy, been accused of rigging the markets, lost momentum on the objective at hand and have a mystery to solve if we're to see any daylight in this affair whatsoever."

"You left out my stupidity," confessed Toto.

Neily paced up and down. He would need all his contacts to shed light on what just happened. He also knew he faced the wrath of Grace. She loathed any social gaffe threatening her standing or associations in society. To hell with what she cared for, at this moment in time it was irrelevant.

"Right, I've contacts. Can get into the backside of this affair; help us find out who's behind it. One thing's certain, that numbskull Prentice was never the mastermind, Skull and Bones member or not."

"Appreciate it," Toto replied.

"Look, I'm going to get onto this right away. I'll go to reception, book a room for you on this floor. No need for you to make your way through the wolves waiting down there. We'll catch up in the morning, see where we go from here."

Relief washed over Toto, as Willy added.

"I'll stay over, so we can sort this all out tomorrow. I'll go check out what damage limitation is needed. So don't worry, you've got a clear head in Anne. We'll meet at breakfast."

With Willy and Neily gone, Anne and Toto were left alone.

Anne sat down on the bed beside him.

"Well you're nothing if not unpredictable. What's going on?"

"You know as much as I do. This guy Prentice set me up. What we need to find out is why. He's the sort of loser, in spite of his name, that will drag dirt for thirty shekels from anyone."

"We need to find out who's after your blood?" Anne suggested.

"That whole pool thing was a set up all along. Someone knew my background with bicycles, as I never mentioned it to Prentice. God, I should have seen the clues when he accosted me in the lift. When we first met he somehow knew I was a war correspondence without my saying."

"Highly suspicious. Best research his connections."

Toto sat deep in thought as Anne gave him space.

He then stood up suddenly.

"Nikola told me to trust no one, he was right."

Anne looked at him.

"Do you trust me?"

Toto was deep in some thought.

"I said, do you trust me?" she repeated.

"What? Of course I do. What made you ask?"

"You just said Nikola told you to trust no one."

"You're different, you're..."

"What? I'm what, Albert?" Anne interrupted.

"You're helping me, working with me, caring for me."

"Caring for you enough to double cross you?"

Toto spun round stunned.

"What?"

"You trust me, yet I could be the hole in the bucket. I could be the one betraying your project."

"What are you saying? How could you, that's just not possible. That's bloody ridiculous."

"If you're not going to trust anyone, then it's rational to discount each and everyone you have a relationship with, to find the culprit."

"For a start, you've been there from the time I came to Charleston, we shared a lot. I cannot think of any reason whatsoever you'd wish to betray me, can you?"

"None, quite the opposite. I've grown fonder of you the more I get to know you. I trust you, Albert, do you not feel that?"

Toto detected a personal agenda creeping in at the worst possible moment.

He fumbled for a response.

"Look, of course I'm fond of you, we make a good team that's obvious. It's just that I really cannot, at least I am not able to deal with these things just now," he countered.

"Perhaps when things settle we can..."

At that moment a knock at the door broke Anne's response.

"I'll get it," she said answering the door.

"Captain Trapman's room is ready, I've been told to tell him."

Toto took this provident intervention and confirmed to the bellboy he was ready.

" We'll pick this up later and thank you so much for your support," he told Anne as he exited.

"Tomorrow at breakfast," he added.

Anne acknowledged the appointment and turned back into the room wondering whether she would ever be able to express what was in her heart.

CHAPTER THIRTY-THREE

The front page of the morning paper stared up at Toto, as he exited his hotel room. It was the last thing he needed to see. It featured his image waving aloft what was pronounced as a sheaf of share certificates with the headline CYCLES THE NEW RADIO. The reference was to a major pool criminally committed on the public previously. On the way down to breakfast the lift operator so cheerful the previous day, having held shares in the disaster Toto was alleged to have fronted, scowled menacingly. Thankfully several other occupants separated them, making Toto's exit on arrival less embarrassing. True to his word, Willy awaited his uncle.

"Not a pretty sight," he greeted as Toto slammed the Times onto the table.

"Ochs got his story but not the one we needed. Ultimately it's blood they feed on, not causes," mused Toto. "Didn't sleep much, asking myself why someone would wish to queer the pitch."

Willy looked sympathetically across the table.

"When money's involved, people turn bastard into an accepted operating currency. Acting civil on the outside inside there's a cold, selfish and emotionless heart. I've encountered it, even frozen it stinks to high heaven."

"Look, I'm only chasing something rightly ours. It's not that we're stealing others' wealth or inheritance. It doesn't add up."

"Perhaps we don't have all the pieces. You're right to look deeper but at the same time it's a bloody mess to clear up."

Across the dining room obvious signs of guests avoiding eye contact with Toto left the two of them on a desert island. A couple of English friends of the family passed stammering embarrassed apologies only the English excel at. Toto cringed and loathed their insincerity. Then the entrance of another figure cracked the collective reserve and had the room twittering like manic starlings before a murmur.

"Cui bono, gentlemen. Cui bono," trumpeted Vanderbilt as he pulled out a chair and sat down. "Who benefits here, that's the real question."

"Trust you to make an entrance like that," Toto regaled Neily, relieved at least someone of stature made it obvious they still retained respect.

"I gave up caring a fig about what people say about me and how they choose to interpret my life, years ago, something maybe worth your taking on board with the flak flying round."

"Frankly Neily, well heeled as you appear, it's easier for you to act out. As you know I had my pants flying on this one and it looks decidedly like I shall be without trousers after last night."

"Look on the bright side. They're all so tied up with chasing the next hundred dollars, the latest Wall Street tip, the next pool, nothing personal," he winked, "You'll be yesterday's story by midday."

"That's supposed to cheer me up?" Toto winced.

"We have to keep moving or the broadside will sink the ship and mentioning boats, I've decided a little cruise with me, away from all this might just be the ticket to get over the whole thing. We can also chew the cud and work out what the hell is behind all this."

Toto's urge to run from disasters attracted him to Neily's suggestion, yet his more developed self screamed to get basic research done first.

"Certainly worth considering," he replied.

Anne entered the room and made her way over to the men.

Willy caught her entrance and stood up, the others followed as she reached the table.

"Good morning gentlemen, a new day a new way," she proclaimed as they all settled down.

Toto admired her bright complexion, soft smile and sensitivity.

"As much as I may be a woman amongst men, I've pondered long and hard on last night's events. As Toto knows only too well my admiration for General Sumter and his tactics came to mind, as I mulled over cause, problem and outcome."

The three men looked admiringly at a power they were unused to encountering in their own worlds. Yet Toto merely recognized a spirit he very much admired. Even Vanderbilt felt he was witnessing something new.

"His fierce fighting tactics," she continued, "deservedly gained him the nickname Gamecock and Cornwallis tells us Sumter became his greatest plague. Rather than retreat with tails between our legs, might I suggest we fight like gamecocks and unleash our very own plague upon those behind this blow," she suggested.

"Madam, I'm rarely impressed beyond a woman's beauty, yet I fear I must make way for a deep impression in your case reaching way beyond the superficial."

Anne turned to the millionaire and with a truly well seasoned Southern lilt replied.

"Well that just dills my pickle."

The whole table broke into laughter. As they recovered Vanderbilt focused on a figure marching purposefully towards them. He nudged Toto, alerting him to the approaching figure.

"What the hell's he doing here?" Toto questioned. The others looked around to catch sight of the figure in question.

"Dear God, your nemesis comes riding a high horse," warned Vanderbilt.

"As if we needed any more problems," Willy sighed.

"Gentlemen, Capitão and Senhõra Anne, good morning to you all and may I be the first to congratulate you Capitão Trapman on the delightful and injurious embarrassment you endured last night."

"If all you are here for is to gloat Barosso, then may I suggest you take your diplomatic arse out of here before I kick it back to Brazil," Toto retorted, standing to meet the sick grin of the consul.

"If it was as empty as that, I would have sent flowers of commiseration. No sir, I bring you something far more poignant, fitting to our relationship and wounding to your life."

For a moment Toto was at a loss to understand what Barosso meant. The diplomat, for his part relished the sight of his enemy squirming uncomfortably in front of so many now turning to the spectacle. It was then Toto caught sight of the jet-black hair of a woman appearing from behind Barosso.

"Yes, Capitão I present my daughter Faviola who I believe you know far better than social etiquette allows tell."

Toto watched as Faviola appeared in full view. Sinuously she walked over to him and like a python about to wrap itself round its prey, slid her hands sensuously round his thighs. She let the torture of her long searching gaze; hypnotize him into a catatonic state of disbelief.

Unaware of the room's full attention he struggled to reply.

"But.... you.... were.... in Colombia."

"And now I'm here."

"His daughter?" Toto croaked in disbelief.

"After you raped and left me, he took me in. I promised we would meet again, my little coward."

She kissed him hard on the lips, tossed her head back and threw him back towards his chair.

"My father is very unhappy about you stealing his baby's flower and when I told him how you came back for more, he swore to bring you down."

Willy and Neily could not grasp what they were witnessing. Anne however paled and recognized any unexpressed hopes had been dealt a mortal blow. Toto looked and felt a wreck.

"How deep my joy to see you lose everything," cried Barosso victoriously.

199

"Now you know how I felt when you took the jewel from my greatest treasure and spat upon all decency, the like this city of vipers parades as morality."

Toto stunned, still managed to address Faviola.

"Colombia, was that all lies as well?"

"A honeypot you freely drowned in, my taking revenge for your taking me in Manaus," Faviola spat at him in reply.

To say the dining room had never witnessed a confrontation such as this would have been the understatement of the century. There were those not knowing whether to satiate their voyeurism, others whose embarrassment blew a fuse as pink as the grapefruit served them and others pretending this particular Titanic had never even set sail. It was Vanderbilt who tossed a lifeboat.

"Senhõr Barosso, if you think this behavior is worthy of a diplomat then I must demand you leave. As for your daughter or whoever this lady pretends to be, I suggest you take her from here or I shall be forced to call the management and have you both ejected."

Barosso looked at Neily with utter disdain.

"No need, I leave having delivered the blow I swore to return when last we met. I care not for plutocrats, pomposity, bankers and gamblers. You may rape and plunder but you will never take our souls."

Turning, he went to leave with Faviola following. As she passed Anne's chair she threw a final pitiful look at the researcher who sat frozen. Tossing her head towards the exit, the Brazilian emitted a loud hiss in her wake.

"What the hell was that?" demanded Willy, utterly out of the loop of the previous minutes.

He struggled to make sense of what they had all witnessed yet added with inevitability.

"So we can kiss goodbye to our coffee venture, then."

Toto grunted.

Vanderbilt tried lightening the air.

"Apart from that Mrs. Lincoln, did you enjoy the show?"

The air remained heavy. A waiter hurriedly brought toast and coffee in a vain attempt to normalize things.

Toto looked across at Anne who was now visibly crumbling.

"This is not what it appears," he pleaded.

She slowly looked up and across at Toto.

"Maybe not to you but to me it appears I have made a terrible error of judgment."

She got up.

"Please excuse me, gentlemen, I must leave."

She walked towards the foyer. Toto swiftly followed her.

"Look I really apologize for what you witnessed."

"I'm not looking for apologies, merely trust and truth. Both have left, as must I having made a terrible misjudgment."

"Hold on, please," implored Toto.

"There's no more to say. Nikola was right. Trust no one. Goodbye Captain Trapman."

Anne walked out of the front entrance and disappeared into the Saturday crowds on Fifth Avenue. Toto, forlorn, returned towards the dining room.

The others, having left their table, joined him in the foyer.

"Are there any more surprises we can expect?" Willy asked. "I sincerely hope that's it, as I for one am exhausted and it's only Saturday!"

"Let's meet later. I shall sniff out what's going on. Barosso, for all his theatrics, never instigated that *coup de grâce* we witnessed last night. As for the trollop, it seems there was unfinished business neither of us were aware of or prepared for," Neily summarized.

"Look gentlemen, I must apologize."

"No apologies needed, Toto, we're here to help you solve the real story behind all this. I agree with Neily. This is greater than the work of a so-called traduced diplomat. Worth more than a business venture in Colombia, to find out what really is behind this. Let's see if we still have wind in our sails and a fleet to float."

"Thanks Willy."

"The boat's there if you choose to cut away," confirmed Neily.

Toto nodded appreciatively as the three parted ways.

Across town, John Rockefeller Prentice, newly in possession of a small fortune from a stock sale executed twenty-four hours earlier, sat down to a long private game of poker he hoped would last the weekend.

CHAPTER THIRTY-FOUR

Ludwig Landmann's tenure as mayor had allowed him privileged connection into the financial world. His desire to make Frankfurt the center of global finance afforded unique access to the controlling families' cartel. Although never privy to informal meetings between the Rothschilds, Kuhn Loebs and Warburgs, he successfully held the ear of those that did. This enabled insights and dot-connecting far more than any press or outside agency had access to. Schacht, as head of the Reichsbank, envied the mayor's position and made sure he developed discreet relations with him so he might himself benefit from drips of insight, before others knew.

It was one such debriefing Landmann headed to as he crossed the extensive grounds spreading out from the Rothschild palace. An assignation with a secretary to the bankers had them meet under cover of a small folly in the park.

"What news do you have to report concerning the family plans?" Landmann asked.

"There's much speculation London is developing a greater interest controlling the markets than anticipated. Warburgs report their assumption of a major readjustment looks imminent," his man reported.

"Anything we should be concerned about?"

"I understand London and Frankfurt are very much joined at the hip, so I imagine a little jockeying for position is in order."

"That sounds encouraging," Landmann agreed with relief. "Is that it?"

"Yes, apart from a brief mention by Warburgs they had sorted out the distraction they had in place. Not sure what that might have referred to but it was something they had running in New York evidently."

Landmann noted the extra information, thanked his contact and the two went their separate ways.

In New York things were markedly different to what had been expected in August. The slowing down of trade in the financial quarter, vacations taken and shoreline residences, sure havens for rest and recuperation were passed up. The happening place was Wall Street. If there were those retiring to their out of town retreats they made damn sure a ticker was present and working full time. The city not only kept trading, but also more and more people from all over the country flooded in to get a slice of frenetic action. Even the weather was unexpectedly cool and dry.

If Toto had hoped his audience would be holidaying, digesting his burgeoning story, the collective distraction of stock madness kept their interest focused elsewhere. He decided to face up the news desk of the Times to find out why they so patently changed tune.

He entered and Graves looked up from his desk, his sheepish expression speaking volumes.

"So what's the fallout?" Toto asked jokingly, as if a hiccup had interrupted the President's press briefing.

"You got a story to file?" Graves replied coldly.

"Only the continuing war of attrition over on Wall," the journalist quipped.

"About your other project," the editor cut in. "We've had orders to shelve it."

"I beg your pardon," Toto's levity dropped like lead. "Shelve it, it's hardly left the starting block. How can you trash it now?"

"From the top," Graves said with a gesture using his hand to imply his throat cut.

"Ochs?" Toto uttered with incredulity.

Graves nodded.

"What the hell's going on?"

"All I've been told is to knock it on the head. We can file stories in your capacity as correspondent, but not your project."

Toto was shocked. A mainstay of his publicity had been pulled.

"Is Ochs around, can I see him, at least find out why?"

"He's unavailable, I am afraid. I've had my orders."

"Just let me see him," Toto implored.

Graves broke into his pleading.

"Sorry, Captain, as I said unless it's in your formal capacity then all bets are off."

Toto became livid. He saw months of effort dissolving in front of him. He wanted to scream. Instead he turned and headed out. Suddenly swinging round to face the editor he barked.

"If it's a war story you want, then war you'll get. Don't hold the presses, you'll know when the real conflict breaks!"

Many in the newsroom looked up from their desks, some stifling giggles and others looked away in embarrassment for the slighted journalist. Toto could not have cared less. He had declared his position and now he was determined to deliver.

He comforted himself he still had Edwin and the film to his cause, in spite

204

of the collapsed launch. He decided to draw up new plans, accept Neily's invitation and make the most of a timely break to get it all refocused. He would also attend the film shoot the following month.

As if to confirm his plans a telegram from Hollywood awaited his arrival back at the club. He opened it with renewed energy and read it.

FINANCE PRODUCTION PULLED STOP FILM CANNED STOP read the curt message from Carewe.

The cool of the summer month instantly turned Arctic. Toto felt like he had gone seven rounds with Jack Dempsey, beginning to feel what Gene Tunney had felt like on the ropes. His plans, dreams, his world were crashing into each other. He had to keep himself together but felt sick to the core. Grabbing a chair, he sat down telling himself to focus. It was imperative to work out what was happening. If any one of these events had occurred on their own, there would have been ramifications. For so many to hit him like a salvo of machine gun fire demanded forensic research.

He had failed in projects before, that he owned. Even without hindsight he had often known precisely why. However something this important, of such worth and time spent in research pointed to an altogether different scale of setback. Yes, he looked an unfaithful idiot in Anne's eyes, yet this was not about his ineptness in relationships. Something in his gut told him there were greater wrecking balls aimed at this particular construction. What he had no idea of was why.

Laying out some sheets of paper in front of him, Toto started making notes of all areas identified as important, all the people involved getting the project to this point.

He stared down at the list of people and scratched through each name.

Anne, that was stupid, yet why did Barosso's revenge appear just now, what were his real motives? The press, Ochs, to pull so suddenly when they backed a good story and Toto felt embedded at the title? Why did Hollywood so swiftly pull out of the film? The about-turn made no sense. Were there hidden hands manipulating these people and if so, why? Thank God Willy was as steadfastly tight and supportive. Then there was Vanderbilt, turning out to be a real friend. It then struck him: that meeting with Rockefeller the morning before the presentation, handing him those stocks, out of the blue, no rhyme or reason. Then the journalist's pointed question that evening, the photos in the next morning's editions showing Toto waving share certificates.

What they made up for sensation, he knew the system, played it himself for the sake of a tag line, but being the butt of the process opened up a whole raft of an empire, whose sole purpose now seemed set to sell a line destroying one side but to whose benefit, cui bono as Neily said?

This wake up call he definitively had not booked, yet in spite of finding himself a target, deep down it offered a key opening a door on an investigation more revealing than any journey so far. He knew he had the wherewithal, now he was being called to hone research and investigative skills to a whole new level.

It was Smokey Greene who wisely stated although a journey may look like holding a specific goal in mind, it could often merely turn out being a station on the way to something far beyond the horizon. That started to make Toto appreciate his position now.

Threadneedle Street in London on an early August morning saw the lanky, immaculately groomed, imposing figure of the head of the Bank of England step from his vehicle to manage the operations expected from a control center of global financial governance. Sir Montagu Norman, utterly recognizable with fading silvered hair and richly pointed beard with matching moustache, could hardly walk an inch within the boundaries of the City without being acknowledged by a tip of a hat or polite *good day* from any who recognized this master controller.

He entered the Bank, greeted by a deferential doorman in dark pink morning coat and tails, sporting the requisite top hat. Early arrivals' good mornings were brushed aside like leaves in the wind as he strode confidently past each of them without the slightest acknowledgment. His return from several weeks in Bar Harbor, Maine had given him good cause for added confidence. An injection of determination, an absolute desire to continue the mission he had set upon from day one coursed through him. His time spent with peers and close friends on Wall Street and the likes of J.P. Morgan Junior, the Astors, Vanderbilt and Rockefellers allowed him to engage with all the various players toward the culmination of a planned operation to control and ultimately impose the outcomes of British supremacy in the financial world. His meetings in Maine with his lifetime friend Benjamin Strong's successor, George Harrison, cemented the same strong bond he developed with Strong. Nothing could have replaced the personal friendship he nurtured with Strong since the former Governor's death the previous year; Norman was in no way minded to cultivate another.

Someone who carried out precisely what he needed was all he looked for from Harrison. His mission required nerves of steel, a ruthless attachment to the goal and the absolute supremacy of managing all the tools at his disposal. Such a tool was Harrison and a phone call with the man later that day sealed a well-cultivated plan for the Governor of the Bank of England. He then made haste to catch the overnight train to Edinburgh and meetings with his Prime Minister.

In New York Toto found himself at the offices of his attorneys and a meeting scheduled with Randolph Mason.

"In light of the unfortunate outcome of your publicity event," Mason informed Toto as they sat in the attorney's office, "I have had discussions with the board as to where we go from here."

Toto straightened in his chair and leaned towards Mason.

"Good, I'm keen to continue this operation, albeit without the sort of support I'd initially envisioned. With your assistance, I believe..."

The attorney cut in.

"That Mister, I mean, Captain Trapman is where I have to inform you differently. It's the considered decision of this firm to have to, albeit with sorrow, decline any further representation in your case, as there would inevitably arise conflicts of interests."

"Conflicts of interest?" Toto queried. "What conflicts of interest would they be?"

He looked shocked and felt a particularly sharp pain in his gut.

"I'm not at liberty to say any more, just that we view your interests to be on a collision course with other interests we represent and therefore have to terminate our relation."

"This is preposterous. What transpired between you taking my brief and today that makes this state of affairs a problem? At least have the courtesy to inform me of that," Toto stammered in disbelief as much as in anger.

"Let us just say the implications of your dealings exposed the other night." Mason shifted slightly.

"Dealings that have no truth to them and even if they did have, no basis of being illegal as you know damn well," Toto retorted.

"As for their illegality, you are correct, pools are not. However the shadow they cast over those looking complicit in bad outcomes does reflect on those advising them, even though indirectly."

"So for being set up, your firm is running for cover on future flak, is that it?" Toto fired back.

"We have to consider our long-term clients against any negative return we may incur through associations with our entire roster."

Mason leaned forward, folded his arms and shut Toto out with body language suggesting the meeting was over.

"So unless there's anything more you wish to say, I must inform you this meeting is over. All costs to this point will be met, under the circumstances, by our firm, so rest assured we are clear on that matter."

Toto was about to explode. He breathed deeply, pushed his chair back and stood.

"Mister Mason, you may feel the treatment of small fry in this manner is acceptable. I would advise you of this. Your baseless and lame excuses to rid yourself of my business have shown me the color of your integrity and loyalty. That for one is enough for me to be happily rid of your firm's services. As for your actions in this, you have foolishly made a foe where there had been none before. That sir, will be shown to be a most ill-considered move on your part. As for the bill owed, you deserve to take the hit on that, as your services have proven wholly unjustified to a cent of worth. I bid you good day and will see myself out."

Toto turned and marched out of the attorney's office past the seat on his right he occupied on his first visit to the firm. He felt the pain, short-lived joy and length of the brief association well up. Something felt terrible, as if the cogs on the flywheel decided to shatter all at the same time. Yet unlike the sickening feelings of desertion he previously encountered as the other links crumbled, here he felt a sense of something bigger playing out. He determined this would in no way extinguish his passion and direction. He also sensed these events begin to take on a format where missing pieces were in dire need of finding, assembling and placing in such an order; he would be in no doubt whatsoever of the image they would form.

For the first time in ages he felt everything directing itself to a place he knew very well. Research. Between exiting the attorneys to a few steps down the sidewalk, he became certain where the true destination lay.

As he walked down the sidewalk past businesses and office entrances, one familiar doorway caught his attention. It was the entrance to the strange meeting he had with Rockefeller Prentice. A pretence of facade, clearly nothing to do with the reality of where Prentice was coming from, colluded with events leading up to it – their coincidental meeting at the Alpha Delta Club, the man's insistence to meet again, prior knowledge of his journalism.

It was then it struck him. Sitting, awaiting the meeting at Fosdicks, the client he had to wait out passed him in reception, catching his eye. John D.

Rockefeller. So was this the conflict of interest, and if so what conflict? The question he knew now needed answering was why.

To begin down the road answering that question, he needed to see Willy first and foremost. Planning was essential and for plans to work one needed trusted partners.

It was not long before he and Willy were getting the plan together.

"What you need to find out," his nephew explained, "is where Vanderbilt sits on all of this. Realize his position as one of the big names, he's got eyes and ears where we might struggle for privilege, so follow up his invitation, get on board with him, physically as well as metaphorically. He likes you, both of you have history and at least we can determine how deeply he's in it with you, with whoever else has an interest and let's start building the picture."

"Quite the sleuth Willy, I'm seeing a different side to you," Toto offered admiringly.

"Nothing more than I'd use in business, find out the full roster of needs, wants, purpose, usefulness and objectives. Finding out who your partners are, potential and existing, is best practice. Any turf not turned may seed revolt, deception or takeover. As for our relations with Fosdick, worry not. We're yet one more small minnow in their big pond."

Toto nodded respecting his young relative's advice. New York honed a fine example of acumen in times decidedly uncertain.

"It looks like," Willy continued, "there's wealth pouring from every orifice out there. The Wall pronounces all sorts of dreams, desires and future hopes and the tickers broadcast them but me personally, I smell something rotten from a mile off. As long as you're not intoxicated with the best of all times addiction, then it's possible to read reality signs."

"That's one reason those share certificates shoved at me are so not me," Toto responded. "I may have been chasing a pot of gold but did so from tried and trusted research into what's owed. I gamble, sure. I've made bloody stupid decisions in my life, we both know that, but this whole big reveal was built on factual research. All of that was systematically brought crashing down, I've been the target of a character assassination and stripped of most support."

Willy's respect for his uncle was transparent. The admiration for a man to go through what he had put himself through and then have the authenticity to be humble enough to own his shortcomings, made him smile.

"Do you find that amusing?" Toto asked.

"Admiration, old man, admiration," Willy responded. "Many in this city professing power of decision making, vast insight on the next great deal, flaunt themselves like peacocks around high visibility joints, beloved of self aggrandizement, yet you've forged away, soaked up the associations you've cultivated, yet always with an integrity so lacking in these parts."

Toto flushed slightly at the compliment.

"Without your guidance it would've been nigh on impossible."

"Nonsense, it needed your ferreting. Now we need a huge dollop of ferreting to get to the root of what's really happened," Willy said, striking the action bell.

"At some stage I'll need to meet with Landmann again. First we need facts established. The plan's this; get with Vanderbilt, sniff out leads here, meet with Nikola and then hightail it back to Europe."

"And Anne?" Willy inquired.

"Looks like I self imploded that one, right and proper. For now matters of the heart are the least of our problems. I'll get up to Maine where Neily's moored," Toto concluded with authority.

"Why Nikola?" Willy asked.

"Nikola is a man deeply connected to my heart. He's been shafted more times than we collectively care to imagine. Gave me insight some while back on the heirloom I carry. Occurs to me I need some more insight into its relevance here."

"Certainly an area you're best suited to research. Keep me posted," Willy answered.

"Don't worry, you've really energized me into renewed action and I'll report as it unfolds."

The two stood up and embraced each other.

"Family's family. We're a family of explorers, discoverers and seekers after liberty and truth," Toto proclaimed. "That freedom is needed now as passionately as my forebear felt for Washington's dreams."

"On that note, are you solvent enough to get through these next steps?" Willy asked sensitively.

"Gambling antennae did register a punt on a whisper I heard. Swiftly turned it round on a massive hike in expectations, creating more than enough for research both here and Europe. When needs must, dear boy!"

"You wily fox, Toto. Well done playing the system to serve you well!"

Both men parted in the best of spirits and Toto knew for certain Willy had his back, whatever transpired.

CHAPTER THIRTY FIVE

Bar Harbor, a small exclusive town on Mount Desert Island in Maine, was the retreat of preference for the glitterati and moneyed society. That Neily's family was part of that set was acknowledged and the house they had a testament to wealth. Neily, however, enjoyed the place for its convenience parking his yacht and the freedom the waters granted access to the ocean. It was to Bar Harbor that Toto finally arrived having taken up Neily's offer to spend time on the boat.

Met by a chauffeur and transported to the quay, Toto was greeted by the waterside concierge. This old sea dog having given up his sea legs long ago, like some ancient mariner stopped the journalist, insisting he carry the researcher's bags.

"Can't I help?" Toto inquired seeing the old salt struggling gamely.

"Oh no sir, it's my task, rightly honored to help a fellow mariner."

"You look as if you ought to be out there on the brine yourself," Toto regaled.

"Been there, got the scars. Seen it all before, now landlocked, by choice. You English?" The old dog asked.

"Yes, you caught the accent?"

"Sure as heck did, like that Limey left a couple of weeks back. Big banker in London, he said. Smart type, grey beard, mighty fine hat," the old man chuckled. "Mister Norman he was, Montagu if I remember, funny name for a banker."

Toto recognized the name, chuckling as to what the old man might have considered a good name for a banker to be.

"We English are funny with names," Toto kicked back.

The old man halted. Toto turned to see why and the mariner looked him directly in the eye, as he grabbed his arm.

"The names we're given reflect our purpose, so names are important. What's yours?"

Toto could not resist.

"Captain Trapman"

"Ah! I thought so, leader of men," the old man replied.

"Don't know about that."

"Wait and see, wait and see!

They stood before Neily's yacht.

"So here's the Vanderbilt berth. Quite a picture, as sailors from Hamburg would say."

The old salt sniggered loudly and sloped away to his seat at the far end of the pier.

Toto lifted his gear onto the yacht as Neily in full kit welcomed him.

"Accosted by the Ancient Mariner who stoppeth one of three?" Neily laughed, greeting his friend.

"Seems it was – or his brother in disguise," replied Toto, giving Vanderbilt a bear hug, before settling on board.

They cast off, leaving land behind as the sun set in the west and the seaboard eastern skies painted a magic hour like no other. The two men sat on deck in wicker chairs, drinks in hand.

The crew, invisible, steered the craft as Neily spoke.

"It's only when I manage to get away on this do I feel totally free from place and position. Here's where I feel truly myself."

"Don't you miss the razzmatazz, people and fun?"

"Toto, if you knew how far from fun all of that really is, you'd understand the relief I experience being as far away from it as we are. Grace spends all the money, I get bored as hell and the only relief I have is this yacht, the mighty ocean, and the call of the gulls. As close to heaven as it gets. Where's your heaven?"

"I'd hoped in the Santa Marta Hills but as you witnessed I was set up like a prawn on a barbecue stick. Memories will keep me aroused for years," Toto confided.

"She was an unabashed beauty for sure, but Barosso's daughter, I find that hard to fathom," noted Neily.

"We met in Manaus when I set up the ill-founded flat bottom boats. A mere teenager, she stirred every sinew in me. Never raped her as he accused, as willing as her beauty was tangible. I truly fell for that girl. What I had not been able to do was say goodbye before hightailing it to New York. Torn by failure and an inability to face the reality of leaving, I good as dumped her."

Toto sat in silence a moment and then continued.

" First time I've shared this in any detail."

"Appreciate your candor. You amaze and surprise every time. No wonder she was so passionately vengeful turning up in New York. But Barosso claiming her?"

"He took her under his wing when I left her first time round. A journalist in Manaus, he took great pleasure ripping my every move apart especially the failure, always a nasty piece of work. Doorstepping was missionary work compared to his vicious reporting. His venom didn't surprise me at all. His timing though, took us all off guard."

The following morning the sun gifted a great day, the waters calm and the yacht making steady progress down the coast towards Boston.

Neily pulled up his favorite chair, drew a table between them, locked it down and mused at the swell in front of them.

"I slept like a baby," admitted Toto.

"That's the ozone. Remember our first adventure on the Lucania, we certainly put on a show there?" Vanderbilt admitted.

"My eyes were on stalks. Never seen so much opulence, you and Grace like royalty. Got a birthday to remember."

"So glad I met you and him together. A good man and left you some fine lessons. Mine loathed the fact Grace and I were together. Got disinherited, disowned and all the other rubbish that wealth and expectation dump on you. Grace, now a shadow of her former beauty, is deeper in love with spending my fortune than ever. Feel I would have fared far better with your kind of upbringing."

"So many crave what you have, the grass greener on the other side," pondered Toto. "You've everything, what's lacking?"

"Happiness. I only find that here, away from the noise. You can keep the rest."

"Your Declaration stipulates the unalienable right of each to that."

"May be considered unalienable but the process of attainment is the hurdle!" Neily admitted ruefully. "One of the family famously admitted inherited wealth was the real handicap to happiness, leaving nothing to hope for and nothing definite to strive for."

"An indictment if ever I heard one. Why do all those Rockefellers, Morgans and Harrimans carve up so much for themselves. Is that their happiness?" Toto questioned.

"First, because they can. It's that simple. Secondly, they're creating slaves of the rest. The people, they're merely financial cannon fodder for more acquisition, more greed, and more financial sport to win. As part of the elite our family fortune, though dwindling, bestows privilege. The bare thread drawing me close to all of that is only held in place through cowardice and conditioning. If I was a man, I'd throw it all away, disappear on this boat to a desert island or endlessly sail the seas."

"Many see that as the privilege of wealth," replied Toto who recognized in Neily someone troubled, tired and at a point in his life where all seemed to be pointless. He could relate to that.

"I've been there in my own way," he conceded, "What baffles me is why I was targeted so precisely at the launch. Looks like a set up."

"Par for the course. When usefulness is spent, they throw out the trash."

"But what use was I? Why use me?" asked a bewildered Toto.

"Truthfully, I can't answer that. I consider you a good friend, so I'll come clean."

"What are you getting at?"

"Some time back I was asked to meet up with James Warburg who insisted I kept an eye on you, make sure everything went well on the project. I thought his interests would benefit your cause, so agreed. Please understand all I did for you was not solely as a result of that request. As you know we go back."

"So you've Warburg asking to look after me, their asset and you agreeing?" Toto suggested in amazement.

"I've no idea what sort of asset you are to the Warburgs, but he certainly wanted to make sure your interests were cared for," Vanderbilt conceded.

"What interest am I to Warburg with the loan repayment?"

"James' father Paul Warburg is a founding partner in the Fed and it would have been incumbent on them to make sure payments were dealt with."

Toto rubbed his chin, looked out to sea, took a long draught of lemonade and replied.

"When I mentioned to Mason we wanted payment in gold, he became very defensive. Told me how difficult it could be, later he suddenly assured me the gold would be less of a problem."

Toto paused to think before continuing.

"Mason worked at the Fed, undoubtedly his connection with Warburg is solid. Warburg and the House of Morgan control most of what goes on in Wall Street. Prentice is sent in to set me up but what's their game, the Rockefellers I mean? I'm a mosquito to their elephantine ambitions."

Vanderbilt laughed.

"Well you may consider yourself a mosquito but even an elephant can get pissed at the humble insect. The question is what service of theirs are you disrupting, to want you off the map?"

"You'd know better than I," replied Toto.

"I may be painted in the same colors but even my position gets me to feel more like a pawn to their King. We all have our place in the food chain."

"Well that puts me way down, just a snack," mused the researcher.

"Some snacks get stuck in the throat and choke even the highest rank so, like the mosquito, we all have our day," Neily chortled. "Anyway the object in life is not to feature on someone else's menu, is it?"

"Hope not. Apart from my culinary usefulness, what else have you unearthed, Neily?"

"Cards very close to their chest. Morgan's been acting as casino head on Wall and as usual margins make them all richer by the hour. So well insulated any fluctuation would never really knock them out."

"Yet the madness and greed of the common stock holder is driven by their every utterances."

"The question is, who's really instructing?"

"The main houses themselves," suggested Toto.

"You'd think so but first of all your venture's zero threat to them, just more advertised bandwagon rags to riches. Second, my interest with keeping in with Warburg, Goldman Sachs and the rest is certainly not to secure the family's fading fortunes but merely to trade favors and keep Grace's excesses funded. You're going to have to solve who ultimately benefits, as I said before. Finding out why Warburg wanted you contained, that would be the best line to research."

"You think the stock and bond frenzy is just a major distraction?" Toto asked.

"To some, not to those believing it's their yellow brick road moment. With Mason telling you your venture created a conflict of interest, there's a big clue right there. Someone else's interest is not served by you being around."

"Darned right," Toto agreed. "Knowing whose interest that is would unlock a lot."

"I'm not much of a businessman. Good at spending it, but from what I can see the volatility, the remarks we heard from the above, that we can expect a crash – may be more than just an enigma. You're best off out of all that, yet if the crash is purposeful, who's doing the crash?" Neily postulated.

"If some were aware of an imminent crash, what's in it for them, where's the profit in ruining a cash cow?" Toto thought aloud.

"Nothing's ever executed unless someone benefits. Find out who and you just might find out why you found yourself in their cross hairs."

He knew Neily had not only been open with him, he had given some good ideas to follow.

Toto remembered boarding.

"When I was quayside the old sea dog heard my accent and informed me Montagu Norman had recently been here."

215

"He's a regular visitor. Seems to love mixing with the likes of Morgan and Rockefeller. Old Jensen, as the local telegraph here, informed me Harrison of the Fed was up here chewing the cud with Norman."

"The fact I join you here and Norman meets the Fed and hobnobs the big wigs on the Wall cannot be coincidence. Could be useful dots."

"As you said, not just coincidence."

Toto smiled.

"Tesla always delights in informing me there's no such thing as coincidence; exists merely for those refusing the math of universal patterning."

"Tell that to the investors and soothsayers," Neily replied. "Sounds like we relax a few days then get you back to the city.

Toto agreed and the two of them put their feet up and prepared for a long and intensive investigation ahead.

CHAPTER THIRTY-SIX

Back in New York, Toto found the madness of speculation, desperation and outright insanity of dealing, buying and selling issuing from every orifice of life in overdrive. The mood had changed from outright celebration to uncertainty, bordering on the maniacal. High hopes vacillated between desperation to purchase and temptation to sell. Struck by statements from founts of wisdom on Wall, reflected in column inches pouring from the press, all finding their targets in craving, desperate minds hoping to ride their increasingly phantom transport. For Toto it sounded even more like propaganda and manipulative motivation, after the clarity he had developed on the high seas.

Arriving at Tesla's offices, he was relieved to enter an environment of sanity and relative stability.

"Don't you sense the world gone mad, Nikola?" Toto put to the scientist.

Beverage in hand, he sat as the inventor moved from tabletop to notebook ignoring his guest. Although others might assume Tesla to be oblivious to the researcher's presence, Toto knew full well the inventor to be very much present.

"You're entering the peripheries of the world I inhabit, where madness reveals itself in what others accept as normalcy and sanity," the inventor replied, carrying on.

"Would I dream to be even a continent close to your habitat, Nikola?"

"The boundary between worlds is diaphanous, if minds just knew it. Most fear these regions, as natives fear the appearance of strangers on their shores where no apparent means of transport is visible. However those of us who straddle them by dint of ability, training or gift have a unique viewpoint from which to assess the madness others accept as real," Tesla explained, writing copious notes emanating a brilliant mind.

"That madness multiplied with the failure of the launch," Toto shared.

"It was to be. You challenged a hypocritical system with truth, it returned mortal fire. What briefly passed as governance, has become a tool with which the plutocrats play us all."

"Why?" Toto asked.

"You, more than most, ought to know the answer to that question. Your experience must expose the power wielded for selfish ends. These are terrible times we live in.

217

"Yet so many think these are the best of times," Toto replied.

"*Quod erat demonstrandum* – precisely demonstrated," Tesla grunted. "We are led to believe this is our good, when the blow about to fall will crush even that false spark of belief."

"To what end is this cat and mouse?"

Tesla stopped what he was doing, walked over to Toto's chair and looked down at the Englishman.

"You ask for justice, then present your proof demanding what is rightly assigned you. They not only scupper that attempt, they take you down as the assassin's bullet took down Archduke Ferdinand. Don't take this personally, even though it hurts, look for cause and reason. It will be found the same as in Ferdinand's case, yet dressed to look like righteous cause."

"My God Nikola, I lived through that slaughter and you're telling me the death of the Grand Duke was merely an incidental triggering that travesty?"

"Contrived! Now you're using your faculties in right research," the inventor beamed. "That's why you, your father and those like you hold my friendship and attention. The rest..."

He turned and walked back to his notes.

"Pffft!" Tesla exclaimed, throwing both hands to the heavens.

"How can the trigger for war, my project's destruction and the madness presently taking place outside be part and parcel of the same thing?" Toto struggled to connect dots Tesla had thrown down, like pearls before swine.

"That one, dear fellow is for you to solve. I have given up any hope these oligarchs have the best interests of us all at heart. My experience shows they just wish to steal, abuse and destroy," Tesla replied in a bitter tone.

"Yet you see things from a perspective others cannot."

"Untrue. Others are afraid to see," replied the inventor.

"Afraid, of what?"

"Of recognizing their own power and at the same time destroying their illusions. Knowing they're the ones with the wealth, the dominion, the control," Tesla repeated with specific emphasis on each word.

"How can it be?" Toto asked, like one bereft of justice.

"When you have little or no idea how powerful you are, yet accept others dressing themselves to look powerful, then vulnerability is an opportunity to be taken advantage of."

"You've been taken advantage of more times than I can remember. Where was your power?"

"In my mind, always with me. Never lost any of that. All they took from me was sharing it equally with mankind. To help each and every one share illimitable power Nature gifts us. The sharing, no less, no more. I work on how to overcome that obstacle. I am an old man and all I have is George to help me in my project."

At that moment Toto became aware of a small curtain parting and George Scherff's entrance.

"George, I was just telling Toto how all my best work is in my head and all the rest you take care of, making sure we continue to struggle against forces wishing to steal and abuse."

Tesla's complexion brightened as his right hand man entered.

"Like a rare treasure we've a duty to protect it against the elements," Scherff replied. "It's good to see you bring a smile to Nikola. He gets weary of the foolishness of those he speaks of. I'll leave you two to put the world to rights and address the oligarchs who plague Nikola. Good day."

Scherff left them, Nikola occupied himself and Toto was left wondering how much of the conversation Scherff had caught. It grated him but he could not put his finger on why.

He got up, moved towards Nikola, leaning against the table, folded his arms and cocked his head and spoke.

"Nikola, I'm leaving New York, heading back to Europe."

The inventor carried on, disregarding the remark.

Then muttered.

"Good."

Toto started a little, perplexed.

"Good?"

"You're needed there."

"How can you be so sure?"

"Because roots run deep and what your forebear helped with here was seeded there. Foot soldiers may parade here but remind yourself the heirloom you carry, it holds the key."

Toto was startled a second time.

"How did you know I was thinking of that, Nikola?"

"I felt it in your mind, its key is obvious. Solve the riddle and the riches of your mind will reveal truth."

Toto took the triquetra from an inside pocket and repeated part of its inscription.

"The torch of mind through whose light I am free."

"Precisely. The relation between the three elements will guide you to the center. Trinity manifests truth, justice and freedom – its opposite reaps a bitter harvest of slavery, dominion and death."

"Its opposite?"

Tesla looked up.

"Light cannot exist without the dark. They maintain equilibrium, knowledge within each other. Tilt the balance everything suffers. What's happening today is a battle for ascendency, dominion. It's been growing a long time."

"Who are these forces?" Toto asked.

"Ancient enemies, old as time. Amongst us today."

Toto considered and replied.

"Are you suggesting what happened to me is somehow part of this battle?"

"Find out why they took you down and it will lead you to the dark players. Your forte is research, drilling down and exposure. Be careful, you're dealing with powers so corrupt, they think nothing of disposing every irritation in their path."

Toto felt excitement and trepidation equally. His instincts smelled a story, his better instinct warned him caution.

"Do those you have dealt with share this darkness? Toto asked.

"Does ice melt in the sun?" Tesla cut back.

"The quality of darkness is obsession with self interest, void of empathy. Always been so, always will be, until we grow our minds," he added.

"How depressing," Toto mused.

"Not as long as those, like you, stand up and shine the torch. Now go, you're wasting time with an old man who never had the strength to stand up to this power. Merely begged its assistance and got fleeced."

"If I can do anything Nikola, it will be to establish your genius so disrespected by the world, so little known by those you wish to help," Toto assured the inventor with passion.

"I believe you, thank you, my friend. Now get to work, your gifts are in your hands."

Tesla turned to his long-time friend and smiled a craggy smile, weary, yet exuding all the hopes he had brought to these shores so long ago.

"Take everything I have, call on me. Use that channel we both have knowledge of, irrespective of distance, I will hear and respond."

Toto thanked his friend, turned slowly and moved to the door. As he opened it, about to exit, he turned.

"You've always meant..."

Tesla interrupted him.

"As you have for this foolish old man. Now be gone with you. My light is with you."

Toto disappeared, missing telltale tears trickling down Tesla's cheeks.

The chaos of uncertainty, mixed with the foolishly misguided hopes of recovery overlay a New York keen to assert its confidence even in the face of impending doom. The American dream felt ever more believable the closer it came to its own nightmare, as October broke through its first week.

Toto met with Willy for the last time before departing.

It was appropriate they agreed to meet at Willy's favorite deli. Toto enjoyed the lack of ostentation his nephew displayed. The two devoured pastrami on rye.

"When you speak with Leila, before I get back to London, ask her to quiz Landmann if he's heard anything on the grapevine?"

"He's got ears and eyes within the inner sanctum of the families which may offer insight into what's going on here as well," Willy answered.

"Undoubtedly," Toto agreed.

He looked at Willy, keen to unburden a weight he had been carrying.

" I have to apologize for getting you all mixed up in this, never wanted you to tarnish business reputation."

"Funnily enough" Willy observed, "quite the opposite. Those taking notice of these things recognize the substantial friends and connections we have. Everyone wants to rub shoulders with the well connected that in turn brush these hiccups very quickly away, for that's how they interpret them. You and I have very little vested interest, having never seriously played the markets. What's important is the underlying movement."

Toto nodded in agreement and much relieved, then added.

"There's a bigger chess board played than the roller coaster distraction of money and stocks. Seems like our little venture served to distract attention. We may not have succeeded in pay back, but instinct points to an even more important story I've yet to uncover."

"That's what I like to see, the investigative reporter rising from the ashes," Willy responded.

Warming to his uncle's call to action, he continued.

"I came here to get away from a financial catastrophe bringing Germany down. Looks like I'm caught up in another developing here. I'm well equipped to ride it out. The question is, if everything happening is for someone's benefit, start stripping away, finding out who that someone is."

"Neily impressed on me elite money does nothing unless there's direct benefit. Finding who benefits from our brush with them, as Nikola rightly said, will open all sorts of doors," Toto admitted.

"And also why, as you admitted at the get go!" Willy added.

Toto's gratitude for everything his nephew had accomplished with him impressed the importance in finding answers for them both.

The few days aboard the voyage to Southampton, several days later, afforded him time to gather his thoughts, set out a plan and prepare to face his family, a different pace of life in Europe and an as yet unknown force.

CHAPTER THIRTY SEVEN

As the train pulled slowly into Waterloo station Toto took down two large suitcases from the rack above, preparing to exit the carriage. It came to a halt, he snapped the door open, jumped down and pulled the cases with him. A porter immediately appeared at his side, placing both bags on his trolley.

"Cab sir?" he asked.

"Yes please," replied the researcher as he locked step with the younger man.

"Off the boat then, are you sir?"

"Yes, came in this morning."

"Bloody mess this Hatry bankruptcy," the well-informed porter continued.

Toto had read how Clarence Hatry, a multimillionaire, had gone down creating a hue and cry in financial circles, causing widespread panic in the money markets both here and across the pond.

"Shouldn't affect you too much then," Toto threw back.

"Well if you ask me these City bankers, stocks and share players just gamble with all our lives without caring how it hits us, the workers."

"You've a point there," Toto agreed.

The porter politely guided Toto to a waiting taxi and loaded the bags onto the open space in front. He drew out a shilling from his pocket and placed it into the porter's grateful palm.

"Very gentlemanly of you, thank you. Watch out for those bankers, sir and keep your wits about you."

Toto got into the two-seater cab, smiling back at the porter who tipped his cap at his departing client. Keen to observe signs and significance, he took the porter's words to heart and promised himself the bankers would become the central focus in his investigations. Meanwhile he guided the cabby to deliver him to a mews house in Notting Hill, a quiet suburb of the capital. A friend of Leila's had offered the property, again his sister delivering when needs must. From there he would lay out his plans.

First he wrote a letter to Adrian informing him of his return and offering a room for when he came down from university. He left it to Adrian when that would be but already had plans to rope him into his work.

As for Smokey, he had been forewarned and Toto knew the man would contact him in his own time.

Across town Sir Montagu Norman entertained Anthony de Rothschild at another of their regular meetings. Having assured the banker there was no worry gold would exit to a now discredited war loan reparation bid, Norman suggested ways of resolving Brazil's lessening need of British influence.

"The national banks of the First Republic bolster their home industries, important we maintain a semblance of control over them," insisted Norman.

"Let's interest them by promising, say thirty million in bullion injected," suggested Rothschild. "It would help them back up the twenty-five million dollar loan already running and at the same time keep Morgan and Dillon's eyes on them maintaining their usefulness as and when."

"I'm expecting to hear from Morgan tomorrow on the state of play in New York. Although not affecting external issues, we could pre-empt any ripples later in the year, be seen to show support in the face of international jitters," Norman replied.

The two men understood their plan to control not only the gold but also the global financial markets, was taking its intended course. The system depended not just on control from the City of London but equal pressure injected from the houses of Frankfurt and Washington. It was present plans being formulated in The Hague that pre-empted that.

"Understand Schacht has regained demands alongside reparations respon-sibility for the Bank of International Settlements initiative," noted Rothschild.

As one of the central cogs of the Rothschild banking arm, it was seen as important for the new Bank to be set up and steer global money needs with abilities over and above reparations.

"I've good leverage with Schacht. What he does, he does in our name, rest assured of that," Norman confided.

In Frankfurt, Wilhelm and Leila entertained Ludwig Landmann at a private dinner in their house. Landmann had the opportunity to share much of what he knew of the banking families' plans and how they impacted Toto's unsuc-cessful bid for reparations of the ancient War Loan. What they did not tell the mayor was that Toto had informed them of his arrival that evening from London. The doorbell rang. The maid ushered in the unexpected guest.

"My dear Toto, what a fortuitous and pleasant surprise," Landmann cried as he stood to warmly greet Leila's brother.

"You know how I love surprises, dear Ludwig," Leila shared Landmann's joy and personally drew the chair back for her brother to sit down.

"A whisper down the line suggested, Ludwig, you've news for me from our friends in banking. Since I was keen to get it straight from the horse's mouth I leapt on the train to be here. So tell all," Toto beamed.

"First of all," Landmann began, "Your attempts at reparations seem to have been used against you as a diversionary tactic."

"That's now amply apparent," interrupted Toto.

"They've been planning a major operation that, as we have just heard, resulted in the blackest few days in American financial history. The crash was a concerted effort from both London and here to bring chaos to the American markets," Landmann revealed.

"As Wilhelm told you our attorneys in New York also work for my nephew and more pertinently for the Rockefeller family."

Landmann leaned forward and twiddled his moustache. His eyes sparkled.

"My dear friends, several things have come to my attention. Thanks to your endeavors in New York, my ears have been especially tuned with events here, as to their impact on a larger scale. With the agreements in Baden-Baden and the new Bank of International Settlements looking to complete, I suspect for our own interest of reparations we could be also the sacrificial lamb to a greater slaughter."

Leila looked perplexed.

"Are you saying the crippling debts we're forced to bear from Germany losing is merely a collar of restraint so the banks can then use us as a pawn in their games?"

"What I'm suggesting, from the information gathered through my informants, is that the Bank is being constructed under the cover of central control for reparations, then acting as an unaccountable house through which all sorts of deals take place."

"That would advantage great power behind the political processes in many countries," gasped Toto.

"It would also steer decision making into central banks in those countries, especially as your esteemed Montagu Norman has been present at several pivotal meetings here in Frankfurt," Landmann confided.

"Are you suggesting the Bank of England is a major cog?" Toto quizzed.

"With the ease with which he commands the attention of those in the States along with the very same families here who initiated the Federal Reserve, I would concur that to be a huge yes!" Landmann exclaimed.

Both Leila and Wilhelm looked shocked as they realized the rising economic chaos engulfing Germany, so swiftly after the crash looked to become an even uglier scenario than earlier years had delivered.

Wilhelm took a sip of his wine and asked Landmann.

"Things have fallen through the floor badly in the last days. Are we going to see the sort of chaos hyperinflation gave us?"

Landmann pondered.

"My feeling is the Nationalists, becoming a stronger force in the country, want to overturn the Versailles Treaty, killing any necessity to repay a single pfennig. That might assuage the possibility. Let's face it, a good crisis always benefits the one seen as the knight riding to the rescue."

"It all adds up to some ugly times ahead," Toto reflected.

Leila agreed.

"Not giving any of us much cheer for what may happen. Tends to support our feeling we'd be better out of the country."

"In my humble opinion," Landmann reflected, "the banks will be the ones who steer the economies of all nations. More so the families behind these banks will and they control the rudder in global navigation. It's that power now frightening me, more than any nationalists, socialists or corporation."

Toto's mind shot back to Wall Street and thought of the nightmare losses hitting so many.

"Morgan, Loeb, Warburg and Sachs would have been lacerated when the markets crashed, surely?"

"It's certainly set up to look like that, but having been forewarned and party to events, heavy losses would have been swiftly hedged. As much as they made certain there appeared to be sacrificial losses, the hit never intended to take down the whole founding structure," the mayor replied with insight.

"There's good reason you were seen as shrewd placement as mayor, Ludwig," Wilhelm noted.

"And yet I still hold the ambition to make this city a true financial center in the world of business, built on ethics."

"I have no doubt," replied Toto. "How does that fit Rothschild, Kuhn and Warburg?"

"May I remind you what Mayer Amschel Rothschild stated, *Let me issue and control a nation's money and I care not who writes the laws,* I believe that answers your question in a sentence!" Landmann retorted.

Toto's time with family and Landmann gave him renewed drive and reason to dig deeper into what was turning out to be a far more complex and enthralling trail. His desire to investigate and use his powers of research led him to believe he was onto a story worthy of his calling.

Returning to London, with more information, he took up his brother's invitation to spend the Christmas holidays with them in Kent. Son Adrian had written confirming he would be there. The economic climate looking unhealthier by the day gave people more reason to feel depressed at what lay ahead. For Toto, he felt compelled to spend as much time as possible peeling back layers of what Landmann had revealed in Frankfurt.

In New York the havoc reaped by the almighty crash in October had the impotent imprecations from both press and politicians that improvements lay ahead, fall on the deaf and dumb. The country was sinking remorselessly into what would become a decade-long depression. J.P. Morgan in a public display of generous cutback donated his favorite yacht to the government. This thread, convincing people they were all in it together, lacked the footnote that his new three million dollar yacht would be delivered shortly.

It would be many months before they got even the slightest whiff of an ever widening and seismic gap opening between the elite percentage and the rest.

In the Trapman household Louis made sure prudence and foresight garnered a family Christmas, far less exposed to the reality of loss many families in the country were experiencing. Christmas turned out to be festive for all gathering round the hearth.

Adrian, fresh down from Edinburgh was keen to make the most of spending quality time with his father. Toto reciprocated by sharing some of the developments he had begun in tracing what sort of power was really responsible for events. He also participated in Louis' display of abundance.

"Looking at us, it's hard to believe we're slipping fast into depression," commented Toto.

"We had a good teacher, if you remember," countered his brother.

"Who was that?" Adrian asked.

"Your grandfather," answered Louis.

"Ah, Paris you're referring to," Toto reminded the gathering. "During the siege of Paris, having sent the family back here, William remained with Michel, Louise's father and traded in the sides of ham they accumulated well before the siege truly set in. Made a tidy penny selling to and feeding the starving French."

"Foresight in stocking up," Adrian noted.

"Your grandfather was more than using his foresight," Louis corrected. "He played the double game in Paris. Being Prussian, the ones laying the siege, yet inside the French camp, he used his foreknowledge to advantage."

"Are you saying he was a spy?" Adrian asked incredulously.

"He was, in his own way using skills at diplomacy to advantage, looking after both sides' interests. He even helped take care the message of their plight reached the world at large, utilizing skills with balloons to get their story to the waiting press," Louis countered.

Hetty, his wife broke into the male dominated discussion.

"It was grandmother Eliza, who encouraged William to share his expertise in balloons with the Confederates before they swiftly left the Carolinas, although never giving ultimate advantage."

"Quite right. Our father straddled all class and persuasion," Louis agreed. "The trick in war, business and finance is to maintain a win, win scenario. Witnessed that in Russia, we saw how and where money and sponsorship for the Bolsheviks came from."

Toto and Adrian looked surprised.

"Louis, explain," his younger brother pleaded.

Louis felt comfortable and in full flow.

"Until it was closed this year, we had a factory in Leningrad and on numerous occasions I heard tell of money and support coming from the West helping the revolution before, during and beyond nineteen seventeen."

Toto saw dots forming.

"Ludwig did remark how the banks and their partners in Wall Street encourage support of both sides in conflict but I didn't imagine it ran to financing the Bolsheviks."

"Articles in both the Times and the American press alluded to that. Seems the League of Nations never took appropriate action and those wanting to encourage exploitation of the Germans and Jews in Russia got away with it while publicly supporting them. There's your double agent working admirably," Louis summarized.

As the hearth fire crackled, the ladies withdrew. Adrian, keen to stay listening to his elders and John, Louis' son, kept a low profile and listened.

Hetty protested.

Louis was final arbiter.

"Hetty, these boys are going to be around a lot longer than us and deserve to be privy to what has been and will be their reality, so as much as I support your views in many things, I feel they're pleasantly disposed to remain and listen."

His wife diplomatically gave way as the conversation continued.

"I don't need to remind you," Louis turned to his brother, "the way the Turks and Greeks set upon each other in the Balkans. Your embedded reporting on that front gave you insight into the disaster."

His younger brother nodded, as he continued.

"Adrian, your study of Amharic at Edinburgh will set you in good stead. Mark my words, we're going to see a royal hue and cry chasing every last piece of Semite land, therein lies wealth for the money masters and their exploitation."

"They've ravaged Africa and its resources well enough," Toto reflected. "Look how Rothschild controls gold and diamonds there. Pretty certain my exploits were more about control of those resources than freeing up the country. Self interest is non-existent for cannon fodder."

Louis looked over to his brother.

"One thing becomes apparent. Whatever petty ambitions a nation wields, their fate is within those holding the purse strings. If this financial disaster is to take not only the wind out of the sails of your project but globally taking control of economies, the question is: whose interests are served for wars, crashes and destabilization to be effective?"

"A wonderful thesis, Uncle Louis," Adrian chipped in.

"Well, your father's on a mission to solve that question. Enlisting the help of one very competent and intelligent son would be a real benefit," Toto suggested, looking proudly at the young man, so long rejected, now proudly acknowledged as his own.

"I'd like that, Dad. The best present I could imagine."

"Sounds like the best present we could all benefit from," Louis concluded, "I therefore call time and wish you all an excellent Christmas with an exciting year ahead."

Jonathan L Trapman

CHAPTER THIRTY-EIGHT

The New Year saw Adrian return to Edinburgh, keen to get into his studies, assisting his newly engaged father searching behind events leading up to the October crash now affecting global political and social affairs.

Toto, pleased to have his son as an intelligent and sharp assistant, launched into the year a determined man.

Prying into the protected corridors of power and money required stealth, cunning, subterfuge and a healthy amount of deception, qualities these entities used with unfettered abandon. Outcomes were their self-service. Outcomes for Toto were everything. He knew the perils pitting expertise against elements thinking nothing in wiping out interference. They had demonstrated their games in New York. For this investigator it would be no game. It would dig into the very heart of the triumvirate of power about which Nikola had warned.

First things first; he had learned the hard way a plan must be ordered. To that end he set out to find key players, their lackeys in the City of London and henchmen in the offices of Fleet Street. Before that could be accomplished he rolled back the years, reacquainting himself with some long ignored companions.

He made his way to Woolwich and the Royal Ordnance Factory. One Thomas Brighton, a colleague from Bicycle Corps days, now headed up a secret development group. Through a circuitous route Toto had traced his whereabouts. An alehouse near the factory was their chosen reunion spot.

"Tommy, you certainly have gone up in the world," Toto noted.

"You know me, always loved pyrotechnics. It's the rockets doing the climbing," the weapons man admitted. "I imagine you're not here to purchase firepower."

Brighton, in his late forties, once and always a military man, fresh-faced with an acute ability to convey deep interest even over the most mundane matter, was the epitome of a general manager of any small enterprise. Irish to the bone, he reveled in the airs a smart plain suit and sharp shoes gave him. He blended perfectly into the normalcy this riverside part of south west London breathed and where the military held sway. His demeanor gave nothing away to suggest his real work developing secret weaponry.

"Perceptive as ever," Toto smiled as he placed his drink on the table. "So now you know what I've been up to since we met last, I want to know whether the Tommie of yesteryear who found nothing too daunting, allowing inventiveness procure results where others saw failure, still beats in that Irish heart. My one question is, have you still got the touch?"

Brighton looked deep into Toto's eyes. It may have been the early evening light but Toto swore he saw a brightness develop.

"Is the Pope a Catholic? What's the craic?"

Toto knew his intuition and memory had not failed. The two spent the next hour reminiscing and for the researcher to convey how the munitions expert could help access the pertinent and tricky to locate information he needed.

Half way across the world, in a Florida mansion afforded through diligent criminality, Aaron Kersh sheltered out of trouble from fallout following the 1929 crash. His foreknowledge allowed him to short the market and enrich himself way beyond trouble. His employees' suffering never gave him one sleepless night. Nothing did. The call requesting him back in New York, he had expected. How else had he been able to reap rich harvests, without those far wealthier than he recognizing his worth?

The Rockefeller premises on Broadway were luxurious and central. As he intended, the family had duly noted the handling of Rockefeller Prentice. He was a past master assuming the role of good foot soldier.

A hard-nosed minder led the speculator into an office where two other men, both recognizable and utterly self assured, sat.

"Ah, Mister Kersh may I introduce Henry Ford." John D. Rockefeller Junior spoke with the powerful, relaxed tone that unassailable wealth offers.

He moved not an inch within the large leather chair he occupied.

Ford and the new arrival shook hands and with little grace Kersh plumped himself into a third chair.

Rockefeller continued.

"I have summoned you here for several very good reasons. First, having so carefully looked after the runt of the litter and guided him wisely, I thank you."

Ford smirked at the plutocrat's dismissive description of the errant nephew. Kirsch returned a passive nod.

"I wanted you to meet with Henry here as we're currently developing stronger business relationships within the European theater and with your roots we considered you might very well be open to helping us move these plans forward."

Kersh sensed he would have little say in what already had been decided. A negative response was not what they had called him in for. It might disturb the plans he had in Florida, but since there was far more power and wealth in the room, he deferred to it.

"Not a man to beat around the bush, Mister Kersh or should I call you Kuterkin, your history as we know makes you an unexpectedly good candidate for us enlisting your services."

Kersh saw the development of an apparently invisible, decades-long alias, have its lock picked in front of him. For the first time he sensed unease, in an environment within which he clearly played second fiddle. He refrained from reacting and lent an ear.

Ford picked up the thread.

"We've manufacturing interests in Germany who, keen to pick up and improve their lot constrained by end of war treaties, have asked to develop our partnership. We agree it's in the mutual interests of both countries to further these efforts."

Kersh wondered why he had been called in. He was neither an engineer nor mechanic. He knew how to swindle, cajole and put up fronts fleecing others but hard labor held no interest. Answering these thoughts Ford continued.

"You of course are an expert in your own field. A field we consider helpful to access, in ongoing relations."

"I know nothing of your field, Mister Ford. I cannot see how I could possibly be of use."

"We believe you're perfect," Rockefeller cut in. "Looking for someone ruthless, focused and able to make things happen be they in the factory, exchange floor or elsewhere, you fit admirably."

Kersh realized there were probably few, if any dark corners, these people had not managed to excavate, and so he relaxed, took the opportunity and cut to the chase.

"What's in it for me?"

"Financially, ten thousand dollars, all expenses and a position as chief negotiator on employment, security and fund management," Ford declared. "You'll have a small, efficient, fully briefed team under you, covering all aspects of the job. Your personal knowledge will be of little importance, except in running a tight ship. Since you still retain your mother tongue, that's beneficial."

Kersh felt relief, a sense of opportunity, yet angered they had the jump on his background. He comforted himself knowing a good job done here would inspire these echelons of power to later ease the door open.

"Your work in security will be to run a small elite team of, let's say, persuasive operators. They will answer to you alone under all circumstances. Any resistance on whatever level would call for your maintenance. Do you understand?" Rockefeller asked.

"Perfectly," Kersh responded.

Rockefeller leaned into his desk, pulled out a large brown envelope and handed it to Kersh.

"All you need for now. We are pleased to have you on board, Aaron."

The businessman and plutocrat were satisfied. Kersh took his exit knowing his power base had been exponentially expanded. Financially he felt comfortable, however the wield he would have access to under his control allowed him a raft of new directions and power.

CHAPTER THIRTY-NINE

Toto missed Smokey's presence since his return, so receiving a telegram from his friend to join him in Ireland he wasted no time.

The west coast of Ireland retained its vision of unimaginable beauty for them both. For Smokey it offered secure, unambiguous freedom and a sense of utter belonging for his creative soul. For Toto its generous coastline looking out over the vast expanse of the Atlantic allowed his own vision to expand and cohere.

As they walked the long strand of beach below the little white and grey slate cottage Smokey inherited, Toto lapped up boundless clear skies and majestic ocean, broken only by spits of grass-topped sand dunes. Soon finding one to sit on they took some moments to tune into natural awe.

"Love sharing these moments," Smokey mused. "Missed our long talks, and all the excitement your life brings with it."

"It's mutual. Feels like just last week we sat looking out over the Wiltshire downs, yet so much has happened. Hearts and plans have crashed, yet I feel more focused, determined to get to the bottom of what's going on."

Smokey remained silent, as Toto looked at his friend, gazing out to sea.

Moments past before Smokey spoke.

"Some believed the world was flat. Looking out over the horizon, if you had no knowledge of what lay beyond, why argue? Lack of knowledge is easily manipulated. It's up to those journeying the unknown to return with knowledge and help enlighten those too fearful or ignorant to break patterns."

"New insights are hard to take on board. They demand cracking comfortable beliefs, breaking down hardened hand-me-downs and lives safe in the trust of normalcy and perceived security," replied Toto.

"The powers that ruled way back wielded heresy as defense against those challenging beliefs and hegemony. Opening minds beyond control threatens every self-serving reality. Maintain power and control by restricting education, writing and promoting the history you want them to believe. Today the masses are controlled by what the press ordains and radio broadcasts. How are new horizons shared?" Smokey asked turning to look directly at Toto.

"Follow the money, expose those who control it and infiltrate minds through the pen and press not controlled."

"There's a start," agreed Smokey. "Books are an excellent way to spread the word."

"That's what I've in mind having collated and solved the present mysteries.

"Your suggestion that the crash was manipulated, do you know how and by whom?" Smokey asked.

"No secret there, Montagu Norman had the Fed under his thumb, still has. Mason alluded to the strength of his relations with Strong and Harrison, his visits to Bar Harbor and Wall Street. On the boat with Neily, he shared his take on the inevitability of it all. The why, I can't answer yet."

Smokey looked out to sea, pondered, then drew a slim pipe from his pocket and a tin of tobacco. He carefully filled it. Toto observed his friend's dedicated process of replenishment, enjoying watching the Irishman's simple efficiency preparing personal pleasure.

Smokey noticed.

"Helps me focus, this ritual does, bit of a meditation." He lit up and drew deeply on the pipe. Exhaling, he continued.

"I'm no way a man of the world like you, but have studied form and visiting London I'm struck by reporting in the papers. Old man Burnham let go the reins a while back, perhaps a visit and chat with him will reveal more. He's long since released the party line. So often freedom of expression with no restriction of office can encourage insights."

Smokey took another long draw.

"Heard from that Landmann fellow in Frankfurt?"

"Met him with Leila. He's got people on the inside confirming my efforts were used as distraction."

"One thing I always ask is: what are they divulging publicly while developing the out of sight agenda? Sounds like the claim was for public consumption, alongside massive stock madness, so no eyes fell on the real agenda."

"Makes sense, but what that agenda is becomes the big question. I'm realizing how used I've been by bankers, Quex and the intelligence services."

"You served the Service well in South Africa, Greece and during the War with your bicycle brigades and journalism. They never forget useful service," the Irishman noted.

"As much as I loved the military, these wars, senseless slaughter of millions, have got us no further down the line. Look at the horrors witnessed in the Balkans, not to mention the trenches in France."

The scenery surrounding the two of them, the crashing waves, screeching gulls seemed a million miles from the horrors Toto witnessed, yet the effect of all he had seen was still as vivid as when it happened.

"Sitting here," Smokey reminded, "It's hard to imagine killing is an everyday occurrence. Empire demands it, constant imposition of will over the conquered.

Today we live through deprivation, depression and the results of a system breaking, yet desperate to reinvent itself. Do those at the top suffer? Of course not, look to those that do. For the most part they accept their lot. Now ask yourself, who benefits from all this?"

Toto was reminded of the conversation he had with his brother at Christmas.

"Louis asked me that. We may not see eye to eye, my brother and I, but his question still rankles. It's never the ordinary people that benefit."

"Certainly not. Control and the flow of money remains the sole instrument of the elite. It manipulates choices. Identify who decides the choices and who finances them brings you closer to answering your brother's question," Smokey offered.

"You're right," agreed Toto.

"Spend a lot of time contemplating the ways of the world from this small piece of heaven. The local library's a good source. An interesting one on the Rothschild dynasty fell into my hands. Their influence flourished, financing both Napoleon and Wellington."

Toto thought how the odds were always stacked in favor of the rich. The biggest pots able bid to win on bluff.

"If you had access to enough resources and could handle losses offset by an inevitable win, isn't that always stacking the deck in your favor?" Toto suggested.

"That's ultimate control," replied Smokey. "In their case they controlled information reaching London, then arriving first, bet against the rumor Wellington lost in the field and wallop, richer than Solomon, proving control of information is a huge asset in the game Made them the controller and masters of the banking system."

"Get everyone fighting each other, set up division then they've conquered: game,set and match!" Toto replied.

Toto felt an enlightening moment hitting him. He also felt distaste for the callousness all this control demanded.

"You're not going to find much compassion in that game," he told Smokey.

"There's no return in compassion and empathy," Smokey replied.

"You're right. No one made a stash loving the enemy. Think it's time to get the inside track from Burnham, at least he's always shown me heart," suggested Toto.

"I'd love to stay a while longer. This place is conducive to the creative soul."

"All the time you like – the Irish air refreshes hidden crevices of insight," the young man replied with a lyrical chuckle.

CHAPTER FORTY

One thing was for sure with Thomas Brighton, he was not the most assiduous fellow when it came to keeping secrets. His work at the Woolwich Arsenal, on secret government projects, therefore could have flagged an oxymoron in process. Yet his remarkable talents as a pyrotechnic genius overlooked apparent shortcomings. That his apprenticeship under one, Frederick Dickson, master gunpowder manufacturer was noted on a curriculum vitae held in some secret government file within the depths of the Ministry of Defence, enabled his employer to overlook this foible.

It also transpired the younger daughter of the same manufacturer, Olga, had been in New York at the time Toto first began his research project. Their meeting, a happenstance generated through Grace Vanderbilt at one of her many social whirls, gave both of them first sight.

Yet it was at an informal garden party, in London's Holland Park, that found Toto renewing this acquaintance, with Olga recognizing him first. As an attentive waiter delivered daintily cut sandwiches to the researcher's plate, she glided up to him.

"I can't help feeling you must be the same Captain I met in New York some time ago."

Toto turned to set eyes on a comely, attractive and slender forty-something of a woman whose attire, floral dress and wide-brimmed hat reminded him of a Degas caricature. Lace-gloved hands held a bone china tea cup and saucer impeccably. A dimple on the right side of her mouth, as she offered a smile, amused and attracted him at the same time.

"Madam, you also remind me of a previous acquaintance, however an unusually good memory for detail has utterly forsaken me."

"Does Vanderbilt ring a bell?" Olga suggested.

"Of course, yes indeed. Olga Dickson. Grace made sure everyone remembered her soirées, yet I completely lost remembering your attractive face," he joked.

His early research had Neily help him with social opportunities, encouraging moneyed interests to his cause. Olga's introduction was never earmarked as financially beneficial.

"I enjoyed the social circuit while furthering business connections the company had with Vanderbilt railroad interests," she answered.

"Well I'd never have thought it."

"Explosives are a global export," she reminded him.

"That they must be," Toto admitted.

"Are you still researching?"

"Author and retired military," he announced boldly.

"Not what my family would have called a profession, the writer you understand, but for me highly romantic," she smiled sweetly.

Whether it was the summer scent of honeysuckle wafting his way or the freedom he felt being around this very artistic gathering of friends, he felt caught off guard and opening to the warmth this daughter of dynamite exuded.

"So how come you ended up here? Not the sort of friends I'd figure you being around," Toto challenged playfully.

"Banker friends of the family live next door and they were invited, so I tagged along."

Toto's instincts pricked up.

"How fortunate for me, such a pleasant re-connection!"

Olga smiled and turned to greet her hosts who had spied the engagement of one they did not know. Toto straightened himself for the encounter, then parried introductions, along with his military credentials and authorship of dogs for good measure.

"Fascinating," responded the banker. "My family have bred Springers for generations. Always knew they were intelligent, the way they chase rabbits round the estate."

"So you find it sustaining as a fine pillar upholding public finance?"

The banker eyed Toto with a shrewd gaze. Years of seeing behind the mask of those who sat opposite him at the bank gave him an unproven sense he maintained hidden insight, when it came to character.

"Since the sixteen hundreds we've served the private interest - that I find sustaining. The unwashed we leave to others. What sustains you, Captain?"

Toto, disappointed at the man's lack of lightness, yet not surprised in the present company, swiftly attempted to bring the women back into the conversation.

"The pursuit of mysteries and research into hidden knowledge."

"Admirable, a man in search of solutions. Something this country is in dire need of at present," the condescending banker shot back.

"Shall we mingle, my dear, as the boys solve the world's problems?"

The banker's wife, keen to disengage from her husband's pet peeve endeavored to prize Olga away. She, on the other hand, was far too interested in developing renewed interest of her military attachment.

Boldly, she joined in.

"Captain Trapman has been researching much more than dogs, Angus, having found fortunes in his ancient lineage's gifts to the States."

She turned to Toto for confirmation. Keen to see to which particular fly the banker rose to, he answered.

"Merely uncovered gold, assisting the rise of that nation, gifted from our family."

It was obvious the hunch played well. The banker's eyes glinted at the mention of gold.

"A good discovery riding the storm a reinstated gold standard has created. So are you looking for a safe investment for that? We've taken care of Olga's business for a good time," divulged the City player.

Toto felt the sport of the line tightening and as all good fishermen realize, play is the true sport before reeling in.

"Since the bank deals solely with the private sector and as you seem to have looked after Olga so well, I'm definitely all ears."

Olga's interest, recognizing her new catch might be able to match her own wealth left to her by her father, marked Toto as a potential catch for her own fishing rights. Toto for his part investigated what might serve as future interest.

"So what advice have you in these austere times?" he quizzed.

The banker already settled into his imaginary chair in the ornate offices on Fleet Street the bank operated, confidently replied.

"As Olga well knows our bank is as discreet as any institution carrying the sort of longevity we do. Her father attested to that," he winked knowingly at his guest. "Your gold would remain a dependable asset for any ventures you feel drawn to finance with Child & Co. As we say, our clients are never treated as child's play."

He laughed loudly at his own joke. Toto swore he had been schooled at Eton, pitied the poor fellow whose own indiscretion suffered one too many whiskies, yet enjoyed playing his audience.

"Sounds like a meeting is beneficial. Where are your offices?"

"Fleet Street," replied the banker.

"Somewhere I've spent many late nights meeting deadlines," teased Toto. "Viscount Burnham can amply attest to that," he added, upping the ante on references.

Both the banker and his wife looked towards Olga, satisfied requisite endorsement for her newfound friend to be in place. It was apparent letting

241

her carry on alone was in her best interest. A hearty slap on Toto's shoulder, which he resented, signalled their withdrawal.

"Well you even managed to impress me," Olga admitted as the others disappeared.

Toto felt he had comfortably set the stage to research this new interest popping unexpectedly into his life.

They successfully arranged to meet again, which suited him. It had become very apparent funds he relied upon for some time were fast diminishing. His research needed a secure financing base and this new spark igniting dormant passion looked set to replace his brother's reluctance in continued funding. It was also time to approach old friend Burnham.

A train from Marylebone Station delivered Toto to Beaconsfield promptly, where Burnham's driver met him. August flourished along the route they took to Hall Barn, the newspaper magnate's estate. Either side of them a quintessential English landscape of dappled meadows and woodlands in many shades of green. The scent of summer was everywhere with hay bales and verdant curb side growth, enticing the senses with rich aromas of country comfort. The manorial pile might have been mistaken easily for a French chateau as it came into view.

Driving through wrought iron entrance gates, past a bleak black and wildly decorative wooden gatehouse they came to a halt at the main entrance. The researcher reminded himself this was the selfsame family friend that in their youth had consistently beaten him and his brothers at tennis during shared holidays in Pau.

Was this the secret to success? he pondered.

Ushered into one of many sumptuous ground floor rooms, he was confronted by an unseasonable fire blazing in the hearth.

"Gives me a sense of homeliness," Burnham quipped as his entrance took Toto by surprise and his gaze away from leaping flames. He made to rise from the chair.

"For goodness sake, put ceremonials to one side. We've known each other far too long. Feel at home, even though you might feel it above your pay grade."

The magnate chuckled as he nestled down opposite Toto into an equally inviting large chair.

"How long since I sent you off half pickled to Euston?"

"Too long, always miss your humor."

Burnham continued to chuckle. Old age seemed to sit well with the man, in spite of physical challenges.

"The older we get I swear we remember even more of our youth."

"Days marked with eventful times in spite of the age gap. We made the most of it."

The elder man nodded in agreement, as his wife Olive entered the room. This time Toto made an absolute effort to stand and greet his hostess.

"Toto dear, obey Harry's orders and don't stand on ceremony. We may look posh but behind appearances we're still the same, frivolous friends your mother and father so cherished."

He had neglected these two for too many years and forgotten the renegades of aristocracy they had always been, away from the spotlight.

"Harry's in excellent hands as always, so I'll let you chatter and get the lunch ready. You're staying for lunch I hope," Olive questioned Toto.

"Of course."

Pleased, she left them to it.

"In your note you wanted to quiz me on several pressing questions, fire away I'll do my best."

"You remember the disaster our presentation turned into in New York."

"Hard to forget, Ochs sending me a cable with multiple question marks attached," Burnham giggled mischievously.

Toto continued.

"The way he pulled all interest in the reparation story not only off the front page but from all of them."

"Yes, rum stuff."

"Seemed mighty queer to me how I lost all traction from film, press and most of the big names supporting, in a flash. It felt the world had fallen through the floor."

"Fickle is what press and plutocracy are by default."

Burnham warmed his hands against the fire. He may have headed up one of the biggest titles in print but was well versed in the treachery and insincerity running the industry, like some dark phantom haunting and seeking out its next victim. It came with the territory and he loathed its apparel.

"I've always tried steering well clear of the obvious pitfalls and demands the establishment impress we deliver, so can imagine you being crestfallen."

"I'm a tough nut when fielding blows but something nagged me right from the beginning of this fallout. Who benefited?"

"Always asking the right question. That's why I saw you as a bright journalist from the beginning. These things are not obvious to the general populace. Let's face it, they're fed what we tell them is truth. Many times frankly, what we're asked to tell is anything but the truth."

Toto shifted his position. He straightened, not wishing to miss a syllable.

"I've been press-ganged into towing the political line, in spite of alliances we, as a news organ, feel close to. Have had to answer to those who stay so far behind the curtain and remain unaccountable."

"What are you saying, editorial decisions don't stop at your desk?"

"Naive to imagine it ever did. Of course we have our political preferences, still try and be even-handed, to avoid being obvious. Rarely works."

"Who is it that's behind the curtain?"

Burnham, even in his own home, through years of habit looked around him before answering, in a hushed tone.

"The bankers of course, the money men. The City of London secret society of financial manipulators, ever was, ever will be."

Toto was shocked, more so from such a frank admission from one he imagined would be comfortable amongst such types. Burnham continued.

"It's always the money. That megalomaniac Norman has much to answer for. It's he that drives the American tank. I'm in no doubt his lust for control was behind the whole crash and now this depression. Points that way, as if lit with theater lights."

"Got powerful friends in Europe who help, according to sources there," Toto noted.

"You've your lovely sister Leila able to listen in at the center and you're correct there are forces wielding huge control."

He leaned forward in his ample chair and continued.

"I'm going to confide some far darker mischief."

Toto thrilled. He had hardly expected the magnate to spill such beans but something cautioned him restrain enthusiasm, listen well and take mental notes like never before. The thread suddenly shattered, as the butler swept in with sherry for them both.

"This will loosen the links," Burnham muttered as he savored the sweet dark wine. "Olive converted me but we can only enjoy it here at home. Too much of a scoop to be seen imbibing this at the Club. Lose my reputation utterly!"

Eagerly Toto wished him get back on track.

"So the darker mischief," he reminded him.

"Yes, where was I?"

"The darker mischief," Toto repeated, fearing Burnham had lost his flow.

"Of course your friend Landmann is a good catch for you. He's seen and heard a lot more than they care he did."

"You knew about Landmann?"

Toto was taken aback Burnham knew of their relationship.

"Still have my sources. I keep an eye on my protégé but never fear I'll never put you on the spot. You're near as damn it, family."

"I take that as a great compliment."

"On me," responded Burnham. "Now where was I. Oh, yes, Landmann has eyes and ears into some deep canyons. I've always considered the man to be someone of the greatest integrity, Jewish, honorable and utterly devoted to best practice in the financial world. Quite a coup getting him his position as mayor. That's why he's so keen to make Frankfurt the major financial world center. An anathema to Norman, who sees the City of London as the original City of Light and revelation!"

"The bond of the tribe and culture is a common one," Toto interjected.

"The difference is deeper than that. We may share common roots and historical culture, yet over the past century or two the true historical base has been infested by cuckoos, dark evil cuckoos."

"Cuckoos?"

"The sort that have no right to call themselves Jews, yet with their money, influence and dark arts and intrigue invade the nest, chuck the rightful inhabitants out and call the tune, thinking they can trade on our universal adeptness in all things financial."

Toto had never imagined Burnham to be so conspiratorial, yet his words reflected much of what his own research pointed to.

"Are you suggesting the families making up Wall Street and the Federal Reserve are such cuckoos?"

Burnham warmed not only by the hearth but also Toto's grasp of where he was going. He felt more animated than he had done in years. It was releasing to vent what he knew and felt in a confessional way, to a long-term friend, yet more importantly to one who would investigate deeper than others, aware of such truths, would delve.

"How good to release what I'm privy to. I'm an old man happy to unload facts hidden for too long, suppressed from being expressed by the very bodies perpetrating powerful control. Imagine it's what Catholics look for in final rights."

"I feel honored."

"Honored, my ass," Burnham blurted. "Make sure you remain the excellent journalist I first glimpsed all those years back. Start getting some truth out there."

The righteous indignation and powerful support he offered Toto acted as an injection of adrenalin he had sought for ages. That it came from this source was as surprising as it was sudden.

"Albert, I want you to take heed very closely to what I am about to tell you. I come from a long Jewish lineage and very grateful for that. Our ancestors wandered like nomads across the face of the earth, as we were destined always to do. These cuckoos have usurped our tribe, claimed it as their own and inveigled their own agendas into the mix. Their plan's an insidious one, so far from the purity we hold sacred. They've taken over the moneyed classes, set themselves to take over the world. It's not new, yet today what passes as news is merely infernal preparation on minds to accept the inevitable outcomes they worked so hard on, since way before you and I came in."

Toto listened intently. Each sentence made more and more sense in spite of the puzzle still defining a hazy image. Burnham continued.

"You and I share a love of all things military. We both found the ethic of the military slipping from service into oppression. Its powers abused and manipulated for the selfish gain of others. Let's not delude ourselves. Empire is empire and at its heart is a military machine. Becoming a Lieutenant Colonel in the war, mentioned in dispatches for things committed honorably, where did it get me? Titles? Got a toy box full of them. They're meaningless on the level it matters. Today I sit here and question what all the slaughter was for, why it followed the path it did."

Burnham paused, reflecting, staring into the leaping flames. Toto responded.

"Leila had unique insight into that farrago. History we're asked to believe is diametrically opposed to her experiences. We did our stuff; acted as the good little cannon fodder demanded of us, or in your case ordered your squaddies to carry out; just look what happened. Millions slaughtered. For why, what, for who?"

"I don't doubt your sister. She's utterly sensible, a truthful weather vane where others might have just accepted to the letter what they were told," Burnham confessed. "I remember when she was visiting Haldane, he asked me along to join them. Shortly before he passed. He shared the experiences of the witch-hunt he'd been subjected to, on account of his sympathies with Germany and reminded me of how that bastard Northcliffe used his press power to set on the man like a pack of wolves. That brigand Turpitz purposely stitched up Haldane's opposite number. There was genuine respect between the two ministers. Events even then were manipulated by dark forces, turning the wheel, bending the hand of history towards a fast approaching midnight."

Toto cut in.

"She felt none of it ought to have ever taken place."

"The archduke's assassination, well that was just the excuse, a *raison d'être* for beginning the whole disaster," Burnham declared.

"Don't misunderstand me, there were differences, they were exploited and used by the controllers of the purse strings exploiting the single biggest casus belli – with economic degeneration fueling the war machine. Lives of millions just bean counters to them. Family pitted against family. Even royals on each side, including the Tsar who'd seen right through them. Callous, ruthless, nothing less."

"The Tsar called them out?" Toto queried.

"Of course! They gave the Bolshies carte blanche to dispose of the whole family. They'd have had my hide if I'd printed that. Too much of a coward to face them with their own deceit."

"And now?"

"Too late, my game's almost up. It's your turn to tell the truth. You always were way more courageous than all the sycophants in Fleet Street, even though I incriminate myself," Burnham grinned.

The two of them sank into silence as the enormity of what they had shared sank in. Both knew these thoughts aired in public would have brought down derision and opprobrium on their heads. Toto comprehended why Burnham insisted they meet here, at home and the privacy provided. He was also concerned as to how the Viscount saw him exposing this out for public scrutiny.

He raised his head and looked across to the elder before him.

"How the hell am I supposed to feed this out and expose it?"

"I've friends and connections who feel as I do. We're not alone, yet the enemy we're faced with is a mighty and powerful creature, cruel, insensitive and lacking any empathy whatsoever. Its desire for its own ends is how it feeds, its self-importance, arrogance and ego blind to everything else. Rapacious, hideous in its world view and evil to the core."

"Sounds terrifying, to be honest," Toto admitted.

"It is, yet it has its vulnerable underbelly as does any monster. It's that underbelly you must address, attack and expose, so it bleeds to death."

"A tall order. What is that vulnerability?"

"Transparency," the old man confirmed.

Burnham looking at his guest saw bravery, a touch of foolhardiness, ample courage and a desire for truth. He thanked his guardian angels for conspiring to make sure the bond between Trapman and Levy was compact, strong and developed early on both sides. The fruits of that higher wisdom looked fair to flourish in the not too distant future.

"It's what brought us together," he continued. "Our shared honesty, love of truth over injustice, on whatever battlefield we participated. Personally I fear I'll not glimpse its fruits, yet my contacts can help unravel things. What trick of fate brought our two families together, I shall soon be privy to. Having been afforded a front row seat in life, I'd like to feel I contributed."

Toto felt Burnham's weariness at having carried such a position. He felt a handing over, a generational gift in process of change. Fear, deep inside, bit. His old friend's expression of obvious relief completed the process.

"I'll always remember your help," Toto assured his mentor.

"It's a challenge no one can attain alone," Burnham cautioned. "What was that line? *There is a tide in the affairs of men, which taken at the flood, leads on to fortune.*"

Toto completed it.

"*And we must take the current when it serves, or lose our ventures.* Always been a driving force for my own life that, despite falling over so many times."

Burnham raised himself in the chair as Olive entered to declare lunch ready.

"I was just saying to Toto, dear, how we all go back a long way to Pau."

"Joyful times," replied Olive.

"Think it would be good if he benefited from talking to close friends."

Olive turned to Toto and took his hand in both of hers.

"Harry and I have little we do not share. I suppose that's been the medicine keeping us strong and together all these years. If he feels you need to talk with others, then indeed you must."

"I appreciate that and our time together. As Harry said, it's not a task we can do alone," Toto acknowledged.

Burnham moved towards Olive.

"Think he needs to speak with Winston."

"Absolutely," Olive agreed.

"Churchill?" Toto queried.

"Yes," they both answered.

They proceeded to the dining room.

"You realize he and I have almost as long a history as you two," Toto shared.

"Well nothing surprises me with your family and the way you cruised social strata," Burnham replied.

They arrived at table and sat down to an abundance of simplicity.

Olive apologized for the seasonal fare. Toto assured her he adored salad, salmon and the early fruits of the walled garden. He then shared history of his acquaintance with the politician.

"Winston for all his bluff and wind knows more than most of what goes on behind the scenes. If you can get anything out that helps, he's your man," suggested Olive.

"Can imagine," said Toto.

"Those playing the great game have already seen his worth," she added.

Toto, struck by her remark, felt compelled to quiz her as to what she meant by the game players. Burnham cut in.

"Best work that one out for yourself."

Toto determined he would and continued his connection with Churchill.

"Ended up on the same train in South Africa. We bicyclists on a spying mission, our wheels adapted for rail, hitched a ride until just before the train got hijacked and Winston earned his famous capture. During the journey I reminded him of our meeting as kids in London. Surprised he even remembered, but his journalism he'd bagged inspired me to follow suite."

"As I said, fate casts a mysterious web over us all," Burnham mused. "Since he's stepped back and is writing more, it's a good moment to spend time with him again. I'll contact him and suggest he contact you."

Toto knew connecting with major players helped – and Burnham was no exception.

CHAPTER FORTY-ONE

The National Socialist movement in Germany had its ups and downs following the general chaos of the nineteen twenties. The uncertainty and rudderless guidance exhibited by a political elite towards a downtrodden, exhausted and supine population created fertile ground for strong shoots to emerge. It was the dedication of its ambitious leader, one Adolf Hitler that saw the National Socialist German Workers Party flourish and grow into the second most popular party at the beginning of the nineteen thirties. This coincided with the arrival in Europe of Ford and Rockefeller's emissary, Aaron Kersh.

Plans were underway to build a vast factory complex in Cologne, where Ford's manufacturing could provide a good outlet for not only Germany but also Europe and South America. In charge of security and appropriate human constituent parts in supporting deals, Kersh, in his role found local members of the National Socialists to have much in common with his own views. The development of a seamless interaction between these members, the party in general and the operations at Ford was quietly acquiesced by both Ford and Rockefeller. Their instinct Kersh could become a useful bridgehead was paying off. Although the new headquarters would not be operational until the following year, Kersh made sure he cultivated and integrated into the consciousness of the local and national members of the burgeoning Nazi Party. This he saw as a bonus not clarified in New York.

In the southern English provincial suburb of Bromley, the relationship Toto nurtured with Olga Dickson back in the summer swiftly blossomed into her accepting his hand in marriage. A quiet wedding, followed by a short honeymoon locally, was completed with the presence of son Adrian, fresh from graduating university, staying in the terraced house Olga had purchased prior to their relationship.

Toto careful to be as diplomatic as possible, endeavored to gauge Adrian's emotional heartland. The two of them sat in the comfortable front room, with his new wife having taken her leave for the night. Toto spoke.

"With all the hustle and bustle we've not had a chance to talk about all this, nor have I asked how you felt."

Adrian clutching a mug of hot coffee in both hands watched the twirl of milk he had poured create a vortex. He felt his father's awkwardness and looked up.

"It's alright Dad, you're happy with how things have turned out and that's the important thing. I've had good time to reflect on how our lives have weaved in and out."

Toto audibly released a sigh as he leaned back in his chair.

"It means a lot to hear that from you. I expected the worst as I have been such a let down and..."

Adrian interrupted.

"I'm not expecting you change, you make an effort and with mother disappearing to Italy, I'm actually happy having you around."

He saw the relief on his father's face and remembered what he had been dying to share. Toto caught the expectation.

"God, I haven't even asked about your exams."

Adrian beamed.

"Got a first with honors!"

"Good God, well done that man. And Amharic, how did that turn out?"

"Best marks of the lot."

"That's excellent," Toto exclaimed, as proud a father as he had ever felt.

Adrian looked at him pretending seriousness.

"Want to know a secret?"

"One more won't break the bank!"

"When it came to them looking for an examiner to mark the paper, no one had bothered to find out if there was an existing expert in Amharic, so they ran an ad in the nationals asking for anyone with good knowledge of it to apply. Since I was damn certain they wouldn't find a candidate, I sent off an anonymous acceptance and ended up marking my own paper."

"You've got to be kidding."

His father retorted, realizing this apple fell as close to the tree as he could have possibly wished for.

"You canny so and so. Think that earns you your first assignment."

"Which is?" Adrian replied.

"Helping me open a can of worms."

"We're not going fishing again, are we?"

"For the truth this time, young man, for the truth."

Toto then filled him in on what Burnham shared, on the information he himself culled from his own research and laid out the approach ahead.

"Uncle Louis gave me an early twenty-first present." Adrian informed his father.

"What was it?"

"Enough to enable me to travel and visit places I've wanted to go."

Toto felt a real pang of guilt course through him, knowing very well he had never been able or present to fund anything during his son's formative years.

"My regret has always been," he began.

"I know, you don't need to excuse yourself. It's more important we move on. At least your brother has been able to help us both. Look on the positive side."

Toto was amazed again at his son's maturity.

It ought to have been he who was giving advice, he thought.

"So where do you have in mind?"

Adrian beamed.

"The Levant has always called me, especially Lebanon, Palestine and Syria."

"When I was in Mesopotamia during the campaign there, got to know the people. They're extraordinary," Toto shared.

"Want to live amongst them," Adrian said.

Toto pondered a few moments and then laid a suggestion to his son.

"Being the cradle of civilization, it's attracted its fair share of empire interference. I've been researching much while you've been in Edinburgh and one of the recurring themes has been rape and pillage. In Africa it's been a foundation stone of the British Empire. The whole Boer War was a smoke screen for ownership of the diamonds and gold down there. If you're up to it, and it'll be good practice for any diplomatic career, you could dig into what's going on with the oil and picking off of ancient civilization's treasures. Whet the appetite?"

"Sounds terrific. I can infiltrate and get more information. Perhaps dress as a Bedouin like Lawrence!"

"He knew a lot of what went on in those parts and knew the Arabs well, unlike the high command who just pushed pencils and agendas. I'm seeing Churchill soon to quiz him on several issues. You know Lawrence worked with him at the Colonial Office?"

"Yup!"

Adrian had studied Lawrence at university and his Middle Eastern exploits. He mirrored his own dreams on the man.

"When are you hoping to take off?" Toto asked.

"After Christmas."

"It looks like I'm heading back over the pond in the New Year, when back we can debrief each other and plan further."

"Why are you going?" asked Adrian.

"Vanderbilt suggested I meet a congressman, Louis McFadden. He's been a strong vocal opponent of the Federal Reserve and not only will we have a lot in common but he's a repository of valuable information."

"What about being newly wed. How does Olga feel about you going off?"

Toto looked at his son and saw the concern another disappearing act from him could be imminent. He needed to reassure the young man he had changed.

"Don't worry, she's fully behind me with this work and we've both agreed it needs to be done for the sake of sealing the money owed."

"The Moore Millions that fell through?" Adrian asked, somewhat confused. "I thought that was a dead duck."

Toto had to make a decision. He knew his son was not stupid, yet he needed everyone, including Adrian, to feel there was still potential and life despite his primary failed attempt at getting Congress to agree reparation of the debt. More pertinently he had convinced Olga the retrieval of riches she believed he was due imminently was still very much alive. He needed her resources more than he needed her relationship at this stage, cold as that calculation sounded. Needs must, he convinced himself, for the greater good and course he was set upon. It would help nobody to divulge these truths, neither to his son or anyone in the family. He made his decision.

"The present project, the reparations and the research necessary are intrinsically linked. Failure in either threatens the other. Those I'm dealing with on both our side and those ranged against us have to be very carefully managed. As Tesla warned me, trust no one. However at this moment I truly need you to trust me. Can you?"

Toto asked with an urgency his son felt deeply. He also realized his past record would impact his son's response. He waited nervously.

Adrian glanced round the room, pausing at a photograph of his father in military attire, taken back in Bicycle Battalion days. He wondered how much of this man's life he would ever get to know. Turning to meet Toto's eyes he felt the sincerity of the question and gazed long and hard.

"I trust you," he replied.

CHAPTER FORTY-TWO

Montagu Norman's bimonthly meetings with the Rothschild banking business and his guidance and manipulated control, through the close relationship he nurtured within the Federal Reserve and his ongoing friendship with Rockefeller and J.P. Morgan, were heavily noted in the credit column of the bankers' overall strategic business plan.

That strategy had successfully executed the crash of 1929. Its pyroclastic flow of after shocks, developing worldwide depression through a syncopated pattern of both agitation and suffering moved forward. This resonated, encouraging a cacophony of chaos. Where there was chaos, fertile soil for tilling dissent, fascism and every excuse for even more war presented itself.

Norman's relationship with Morgan had them meet often. Ford and his fellow industrialists, with the encouragement of Rockefeller and others, developed industry and assistance in Germany. Norman made sure he was positioned at the center of the creation of the Bank of International Settlements. Its initiation earlier in the year enabled the main players to manipulate its overt utility in reparations management into a more covert central bank for central banks around the globe.

An internal coup in Brazil offered Rothschild and Norman an opportunity to develop yet another central bank. For Norman here was an opportunity restoring far better commercial advantages for British industry. In the ongoing search replenishing gold reserves, a gold rush in the north of the country attracted a curious collection of European gold seekers. No surprise therefore finding unsavory interests both from Britain and Germany among those rushing to win gold.

Whilst Norman and his partners organized a Brazilian adventure, Toto answered a promised connection made through Burnham to visit Winston Churchill.

A letter arrived from Chartwell, Churchill's home. It requested his presence at the house the following day.

The sun warming an otherwise chilly late November day, encouraged Toto to make the fifteen-mile journey by bicycle. Olga considered the idea lunacy of the first degree, but clad in a warm brown suit, clipped leggings around socks and a matching cap, he set off to arrive a couple of hours later at the home of the resting politician. As he dismounted a cheerful Winston, wrapped in a light overcoat, walked from the garden up the steps to the driveway to greet him.

"Your escapades in South Africa haven't dulled a passion for two wheels.

Persistence, a quality I much admire," the politician noted, remembering their railcar meeting during the Boer War.

"Surprised you remember the journey together."

Churchill shook Toto's hand and gave him a friendly pat on the shoulder.

"Blessed and cursed with a photographic memory. Heard whispers your lot were on secret reconnaissance there."

Feeling the chill of the morning, Churchill was keen they both got inside.

"Your efforts deserve a stirrup cup. Let's get in out of this beastly cold and meet Clemmie. Apart from the staff we're the only ones here at present," Churchill offered.

Toto swiftly agreed as the ride's energy fast dissolved now static. Entering the house, he met Clementine, Churchill's wife, who ushered them into the drawing room.

"Harry reminded me you also pushed a pen on the rag," Churchill noted.

They settled down into comfortable chairs, facing an open fire, above which hung an oil painting of a fine racehorse. Toto wondered if his host had painted it.

"As war correspondent for them in Europe and recently the States."

"Never knew we were at war with America," chuckled Churchill. "Had hoped King George learned that lesson first time round."

"Covered the odd skirmish in South America, fracas in Canada and New York where, like yourself, I got most pleasure writing books," replied Toto.

"Never one for remote reporting. In the thick of it was where I operated best," Churchill barked. "The uncivilized tribes can be wretched bother, best dealt with swiftly and reported later."

"As I found reporting from the Greek side in the Balkan war."

As Clemmie brought a whiskey for each of them, Toto acknowledged gratefully.

Winston took up the conversation.

"Newspapers hold great power. Burnham would second that. Put out powerful stuff and people, over time take on the message. Control the press and you've the ear of the people. Something political parties would do well to remind themselves."

"The pen as sword and all that," Toto added.

"The pen's essential yet where we find in our territories a strong aboriginal propensity to kill, our faith must always exert a modifying influence, protect them from their more violent forms of fanatical fever and where necessary exterminate such brutish behavior," Churchill replied.

Toto was reminded not only of the revulsion felt in the Balkan catastrophe but the supremacist attitude his host was noted for displaying.

Was empire bettered by such thinking? he wondered, *killing men, women and children whatever their ethnicity never proved a solution in his experience.*

In the quiet and beauty of the Kent countryside, listening to the politician declare the rights of an empire as excuse for such slaughter seriously grated his present sense of direction. He decided swiftly to change the subject.

"Burnham suggested you might enlighten me on details I'm uncovering. With your experience at the coalface, he suggested you might shed some light on them."

"Sitting out the front benches at present, away from the fray I'll do my best."

"Following my unsuccessful attempts at reparations, it's apparent some were hell-bent manipulating events with this present depression. Much of it looks European based with Norman at the Bank having profound influence in these things."

Churchill looked fixedly at Toto and listened intently as he continued. He lit a cigar, ruffled from a box on the table beside him. Then methodically took a long, slow draw on it before replying.

"That man I have neither time nor liking for. Persuaded me to reintroduce the gold standard, which I now deeply regret. Norman takes no prisoners where motives are concerned. His self assurance and arrogance make him more enemies than friends."

He took a long draught of whiskey as Toto wondered how much respect Winston held for the maverick banker.

"Do you respect him?"

"In as much as he carries traits I happily own, yes. His persistence in believing means justify the end," the politician continued, "I cannot swallow. Have faith in a cause and an unconquerable will to win but beware the means do not scupper victory."

"Where might this not apply?" Toto asked, inquisitive to know to what lengths Churchill was prepared to go.

"When it defines protection of freedom and life. Then all bets are off," he stated with absolute conviction.

"So the course Mussolini has taken in Italy: your public statements seem to suggest he's got it right," Toto pressed him.

"Yes I did sing his praises and Fascism has rendered a service to the whole world, showing a way to defeat the bestial appetites and passion of Leninism."

The growing fear of Communism skyrocketing since the revolution was a fact. Churchill's well pronounced hatred of it was common knowledge and had added constant fuel to that fire. Was there an agenda here he was not yet aware of?

"The perils of communism, how do they stack up against what we forge in the West?"

"The West?" Churchill rebutted with passion. "The West *is* Great Britain," he declared emphatically. "We are the empire, east, west, south and north. Bolshevism is a disease, not a creed, but a pestilence. We can never afford to catch its virulence."

The researcher realized Churchill's stay away from the political hub had in no way diminished his own virulent hatred of Bolshevism. He sensed something prizing itself open from within this obsession.

"Sub-human goals and ideals are set before these Asiatic millions. In Soviet Russia we have a society that seeks to model itself upon the ant – a hive mentality. From the days of Weishaupt to Marx, Trotsky, Bela Kun and Rosa Luxembourg, this worldwide conspiracy for the overthrow of civilization and for the reconstitution of society on the basis of arrested development, of envious malevolence, and impossible equality, has been steadily growing," Churchill continued in full flow.

As he paused to take a drag on his trusty cigar Toto tried to intervene. Churchill preempted him.

"With the exception of Lenin, the majority of the leading figures amongst the Soviets are Jews. Litvinoff, Trotsky, Zinovieff, Krassin and Radek – all Jews. In the Soviet institutions the predominance of Jews is even more astonishing. And the prominent, if not indeed the principal, part in the system of terrorism has been taken by Jews."

Toto was getting a better handle on many of Churchill's obsessive outcries against Bolshevism. He wondered whether this was what Burnham alluded to.

"Burnham talked of hidden hands, dark forces manipulating the actions we're exposed to. Are these the ones you're referring to?"

Churchill drained his glass, refilled it and offered the bottle to Toto who declined. His host placed the bottle close to him, on a round Georgian table, took another draught and answered.

"I'm not talking here of the national Jews, those whose like we accept and include in our society. Nor the Jews desiring a new home in Palestine. There is an international Jew, one so far removed from the historic one. These are the roots of the Bolsheviks."

"Burnham refers to them as cuckoos," Toto broke in.

"Damn fine description," Churchill agreed slapping his knee in approval.

"When Balfour put the offer to Rothschild for the delivery of a promised Palestine to the Jews in his letter a decade or so ago are you suggesting he created a promissory note for a future home for Jewry?"

"Merely reward for persuading American intervention into the war, yes. Of course, my tenure as Colonial Secretary enabled my substantiation of that offer. In whatever way, I supported the gesture."

"Such displacement of indigenous peoples would be heavy-handed and none other than an act of aggression on an autonomous people, to say the least," Toto interjected.

"Don't forget, we own Palestine and in mitigation I assured them not to take for granted the local population would be cleared out to suit their convenience. They may be barbaric hoards, the Palestinians, who eat little but camel dung, but British fair play can still be exhibited."

Toto was horrified but hid it well. His visit to this loose cannon revealed some very dark and dubious thinking. His journalistic instincts demanded he stay objective, clear and note every word spoken. When in the inner sanctum, silence delivered appropriately often reveals more. He steered the conversation to a more personal level.

"Leila, close to the Kaiser as you know, always said he wanted nothing other than peace in nineteen seventeen, so why did the war not end there?"

Churchill's eyes sparkled as he replied. Toto could not work out whether it was from the whiskey or from knowledge well hidden.

"Haldane shared his adoration of your sister's skills and insight. I once had the pleasure of sitting next to her at dinner in London and was most taken by her manner and political acuity. What she had little idea of was the strength a Rothschild whisper in an American ear encouraging entry has on things. The establishment of the Federal Reserve had already sealed the fate of any refusal to enter the fray."

"So had the Americans not appeared, the Kaiser would have obtained the peace he had been bullied out of and millions of deaths would have been saved," Toto concurred.

"War, it seems, is the oil lubricating the world. A fact we all loathe to admit and a truism the Bolsheviks try so hard to override through their collective slavery."

Toto felt the sharp end of Churchill's persuasion to conflict, yet wondered whether it was merely a personal conviction.

"Are these the dark forces Harry talked of?" Toto queried.

"Always a banker's war. We can play our political hand, hold lofty perspectives on a world order but control of money will always be the tune we pay the piper," Churchill admitted.

"So where does that leave the National Socialists and Hitler's popularity?" Toto asked, keen to gauge the statesman's European stance.

"In a world of barbarous peoples, the Aryan stock is bound to triumph. It is sheer humbug to pretend Bolshevism is not far worse than any German resurgence, let alone the hope and self-belief Hitler inspires in the people. As a check on the Bolsheviks, it can only be encouraged."

It was apparent Churchill had an alternative vision for what his sister and brother-in-law both felt were developments of the worse kind, taking place in Germany. What was it from the politician's perspective that drew him to see German resurgence in its present form as benevolent?

He decided to ask.

"If we look at the crash, how that was created, then follow the results that included a depression Germany got yoked into, on top of the anvil the victors' exorbitant reparation hammer forged, was it not this straw that broke the camel's back, fermenting the very desperation, destitution and climate encouraging a strong leader and desire for restored self image?"

"Undoubtedly," replied Churchill. "However a stronger Germany also offers the best bulwark against the Russians. Playing each against the other, while supporting a growing industrial base for Germany, requires deft skill and profound oversight."

"So who precisely would engineer that?" Toto asked, swiftly joining dots. "The bankers?"

"Obviously, since money oils the wheels of economic progress. Norman scurries around, making sure key players are under his thumb, is key in the creation of the Bank of International Settlements, committing centralized control over central banks, handing powder and fuse to the likes of Schacht, Warburg and the City of London. He feels his omnipotence strengthened as he handles a global instrument of great influence."

"Do the people understand they're being mobilized and used in this equation?"

"I doubt it, as in war they're incidental to the greater plan, though we do offer them the vote and call it democracy," replied Churchill.

"Incidental?" Toto queried, shocked at the ease his host brought the statement forward. "I was under the impression we fought the last war for the sake of democracy's freedom."

Churchill took a puff on his cigar and chortled.

"The best argument against democracy is a five-minute conversation with the average voter. Yet let them feel they're sovereign and whatever result transpires they'll accept."

"Are we to believe political decision makers are in control of their countries' sovereignty?" Toto rejoined.

"Yes, we're asked to believe that. Who ultimately controls is a question long on the lips of those seeking change."

Churchill paused, but not long enough for Toto to cut in.

"We're both journalists. We know how the page provides a clarion call to support as well as persuade. People look for strong leadership, both in war and peace. As civilized nations become more powerful, they also become more ruthless," he declared.

His enjoyment at holding court was apparent.

Toto, moved to his view on the recent war's near miss for peace.

"The refusal to find the peace, are you suggesting that was an example of becoming more ruthless. When there was obviously a possibility for peace, why the prosecution of more war with people hoodwinked of any potential?"

Winston glared at his guest. He knew their historical tracks had parallels. He also saw Toto, an outsider, unaccustomed to strategic and political realities he himself so willingly had immersed, hampered his overview.

"In war-time, truth is so precious as to always be attended by a bodyguard of lies. Sometimes to further outcomes we must create our own disappearing act, as the conjurer deceives the audience."

"Reminds me of Bismarck's - *People never lie so much as after a hunt, during a war or before an election* - Does that not smack of Norman's means to ends?"

The politician stopped puffing his cigar, held his glass firmly and looked directly into Toto's eyes. Toto felt it forcibly, yet held his ground. Something had changed very suddenly.

Had he prized open a small but important fault line in the man? he wondered. Churchill, professionally, covered himself.

"Bismarck was truly a great statesman."

All the time he kept his eyes glued on Toto. The room they were in was warm in spite of the weather and month, yet a perceptible chill ranged around its length like some wraith of wrath seeking out its target. Toto felt the confusion, let it go, determined it should not interfere with his focus. He made it his turn to cover himself.

"Way back in Hyde Park when Louis, Arthur and I arrived at your birthday party, I remember how attentive and caring Mrs. Everest was to us all. So optimistic, so compassionate."

Churchill reacted like a trout entranced by the fly. Leaping at it from the depth of a still dark pool in his mind, he was snared at the mere mention of his beloved nanny's name. Its resonance crashed through ages, smashed through structures the present had formed and threw him back to his eleventh birthday party at the house in London. Privileged, dressed to the nines and king of his miniature kingdom, with his plump and cheery guardian perfecting the sole resource of love and attention he had enjoyed in those years.

"Ah, Woom, blissful days!" he murmured, delivering the nickname he never failed to use. "How swiftly time forces us to let our hearts break asunder through loss."

"Winston, I can't help but note the strands of similarity woven across our lives. We both had mothers who married three times. Both of us journalists, army veterans and authors. Your family way back in service to the Crown, mine in service against the Crown through assisting independence for the colonies and today, sitting here discussing where the journey moves to."

Churchill shifted lightly in his chair, turned towards his visitor and replied.

"The fault, dear Brutus, lies not in our 'stars' but in our selves that we are underlings. It's how we venture forth and within the remit we've carved, make changes in the world for better or worse. Do you consider yourself an underling or a leader of men?"

Toto knew he was not going to extricate himself from this master of debate easily. In his ear he heard the words of Tesla. *Trust no one.*

He wondered, *did he trust himself, his life, everything gone before that had brought him to this place, with a man of wit and maneuver far greater than his?* Yet a man who could well point him in a direction discovering hidden truths. He bet his host enjoyed being tested.

It was then he had a thought.

"I cannot predict if I'm an underling or a leader of men but what I do know is I have a destiny, handed to me by my father when still a young man."

Toto opened his shirt, under the brown jacket he wore and from round his neck, carefully extricating the triquetra, leaned towards Churchill, holding it in his palm.

"My father gave this to me, saying when I discovered its meaning I would discover not only my purpose but our generational journey."

The object presented captured Churchill's eye and interest.

"May I hold it?"

"Certainly," replied Toto, taking it off.

The politician took it and read the inscription.

"A powerful message and one of great significance. Your father's Prussian side spent many years in service to diplomacy."

"You've a good knowledge of our history," Toto noted with not a small amount of surprise.

"No good being ignorant of those seeking you out. My office had good resource to the services we rely on for knowing both our enemy and friends. Not unfamiliar territory within your family, as I recall."

It would have been foolish of Toto to have ignored the fact Churchill's former positions would have had him able to pull strings and files when needed. He was reminded of the man's assiduous ability to brief himself.

"Our diplomatic status served us well on both sides at times," Toto confirmed.

"So your quest to find out who could be oiling present circumstances might well benefit you investigating who is strengthening their position in respect of resources," Churchill offered his guest.

"What are you implying?"

"I merely suggest you meet our mutual friend Hugh Sinclair. He may have some interesting avenues to research."

"Quex?"

"Of course. I understand your previous services there were highly regarded and as we both know, it was what got us reacquainted."

Toto began to appreciate he might be revolving in interesting circles.

Clemmie's entrance to call Winston to the lunch table was the cue for him to leave. Bidding them both farewell and thanking the politician for a resource of useful information, he donned bicycle clips, put his gloves on and left for the return journey.

Within Chartwell, Clemmie asked her husband.

"Will the poor man not be chilled to the bone, out in the cold?"

"Quite used to it, for sure. He's placed himself out there for some time now," he replied taking the phone and making a necessary call.

CHAPTER FORTY-THREE

An invitation from Whitehall came by telegram to Bromley. Toto caught the London train and made haste to the meeting with Quex.

The head of service was professional and to the point. He paced up and down behind his desk, in an agitated state, as Toto entered.

"Good man for dropping by," he greeted, showing relief yet no acknowledgement it was he who issued the invite.

"There's gold in Brazil, could be going to the Bolsheviks. Need the right man there to keep us informed. You want to take it?"

Quex's manner was curt. Toto, aware no pleasantries would be forthcoming, realized this was not a request.

"Yes, happy to oblige."

He swiftly assessed this would fit into other plans.

"Dangerous part of the world, wretched insects, malaria, natives and other paraphernalia but you've done India and Mesopotamia, so this will be a walk in the park, or should I say jungle?"

"Could well be!"

Toto, drawn to share that South America was nothing like the examples given, realized the head of the Service was in no mood for splitting hairs.

"Had word the Soviets are building their gold reserves. We need to make sure the Germans hold a decent enough buffer zone against the Reds. Who's doing what and where? You know the drill."

Toto nodded.

"Another thing, between you and I, that man Norman has been poking his nose in over there with Rothschild. You'd do me a big favor if you found any dirt on his hands. He's been giving the impression he knows our team better than we do, but you never heard that from me. Not part of the brief but I'd appreciate anything you dig up. See Evelyn on the way out, she's all you need."

"I'll do my best."

"You will. Forgot to thank you for the Colombian assignment. Good work."

Quex added, quickly diverting his attention to some papers on the table, which was his way of closing meetings.

Toto made for the door. As he reached for the handle, his operational head added.

"Winston assured me, you understand the urgency. Seemed to feel you were the man for this. Good luck!"

Toto thanked Quex, closed the door behind him and confronted Sinclair's sister, Evelyn, standing directly in his path. Caught off balance, he complimented her on her fashion sense. She smiled, handed him papers, brief and travel documents.

The family resemblance was obvious, along with a healthy dose of eccentricity, he told himself, unlike the reality of her attire which was as far from a fashion statement as he could imagine.

"The Passport Control Officer in Santa Marta will be your contact," she advised him, still smiling.

It was as it always had been. He was not the first to recognize that. The passport control cover had never been redesignated, even though this so called secret was as open as if it had been headline news. Funny how unwilling Quex was to change protocol, even when covers were blown. No wonder Norman found it easy to extract information from some agents, while Sinclair, oblivious, took great exception to what he felt was a tight ship.

Dread washed over Toto imagining the twerp Buffett, who accosted him first time round, may have pushed up the ranks to agent in situ.

Anything was possible the way Quex controlled operations, he pondered, making his way back to Bromley and Olga.

His plan to tell her he was continuing the search finalizing the gold recovery was swiftly approved. Her fronting expenses involved in his cross-Atlantic adventure surprised him and meant financial security guaranteed, as an inflated figure covered any eventualities. The upcoming holidays afforded time with Adrian, an acceptable period of marital presence and for plotting the road map.

He briefed Adrian on what he could do in the Levant, especially Churchill's connections with Anglo-Persian Oil. He knew his son not only needed and deserved the break, but that he himself had to gather more material before he could usefully employ their twinned capabilities.

He wrote to McFadden, the contact Neily suggested, as the congressman had spent many years railing against the Fed. He informed him of his journey, promising to give notice when and where they could both meet. A long update to Vanderbilt also sent, as well as a note to Landmann suggesting they meet on his return in Frankfurt. Both Leila and Wilhelm had fled Germany, escaping the growing rise of the Nazis and Wilhelm had accepted a proposal to work with the League of Nations in Geneva.

The banana boat he sailed on, once again out of Avonmouth, afforded time to reflect and correlate research including where he was with his own life.

It was clear from his meetings with both Burnham and Churchill, there were powerful forces behind both political and financial control. He witnessed the machinations and power of the Rockefeller influence. It was obvious now they had been behind his failure. Those ranged to help him had turned out to be either directly in the pay of these forces or under enough control to do their bidding, in exchange for selfish ends. His greatest disappointment was how the press had been so fickle and so easily in the pay of power and influence. Yet Burnham's admission control for major decisions no longer stopped at the proprietor's desk confirmed these hidden hands working.

McFadden would be able to offer tremendous insight into the role of the Federal Reserve, its influence and dealings, so tightly operated through European founder members. Its pretensions, to be seen as an American arm of governance, were as laughable as if he declared himself a member of the Royal family. Why people seemed to be oblivious to this glaring anomaly would become clearer when he met the congressman.

Neily remained a trustworthy ally throughout. By his own admission he no longer wielded the financial clout of his peers, well aware Grace continued to make his lessening worth less influential by the month, yet his name still held currency. There was much Toto felt gratitude towards his American friend. Recognizing his own folly over the years, having given more than enough blind trust to those who later failed him, he recognized the area he was venturing into was one demanding utter discrimination, if he was to negotiate a way through. It looked to be a minefield, requiring skills second nature to his colleague, Thomas Brighton, the munitions wizard. If the family's genetic prowess in diplomacy were to prove an asset, he needed to access it in his own genetic strand and fast. He took comfort his antennae had sharpened considerably since his association with Nikola and the scientist's own unique observations and insights into the inter-connectedness of creation and its creatures.

His present involvement with the Secret Service made it clear both parties served mutual interest. That Norman was irritating Quex revealed the power base of the secret service was a leaky bucket. Not that he cared overly about the inside games played; he appreciated there were dirty players forcing through their own agendas. Claude Dansey was one of them. He hoped their paths would not cross again.

He was immensely pleased he and Adrian had reconnected. It gave reinvigorated purpose. Brother Louis and sister Leila had been there when he needed. Now they both set their ways on quiet retirement for one and release from a growing nationalist threat for the other. His present mission launched his own strength with an authority and conviction securing more reality than any past dreams he had conjured.

As the vessel pulled into Santa Marta, memories of Faviola flooded back. He had promised to return and be with her, yet that dream shattered when she broke his heart in New York. Barosso's mortal wound to his plans had never lessened the loss he felt at Faviola's betrayal. Perhaps the process he first came across, stationed in India, was kicking in.

Karma had sharp teeth he brooded.

Passing through immigration his fears were realized. Drayton Buffett, as cocky as ever approached him, grasped his right hand and welcomed him to Colombia.

"Follow me, we can get you on your way in no time."

Toto dreaded another wild ride through the streets of Santa Marta, so was surprised when he was hurriedly ushered to a chauffeur driven car and bundled into the back followed by Buffett.

"Got a brief from London, organized for you to fly down to Manaus, where our people are expecting you. Sorry about the haste but head office insisted it was urgent. How you managed to wangle a plane, I'll never know."

Toto himself was completely taken by surprise. However Manaus suddenly conjured all sorts of memories, most of them littered with the body of Faviola. Not expecting to be shuttled at such a speed he requested a favor of the go-between.

"Before we set off…"

"Just you, old man. I'm staying."

Toto relieved he did not have to spend any more time than necessary with this operative, continued.

"I need to contact one of my people here as soon as possible before flying."

"Of course, tell the driver where to go."

Toto did just that and the car sped off round a bend, across a small square and a few minutes later stopped outside a small indistinguishable entrance on a back street, far from the plush house the two had previously occupied. Toto got out, entered the building and allowed his eyes to become accustomed to the low light level. A shuffle of feet on stone floor raced to him from a side room.

"Capitano, welcome back," an old man's voice greeted him.

"Juan, it's good to see you again after all this time."

They embraced and Toto received a kiss on each cheek from the old retainer.

"*La signorita* said you would return. I also knew you would."

"It was a close call, Juan, and much has happened. Unfortunately *la signorita* is no longer part of my life."

"No longer?" Juan looked horrified at this news.

"She and Barosso arrived out of the blue in New York and put paid to my plans," Toto explained briefly, catching the old man's distraught look.

"This cannot be so."

"I'm afraid it is," the captain replied, not wishing to hurt the old man who had been so much part of his life in South America, as well as a solid support when he last was here with Faviola.

"I came here, hoping you were still here. I wanted to leave you a gift. Something I wished I'd done before. Something for your comfort in retirement."

Toto slipped an envelope containing twenty pounds, a small fortune locally, into Juan's hand. The old man trembled and endeavored to pass it back.

"No, it's the least I can do for you," Toto insisted.

"But you are wrong, Capitano."

"No, you deserve it," insisted the Englishman.

" You are wrong," insisted Juan, "about Faviola."

He pushed a smaller envelope into Toto's hand.

"Read, read!"

Toto obeyed and moved to a small window where the shade of a wall opposite reflected a soft light into the room.

He drew the note from the envelope and read words he never in his life would have imagined to be reading.

I knew you would return. I wait for you. New York was not as it seemed. You have NEVER broken my heart. Hurry to Manaus. You know where I am. I need you more than ever. Do not delay – Faviola

"When were you given this, Juan?"

"She left it for me when they came back from New York."

"They?" Toto queried. "Was Barosso with her?"

"Yes, not nice man, not nice man," spluttered the go-between. "She hurt bad, I cry," he added.

Toto was confused. Yet the elation of this news calmed his fury at what Barosso must have done and it made him even more determined to get to Manaus as soon as possible.

Good God, he thought, *what a stroke of luck to have wings with this as an imperative.*

Toto took the old man and hugged him again, with a gentleness Juan melted into.

"You know we may never meet again but I'll be eternally grateful you entered my life, an angel with such news," Toto shared feeling a deep connection.

The old man, to an outsider, may have appeared as just another worker, but his constancy and help earned him a special place in Toto's affections.

"I know, Capitano, I know. I thank you and may Santa Maria guard you on your journey."

With that he guided Toto to the entrance and waved him away until the car disappeared in dust and round the corner at the street end.

A small airstrip acting as the local aerodrome held the Junker, already ticking over. Buffett walked with Toto to it while outlining his itinerary.

"This will take you to Maracaibo in Venezuela and then on to meet a boat at Puerto Cabello. That will get you to Belém where we've organized another plane to take you to Manaus. Damn distances, anywhere takes ages. Gives you a week or two to get acclimatized. Any problems telegraph me."

Delivering his luggage to the handler, Toto was soon on board and on his roundabout way to Manaus. Divesting supplies and two other passengers at their first stop, he accompanied a virtually empty craft to rendezvous with the vessel, a cargo ship plying its way down the east coast.

A successful tie up at a very busy Belém hub with another Junker saw him arrive a couple of weeks later in Manaus. He reached the small hotel previously his base during his first unsuccessful project with glass bottomed boats. The owners greeted him as if his absence had been only months. Hard to believe it had been well over five years.

"Welcome Capitão, your room, as always, available," Estela, the plump yet bubbly wife of the owner, greeted him.

Happy to be back among such warm and kindhearted people, he was struck by how much he had missed this place. Outside the ever-bustling activity of a vibrant and courageous community refused to cower into accepting onerous conditions the Ford rubber enterprise forced on them. Its failure to appreciate not only local agriculture but also customs were to doom its growth. An invasion of American industry had developed mistrust and loathing of its inevitable exploitation. From Belém, Fordlandia to Manaus their offices found it more and more difficult to engage a workforce proud of its own identity. Local enterprise, and the welcome Toto received as a prodigal member of this community, confirmed his impression these people would be a hard adversary for even corporate giants to break.

Keen to reunite with Faviola, he determined to sort out transport needed to move into the interior where he had been instructed gold prospectors were at work. Estela could read his mind. Passing him a note, along with his returned papers, she winked knowingly.

"Now Estela she know what is written but word of warning: Barosso, very jealous man. Senses you come."

"Thanks for the warning," Toto replied.

He knew both Estela and her husband were steadfast in their loyalty to him. When his cowardice had him running from here, it was their united understanding that hearts are irrational, which supported the plight of both himself and Faviola, without judgment.

"I must first sort out the journey then meet with Faviola," he reassured his host.

She understood perfectly.

For all his arrogance and privileged colonial superiority, Toto granted Buffett kudos for somehow organizing a seamless connectivity for his travel arrangements into the jungle. This new link in the chain bagged him useful wings with water landing gear that would get them up the tributaries of the Amazon with ease.

He arranged to meet the flight crew at the aerodrome. There Arnaldo, the interpreter, speaking several tribal dialects which were essential for traversing and gaining permissions through their territories, gave him the rundown for the journey. All concerned had been briefed that Toto was a reporter from England chasing down the story and disappearance of Lt. Colonel Percy Fawcett, an archeologist and explorer last seen disappearing into the Amazon jungle in search of a lost golden city some years back. It was both handy and good cover for any enquiries he made around gold. The destination of Cuiabá, in the state of Mato Grosso, acted both as the kick off point for the explorer and also gathering point for the many *garimperos* attracted like moths to the gold flame of riches. These *garimperos*, as the locals called the prospectors, were eyed with both suspicion and contempt with the single saving grace they could offer work to otherwise unemployed local hands.

Toto, arrangements completed, decided a few sentimental days in Manaus, discovering the truth around what Faviola had indicated would be in order. However the bush telegraph had worked its usual efficiency and returning to the hotel he entered his room to find her perched on the edge of the bed. She looked dreadful. Her face, bruised, red and beaten made her almost unrecognizable. Toto was horrified. This was not the treacherous betrayer from Casa

271

Cauca, more a mortally wounded doe after a chase.

"What the hell happened to you?"

"You got my note?" Faviola asked, not taking in his question.

"Of course I got your note. Who did this to you is a far more pertinent question," he replied, pointing to her injuries and angry at her treatment.

"Are you angry?"

"Yes, at whoever did that to you. Who was it and why?"

He was as far from angry with her as was possible. Yet livid at what he saw in front of him.

"Tell me, how did you get into this state."

"Come, sit down. It's a long story."

"I've got time," he replied, impatiently pulling up a chair.

Faviola took his hands in hers, quite expecting him to withdraw them. Toto knew that was not going to happen, but was itching to hear what had happened.

She looked at him directly. He recognized the tenderness of all those months of morning love making in Colombia.

"Everything I did and said in New York was a lie."

"A lie? For God's sake you ruined everything I had there: reputation, relationships and prospects of returning a fortune to the family. You call that a lie?"

Toto tried to restrain himself, recognizing the anger he was resorting to had everything to do with what she had endured and nothing to what transpired in New York.

"Please listen," she implored, aware her explanation needed to be swift.

"I'm sorry, the anger was not meant against you but whoever did this to you," he assured her.

" Barosso. He blackmailed me."

"Blackmailed? More like beat you black and blue. Why?"

"He heard you were coming. I smiled at the news and he beat me. He has our baby kidnapped."

Toto was stunned, unable to take in what she had just said. His anger for Barosso was making him apoplectic on top of an admission out of the blue. He fought to control himself.

"Our baby, Barosso, kidnap?

Faviola realized she had laid too much on his plate. She breathed deeply, curled herself into a squat position on the bed and addressed the revelations one by one.

"Yes, your daughter from Manaus. She is the gift of our relationship," she admitted.

"My daughter?"

"After you left and went to New York I gave birth six months later. Barossa took me in and looked after us both. I naively felt it was best for Catarina. That is your daughter's name."

Toto was both shell-shocked at the revelation and confused about his nemesis, Barosso.

"You never told me any of this in Colombia. Could you not at least have admitted I was a father?"

"I could not. Barosso had her, swore she would be killed if I told you anything. I was so afraid, caught in loving you, yet unable to tell the truth."

"The old man whose plantation it was, that's a lie also or was he Barosso?"

"No," she replied softly, he was connected to him and was persuaded to teach me all I needed to know, I found out later. He really taught me the trade."

"So let me get this straight. Barosso took you in, used the child, our child as hostage to get you set up in Colombia, to be there for my arrival. I come looking for suitable partners for our coffee venture and just happen to land on your doorstep, very convenient. My question is: how the hell did Barossa know I would be coming, give you time to train up and be ready to set me up again?"

"You did not know I was there?"

"How could I? You were the last person I expected to see. Why the hell would I expect you in Colombia? I was there to get a business rolling, after you and he ruined me in America. Seems Barosso was not content to let me off with killing one business project. He was after so much more. But why?"

Faviola, in evident distress, started to see the web of intrigue open before them.

"How did you land on my estate? That seems pre-planned."

" I had some contacts from Willy but your whereabouts were not part of his list."

"Then your Wilhelm can be ruled out," she added.

Toto started at her use of *your Wilhelm*. There was innocence in her describing Willy that way.

"He would be the very last person to betray me. Inconceivable. No, it was," he thought a moment and then the penny dropped. "Yes, that's it, Buffett gave me a couple of contacts he said London asked to investigate, when I

273

arrived in Santa Marta. Yours was one. Shit, I don't believe it. Never had a good feeling about that prat."

"Why would he do that?" Faviola asked.

Toto wondered why the hell Buffett would have reason to be involved. Was he merely a new Service placement?

"You knew this man Buffett?" Faviola asked.

"No, only our second meeting. Never did warm to him."

Toto's mind was spinning wildly.

"Who in London would get involved in this, pass on the information and why?"

"These people in London. What do they do?" she asked.

He had not counted on telling her that part of his involvement with the Secret Service. It had seemed irrelevant. Yet looking at her sitting there black, bruised and the result of his association somehow now bringing her into that part of his life, he decided to tell her.

"National security."

Faviola gasped, not quite understanding but took a guess.

"National security? Does that mean spy?"

"For a country girl you're pretty smart," he replied, finding himself smiling for the first time since they met.

"We have spies here as well. Especially Americans arriving from the rubber plantations."

Toto realized this woman to be someone very special. He began to appreciate how he managed to catch up with her, in spite of circumstances presently looking so inopportune. He looked at her, feeling the love for her, then acutely realizing she needed someone to tend the injuries.

"Oh, God you need to have those wounds looked at. Is the rest of your body in good shape?"

She smiled.

"I have dreamed for too long to show you my body. As for my face, it's fine. It will heal, not the first time. That *desgraçado* will pay."

"Probably understand what that means without translation."

"Bustard, you say?"

Toto laughed.

"I think you mean bastard. Bustard is a bird and Barosso's no bird. He's a pig and they don't fly."

Her laughter at his image lightened the mood. Toto got up from his chair and moved to the window looking onto the street below. Women carrying wicker baskets of fruit on their heads, wearing multicolored dresses, swept along to the square where they would replenish their pitches. The morning heat set its mean to last the day. Others scurried along, as he half expected to glimpse Barosso's men staking out the hotel.

"Does he know you're here?"

"I made sure no."

"Is he holding Catarina?"

"He never lets her out of his sight. I told him I was going to the market and slipped out without anyone seeing."

"You've got to get completely away from that man. Your, I mean, our daughter as well."

He could not quite get used to owning his own creation but he knew this time he had no intention of not doing so.

She looked to him, helpless, unable to construct an answer.

"This is what you're going to do," he continued, fully owning actions as events demanded. "You're going to go back."

"No please, I cannot, please," she implored.

"You have to, for Catarina," he ordered. "Go back, collect some fruit on the way, act normal as if you have done what you said you'd do. Is there anything apart from the child you need from there?"

"Nothing," she replied. "Just you, me and Catarina."

"I'm going to get Estela to find some clothes for you both. She knows you well so no problem there. Also we must get some suitable clothes for the jungle."

"Jungle?" Faviola gasped.

"Long story. There's plenty of time to tell you why, as we fly. Important thing for now is to get you far away from that *desgraçado*."

Faviola smiled at how he took so easily to her tongue and admired him for it. She also felt far better protected now he rose to the challenge of devising escape from a torture she had endured for years.

"Does Barosso go out on his own during the day?" Toto asked.

"Every morning. He goes to the cantina for coffee and meets close associates."

"Every morning?" Toto quizzed. "At what time?"

"Yes, at seven thirty, except Sundays when he goes to church for confession."

"The priest must work overtime with a whole dossier on his sins! This is what we do. Tomorrow, when he leaves for the cantina, I shall pull up in the street behind you and we'll go straight to the aircraft."

"We fly?"

"Yes, we fly"

"Never flown!" Faviola mouthed with trepidation.

"There'll be many things from today you have never done before," he reassured her.

On that she trusted him implicitly.

"Tell me, everything we did in Colombia, was that real?

"Every little thing," she replied with the reassurance of a kiss blown across the room. He moved towards her. She rose and they met. He ran his open palm cautiously over the bruises and marks on her face, so gently as to not draw pain. He then drew her closer and kissed each mark.

Her eyes met his. "Medicine?" she asked.

"Healing," he assured her as their lips met and they embraced with passion. As they broke a long hold, Toto moved to open the door.

"Let Estela take you through the back, just in case eyes are on the front. Hurry, collect some fruit and vegetables and I'll see you at just before eight in the morning.

Faviola left.

He gathered his things and went down to rejoin Estela who had ushered her out through the back door.

"Capitão, if only I had a gallant knight as you."

"You have Ernesto, a fine man and dutiful. Both of you are angels on earth."

Estela made to swoon at his poetry as he offered a peck on her cheek.

"Now we need clothes for the two of them, not too many but good for travel and I'll also need Alberto's services tomorrow early to drive us. I'll inform the others we leave in the morning."

He turned to walk over to where Arnaldo was staying. As he passed familiar haunts he had got used to when gearing up the tourist business, he remembered the virulent hatred even then Barosso had thrown in his path. At every turn the journalist had resented his English counterpart's success integrating into the local society.

How had he then weaseled his way into a position of consular activity in, of all places, New York? Toto wondered.

Undoubtedly offered all sorts of inducements to grease his pole. Well, if all went well all three of them would be rid of him for good in a day or so.

The next morning Toto stood at the desk, with Estela handing him a strong travel bag containing everything the other two would need. Alberto outside waited for his ride.

'This telegram came early," Estela said as she handed a sheet to Toto.

"We'll miss all of you, keep us informed where you are, even if it's the other side of the world," she pleaded with a little tear in her eye.

Toto pocketed the message.

"*Muito obrigado*, dearest Estela for all your loving help."

"Capitão Trapman, it is you we should be thanking. Our dearest Faviola can at last be where her dreams have rested all these years. Remember us to Catarina, she will become as beautiful as her mother," she replied, pressing softly both his arms with her overworked hands.

Toto hugged her and held her for a few moments. Ernesto entered from the back and placed a large, all encompassing embrace around the two of them.

"We have a saying in Brazil," he offered. "*Que saudade*, meaning we miss you terribly already, but now you must rush. Alberto will take good care."

Toto grabbed the bags, slipped an envelope into Ernesto's hand, got into the passenger seat and the two of them drove away. As they made their way along the street behind Barosso's house, a man in a white suit walked past the alley he knew Faviola would exit. The white suit looked back as the car stopped and then resumed his journey.

"No problem," assured Alberto.

As arranged Faviola swept out from the little alleyway, holding the hand of a dark haired, light complexioned beauty of a five year old and a small case in the other. Toto's heart stopped.

My daughter, he marveled, *my daughter*.

Faviola leapt into the back seat with Catarina slamming the door closed and Alberto sped off.

They were soon beside the plane on the grass runway and before they placed all the bags into the hold, the pilot had started to warm the engines. Arnaldo urged them all to climb in and moments later the plane left the runway and circled over the vast expanse of the black-brown confluence created by the Rio Negro and Rio Solimões.

"Have you seen anything as beautiful as those twins birthing the Amazon?" Toto asked as Faviola and Catarina's eyes were both on stalks, at an unimaginable sight neither ever considered would have been their experience. Catarina squashed her nose on the window as the plane banked. Almost as if she wanted to burst out and fly into the scene below. She settled for rounds of bubbling giggles.

Faviola drank in the magnificence of the meeting of the waters before turning to Toto and replied.

"Yes I have. The three of us together."

She looked down at Caterina, who had fallen back into her seat, wearing the biggest smile. The little girl began to stare at the stranger sitting opposite her. She scrutinized Toto in detail, from his hands to feet and up to his head for a full minute.

"Papai?" she finally asked.

"Yes, Catarina, I am your Daddy. Papai!" he answered with immense pride.

CHAPTER FORTY-FOUR

A telegram arrived from London and waited at the port office where it was collected later by Buffett. He read it, ordered the clerk reply immediately and handed back a hand-written note:

CONTACT ADVISED STOP TARGET IDENTIFIED STOP WILL CONFIRM LOSS STOP.

He sauntered over to the bar, close to the customs house and threw a snort of tequila down his throat for a job well done.

Barosso arranged two of his men track Toto's movements and report back when they had discovered his itinerary. Returning home, he called to Faviola to prepare lunch. He was met with silence. Moving from room to room, his irritation rose with each empty space. Racing upstairs he was confronted by Catarina's unmade bed and several articles of clothing strewn across the floor of the bedroom where Faviola slept. It was obvious they were nowhere to be found. Returning to the ground floor, he shouted to the cook.

"Where the hell are they?"

"Eu não sei!" cried the terrified cook, knowing ignorance of their whereabouts could easily elicit a sharp slap from Barosso. Too agitated, he rushed from the house, just as one of his henchmen ran towards him. He knew the news was bad.

"The hotel staff said the Capitão left early this morning with all his bags."

"Check the aerodrome. See if the flight has left."

The man stood his ground.

"Get on with it," Barosso screamed.

"It left with four passengers, senhor, three hours ago."

Barosso knew exactly who three of them were.

"Get Rolando and a plane here immediately. Get their flight plan from the air controller now!" he screamed.

As much as planes were not common currency in these parts, he had enough clout with the staff at the Fordlandia office to make sure the plantation made one available when he commanded. He also knew his coffee that morning had cost him at least a two-day head start as well as any last vestige of control over Faviola and her daughter.

Toto, well aware his rescue of Faviola would certainly elicit revengeful action from Barosso, covered them all by slipping the air controller a handsome bung instructing him to advise anyone asking after their flight plan to say they disappeared in the direction of Cuiabá. They meanwhile headed to Itaituba on the banks of the Tapajós River. Here Arnaldo arranged to pick up boats and several local hands that would accompany them up river towards where various prospectors had been observed heading. Those returning from Fordlandia spread news there was gold to be found in the sandy banks and tributaries running into the river. Toto also heard through European contacts that amongst those looking for gold were indeed insalubrious creatures happy to be in the pay and supply of both Bolsheviks and Nazis alike with their trove.

The plane dropped them then headed back the fifty odd miles to Fordlandia, where its flight went relatively unnoticed. Toto and his party made their way by boat up river, to investigate. For little Catarina the flight, although a life-defining moment, took second place to her love of the river. Both adults knew it was impossible to dissuade her presence on the journey upstream.

Arnaldo's knowledge of local tribal dialects helped them tap local knowledge. Equipped with essential supplies easily sourced so close to the rubber center, they set off with provisions, tents and protection against the usual suspects of the forest. The appearance of what might well have been taken for a family day out along the banks of the upper reaches of the Thames, here in the Amazon fell into the category of lunatic *brancos* in search of impossible dreams to invisible eyes of tribesmen tracking them along their route. Since leaving the relatively populated lower reaches of the river, those with far greater right of residency observed every movement from deep within the jungle.

"I don't wish to frighten you but there are eyes watching us."

"Eyes?" Toto queried.

"Yes. They've followed us for the last day or so."

"Who?" Toto asked.

"I cannot be certain but likely the Munduruku. It's not surprising, as we're in their territory. As long as we keep ourselves to ourselves there's no problem."

Toto felt reassured, though he had no compass to measure that against, save Arnaldo was an honest type.

Their journey up river took several days to reach tributaries flowing into the Tapajós. Reaching one of them they steered the boat towards the bank, climbed out and made way on foot along its edge. One of the men sent scouting ahead returned later with news of a group of *garimperos* camped further up employing a dozen or so locals to pan in the water and sandbanks. They pitched camp well away from them and Toto and Arnaldo, equipped with pistols and some surveying equipment, brought along as cover, investigated who these people were. Faviola and the rest remained in camp.

Being surprised by unannounced strangers made even the most honest prospector highly nervous in these regions, so the two of them decided to call out before they were spotted. It had the effect of bringing two heavily armed Europeans racing to where their cry came from. Coming into view one of them, seeing Toto, asked in German what the hell he was doing there. Arnaldo looked to Toto to manage this language barrier. Toto replied in English, feeling it diplomatic and also to discover if the fellow spoke it.

"We're here on a survey of local habitats," he said with as much seriousness as he could muster.

"English?"

"Yes," replied Toto having established the German could.

The prospector was a solid built, brute of a man, with few softening features. A pockmarked face gave no indication whether he had collected years of attack from the insects in these parts or were merely birth defined. Either way he was not someone Toto wished to mess with. His sidekick was shorter and stockier and made up for his stature adopting a bellicose attitude, encouraged by two revolvers, one in each hand.

"I'm sorry to come upon you like this, we're not here to cause trouble. It'd be good if your friend there could drop his guns," Toto implored the taller of the two.

"We don't appreciate strangers here," he said firmly. "Especially Europeans like yourself. So it would be best for you to turn round and go back from where you came."

The menace in his voice was not encouraging. Arnaldo followed as much as his little English allowed. He spoke softly in Portuguese to Toto.

"Tell him there are Indians watching us and best we not argue amongst ourselves for everyone's safety." Toto caught the drift of what he was told.

He realized the German and his sidekick had no knowledge of the language and conveyed what he understood the message to mean. It spooked the two of them and their attitude relented.

"So how can we help you, then?" the man replied.

Relieved he had broken ice, Toto suggested they join the campfire in the distance and get to know each other over a brew. With that he theatrically withdrew a small tin of tea from his pocket and presented it to the German.

"Bloody British, you die drinking tea," he said bursting into laughter.

The Englishman hoped he would not and diplomatically also laughed. Arnaldo, once again, impressed by his white man's creativity at moments of potential hazard, laughed as well.

Arriving at the campfire, with the workers panning endlessly ahead of them, Franz, the taller prospector gave the two visitors a potted history of their attempts to find gold along this part of the Amazon. Comfortable neither of them were interested in the same line of business, his mood became much more amiable. His sidekick remained on taut guard.

"Don't worry about the Rottweiler," he said pointing to his partner. "He neither speaks English nor drops his guard. A useful man to have at one's side here."

Toto could agree with that, as long as he was not on the receiving end.

Franz continued.

"These alluvial banks hold good deposits. It's what attracts many to infest these rivers. The water is high at this time of year making tributaries deliver more."

"Are you collecting for yourself or do you sell it on?" Toto casually inquired, having listened to Franz dispense enough of his own tales to be more relaxed to an inquisitive stranger's digging.

"Of course, I keep some but most goes to those who pay us good money for weight in Fordlandia."

The name caught Toto's interest, hoping not to show his host further interest, asked.

"So rubber has sidelines?"

"*Ach nein*," Franz slipped back into German. "There are those who are far more interested buying as much gold as they get their hands on from prospectors, to take home to Germany."

"I thought Fordlandia was an American set up?" Toto queried.

"That Herr Ford has very close associations with our leaders, so do not be fooled it's just American interests. The company has huge investments growing in Germany and the rubber here is needed both in the States as well as Europe, so becomes a useful channel for gold."

"I suppose so," replied Toto nonchalantly, happy to establish solid evidence the reports of gold had been substantiated. He was keen also to find out how much the German himself had found.

"I've been working for eighteen months in this hellhole and have made it worth every mosquito bite," he admitted, helping Toto understand his hunch to be correct, not only concerning the quantity of gold but also his complexion.

"You go upstream and there are at least nine other large prospectors at work," the gold miner added. " We keep a good distance between us, although working for the same purchasers, our finds are our own."

Toto was very grateful to Franz for saving him a lot of legwork. He knew a trip to Fordlandia would easily confirm not only the buyers but also expose precisely who were the end users.

Arnaldo, having drifted away from the others, returned with an obvious urgency. He directed his concern to Toto.

"There's movement in the forest. I don't like it. We need to move back closer to the main river. It's soon dark. We must be quick."

The Germans picked up on his anxiety.

"What the hell's going on?" Franz demanded.

Toto explained and suggested they all move back towards the river for the night.

"We have guns, those natives will be no trouble," the prospector stated with an arrogant confidence.

"We're not talking about a few," Toto informed him. "These are people utterly at home in these conditions and there are many of them. Safety in numbers always worked for me and that's been true wherever I've found myself in the world."

The German, impressed with Toto's authority, reluctantly agreed and they struck camp and headed back to where he had left Faviola and the others. Although surprised to see a woman and child, the prospectors felt a lot safer with their greater numbers. Arnaldo proceeded to post lookouts throughout the night and the group was able to rest soundly.

It was not the normal jungle cacophony of nature arousing Toto from sleep the next morning. A distant drone caught his ear and was anything but natural. He was not alone in catching it, as the two Germans, already up, were alerted by it. Sending three of the workers to the main river to investigate, as the sound became louder, Franz immediately recognized its provenance.

"That's a Junker engine or I'm a cabbage," he announced in German.

Toto smiled at the fellow's unwitting self-deprecation at the same time wondering who was arriving. By now the others were awake and already by the fire helping themselves to coffee. He decided it best to go down and investigate. Franz insisted accompanying him, even if just to gather his workers back.

Faviola pushed a mug at Toto, insisting he drink before venturing out. He took a gulp and together the two men set off towards the growing volume emanating from the river.

Just before breaking through, arriving at the bank, he parted dense vegetation to see the three workers gesticulating towards an aircraft, complete with floating landing gear, make its way towards the river's edge. One passenger, standing on one float, shouted directions to the pilot. The nose edged round and made for a sandbank near where the workers stood. As it grounded the navigator jumped down and secured an anchor into the bank as a precautionary measure.

"Those don't look like prospectors nor from the rubber plantation," whispered Franz, cautious their presence would not draw attention.

Toto's face reflected horror as he recognized the next one to exit the plane, followed closely by a heavyset gangster type.

"Shit," he exclaimed.

Franz turned to Toto, whose complexion had lost any color.

"You know these men?"

"Too bloody well I do and they're real trouble. We must to get back to the others."

As he said that the two heavies approached the three workers who immediately pointed towards where Toto and Franz were hidden.

Toto grabbed the German by his sleeve.

"Get out of here now. *Schnell*!" he hissed.

As the two of them turned and raced back, three shots rang out.

Breathing heavily they arrived at the camp, where the others, startled at their sudden reappearance, rushed to them.

The short German looked at his partner.

"Where are the others?" he blurted in German.

"Dead," Fritz said, still stunned at what he had witnessed.

Toto grabbed Faviola.

"We have to get into the jungle. Barosso has bloody found us."

"How, what, it's not possible?"

"I don't know how but he's here. They've just shot the three workers in cold blood and they're coming for us."

"Mãe, what's happening?" Catarina tugged urgently on Faviola's arm.

Faviola, confused and scared in equal measure at the proximity of Barosso, changed gear and responded.

"Come, we're going to play a game in the forest," she told her daughter.

Arnaldo, used to sudden preparedness, grabbed his weapons, instructed the helpers to go with Faviola and look after them, no matter what. He then gave them each pistols. The remaining workers rushed back towards where their own camp had been, as Franz, his gun-slinging partner and Toto, hid from view.

Faviola cast a last look at Toto, before he gesticulated they disappear deeper. Arnaldo stayed beside Toto.

"No, go with Faviola, I trust you better looking after them and you've firepower. Now go!"

He obeyed, disappearing with the others into deep undergrowth.

Toto could hear Barosso shouting at his henchmen as they clambered through the bush towards the camp. They arrived at the burning fire.

"They're here, spread out and bring me the Englishman. He'll watch as I kill the woman and child," roared Barosso.

Franz's Rottweiler could take no more. Without a word he burst cover and shot dead the hulk that had left the aircraft last. He rushed Barosso but was cut down swiftly by a bullet from the other gangster.

"They're there," cried Barosso, as the two of them stormed towards the spot the German had rushed out from. Toto and Fritz already knew they had to get the hell out of there. They rushed at an angle opposite to that Faviola had taken, as Barosso chased after them. Both men struggled to make it through the undergrowth. It became more impenetrable the deeper they went. Barosso's screams were close on their heels. Suddenly a very thin and trampled path confronted them.

Was this made by the natives? Toto found himself thinking.

No time to wonder about that, he told himself, *just run.*

Shots whistled past them.

"That's close," Fritz shouted, as the two men scrambled deeper through the undergrowth.

Although still early, the humidity caused them both to sweat profusely, along with the exertion they had to make.

"Split up, you go that way," Toto ordered, pointing to his right.

They split in a Y direction from each other. Somehow, Franz found himself doubling back and running towards the two pursuers.

"*Scheisse!*" he hissed, crouching down.

The goon with Barossa cut through the undergrowth in front of them and came into view. Raising his pistol, having spotted Franz move, the German stood up and got his shot in first. The goon fell hard. Barosso shot right back and Franz fell dead onto the jungle floor he so loathed.

Toto heard the shots and stopped. Should he turn back and investigate who was dead, or keep running? Where the hell was he anyway? He could hear no sound from Faviola. Then, as if to make up his mind for him, undergrowth crackled on his left. He ran away from it, towards what he imagined to be the river. Crashing through the undergrowth, plants whipped his body and slapped his face. A gunshot cracked behind him. He felt the bullet whistle past him. Suddenly his foot hit a small branch lying in his path and sent him flying. His ankle shot a lightning bolt of pain through his leg.

"Bugger," he cursed, realizing his mobility was ruined.

He rolled over onto his back only to come face to face with the sickening grin of Barosso wielding his revolver above him.

"You bastard Capitão, looks like this godforsaken jungle claims another *branco* for its own. Pity, I would have loved you watch your love slaughtered in front of you, alongside that little bastard child. Still I shall find her soon and tell her you squealed for mercy before I shot you."

Toto felt for his weapon. Barosso raised a foot and kicked it away into the bushes.

"Well, I shall not be sorry to lose this bullet," exclaimed the diplomat.

He raised his gun – Toto mentally shot a message of love to Faviola and resigned himself to the inevitable *coup de grâce*. He stared defiantly at his nemesis and the finger on the trigger. An audible hiss followed by an immediate, heavy thud presented Toto with the image of Barosso standing rigid with a near six-foot arrow passed right through him. He rolled away as the man's body fell heavily next to him. It was one of the very few times he decided to offer up a prayer to Santa Maria or whoever else he ought to direct his gratitude to. It was then he realized his face was buried deep in the forest foliage and several ants were becoming far too interested. Struggling to raise himself onto his knees, a hand grabbed him. Looking up, he came face to face with an Indian with painted face, feathered headdress and a quizzical look toward him.

"Useful to have eyes in the right place," he heard Arnaldo's voice utter from behind.

He looked round and sure enough there was Arnaldo. Behind him Faviola, who rushed past the guide towards her man, supported by the Indian.

"Are you shot?" she asked, frantic with worry.

"Twisted ankle, I think. Not shot," he replied overjoyed to be reunited with them both.

Catarina wandered over to where Toto stood, looked up at the painted

Indian and giggled. The tribesman looked back at her and smiled.

"How did you find me?" Toto asked, trying to understand how his luck had been served.

"We heard shots, ran in their direction and came across these Munduruku tribesmen. This warrior ran fast and dealt the blow, having understood Arnaldo's explanation that Barosso was the evil eye. "

"God, I'm so happy Barosso didn't shoot, as he assured me he would then kill the both of you."

"It's over. Now we must get out of here as quickly as possible. This is not somewhere we want to live!" Faviola smiled at her lover.

Arnaldo came over.

"I cannot thank you enough," Toto said.

"What happened to the Germans?"

"They were both shot," Toto replied. "If we hurry we can persuade the pilot to fly us all back to Fordlandia. Our work here is done," Toto suggested.

"I've already sent the men back to hold it for us."

"Good man Arnaldo, I knew I could rely on you," Toto thanked him as Faviola relieved the Indian of her man.

The Indians swiftly disappeared back into the forest, leaving Toto and the others to return via their makeshift camp, to collect what remained, then back to the river and out of there. Arnaldo accompanied them, instructing the others return by the boats. As the plane lifted off from the river and began its turn around back towards the rubber factory, Catarina played with a rough pouch.

"What have you there?" asked her mother.

"Stones," she replied, opening the pouch.

With her little hand she took her mother's palm and opened it. She poured some of the stones into her open hand.

Toto looked over and recognized a handful of what he immediately knew to be gold nuggets.

"Where the dickens did you get those?" he gasped in surprise.

"The big man's tent," she replied innocently.

Faviola looked at Toto, as she translated. Toto stared back at her, amazed at his daughter's audacity.

"She certainly learns early how to look after her mother!" he admitted.

"And her father," Faviola added, kissing him gently on each cheek and hugging him.

CHAPTER FORTY FIVE

Fordlandia afforded enough time for Toto to ask a few questions, determine the gold shipments were destined for Germany, not Russia and, using Faviola's charm and beauty, an opportunity to wheedle out of the transport department the full log of receiver details in Hamburg. She also squeezed out of their unsuspecting, yet salivating accountant passage for all three of them on a chartered tramp steamer about to leave for Rio. That rounded off mission success.

The slow boat down the coast to Rio afforded ample time to plan next moves. On arrival in Rio they made their way inland and behind a small community at Magé, purchased a smallholding, thanks to the find Catarina had sequestered from the dead prospector. Here Toto and Faviola settled, spending several months rebuilding the relationship both felt had been lost forever. Toto expanded his research on the elements of financial and political control he had uncovered.

His trip to the States and a meeting with congressman Louis McFadden was essential. Correspondence confirmed they meet in Key West and with a flight arranged he was ready to leave. He shared his whole story with Faviola, a decision he came to, following his departure from Colombia. Informing her the marriage he had with Olga, would end and they would be free to be together. Well aware of the dangers she faced, Faviola released him in full confidence that would be the outcome.

"We came away with gold in the end," he reminded Faviola, "perhaps not the fortune owed us, but more than enough to take care of you while I'm away and serve us on my return."

"Wish you would stay, we both do," Faviola pleaded.

"I must finish this work, too many depend on this getting out. Here the government is already imprisoned with Rothschild and Norman loans. We have to stop these banks subjugating freedom into debt."

"I trust you to complete this. Just return soon."

"I'll be back in the spring," Toto assured her.

"Come back, Papai, teach me more English," Catarina implored him.

Congressman McFadden had been a thorn in the side of the Federal Reserve Bank and its founders, since inception. For a decade as Chairman of the House Committee on Banking and Currency, he had watched how the Fed manipulated power, increased its cajoling of Presidents creating laws and amendments assuring their ascendency.

In a letter to Neily, Toto told him of arrangements to meet McFadden. Vanderbilt offered the yacht as a meeting point, the congressman happily agreeing. Indulging in the service PanAm offered of a flying boat to the Florida Keys, Toto met the others. The yacht then cruised up the coast, as all three relaxed into days of sharing their collective research. The sky played out symphonies of dusky colors, reflecting evenings of stunning October canvases, offsetting clear blue days.

McFadden, away from Washington and his oversight, relaxed and opened up on observations of the Fed. Normally fastidious in his presentation, reflecting many characteristics common to having spent a life in and around banking, this break on the high seas allowed him to crack the mold.

"You realize this whole thing was no accident. It was a carefully contrived occurrence. The international bankers sought to bring about a condition of despair here so they might emerge to rule with an even tighter grip on us all."

"Everything my research unearthed brings me to the same conclusion. True both in England and Europe," Toto replied.

"They're hell-bent on creating a world system of financial control in private hands able to dominate the political system of each country and the economy of the world as a whole," McFadden explained.

"What's their end goal?" Toto asked.

"To create a single system where everyone is controlled in feudalistic fashion by central banks of the world acting in concert, through secret agreement. It's why the Bank of International Settlements was set up in Switzerland. An *über* bank, if you will."

Neily listened to his two friends, preferring not to participate; however McFadden directed his next offering to him.

"You realize Neily most, if not all, of your peers to be puppets of this whole charade."

Neily shifted uncomfortably.

"I realize big money always looks for its own interests and the Vanderbilt name is considered part of that big money."

Toto recognized Neily's position and asked.

"How do you feel with all this, being in the camp of the problem?"

Vanderbilt smiled.

"My family's up there with the Rockefellers, Harrimans and Morgans, sure. However although the blood runs in my veins I am, and always have been, the black sheep. Started when I married Grace. I suppose you could say she became the drain into which any wealth I inherited began to disappear. As a rather devout coward, I have this yacht as my escape from all I loathe and she loves – so gentlemen you can see I'm hardly an appropriate chip off the old block!"

"We entirely appreciate that," McFadden responded encouragingly. "Confronted with such evil, everyone who can must play their part overcoming it. Albert has done sterling work complimenting my own research."

He proceeded to remove his studious-looking round spectacles, balanced on his nose, polishing their lenses with a handkerchief. He may have enjoyed sporting casual shorts and a light shirt, but the habits of keeping clear focus remained close at hand. Dusk's chill and sea breeze had him reach for a jacket he brought to the table. Toto raised a glass of chilled Chablis procured through Neily's contacts and took a satisfying draught.

"I've respected, for some time, your tenacity in seeking accountability for these forces, Louis, and for my own part been lucky enough to have the likes of Churchill help me understand more about the global implications."

"Beware wolves in sheep's clothing, Albert," McFadden cut in.

"What are you implying?" Toto answered, surprised at the politician's remark.

"Did it ever occur to you Churchill is virtually bloodline to Rothschild? Father died owing nearly quarter of a million dollars, mostly loaned him by Natty Rothschild. Then Winston, when in government, paid back favors by re-equipping your navy to run on Rothschild oil interests."

"My research is slipping. Of course that's why Churchill had such a close association with Anglo-Persian oil!" Toto admitted.

"The Rothschild family is one major force behind all this, controlling, their American lapdog, Morgan and their parasitic money men. Rockefeller dances to their tune for the usual kickbacks and the hyenas on Wall Street concoct a crash, driving the country into a depression large enough to sink us and fill their pockets."

"Are you saying they control that much of the political establishment?" Toto remarked.

"They're everywhere, are they not Neily?" McFadden turned to Vanderbilt.

"I've seen with my own eyes, heard those supported by the eight families conjure up all sorts of nonsense to persuade Congress and our representatives to pass everything, making it easier for them to get richer. Blackmail is a most regularly used tool of convenience. With so many compromised and held to ransom, their task of persuasion gives them a relatively smooth ride."

"Neily's correct," agreed McFadden. "Most people think the Federal Reserve Banks are United States Government institutions. They're nothing of the sort. Owned by foreign interests they're the very treason our founding fathers warned us against. They're private monopolies preying upon the people for the benefit of themselves and foreign customers; foreign and domestic speculators and swindlers; rich and predatory moneylenders. Do not think for one moment they look after the common people."

"Churchill told me Baldwin's promise to Rothschild of a Jewish State got you lot to come in to lengthen and win the war," Toto shared, enjoying freshly caught lobster laid in front of them.

McFadden's mood became noticeably livelier.

"Not only that, apart from there never having been a need for us to get involved in that fiasco, just more manipulation. Today, the amount of gold bleeding from our coffers, exported to Germany, in quiet support of Hitler, is criminal."

"I witnessed Germans scratching for gold in Brazil," Toto shared.

"That compared to the billions in gold from here is peanuts," McFadden added with a mocking laugh.

"How do we alert the American people to this travesty?" Neily asked.

"I'm concluding my research, now unhampered with chairmanship, and will place all my findings before Congress very soon," the congressman assured him.

"Once I've dug into what's going on in Germany, the relation the City of London has and Norman's meddling, I'll get my findings published," Toto assured the others.

"I can tell you" McFadden confided. "That man Norman is so deeply ensconced with the families. His manipulation of Strong and Harrison and with Rockefeller's help was what brought it all crashing down."

"No wonder my little escapade was just smoke and mirrors," Toto added.

"Damn right it was. You still deserve repayment, but with what they're now spending on gearing up for another war..."

"Louis, are you telling us there's going to be another war?" Toto asked.

"Well money was never so well invested as for war."

"Well invested?" Toto butted in incredulously.

"Please Albert, don't be so naive. The only ones making money, ever, in war are arms manufacturers and those backing both sides in the conflict," the politician confirmed.

"Rothschild played that game with Napoleon against Wellington, and had their fingers in every other conflict since," Toto replied.

McFadden, pleased to be amongst friends who could see the destruction wrought on his country, felt reassured.

"The Federal Reserve, executing orders of the Rothschild cartel, has cheated the Government of the United States and its people out of enough money to pay the national debt, probably several times over."

"Hardly Federal," added Neily.

"Nor anything like a Reserve!" McFadden added, with great bitterness.

The three of them agreed to Neily's suggestion to tack up the coast, back to New York under Vanderbilt colors.

Shortly before reaching New York, Toto, arranging his things, dug into a pocket of trousers he had with him since Manaus. It revealed a crumpled telegram. How it had been overlooked, he had no idea. He read it and could not believe his eyes.

UTMOST CAUTION STOP BUFFETT WORKS FOR ROCKEFELLER STOP NOT SERVICE STOP Z.

He had completely overlooked what could have been life-saving information. It was signed Z – being Dansey's code name. Why would he take such a personal interest, let alone care, as well as know his movements. Last time they met, he swore he never wanted to see Dansey again. Apart from this reappearing ghost, things were falling neatly into place. He climbed back deck-side. The other two beckoned him over. Both were in good spirits.

It was Neily who picked up Toto's concern.

"You look like you met a sea monster down there," he joked.

"A monster for sure," he replied, drawing up a seat.

"You know I told you about Barosso meeting a sticky end chasing us into the jungle, well I just found this."

He pushed it across the table.

"Received it shortly before leaving Manaus, stuffed it in a pocket and forgot about till now, months later. How I never spotted it sooner I'll never know."

"Maybe clean your pants more often," Neily laughed.

Toto appreciated his lightness.

"Who or what is this Z sign off?"

"It's the code name of another agent. One I had no desire to hear from, but that's another story."

"Well he was happy to contact you from London."

"No, he's in Italy. Assigned there," Toto corrected.

"So he's an agent, seems to know what's going on and felt for your safety enough to warn you." Neily summarized.

"Sort of chap I'd be grateful to have my back," interjected McFadden. "With as many daggers aimed at mine each time I open my mouth, I'd appreciate that sort of warning!"

They all laughed.

"Explains why Barosso hadn't finished with you," Neily continued.

" Looks like he already turned Buffett the first time you arrived in Colombia, then set you up when you returned. Heard you were coming back, deduced you'd be curious locating Faviola. Your note from the old man confirms that. Once you left, Buffett telegraphed your arrival."

Toto pondered the chain of events.

"Barosso set me up in New York. Buffet works for Rockefeller who gets Barosso to ruin my plan, while getting his revenge, gets me out of the way, crash runs its course Boom! Boom!"

McFadden listened, intrigued. He felt it time to introduce some further jigsaw pieces.

"You were sent out there, as you explained earlier, to find how much gold was shipping to Germany and Russia. We get our crash, gold leaves here in its millions, engineered by Rothschild's. Ford, Rockefeller and other corporate interests push their agendas in Germany. Is there no end to these blood suckers?"

Toto nodded in agreement.

"In your position watching the bankers, getting to know their underhand plans, I can understand why they have it in for you."

"Not only that Toto," Neily chipped in. "So much business is transacted in the club. If you're not part of the club, then get a whiff of what goes on, most times you're toast."

Toto brightened.

"No wonder Skull and Bones, Delta Pheta and the rest become breeding grounds for suitable frontmen for their plans, yet the real club and influence is within the eight families."

McFadden shifted in his chair, straightened and leaned forward.

"Gentlemen, I've spent the last two decades battling the invasion of these vultures. Our American aristocracy may play with their secret societies at Yale and Harvard, however these are the true pariahs creating the yolk holding this country to its own serfdom. Freedom is the illusion they tease us with. The right to create wealth for all entering the land of opportunity is the hook, yet their single purpose, their self serving means has but one objective: to own, control and ultimately rule everything that passes off as free enterprise. Like all good Ponzi schemes, they make it appear that enterprise is an autonomous, individually driven result of personal creative endeavor."

"Are you suggesting the land of the free, home of the brave is one huge marketing ploy?" Toto asked.

"It's become the useful selling tool for every immigrant landing on these shores and everyone here believing the American dream to be alive and well. A dream the founding fathers would cringe to witness in its present incarnation," replied McFadden. "They warned us against the bankers and foreign interests, in no uncertain terms, how given half the chance they would usurp the whole operation, sending our hard-won freedom back to old world slavery, ironically the ones financing the slave movement in the first place. We're talking the long game here, gentlemen. Let's not be romantic and fall into the Hollywood vision we've been served. I've been fighting that reality ever since they created the Fed."

"So how do we expose this treachery?" Toto asked.

"Keep it in the public eye," replied the congressman. "Not easy when you have press barons more interested in serving these masters rather than the people."

"Something Burnham warned me of back in England. It's a universal disease."

"Toto, you're as independent as they come, how do you intend to expose this to people?" Neily asked.

"Writing, as I said, researching it and gearing those with influence, helped by present austerity, to awaken those open to hear truth."

"You're up against a formidable foe," warned McFadden. "They'll hunt you as they have me. They also have the public so deeply asleep in dream land, you'll need the trumpets of Joshua to help wake them!"

"I'm no stranger to their jeopardizing plans. Perfectly prepared for whatever they throw at me." Toto replied.

"You're right, in your position, to keep reminding people of the terror they allow, having the eight families take over the money system, Wall Street and the economy. It's treason writ large, this whole charade. Your man Norman being one of their main officers," McFadden noted.

"His connivance with Rothschild was one reason I accepted the Brazil assignment, to see what they're up to. Yet what bugs me is why and how Rockefeller, Ford and Rothschild pump up the National Socialists and Nazis in Germany, rearming the nation, ignoring everything laid down in the

Versailles Treaty."

"Money, profit and to hell with how it's created. They even engineered the war. To think I was fool enough to go fight it, Rothschild twisting the President's feeble arm to join in," Neily confessed.

A veteran on the receiving end of subversion, implication and dirty dealing, McFadden turned to Toto.

"Albert, have you wondered why your secret service asked you to go to Brazil. Over and above it fitting nicely into your plans?"

Toto thought back to all the events leading up to the decision. He remembered his conversation with Churchill, suggested by Burnham, followed by an invitation from Quex to see him. Were all these merely coincidental or was a powder keg trail being laid?

"I keep hearing Nikola's warning that there are never coincidences and when looking at how my trip to Brazil and its outcomes turned out, it does make me wonder whose interests are being served."

"You're right to wonder, Albert," the congressman agreed. "I'm strongly convinced Rothschilds and their Khazarian mafia are so deeply interfering and influencing our country, through financial invasion, they'd go to any lengths to get what they wanted. Burnham, like so many press barons, must also be influenced by their desires. I've already expressed my views of Churchill's connections to the Rothschilds, so what's the important link connecting the secret service and Quex into the scheme of things?"

"Maybe the warning from Dansey indicated foreknowledge you needed to know," Neily threw in.

"He's never embraced Quex's way, especially how the service is run and has no reason to look after my interests."

"Are you sure about that," McFadden asked. "Sometimes our own perception of someone's motives hides an intention we're better off heeding."

"Worth getting in touch with Dansey finding out a bit more how he interprets these things," Neily suggested.

"Damned useful having you guys to talk things through. Really appreciate that."

"We appreciate what you've been digging up," replied McFadden.

"Second that." Neily added.

By the time they arrived at Rhode Island, accepting Neily's invitation to stay over at Beaulieu, his summer residence, it was agreed Toto would return to Europe, meet with Landmann, develop leads McFadden helped forge around the core Rothschild guided banking interests.

The congressman drew Toto aside before they went separate ways.

"Remember to look into the role of that snake Norman and get Landmann to help you uncover the depth of investments U.S. corporate interests hold in their supporting Hitler and rebuilding. I may be going out on a limb here, but with what I know of the corrupted system we're tied into, it probably has more currency now than ever."

"What are you saying?" Toto queried.

"I'm suggesting with all our corporate interest, the way the money steers the movement of people, agendas and politics, the pressing question must be, who's really behind Hitler's rise and the whole National Socialist movement?"

McFadden paused, reaching deeply into Toto's mind.

"Both on this side of the pond and in England there seems to be a considerable acceptance of his rise in quarters better served being far more wary. The tide will inevitably turn, I'll wager, that's tactics, yet believe this: before the scapegoat is loose on the field of combat, playing its part, the lines, the channels and support system have to have a solid base. Ask yourself, whose interests are best served committing the world to yet another round of devastating warmongering and cultivating a deadly crop harvested in the killing fields? In my experience of finance, there's only one answer – follow the money!"

"I'll certainly look into that," agreed Toto, now armed with a far clearer picture of what was in store. That it looked, even from this perspective, a sorry sight, urgency to get it out into the public domain was an imperative more pressing than any burrowing for ancient reparations. Toto felt this mission to be the reality he had been cast for and sworn to complete.

Neily saw to it that both congressman and researcher were taken to the city, where Toto managed to spend time with Willy. He booked his ticket home under an assumed name, to avoid any prying interests on his movements. If Norman could get away with it then so could he. As few people as possible, knowing his return, would, at this point, work in his favor. He needed to stay as far out of any spotlight as he could, while monitoring contacts with all those tied to wanting rid of him.

A visit to his munitions expert Brighton offered the best solution to finding Dansey's whereabouts in Italy.

CHAPTER FORTY-SIX

Returning to Bromley, he found the reception to be less than welcoming. His lack of communication from South America created irritation in his wife's attitude towards his adventures. Olga, as holder of the purse strings, laid an absolute embargo on future funds. That came as no surprise. His lack of information had been purposed, as reuniting with Faviola, the usefulness of this cynical relationship had run its course.

For her part Olga had not, it transpired, hung around the tree of faithfulness. Rumors of dalliances supported Toto's decision to part ways. For purposes of appearance, Olga wished her husband maintain the appearance of a marriage. He agreed, as it cost nothing.

Thomas Brighton was pleased to see his old army chum again and eagerly embraced a suggestion of bicycling round the Surrey hills, including a watering hole or three.

As Toto refilled their glasses, he sat down beside his munitions friend, keen to find out how close to the service Brighton could finagle himself to procure what Toto needed.

" You want me to dig up Dansey's whereabouts, then?" Thomas queried with an enthusiasm more in keeping of an errant schoolboy, eager to commit a foolhardy dare.

"As much info as you can on him would be great. Make sure Quex has no idea we're sniffing around. That's why I can't just march in and demand the information. I've little idea of the stability of the present hierarchy but getting to Dansey behind all that would be pukka."

"You've been away too long, me old china!" Brighton confided, with a nudge in his friend's side.

"From what I've heard on the grapevine," he continued, "Dansey's Z division has become a direct challenge to HQ. Things are pretty porous presently, so getting you details without raising alarm, well, trust your Irish, he'll deliver."

"I do," replied Toto in full confidence.

"Will you be needing a friendly blast to waken the lords and ladies?" Brighton asked, itching to put his expertise into practice at any opportunity.

"Our explosions are going to be a tad more refined, but keep your hand in for later," Toto encouraged.

Brighton grinned like a Cheshire cat.

Next stop was Tunbridge Wells and brother Louis and sister-in-law Hetty. He had no wish to confide in his brother all the events of the past months; more the realization his future would have him lose all physical contact with close family. He respected and honored Louis' assistance along the way, it was only right to make one last connection. The house was as welcoming as ever. Young John finished schooling and was preparing to go up to Cambridge. Thrilled to see his favorite uncle, Toto saw the blossoming of a strong soul and made sure they had moments together.

A clamber over the local sandstone rocks offered a good opportunity.

"Uncle Toto, your escapades all over the place look pretty romantic from where I'm standing!" John shared.

"You remember all those battles we fought on the playroom carpet and how I told you it was the taking part that really mattered and not the winning?"

"Yes, never forget."

"Well, in life, progress and the right to change the rules means I'll reassess the advice."

"Fair enough," John agreed.

"You see sometimes life throws you a curve ball."

"Curved, what like a rugby ball?" John interrupted unaware any ball apart from a rugby ball was indeed curved.

Toto chuckled, instantly reminding him of the joy being around innocent, inquiring minds.

"An expression I picked up in the States. Comes from a baseball throw meaning something arriving unexpected. Over the last little while I've received loads of curve balls. Whereas taking part is all well and good, sometimes we have to get down, get dirty and act to root out what's taking us to war. Prevent us having to fight at all, which frankly is the stupidest act humans ever partake in."

"Having been in as many war zones as you have certainly makes you the expert."

"I'd have preferred not to have been. It's not the sort of education any of us need."

"I've ever been through war, always feel there are better ways for people to sort out differences."

"Precisely, John, that sort of thinking's going to help keep the world sane. However, my research has uncovered a madness none of us wish for and it needs exposing, so the likes of you and your generation might be saved another atrocious slaughter, worse than the one we've just been through."

John pondered his uncle's words as they both sat squatting on a large sandstone outcrop, looking across the fields towards the town. The young man had done a lot of pondering in his short life. Sitting here with his favorite uncle, it felt most appropriate to mull over the big questions.

"I often come here clamber, climb and challenge myself," John shared. "Mother always tells me to be so careful, she's very protective. All I want to do is push myself to the limit, see how close I get to falling down."

"I can understand that. Like my life, and I've fallen down loads. What I've learned is picking yourself up, brushing down and moving forward is the solution. The only way to learn."

"So do you think there'll be another war, uncle?"

"I hope to God no, but God never decides these things. Arrogant delusional men do, seeing so much profit in war, caring nothing for the cannon fodder. They chase greed-filled goals, sacrificing everything sacred, for power and wealth."

"You're going to stop them?"

"Till my last breath, though I can't guarantee alone I'll succeed. It's a joint effort. It's up to you and your generation to keep demanding peace."

"As long as war is regarded as wicked, it'll always have its fascination. When looked upon as vulgar, it'll cease to be popular," John replied.

Toto looked amazed at his nephew.

"Where did that come from? It's so true."

"Oscar Wilde, fortunately. I've nowhere near his erudition, just love his work, encouraged by Alf, my teacher at school," John admitted.

"Lucky you, wise teacher," his uncle added.

He turned to his nephew.

"John, I'm going to be going away."

"What's unusual about that with you," his nephew shot back, chuckling.

"You're right I'm always going away, but this time I won't be coming back."

John looked at his uncle, sadness rising at the news.

"What never?"

"Never's a long time, though it's quite possible," replied Toto.

"I'm going to be upsetting a lot of people," he explained. " With what I'm about to do, I'll have to make myself scarce, which means disappearing. Do you understand?"

"I suppose so, but what about the others?" John asked, curious as to how everyone else might react.

"I want you to keep this a secret between you and I. Your father need not know and your mother would not want the concern, would she?"

"You're right. So where are you going?"

"Back to Brazil, then who knows, first off I have business to clear up in Germany, a trip to see Smokey and then make sure that cousin of yours is primed for his first diplomatic post in Addis."

"I'll miss you."

"Miss you too, young man. So you'll be off to Cambridge, then what? Do you have plans, travel and marriage, become another writer in the family? Where are you headed?

"To retain a free spirit like you and become a farmer," his nephew revealed.

"The world needs feeding. Tell you what, you attend to the physical and I'll stimulate the mental. Deal?"

"Deal," John agreed.

Together they clambered off the rocks and made their way home.

Brother Louis repaired, after another good dinner, to the drawing room and looked out over the garden, lit under a watery winter's full moon. Toto sat next to the blazing hearth, enjoying the warmth. Everyone else had retired.

"So what's in store for you and Olga, now you're back from gallivanting around the world?' Louis asked.

Toto caught his brother's tone of jealous resentment at the freedom he projected. He had no intention to inform him of the changes taking place. Louis would only see it as another failed marriage, so he changed the subject.

"John informs me he wants to be a farmer, once he's finished at Cambridge. Would you like him enter the Morgan Crucible business?"

"There you go again," Louis shot back, raising his voice as he turned from the chill scene outside. "Avoiding my question. I'll ask you again, what are your plans?"

"Probably carry on writing, keep the press stuff coming and take holidays in Bognor, since Olga has banned funding extravagant lifestyles."

"Something maybe your sister and I should have heeded earlier," his brother threw back.

"You saying you've wasted resources on me all these years?" Toto responded sharply.

"Always told your sister we were throwing good money after bad but as you know she's got a very soft spot for you."

"Good money after bad? Thanks!" Toto winced at his brother's revelation. "Yet you'd have been the first to claim your part had it gone the distance."

"Your life has been an unremitting flow of disaster after disaster. The only thing you ever got half right were your escapades with bicycles. Even your book on dogs became an excuse to chase rainbows."

"Rainbows?"

"Yes, pots of gold at the end of a fruitless quest!" Louis emphasized.

Toto sat in his chair, staring at his brother, who looked older now than he had ever noticed. He saw an old man, bitter at having never really taken bold steps to veer from a predestined course in the City, as a company man. Unlike their father he had chosen to resist the pull of the diplomatic corps. What he saw in Toto were the dreams he himself had let go in pursuit of stability.

"You personify an elder brother's role, safe rather than bold, grudgingly supportive, more than likely so you can assuage the jealousy. It's abundantly clear any filial support for how I charted life has been skin deep," Toto hit back.

Louis paled and Toto saw he had hit a tender point.

"Your boy Adrian suffered much because of you. We're all surprised he turned out so balanced. At least I took in those not my own, brought them up to know what family is. I never left them to fend for themselves, bereft of a father, whereas you just disappeared, leaving both wife and son to fate and fortune."

Louis suddenly felt the tiredness in his years encroach and used the mantelpiece shelf above the fire to support his tall frame.

"I'll have you know my son and I have found each other, in spite of the past. As a father I am as proud today as I have ever been."

"Perhaps then, from now you might take more responsibility," replied Louis. "Begin to make something of your life before it's all too late."

Toto felt himself rise to the fly his brother cast. He had to maintain all his inner strength resisting replying. He knew otherwise he would say too much and compromise everything he was engaged in.

"The pity is Louis, you may only get to know what I've been doing once it's too late. I can live with that. Can you?"

"I know what a hash you've made of it all so far. No secrets there. All I hope is you redeem yourself in front of your son, as it seems it will never be possible for the women in your life to be afforded such redemption."

Toto's heart flew to Faviola and he knew all he had accomplished in the area of women had led him finally to find his true heart in beauty that would always remain hidden from this life in Europe, his family and those who wrote him off as without real results.

Toto looked at his brother, remembered Arthur and the other siblings. Childhood seemed lost in the mists of another lifetime.

"You never got over Arthur's suicide, did you?"

"It was his own choice to quit over that woman. One not worthy to be seen responsible for a bad decision," his elder brother mused.

"We all make our decisions, bad and good, I have come to believe both drive us forward, as long as we maintain full responsibility for each decision and learn from them at the same time," Toto reflected.

'I truly hope you live that belief, brother. It's something I wish my own son carries with him, continuing the path I've forged."

"Have you shared that with him?" Toto challenged.

"There's much I wished I'd shared with him of life but some things remain hidden."

Too true, Toto thought.

"That unfortunately is the legacy of our times," agreed Toto. "One, like our increasingly archaic system of class, rights and privileges need to be shaken out like an old carpet needs ridding its dust."

"You and I have many things we differ in. The belief in the strength of the system of governance is one. I believe it's the very strength built up over centuries that keeps us together," Louis cut back.

"Who runs and rules such a system?"

"Why, those we vote in. The ruling class with their heritage and wisdom make sure the glue of ages holds the ship afloat."

" You have absolutely no idea, have you," Toto admitted with shock at his brother's allegiance to the status quo that he was now exposing to be rotten to its core.

"Can you not see the bankers and plutocrats control the whole show?"

"Rubbish, fellow, it's those very bankers drawing us back from the pit of depression, as we speak. They know far more about finance than you will ever learn, believe me."

"I entirely disagree with you. Having seen and dealt with some of these bankers first hand, I can categorically say I found the opposite. We're being roped into more and more chaos at each turn just to line their fat pockets with even greater wealth. Do you suppose that will enhance the worker at the mill, the miner, shipwright or farmer? Of course not; they're financial cannon fodder making the money machine churn out greater and greater wealth for a few."

"Now you're sounding like a Bolshevik. Get some sense into your head."

"I fear nonsense has glued your allegiance to a ghost, a ghost parading as a sentient, healthy being. Who do you suppose created the crash of twenty nine?"

"Economic uncertainty, no more," Louis replied, agitated at his brother's insistence on hidden hands.

"Manipulated collusion of the worst kind. Its roots spread into the City here, if people knew," insisted Toto.

"Another dream of yours and conspiratorial journalism," the elder man shot back. "You're better off with facts, not this fiction you continue to expound."

"Trust me, there's another bloody war around the corner, first attempts only got a third of the way."

"Good God man, the cold's got your brain or the brandy's working, the last was the final one, we all know that. No one can withstand another such bloody event."

"Create depression, scapegoats, agitate for change, cover up utter failure of economic models. What's used to cover all these failures, masquerading as a final solution? War, that's it, plain and simple. History proves it's the engine of first choice for the powers that rule. When they feel they're losing their grip, need more wealth or the scheme's run out of steam – bang, divide, rule then manufacture excuses for war."

"And you think you're going to do something about this, do you? With all the success you've garnered, you feel you're best positioned to direct the future? Your grasp on reality has got lost on the way, on your travels."

"I've never been more certain, never clearer and focused in all my life, Louis. As I said, I'm not looking for approval or belief. From here on in it's my journey, my evolution and my discoveries."

His elder brother saw only a man, some twenty years his junior, deluded beyond hope. He felt he had now lost two brothers, even though one still remained extant.

"I may not believe in what you say, but defend with my life your right to say it. You'd best get back to your wife and son, they need you more than anyone," Louis said with an air of cool dismissal and finality.

It was with deep sadness Toto left the following day in the knowledge he would never revisit nor see these members of his family again. It saddened him, though he gave no outward sign of it.

As he descended the front steps to the waiting car Rumens had ticking over, he looked back. John, from an upstairs window, discreetly waved him off. The rest of the family had already bid him adieu.

CHAPTER FORTY-SEVEN

The neo-Baroque facade to the railway station in Basel lent an air of magnificence for any traveler arriving or leaving. To Montagu Norman, a regular arrival point on his many visits to the central bank of central banks, the BIS, it meant very little out of the ordinary. Such sumptuous surroundings he took as normal, accepting the waiting car, to deliver him to the annual general meeting of the bank.

As Governor of the Bank of England and more importantly a main player in setting up the Bank of International Settlements, he wore his responsibilities as might a hero wear decorations for bravery. Norman's medals veered far more toward the edge of treachery than bravery. Alongside his founding partners, the objective was to steer a central serpentine coil, delivering power and financial life juices throughout a globally controlled banking cartel. In a world fast approaching financial enslavement within the claws of an elite's banking control, Norman assumed his position of maitre d'. Whether he merited it could be disputed, yet his skill handling important duties during the crash and subsequent manipulations had not gone unnoticed by those at the zenith of this powerful construct.

Entertaining several shadowy members of the family of eight prior to Basel the previous Easter, in the South of France, made sure he was backed to the hilt on proposals laid out at the upcoming AGM.

It was to the Hotel Savoy-Univers that over sixty representatives gathered to report, be reported to and generally gain global awareness of the financial controls held over individual governments and countries. Once the general meetings had taken place, warm greetings exchanged and unctuous promises made to those less important in the chain, a select few, including members of the Rothschild, Kuhn Loeb, Warburg families and Norman's compatriot from the Reichsbank, Hjalmar Schacht, gathered for a private session.

During the intense meeting, two of the French Rothschild chaired discussions. At a given signal the elder stood up. Impeccably dressed, sporting an expansive moustache and a complexion indicative of a love of outdoor pursuits, he brought instant attention to himself.

"Gentlemen, as always a huge pleasure to have you all here. We're on the brink to finalize a dream nurtured over many generations. This extended family of finance, in the immortal words of Mayer Amschel, has the power to issue and control every nation's currency. As to its laws, we have in place those exercising our bidding and where we do not, it hardly matters. We will guide, transform and be guardians of a future, so rewarding, so generous to us, who have worked hard attaining these Elysian heights. Our grandchildren will be masters and owners of these divine fields. I therefore present you with our most respected elder."

The room remained silent, unaware what was in store. All eyes fixed on Rothschild's next move. He, acceding their expectations, turned and signaled a solitary doorman open the entrance to an adjoining room. Silently the door opened.

From a dimly lit interior walked an aged figure. His acutely coiffed white beard, moustache and piercing eyes of a hawk, lent an air of total nobility. Walking carefully, with authority to the table, a chair was pulled back for him. Brushing the help aside, he placed it in front of him, leaning gently forward. Slowly and deliberately he took hold of its back. Surveying each and every one around the table, he finally addressed the room.

"We are here to advance the plan. An old man graced with sight of what the family knew to be inevitable. Gifted the pleasure to witness the birth and formative gestation of this project is a miracle rightly deserved."

The whole room hung on his every word. Baron de Rothschild continued.

"As most of you are well aware, the journey to this promised land is nearly over. Return to that land of milk and honey made sweeter by our results. Rewards, we are told, await in the Kingdom of Heaven, yet today we can truly say we have created heaven on earth."

He paused, remaining upright, surveying the whole assembly a second time.

"Funding the dream that will become the State of Israel continues. The influence we bring to bear on each and every land will laud and give eternal thanks to us, the bankers and financial guardians of this world. We shall nurture its existence, reflecting undying endeavor towards absolute control and global power of people and dominions of life alike."

Concluding, he deftly twisted the chair round behind him, with a skill someone half his age would have found tricky. Positioned in front of the chair he sat with an authority only great wealth procured.

A spontaneous applause rang through the room as all stood to congratulate a beloved elder of the House. He allowed it for a good minute and a half before abruptly raising his right hand.

As one, the room fell silent. He lowered his hand and all resumed their seats.

" I will now observe the younger generation finalize this meeting and then, gentlemen, we move to the next stage."

Anyone not present in the room would have been unaware of what that next step was to be. Everyone in the room knew precisely their individual tasks awaiting them. Montagu Norman at that moment recognized he had attained a position of trust cementing his name to posterity, a posterity that would rue this day when all present would be long dead and gone.

The actions they were to initiate would, like ripples in a pond receiving the pebble's drop, move out and reverberate across time, space and a future world of generations to come. Something so terrifyingly awesome, future histories would be reticent to record and generations beyond would be stupefied to comprehend.

The attendant at the door discreetly closing it behind him, left the meeting room. Under direct orders, he stayed within earshot of the room beyond.

CHAPTER FORTY-EIGHT

Toto made the decision to visit Leila and brother-in-law Wilhelm in Switzerland. Having cut their final cords with Germany and Wilhelm, securing a good post at the League of Nations in Geneva, he felt he owed it to her and their life long devotion, to visit her one final time.

As the members and shareholders of the BIS left Basel, heading back to their various seats of operations, Toto arrived in Geneva. Meeting him, his sister brought them to the simple, well-appointed apartment overlooking the lake they now lived in.

"What brings you to Switzerland," Leila asked eagerly as they settled into what would be a long and informative conversation.

"I have to visit Landmann in Frankfurt. Knowing you were no longer there I had both time and inclination to visit you."

Toto filled Leila in with as much detail as he could, concerning the months away. Ostensibly, the Brazil trip was part and parcel of securing a better vantage point for renewed chasing down of reparations, yet it was obvious his sister knew him better than he had wagered and bought none of it.

"This repayment, dearest brother, is as dead in the water as that old swan out there being put to final rest by the lake attendants," she chastised.

She pointed to the efficient parks and lake service employees, clearing nature's cycle of birth, life and in this case, death.

"We've been so close all our lives and your sister, as you're well aware, has a sixth sense even she would wish away. Let's have the truth of the matter, shall we?"

There was no getting round it; he could never have been able to lie to her, had he spent a university education on the art. Her uncanny ability to see behind masks, express herself frankly, from an enormous heart that so endeared her to royalty, dukes, duchesses and commoner alike. He loved her intuitive compassion she wrapped around all those encountered.

"Olga, as you may have guessed, has been a disaster. Well, correction, it's been yet another failed entrée into romantic affairs for your brother."

"Saw that coming, only in it just for her dowry!" Leila smiled sweetly.

He accepted her correct assessment, without a jot of unease.

"Neily introduced me to and I met McFadden. We all three sailed up the East Coast where the politician furnished me with insights and information that frankly changed my whole approach."

"Willy wrote to me with a few details you shared with him. Louis

311

McFadden, now there's a brave soul, utterly misunderstood by the power brokers over there and as courageous as they come," his sister added.

"Telling me, a true fox in the hen house of DC," Toto continued. "You knew I 'd dropped the search for gold!"

"Yup!"

"My energies are into cataloguing, researching and exposing the role of the bankers, their collaborators and the money so obviously behind every nook and cranny of what they sell us as depression, austerity and hardship."

"My brother is awake, what joy!" Leila cried, beaming at her sibling's revelations.

"These people are flooding Germany, fuelling the rise of Hitler and his Nazis and for what?" he asked rhetorically.

"We could stand it no more. Had to leave as it broke our hearts. The Kaiser first got shafted, exiled to Doorn, forgotten. The people then suffered the worst insolvency a country could endure and, through that poverty portal, they inveigled a maniac to rise. To all intents and purposes, the German people are at the mercy of something far more evil than an egomaniac."

Leila allowed her sorrow to vent fully.

"What do you expect with a treaty so onerous, it bleeds the life blood from them," her brother replied.

"The same way constant censure and punishing children for offences they feel they never committed will always give rise to ruining their character and festering a 'don't care' attitude of revolt. Lumping the total blame for the war on the German people, alongside that onerous treaty at Versailles, planted a canker in the German psyche, which only assured violent reaction. They did it to the Emperor, now they're doing it to themselves."

Toto's heart broke for her. He knew how much she had loved the Emperor, Empress and whole family, the locals, sharing their life, who together had endured the injustices of a war traduced into loss, the demeaning way her own family suffered under French occupation in their district, following defeat. Once again she was leaving a country and people she loved. He loved that she herself saw behind the veil, reward for having been so close to the former seat of power.

"That's what I'm going after," he answered.

"The Nazis?"

"No, the banks and power behind them. Landmann's stayed closely in touch along the way. I just got word he's news directly from Basel."

"The Bank..."

"Of International Settlements. Precisely. The families behind it are the ones to investigate."

"You realize how powerful they are and how many avenues they have and dark alleys they control?" Leila asked, not hiding her trepidation for her brother's intended actions and safety.

"Brazil showed me that, didn't it," he replied.

Leila took her brother's hand, stood up and looked down at him. He sensed she had something important to share.

"There's something I've never shared with you. I think it's time now," she began, with a seriousness taking her brother aback.

"What sis?"

"It's about our father."

"What about him?"

"About his former life, the life before you and I were both born."

"In the States?" Toto asked, eager to know more.

"Then, before and after," his sister replied, somewhat enigmatically.

"There's more than a few years in that answer," he advised, chomping at the bit to get more detail.

"Father told us of his encounters with Eliza on the boat as they fled Charleston."

"Of course, loved that story, hounded by the Yankee secret service as spies," Toto added, as a dim spark of awareness lit, deep down.

"Spies, precisely, they were. Well, he was. Sent the family back from Paris, to the grandparents in Cheltenham, under the pretext of not wanting us placed in danger, as the siege became inevitable."

"I remember," Toto replied.

"Well, the Prussians bore down and the fall of Paris was assured. Have you ever wondered how father, a Prussian, was able to be not only holed up inside Paris but to have had access to all those sides of ham. How he used these as currency on a starving population?"

" I always thought it was particularly genius of him and Michel. Then Michel killed for a leg of ham brought Louise to us."

"Of course, Louise came into our family and your heart opened for the first time," she reminded him.

He felt his youthful self loved.

"More importantly father came home," Leila continued, "pockets bursting with money earned from rich Parisians thankful for not being starved. He survived of course."

"Always the hero," Toto smiled, memories as fresh as the lilies in the jar next to him.

"The truth goes a whole lot deeper, Toto. He once shared on the promise I'd never divulge this to you, mother or any of them. Interests in Frankfurt had contracted him to apply his skills infiltrating the Parisian ranks, ostensibly to be a man of means and ham. Also using some of the balloons he'd helped Parisians get their plight and daily message out to the outside world, sending others to the very interests that placed him within. Their objectives were far from aiding the plight and condition of the besieged."

"Are you telling me father was a double agent?"

"Yes," Leila replied bluntly.

"Good God, things begin to fall into place. I sensed he'd been that but during the Paris siege, that's shocking. Were these interests the Rothschild mob."

"I believe so," confirmed his sister, "though you'd do well to cross check it.

"The vast billions of francs the French were ordered to pay at Versailles in compensation *were paid* by the Rothschilds. They'd never pay unless they had their arse covered. Once again robber bankers betting on both sides and still profiting. Father was involved with them?"

Toto, still holding his sister's hands, let them drop. He looked out of the window at a scene of young children, accompanied by nannies and nurses, throwing crumbs for the living swans and ducks eager for a free meal. Would that his father had been as generous to the starving masses. His confusion over what he had always believed and the reality his sister shared, hit him hard.

"God, I don't know what to believe now. So many lies, so much disinformation and tracking right back into the heart of our own family."

He felt the emotions welling up inside. His childhood memories, cherished for so long, began to shatter.

Leila saw what was happening and knelt beside him.

"Toto, we all have to hit the reality of truths untold, the errors our parents made, so often committed with best intentions. It's imperative not to throw everything away with these revelations. Our father and mother were incredible. What they taught us, showed us, enabled all the children to experience a life we may never have had the fortune to otherwise experience. Even through Arthur's suicide, mother's subsequent decline, making things that much more vulnerable, they were our spine, our love, our foundation."

"I recognize that entirely. I suppose having matured, pulled through failure after failure does demonstrate that inheritance," he reflected.

"Your inheritance, that's far more value than simple money, Leila emphasized. "I realize your ambitions to find gold at the end of the rainbow never matured, yet today you're delving into something far more valuable, vastly more important to the world. Make that your recognition and acknowledgement of our father and mother."

He knew she spoke truth. He recognized something greater than family, that only could have been born through family. He felt it in the support she always afforded him. In spite of his brother's doubts she always felt his power to survive, to break through and deliver. It was what he was to deliver that had been hijacked by his selfish desire to match others' wealth, others' lot in life that haunted him. Now he saw how they had become the biggest barriers imposed by himself.

"You're right, I've that goal. I have reason and motivation beyond and above my own interest."

"That," Leila noted, "is what will allow you to win over even the richest, meanest, most selfish opponent. Selfless service for others is a weapon we all have at our disposal. How we recognize, use it and achieve results, is down to each in their own way. He may have worked for the lords of greed but our father was selfless in his love and devotion to the family, its safety and well-being."

"You're so right, as always. I begin now to understand how the whole circle of connectivity was as wide as my most expansive, youthful world view. How we mixed with Vanderbilts, Nikola, aristocracy, political figures in England, France and plutocrats everywhere. The ease of movement through these as well as the common men and women connecting us."

"We were and still are, never 'them'. We have always been outsiders, roaming from place to place," reminded Leila. "Connecting, infusing creativity, concern, interest and communication. For us borders have always been merely way stations on our travels."

"I wonder how much Nikola has been manipulated by the power behind the plutocrats?"

"I'd wager he's been given opportunity and been exploited in equal measure. Those offering so much to the world are always the easiest to subvert and steal from. Their innocence and trust in human goodness hits an impermeable wall of zero empathy. These are the creatures we all need to be wary of. They are creatures from hell growing ever more vicious and powerful, as we stay mute and subservient. They will have their day, unless we recognize them, rise up and stop them."

She looked across to her brother who had got up and walked over to the picture window of the apartment. He gazed out at the lake and the mountains behind.

Such beauty he thought, *how could people discard such beauty and at the same time hoard it for themselves.*

"Toto, I'm getting a very strong intuition right now. You need to go and see Landmann. He holds a key."

" I hear you," he responded.

Unconsciously his fingers caressed his upper chest. He felt the pendant he always carried round his neck. He stopped, as if confronting a ghost. Leila caught the change of mood.

"What is it?" she asked.

'This," he replied as he dug his hand behind his open shirt and pulled out the triquetra. He passed it to his sister.

"Wherever did you find that," she asked in amazement.

"Well perhaps this is my secret father wanted me to hold. He gave it to me on the American trip."

"The wily fox. He most likely left a little mystery for each of us to hold, but this is delightful. You'll have to explain what's inscribed as unlike you boys my classical education fell way short!"

Toto translated.

"Father also told me once I came to understand the meaning behind the symbol, the inscription will be revealed. When Nikola saw it he gave me a clue. He told me the three points hold the dimensions of space, thought and thinker. Past, present and future. Penetration, procedure and pervasion."

His sister marveled at the piece.

"Quite a bundle of meaning. What's your interpretation today?"

Toto smiled at her and looked down at the symbol in her hands.

"I believe the key the triquetra offers are the two opposing forces in nature. One made up of deception, division and war, the other truth, unity and peace. These two forces not only hold the balance but are in constant struggle and flux with each other. My purpose is to reveal and guide others to that middle place where balance, order and containment hold the gossamer threads in place."

"So you feel it's the bankers, the elite holding physical power over a world at the mercy of their greed and selfishness, that spawns deception, division and war?"

"Let's face it: war has always made money for those who care little for the whole. Weapons, blood and loss are incidentals to the end of a profit margin. Look at the American corporate assistance ploughed into Nazi Germany. That's not inspiring peace, it's preparation for an even more futile war. They spend time dividing us all, race against race, culture against culture, religion against religion. The British Empire has been a past master creating division and deception. We've so much blood on our collective hands, no empire with that much blood ought to be in any way proud of its record, nor feel its exceptionalism is anything to brag about."

"You who loved the military, as well. What changed your tune?" Leila questioned.

"Call it the hopeless youthful dreamer, the kid who was never educated to truth, to the facts. I'm not heartless, none of us are, yet we're crammed full of victor's history. The truth of right and might is merely a historical interpretation, not truth. You can recognize that from what Germany suffered through the last carnage."

Leila had to admit her brother was right. When peace was in the lap of Germany, with the Kaiser begging his cousins to cease the senseless slaughter, the British were persuaded to deal, bide their time till the Americans were cajoled to enter the war.

"Do you realize who persuaded the British to stall rather than pursue peace? It was Rothschild."

"We could have saved millions of wasted young lives. The Kaiser always knew he was being swindled out of sense and thrown to the wolves of madness, a madness and fate today having the German people suffer cruel injustice. So history looks to repeat itself."

Toto nodded in agreement.

"Now you understand where I must go."

Toto turned to receive the triquetra from his sister. It was then it hit him.

"My God!"

"What?" Leila asked, astonished at his outburst.

"This symbol handed down through generations, each one passing it on for the next to realize its true meaning."

His sister listened intently.

"Its meaning lies in truth, peace and unity. Within the confines working with the master bankers, father was never one of them."

"As I said we're outsiders," his sister reminded him.

"Exactly! Working on the inside he maintained that gossamer thread of life. A specific space, time and precise location demanded it."

"That was the true gift given by William and our forebears. The true gold gifted," Leila recognized.

"This symbol represents the pivot between light and dark, good and evil and being handed down, he saw the role I must play. Can you see that?"

"I can and thanks to our father we've both been able to have our eyes opened."

Just then the living room door itself opened and in walked Wilhelm.

"Toto, my fellow, what a pleasant surprise to have you visit."

Wilhelm, delighted to see his brother-in-law, walked stiffly across the room and gave him the biggest bear hug.

"No ceremony here," he chuckled. "Looks like we left all that pomp and circumstance back in the fatherland."

"How are you, Wilhelm?" Toto asked, noticing the heaviness of movement and tiredness in his sister's husband.

"*Ach*, these *verdammt* committees, the endless round of talks and more talks. What we thought was to have been a marvelous opportunity to make the world a better place is overrun by those with interests totally opposed to such high ideals. It exhausts me, no end," Wilhelm admitted.

He pulled up a seat next to Toto, by the window.

"At least the view is pristine and beauty herself untarnished," he added with resignation.

"All these talking heads yapping like pointless dogs," Leila continued. "On and on, defined by their endless sense of self importance. They treat us Germans like dog mess on their shoes. Why ever we were invited to join, with that attitude, I shall never know. These talking cabinets remind me of Bagheot's aphorism: *Never forget that twenty wise men may easily add up to one fool.*"

Leila smiled at one of her favorite quotes.

"You see why I married this girl, Toto. She is my compass in all seas, my refuge in all weathers," Wilhelm managed to utter before being overtaken by a rasping cough.

"*Mein lieber*, rest now and we'll talk later. I'll prepare something to eat and you boys muse over *les temps perdus.*"

Over the next few days Toto made a point of giving his sister and brother-in-law his complete attention. The rest, tranquility and sight of the Alps insured a very rested traveler continued his journey to Frankfurt and the meeting with Landmann. With Wilhelm brought up to speed, Toto felt reassured that if two people could have kept some of his better-kept secrets in trust, it was Leila and Wilhelm. What worried Toto more was Wilhelm's health. He hoped the Swiss air could stimulate a return to full health and assure a long life with his adored sister. It was not to be as already on his way to Germany, Toto would never be privy to such vicissitudes.

Landmann, as good as his word, welcomed Toto with a warm embrace and invitation to stay with his family. Over supper, he shared his discoveries.

"Those that seek to rule over us had quite a meeting back in Basel. My source brought most fascinating news," he confessed, as Toto listened.

"It seems the beneficent hand of our guardian bankers holds a viper or three."

"What do you mean, Ludwig? I'm fascinated how your source got news from such a private and closed meeting?"

"Walls have ears, dear friend, though in this case it was a door. I had found out one of the private staff accompanying these vultures was none other than a young man with a predilection for young boys around these parts. So playing the gambit of using the methods of your enemy, I owned a small blackmail of my own. I informed him unless he brought back a complete transcript of what went on behind that door, his little dirty secrets would be in the Frankfurt press quicker than he could say, *nein*. Some of these rather weak characters are like putty in the hands of a professional handler, *ja*?"

"I would take my hat off to you Ludwig, if I was wearing one! So what transpired?"

"It seems there's a desire to not only extend as much financing to our friend Herr Hitler but plans are in motion allowing certain foul Zionist parties to assist him in his ultimate goal of taking Germany forward into a new era. In time-honored tradition these snakes will be funding each and every party, so whichever way divisions appear, as they fully expect them to, their money is on the winning horse."

"What a war horse that'll turn out to be. This is scandalous beyond words. Was the slaughter of the fourteen eighteen carnage not enough for them? I suppose the corporate interests in the States can be assured of an excellent bonus package," Toto noted gloomily.

"Not only that, it seems our friend from Threadneedle Street has carte blanche to play his numbers across the board. The Rothschilds and he, in England, will be constructing a merry little empire of gold manipulation and further trimming of essential infrastructure, as reward for services rendered."

"This is dynamite. We can expect see riots in the streets," Toto mused.

"Unfortunately they've stifled the press and bought them off long ago, along with other means of widespread dissemination. That, my friend, is not news."

"So how can we get this sort of thing into the minds of those looking for peace in our time?" Toto asked.

"On that I'm uncertain; however you're the creative one. Maybe it's one person at a time, one group and one community. A word of caution here, these people have such an array of spies, contractors and the like, you'll need to watch your every step from here on in. If they get a whiff of what you know, that is, anything at all, they will be onto you like a cobra."

"I assure you I'll be as careful as I possibly can. What about your own safety?"

"At present the Nazis, as grotesque as their black shirts are, have no orders to seek out and make an example of us Jews. Those cuckoos they partner, in a strange way, are our ring fence and protection. However no true Jew is fool enough to believe they have our best interests at heart. With not one drop of Semite blood in their bodies and as long as they partner the Socialists, we're relatively safe. However I've no idea how long that might last."

"What about your informant. Will he squeal? He seemed pliable enough under your pressure, what if they do the same?"

Landmann smiled a knowing smile. "The reason so many dislike the Jews, unreasonably in my honest and unbiased opinion," he chuckled, "is we seem to be always a step ahead of the pack. So to answer you, again I took a leaf out of the criminals' book and applied it to our source. His silence is assured on pain of losing his manhood."

"You mean he'd have to convert?" Toto threw back.

Landmann nearly split his sides with laughter and they spent the rest of the evening developing plans as to how Toto's son, Adrian, could bring a swift peace to the Middle East with his freshly developed diplomatic skills alongside Ludwig's insights.

Toto left Hamburg a few days later, making sure he was in no way tailed or followed. Finding several underused skills he had learned in service to the King, he enjoyed playing mouse to unseen cats. He wondered how long these invisible feline followers might take before exposing themselves.

The ferry pulled into Dover and the reassurance of hitting home turf enveloped him.

He utterly missed noticing a fellow passenger shuffle past only to be harassed by the customs officer waiting ahead of them. Walking by, making no eye contact, Toto headed for the boat train to London as the new arrival made sure he clocked the Englishman.

CHAPTER FORTY-NINE

Adrian's escapades in the Levant sparked a burning desire to revisit the Middle East, under diplomatic colors. Apart from being fascinated with the whole area, he brought back with him interesting detail his father would love. As he prepared for Toto's imminent visit to his new digs in Bloomsbury, the epicenter of arts, crafts and alternative lifestyle in London, he made sure everything in the apartment was suitable to impress a parent.

The ring of a bell heralded the arrival. Dusting down the table set for tea, arranging the cakes just so, having lovingly sourced them from his local pastry shop, on a metal golden platter purchased from a flea market in Damascus with Lebanese tea pots on top of each other, he hurried to the door. Opening it he confronted Toto, in white suit, Panama hat, carnation in his right button hole, bearing a scroll under one arm and a walking cane in his other hand. His son stared in amazement at the apparition. He surveyed him from top to toe. At said toes his father sported a pair of spats Al Capone would have killed for.

"Have you gone mad?" Adrian stammered stunned at what stood before him.

"Let me in quick," whispered Toto, leaning forward and letting his lips keep as closed together while still maintaining an ability to enunciate his words.

"But...!"

"Quick, man, they're everywhere," Toto continued with urgency. He began to lean on his son, pushing him back indoors.

Adrian could not resist, let go the door and they both bundled back inside as Toto deftly slammed the door shut with a swift movement from his left Al Capone.

Immediately straightening up, he whipped off the panama and threw his hands in the air.

"Ta-ra!," he shouted, as if some magician had performed an amazing stunt for his audience. "I'm home!" he cried.

It took a moment before Adrian could pull himself together. Was this the father he barely knew for years or a clown fresh off Covent Garden's vaudeville?

"What the dickens...?"

"I'm being followed," his father preempted. "Disguise the better part of valor, what?"

"You've lost your mind."

"No, just the buggers following me," replied his father.

"Dressed like that you're a sitting duck. No one could miss you in miles," suggested his son.

"Precisely. Reverse psychology. Be so far out in the open, they'd not dare attack, take action or expose themselves."

"Who?" asked a perplexed Adrian, "Who would possibly be following you?"

Toto grabbed his son's arm and guided him into the front room.

"Presume this is where we're gathering. I'll explain everything over tea."

This was definitively not the parent he had expected to walk through the door, but it certainly was his father and he was intrigued to find out more of what he never would have imagined a father of his could become.

"So why the guise?" quizzed Adrian as they settled into two very comfortable chairs around the well laid out presentation of English tea with Eastern promise.

"You've been infected," replied Toto.

"Yes, but why the guise," answered his son, not wanting to be railroaded off topic.

"They're following me,"

"You said."

"So if they are, then be a bloody lighthouse and stifle their plans."

"But who are *they*?"

"The Khazarian Mafia," his father enunciated.

"The who?"

"Rothschild Khazarian Mafia."

"Who the hell are the Rothschild Khazarian Mafia when they're at home?"

"The same as those meeting in Basel, that control all central banks, Anglo-Persian oil wells and so much more, the founders of the Fed in the US, the stick behind every revolution and revolutionary in the modern world and their fingerprints are all over the Bolshevik puppets that slaughtered the royal line in Russia, starting that revolution."

"Wow, so no two-bit street corner mob then!" Adrian replied, somewhat aghast at this revelation, yet finding it hard to take his father too seriously.

Gathering himself back and putting his logical hat on, he replied.

"And you've proof of all these explosive exposures you've intimated?"

"Proof? What do you honestly think I've been doing all these months and years researching, dear boy?"

"I knew, as a researcher you're hard to beat and previous conversations showed me a lot behind the curtain but what you're telling me is, frankly, mind boggling. If I've got it right, there's a concerted effort by secret parties to take over the running of the world by fair means or foul."

"Precisely. Most likely foul. What you and I are shown in the open, what we're told as truth, history and events guiding this world, is mere fiction for its better part, or at best a simulation of the true picture."

"Are you telling me they've been lying to us, traducing us into this present austerity and downright misery just to make us compliant?"

"As good as," replied his father, helping himself to one of the best looking cakes in front of him.

"How's that possible, without anyone stopping to shout fraud or, like us, seeing the travesty performed to our face?" Adrian asked, serving tea at the same time, to his father's cup.

His father smiled one of those ever so proud to be your father smiles and answered.

"They can lie to our faces as most of us never conceive being lied to by those they consider to have our best interests at heart. Best interests, my foot. The only interests they have are their own. We for them are merely bait to lure their end goals. The more we remain compliant, the easier it is for them to lie and reach their targets."

"Outrageous!" Adrian exclaimed.

"Of course that's why it's so important for all of us to challenge everything. Question more and refuse to comply until we each feel satisfied our interests are served."

"Obviously!"

Toto leaned over to Adrian.

"I haven't told you this often enough but you're a brilliant, bright and an extraordinary young man, who happens to have turned out to be my son. The pride I hold for you is virtually inexpressible. That you've got this most important point is testament to all you've become."

Adrian listened to his father and all the years of resentment, all the feelings of being cast aside and forgotten just washed away, finally. Before him he saw, with equal pride, someone he so wished to emulate, become and help carry forward the work he now, comprehended and admired. He was lost for words and just replied.

"Thanks Dad!"

"Thank *you*, son," replied his father, basking in admiration.

They both luxuriated in a moment of mutual recognition then, as if fire had been set off under them both, returned to the conversation.

"You asked how it's possible, well it's absolutely possible when you grind a people down – not the elite, you understand – they are in utterly different pastures. Grind the populace down, deny them hope, ravage their savings, destroy their falsely built up dreams, as the crash did and take every ounce of energy and self dependance from them. This makes them not only pliable but susceptible to every belief, thought and directing action."

"That's when propaganda starts its insipid invasion," Adrian broke in.

"Correct. I can't help being reminded what that puppet Hitler wrote in his little book, Mein Kampf – *The most brilliant propagandist technique will yield no success unless one fundamental principle is borne in mind constantly and with unflagging attention. It must confine itself to a few points and repeat them over and over. Here, as so often in this world, persistence is the first and most important requirement for success.* That's why we all accept the lies and rot our leaders repeatedly throw out at us."

" I suppose it also helps to throw the patriotic rah-rah everyone laps up and our continued trust in empire and exceptionalism," Adrian added.

"My son's sounding more and more like a communist. That won't help your case in the diplomatic service."

"My qualifications will and, as a good diplomat, I know when to keep my mouth shut!"

"Darned right. Now tell me, what discoveries did you make to help fill in the pieces, in the Levant?" Toto asked, eager to find out any good points Adrian might have unearthed.

"One thing for sure. The Levant or what remains of it is in a mess. The way the French and British have been using it as their chessboard for their power games is horrendous. King Faisal's furious at the way both Iraq and Syria have been pawns in their game. I know Lawrence, my hero, had a relationship with the Arabs and knew the precise set up. He was exemplary. As always his superiors have just ridden roughshod over far superior experiential advice."

Toto admired his son's depth of grasp on Middle Eastern politics. Balfour's promises to Rothschild acceding Palestine to the Zionists when it became viable was a crime waiting to happen.

"Leila was telling me how neutered the League of Nations has become and any expectations of any part of the Levant being brought in is as good as meaningless."

"People in Syria and Lebanon are so ethnically diverse, so many wonderful cultural mixes. They're happy to integrate the French influence yet feudalism, community and kinship will always be a stronger glue and anathema to the West's ambitions," observed Adrian.

"Western interests look like controlling every move towards autonomy." Toto replied.

"As long as they can trade, get on with their lives and customs they're happy. Geopolitics is no great thing for them but their own identity is. When that's interfered with, we can all expect trouble, and rightly so."

Toto could tell that his son's heart had been touched.

"Do you intend to set your sights on Iraq and Syria?"

Adrian looked up and smiled.

"Absolutely, that's my dream!"

"Then I'd better fill you in on some of the research I have and who might be interesting for you to follow in your work."

He then proceeded to recount a complete overview of what he had discovered, been told and conclusions arrived at. It was dark before he wrapped it up and many cups of excellent Lebanese brew had been taken.

"Whatever tricks the British, French and Russians hoped to achieve after the war, carving up Palestine, Syria and Iraq to suit their ambitions, today the bankers and their patsies want all the natural resources the Middle East nest offers."

"That's why I call them cuckoos. They've no right to be there yet bend British, French and American influence at the expense of the Semite Jews and Arabs," Toto added.

"No wonder they find you a nuisance. They'll have to take me out as well, as I'll be just as much a nuisance!"

Toto sat back and looked long and hard at his son. He had never been as proud to conceive such an inheritance as he felt at that moment. He also knew it was right to confide greater secrets.

"Since you've inspired me so much taking on board my work, I want to share something. Have to admit, it wasn't sceduled. You've proved to me you deserve to know."

Adrian had no idea what might be forthcoming. He just trusted it must be important.

"You have a sister."

He never saw that coming.

"What?" he exclaimed in utter astonishment.

"You have a sister. She's five, her name is Catarina and her mother, Faviola is the single most important thing that has happened in my life apart from you," admitted Toto.

Adrian was stunned. He processed the information that, like a bombshell, exploded so many synapses across his comprehension of his father. Yet what he heard loudest of all was the love Toto held for him over and above what he now described in Faviola. He felt his heart open, soften and allow his father to fully flow into his whole being.

"I'm stunned," he admitted, still, processing what he had heard. "Yet so thrilled for you, for us and funnily overjoyed to have a sister!"

He laughed spontaneously, got up and moved towards his father.

Toto stood up, not quite knowing what might transpire. Adrian opened both arms and grasped his father to him and wept copiously. Toto brought his arms round his son and started to mumble.

"I really didn't mean to upset you."

"Tears of joy, Dad, tears of joy."

Toto instantly had tears flooding down his cheeks. After a moment they pulled apart and looked at each other.

"Two sodding soppy men in tears. Who bloody cares, we all have hearts and I'm so happy to still have yours," blurted Toto.

"If I'd believed this would be the outcome of so many estranged years, I would have told myself I was dreaming, yet here we are, reality and I've a sister," exploded Adrian as he released his father and did a jog around the table, the chairs and each corner of the room.

Toto watched, a beatific look shining from his face. Both proceeded to dance around together in abandon and joy so many estranged years had been healed.

A sharp knocking on the ceiling indicated, along with a rude reprimand for quiet, someone above was in no such mood to join in.

The men stopped, looked at each other and broke down in giggles, like naughty children.

Staying over, sleeping on the floor reminded Toto of his army days. As they both surfaced the next morning, Adrian stumbled on something lying under the table of their long evening, the night before. He recognized it as something his father carried in under his arm the day before.

"Dad, what's this," he asked picking it up from the floor.

"Ah, glad you found it and reminded me. It's something I want you to keep."

"Really, what is it then?" Adrian asked, like an eager child at Christmas.

"It's our family."

"Our family? How so?"

"I never told you, did I? When doing research into the Moore Millions it triggered a huge interest into the rest of the family and roots."

"Like a family tree, a sort of tree of our life?"

"Exactly. My ferreter found every excuse, be it here, Germany, Paris, the States or Italy, to research the family line."

"Is it interesting?"

"You bet it is. After years of research this scroll gives you the complete family tree right back to Beli Mawr, King of Britain around seventy B.C."

"That's some research. Does it mean we've blue blood?"

"That's part of it but much later. What it does show is that we're the issue of an illustrious and infamous long line of destiny making the work you and I do now truly..."

"Revolutionary?"

"Got it in one. We may have helped the founding fathers achieve their goal, but now we know we've the heritage, stamina and blood to straighten up the present world and help re-establish peace unity and truth. You on for that?"

"You bet!" Adrian agreed.

"Another thing uncovered, to mark our genetic credentials, our ancestor from your Aunt Rose's marriage happened to be the original Scarlet Pimpernel. So we've much to live up to and emulate."

"Count me in Dad, let's go!"

His son's remark took Toto back all those years to a bedroom in Suffolk where, as an expectant son of a diplomat, spy and global trader he yearned to hear stories of derring-do, pirates and victories on his father's every return. Here he knew now he had his own son, equally eager and equally a chip off the old block. He smiled and handed Adrian his family opus.

"Be proud, young man, be proud of where you come from."

"That I will be, every second of my life remaining," his son replied.

With that the two of them, happy as Larry, made comfortable progress to Paddington Station where Toto would catch the train to the West Coast and a ferry to Ireland, where he had arranged to meet with Smokey. With Adrian in his dark suit and Toto still sporting the white number he arrived in, they stood out like a sore thumb as they walked, caught the bus and made their way across town. Both hyper alert, they kept an eye out for anyone looking like taking too close an interest in their journey. None appeared to and as Toto retrieved a couple of large cases from the luggage claim, father and son bid each other farewell. He mounted the carriage and turned to Adrian on the platform.

"You know Smokey and you ought to see each other more often. He's such a source of similar wisdom you're developing."

" I will, his visits have been almost as infrequent as yours!"

"I'll be back soon and before I head off to Italy will use that floor again, alright ?

Adrian looked at his father and smiled.

"No, you've earned yourself a mattress.

Toto laughed.

"Honored and accepted!"

"Have a great trip and remember me to Smokey," shouted Adrian as Toto hung from the open window, while the train pulled slowly out of the station.

"Will do," promised his father.

He knew he would never have any reason to disappoint, break promises or lie to his son ever again.

CHAPTER FIFTY

As good as ever to his word Smokey waited for his friend on the quayside at Rosslare Harbor. What surprised Toto was the vehicle in front of him.

"How the hell do you manage to afford a Bentley," choked Toto as he deposited himself in the eight-liter beauty Smokey had so ostentatiously arrived in.

"Did I never tell you the roads of Ireland are paved in gold?"

"You most certainly did not, young man, now come clean where did you nick this from?"

"Shame on you for casting aspersions on an honest man!"

"You're now going to tell me you earned it with your own toil, right?"

"That I did not."

"So you did steal it, you scoundrel," gasped Toto.

"I did not and so, I borrowed it from a friend who most certainly did purchase it with his own money."

The car started with a purr only huge money could buy. Toto loved his style but was utterly mystified as to how Smokey came across this man of means. As if reading his mind, which the researcher knew damn well his friend could do, Smokey replied.

"Met him at the race track in Killarney. Had a nag racing, gave me a tip and I told him a few home truths, I did."

They were now racing along the road to Cork, enjoying each other's company like brothers.

"You gave him a bit of your insight then, did you."

"That I did. He was impressed, which surprised me as what I told him was dark and not the sort of news you'd normally appreciate."

"What did you tell him?"

"I told him his wife would be dead within three weeks, his daughter would marry a wastrel and his business would flourish like no other business he ever owned."

"You did, did you?"

"I did indeed. You know what, he returned a few months later, in this car, told me I could look after it for him until he needed it back and that everything I'd told him came to pass."

"Good God man, you're a seer, by heck."

The road ahead started to blast them with a beauty only this emerald isle could boast. Toto's heart filled to bursting. God, this land, this man beside him, had delivered so many moments of unadulterated joy. He felt privileged Smokey had entered his family's borders and stayed.

The young Irishman continued as he negotiated passing a horse and cart.

"I used to be as happy guiding one of those down the road as I'm presently behind this wheel."

"So tell me more of this fellow who donated the car."

"Yes, I will. He loaned me this because his wife died to the day three weeks were up. He was pleased as he'd grown out of love and his mistress begged him marry her. I didn't inform him she'd fly the nest expensively a few years later. His daughter eloped with a gambler never to be heard of again, along with a good wodge of his cash which he never cried a tear over."

"And his business?

"Now there's the thing. He had a small armaments firm, making handguns. The Ministry of Defence came by one day, asked if he could manufacture cannons and aircraft mounted machine guns. He said sure he could, lied through his teeth and got the contract. Worth a fortune would you believe?"

"Does he still race horses?"

"More than ever, with Irish trainers and successful."

"You amaze me Smokey in more ways than I can express."

"You know, I amaze myself sometimes and makes me wonder who the heck gave me the luck of the Irish in one bundle."

"You, more than anyone know you've had to earn it."

"Now there's truth speaking," Smokey confirmed.

On their arrival at his small cottage the giant Bentley looked so out of place it was almost laughable, yet contrary to finding the locals jealous, they held Smokey's acquisition as perfect for their man. His reputation as a soothsayer had already captured hearts and minds and they treasured him with the protective care normally reserved for crown jewels.

He and Toto settled down and the Englishman related everything including Brazil, his relationship with Faviola, Catarina and the adventures with Barosso. Smokey sat spellbound.

Eventually when a pause was made for a brew, Smokey spoke.

"I'll tell you one thing. I knew Barosso would come to a sticky end. Nasty piece of work that but without his interfering, jealous ways in Manaus you'd have never got your backside up to the library in New York and started your journey, would you?"

"You're right. There are so many things in life looking like the last thing we need yet when they turn out to be the very thing we really need, there's hardly a word of thanks. Diamonds in horse shit are rarely found, far less appreciated when they are."

"Steady on, I'm meant to be the poet here," Smokey chided with humor.

"So tell me, what's it you want to know?" he continued.

Toto knew the moment had arrived. He crossed the room and retrieved one of the bags he had with him. Opening it he turned to face Smokey.

"Are we going to succeed with our mission?"

"You and Adrian?"

"Yes, and others determined to crack this case."

Toto listened as Smokey continued.

"There are a lot of variables. People have to be committed. They have to own their desire strong enough to die for these things. History shows there are few prepared to go that distance. Are you?"

"Absolutely!"

"Even if it meant Adrian had to be sacrificed?"

Toto paused, not relishing the thought one bit. Yet he knew Adrian would have cried out yes at that point, so committed was he now to his father's work. Yet he himself found it to be a loss difficult to stomach.

"For myself it'd break my heart but I know he'd say yes."

"That commitment is what's demanded. Whether the result need be so terminal isn't up to any of us to know, foresee or cater for. There's a power far more knowledgeable, more compassionate weaving the lace of destiny."

"So is that a yes, in your opinion?"

"Success is relative, so subjective. The world evolves and your work will help take it many strides forward. That by itself is success. Does that help?"

"It encourages," Toto admitted, knowing in his heart it was not for another to determine his fate.

It was and always had been his choosing.

He looked at the contents of the case.

"Smokey, whatever happens over the next period of time, I have a commission for you to accept or not."

"Accepted, you know that without asking," replied his friend without a moment's hesitation.

"Yes, I realize that was a somewhat superficial question but I had to ask. I've got a box here with papers, research and everything I've collated concerning the work. I want you to be guardian of these things. Do you accept that responsibility?"

"I do," Smokey replied again immediately.

"There'll come a day when you'll know to pass these artifacts on. To hand them over to one who rightfully awaits them. They'll discover what they are, what they mean and what they must do with it all. As much as that sounds as if I've caught your insightful ways, it came in a very profound dream I experienced, one I knew even more I had to deliver on, an absolute. It was a dream I know will become reality, though not in my time. It'll be at a moment within these times and tides of men, the baton will pass. This, Smokey, my dearest and trusted friend is your burden, your task and your part in the fabric of this ongoing story. Do you accept?"

Smokey felt the energy rise. He felt the numinous waves of the beyond wrap themselves round both men as well as the property, the car, the surrounding land. It held them with such strength, even he had to allow tears to fall silently. He watched as his friend, standing before him, became translucent, radiated like nothing he had ever witnessed. The sounds outside, the birds, the distant shoreline, the waves and ocean beyond, merged with them. The sky burst through the old roof and flooded each and every pore of material existence. They both hung in absolute nothingness, transported everywhere and nowhere at the same time. It seemed timeless and forever, yet as it melted away, it became unclear if it had even happened at all.

They stood there staring at each other, without words. The silence fed them both.

"Shall I take that as a yes?"

Smokey not at all certain Toto had consciously experienced the like of what he had, paused before answering, deciding time would answer that mystery.

"Of course," he replied. "I'll do whatever you bid me do, and with the greatest pleasure," he added.

Toto then dug the casket from the case, collected the files of papers and handed them to Smokey. As he passed them over a huge weight lifted from him. He felt energized like never before. He knew for certain something completed and something finally delivered. The joy of stillness itself coursed through his whole being.

Was this how success felt, he wondered as the thought passed through him.

He remembered what Nikola had shared with him.

It will be in the stillness of all things that you will hear my voice and I will hear yours. No need for machines of men to connect our souls.

He thanked Nikola for everything, for all he had been privileged to share with the great man. He remembered the conversation with his sister. How she saw him abused by the powers funding him. He sent a wish he would be recognized finally for the gifted and selfless inventor he was. Instantly he heard Nikola's words return to him.

I am the gift, we are the reward, there is only one and we are each a part of that whole. No one can ever steal or abuse what is theirs anyway. They merely chose to interpret it as they will. All results are part of the creation we are masters of, and answerable to.

Toto smiled, aware of so much more.

Smokey took his delivery and placed it all on a side table. The two of them spent the next days by the shoreline, walking the strand for miles, reminiscing and sharing as much as two great friends can share given a small window of eternity, left wide open to flood their companionship.

Once again they traveled back along the same road they came on, to the harbor. This time sitting in silence, contemplating their time together. Hardly a word passed between them, yet they shared so much.

At the quay, below the steps leading to the embarking deck, farewells were exchanged.

"I feel no sadness at parting, dear friend as I know we'll see each other before long," Toto said, holding both of Smokey's hands in his.

"You know, I'm with you on all your journeys, yet your path is a sacred one and we can only walk alone that sacred path, even we have the hosts of the beyond to guide and support us."

"I know," Toto replied simply.

The ferry hooted and the traveler bent over to take up his cases. As he did he felt the triquetra against his shirt. Putting the cases down he undid his shirt and extricated the pendant from around his neck.

"I almost forgot the most important piece of guardianship," he apologized. "This will pass on the mantle of Elijah to Elisha. It has served its time and purpose. I know its meaning. It's for another to find and pass it forward."

"I know, too" shared Smokey. "I will keep it for the Outsider to collect."

Toto moved forward and the two men embraced as men, fully cognizant men would one day be as at one with their nature as to recognize war as wasted time, energy and creative impulse.

The ferry blasted its klaxon, Toto mounted the steps and this Outsider disappeared within.

CHAPTER FIFTY-ONE

A drian's floor was softer than he remembered. Deferring a prior offer of the mattress, their time together was even more fruitful. Plans made, agreed with both knowing instinctively they would never meet again. They also knew their work had only just begun. Toto's somewhere else and Adrian's in the Middle East.

There were no tears as the Bromley train pulled away from the platform at Victoria. Trains broke them apart and had now brought them back together. As Toto leaned out of the window, back along the platform, he saw a young lad transformed into a man. He saw his son standing tall, waving him off into the unknown. He felt himself reborn. What he failed to see was the enveloping smoke, wrap over him from the engine and take all from view.

At his destination his trusty bicycle, still where he had left it, awaited his arrival. Strapping the case onto the carrier, his determined peddling swiftly brought him to the house. As he entered, there was complete silence. He had not alerted Olga of his return.

Why need he have done, he thought. He was not staying.

Making his way upstairs to what had been their nuptial bedroom, everything was neat, tidy and in very precise order. That was Olga, he heard himself say. Too bloody tidy, too bloody neat for his liking. There had never been any room for happenstance. That was what really bugged him about the relationship. Yes, he could feel that now. He had been blinded by the restrictive life she represented, from day one. He squirmed to think he shared this bed with someone so inappropriate. What the heck did she want from the relationship? His gold? The wretched gold he had spent so much time chasing. Well, she never got her gold as the real gold was hidden in the journey; in the experiences he had been satiated in, burnished through and arrived out the other side wiser from.

He only wished she might find the sort of contentment he felt right at this moment, in spite of the place, in spite of circumstances. He truly wished for her happiness.

Meanwhile he had a mission to complete.

He left the room, walked along the landing to the spare room. Under the carpet and beneath the floorboards, accessed through an almost invisible small trap door, he withdrew an Enfield revolver, enough rounds of ammunition and a creation of young Brighton's own invention quietly

335

commissioned a while back. He smiled wryly as he knew his army compatriot would have loved to witness the results of his handicraft.

"This one's the one that got away, Thomas, the craic's all mine," Toto whispered, as he collected his trove and placed them all into a case.

Along with clothes, wash things, notepaper and pen, he closed the case and made to head out. As he reached the stairwell, he remembered.

Returning to the shared bedroom, he made his way to the dressing room. Under the small side table he felt for a secret latch. It clicked and a hidden drawer popped open. Inside was a fine collection of expensive jewelry. He had known for a long time, this was where Olga invested what remained of her inheritance. She had locked him out of enjoying or utilizing any of it. Now, however, was the time he needed it. Scooping three quarters of the drawer's contents into a velvet pouch, he closed it and the drawer. Fetching a screwdriver from the spare room, he returned and forcibly prized open the closed drawer, imitating an intruder's work.

He left the house, without anyone noticing, leaving the door unlocked, as it had been on arrival. Back at the station, he bid a fond farewell to his trusty two wheeled stead and was on the train to Victoria and the boat train to France, and onwards to Italy and an assignation with Dansey.

The boat crossing was rough, unusual for a summer's day. The usual holidaymakers heading *en famille* to Le Touquet, Wimereux or en route to the south. Perhaps Pau, Toto pondered as he remembered the family summers spent there. Halcyon days with the Burnhams, American and English aristocracy and so many who had touched their lives.

Young children, broken away from the confines of their wards and nannies, rushed passed, giggling excitedly at the prospect of endless days of sand, sea and food. He wondered what lay in store for their generation, one never having faced the horrors of death, slaughter and senseless attrition. He secretly hoped they would never go through the lunacy, yet knew his research pointed otherwise.

Hope springs eternal, he thought.

As the sea became more aggressive, children were corralled and recuperated before being herded down below, along with those adults, bravely having enjoyed the ride, yet now falling prey to pale, sickly complexions. Toto stayed atop, enjoying being tossed left and center. He looked forward to connecting with the Venice Simplon Express at Calais, a journey he had taken once before, yet now could savor in first class.

As he disembarked, making sure to keep his bags close to him, he headed for the waiting train. Out of the corner of his eye he spotted two passengers who, he was aware, had thrown glances his way during the crossing. Careful to hide their interest in him, they engaged one of the coach stewards.

Perhaps merely inquisitive travelers, he thought, *but caution was the better part of valor*, he reminded himself.

He mounted the train, as a steward led him and the case he felt comfortable releasing, to his assigned compartment. Private, alone and luxuriously appointed, he settled down.

The train left punctually. Toto headed to the dining car which buzzed with expectation, relaxation and a myriad of wealth and opulence. He was guided to a table occupied by an elderly Hungarian couple, returning to their homeland. The orchids decorating the center of their table lent the desired oriental effect, whereas the table settings, in silver, added to a general appearance of luxury. Toto was amused as to how determined people were to be supported by such extravagance. The wife opposite lent forward and interrupted his observations.

"We're returning home, having spent time in your country," she declared in excellent English.

"Would that be London?" Toto asked.

"Oh, no New York," she replied, surprised she had misread him and apologizing profusely.

"No apology necessary. I've spent quite some time there so probably still carry the scars," Toto replied jokingly.

" You were attacked?" the wife queried, with deep concern.

"Only by the stock market," he lied.

"*Mein Gott*, as we were also. With the pittance we rescued, we spent it returning to England, living off favors of relatives and now, one last blast of style, returning to the small farm we left outside Budapest."

Her husband looked up, revealing the shame around revelations his wife admitted to.

"A gamble that did not pay off, sir," he shared, his features showing tiredness from several years of diminishing returns.

"I can understand your journey," Toto admitted. "I've had similar ones myself."

The two opposite looked intent. Their expressions lightened a little witnessing the confidence their table guest exuded, against what must have been equally harrowing circumstances. Perhaps they might learn ways through.

"Yet you look to have survived well," the husband complimented.

His wife smiled sweetly, eager to catch pearls of sustenance falling their way.

Toto noted their interest and felt compassion for them both.

"Let me first of all offer you the champagne for tonight and then if you wish I can share how I managed to find ways through to more fertile pastures."

The Hungarian's wife looked at her husband with an expression of hope the Englishman had seen too often in the eyes of those around New York stumbling across opportunity, where before only despair existed, in the heady days leading to the October disaster.

The sommelier arrived, Toto ordered champagne and his fellow diners settled into a tutorial of success over disaster from an expert in these matters. By the end of the meal both elderly faces had brightened considerably and they took their leave retiring to their compartment, a carriage before his.

As they parted Toto noticed the wife's handbag slightly opened. He dipped into his jacket pocket, where he had placed one of Olga's rings. Deftly picking it out, he dropped it unobtrusively into her handbag. Perhaps they would now be able to afford reinstating a small dairy herd for retirement.

Reaching his compartment, he entered and made to settle for the night. The train would shortly pull into the Gare du Nord, where it would then find its way round to the Parisian southern terminus and on to Italy, his destination.

A couple of hours later, as they pulled into the northern terminus he was alerted to a disturbance outside the compartment. Pulling the door open he confronted a young woman arguing wildly with what appeared to be her companion. Their altercation aroused others. The girl, seeing Toto's face peer round the door, turned and spat an invective in a language he had no knowledge of. Her tone needed no translation. About to close his door, deciding the best action was to absent himself and let it run its course, a man appeared to his right. He pushed Toto back with his elbow, into the compartment. The Englishman struggled to retain balance. His aggressor launched at him with a fist and before he knew it he received a painful blow across the jaw. Unable to hold his own he fell down against the bed as the other man leaned over grabbed his collar and dragged him up. Petrified he was about to be hit again he spied one of his cases lying on the seat behind his attacker. He swiveled round, using the weight of the other man as balance and grabbed the case. With a swift and accurate swing upwards, he caught his assailant on the side of his head with the sharp edge. Immediately the man fell heavily, releasing his grip.

What the hell's going on? he thought, *and where did he come from?*

The compartment door burst open. One of the men he had seen following him earlier burst in. His heart stopped for a moment. He realized instantly certain moves were being calculated in his mind. It was as if something had overridden normal responses, over and above fight or flight. It had a sort of out of body experience he had never felt.

The actions of the man entering the compartment slowed inextricably, as if he was witnessing a movie where the bulb burned the celluloid and the images slowed to a crawl before combusting into smoke. This action was not going up in smoke, it was elongating, allowing a part of his brain to calculate distance, timing, opening and retrieving the Enfield in the other case. It was surreal. He knew he could never have been capable of performing this under normal circumstances yet here he was assessing the possibilities of the impossible within a timescale hardly existing. He bet on it and flew into the air, grabbed the case, switched the catches as the gun flew out, semi loaded, as he had left it. The second intruder must have felt he had entered the gates of hell as the butt of the revolver hit his temple and he fell dead weight onto his companion. Both would not see daylight for many an hour.

Still in this zone of impossibility, Toto gathered all his belongings, leapt over the human detritus and fled through a now opened door to the platform. He did not stop running till he had seated himself in a waiting cab. Ordering it to the Gare de Lyon, for the first time in what seemed hours but were mere minutes he leaned back and felt the normal run of time realign itself through body and mind.

Again he asked himself the question – *what the hell's going on and how did I extricate myself from all of that?*

Looking in the cases, all was as it had been. A small dent and a microscopic strand of hair were all that remained to remind him of the events he had just experienced.

Someone most definitely was keen to see he never got to Italy for sure. He knew he had to take a completely different route to his meeting with Dansey, if he was to complete what he had planned.

"*M'sieur, nous sommes arrivés?*" the driver alerted him.

They pulled up in front of the southern terminus. Toto settled the fare, leapt out and hunted down a slow train to Avignon. Ticket in hand, he boarded the overnight milk train, in the certainty no one would have had the intelligence to work out his new itinerary.

He was correct. The next morning in Avingon, he took the opportunity to purchase some ordinary clothes, to look to all intents and purposes like any other southerner. He dropped into a cafe, ordered a dark, strong coffee and checked his face in the mirror hanging next to the table. Perfect, it was bruised but added that fracas-attracting allure associated with being caught red handed by a traduced husband, of his wife's infidelity. That would be the cover, just in case.

It was not long before his onward journey had him crossing the border at Menton into Italy. Dansey, based in Rome, had suggested they steer well clear of his base and meet somewhere far from the Eternal City. It was Fiesole, an ancient hill town a few miles from Florence that was their chosen rendezvous.

As Toto waited in the *pensione* he had chosen, he treated himself to some pasta and an excellent Tuscan red.

Under wisteria-laden trelliswork, looking out over the valley to Florence, in the distance, the Duomo pinpointed its magnificence and identification of the city's representation of renaissance art and culture.

It was good to be back among these things, he thought.

"Picture postcard, isn't it?" a voice uttered from behind.

Toto turned and Dansey stood there, dressed in an inappropriately dark suit, round spectacles covering mean eyes and a cane in his left hand, supporting a theatrical tilt.

"You normally surprise your visitors with such stealth?"

" Albert, you should know my panther like qualities by now. How else can an efficient secret service operate?"

The two looked at each other with suspicion, as Dansey advanced, pulled up a chair, sat and pretended to admire the Tuscan landscape. A waitress appeared delivering tea, china service and biscuits to the new arrival.

"See you keep your English addictions," Toto remarked, as Dansey's order was laid out.

"Beastly habit to break. Not the sentimental type, just like things to run smoothly, with few hiccups."

"Was that why you sent me the telegram?" Toto cut in.

"Look old chap, I realize Quex sent you on a wild goose chase but I knew that queer Buffett was double-crossing you with Barosso."

"How did you know that?"

"I do run a secret intelligence service."

Toto disliked the arrogance of the man and the attempt at saving his life, which he never did, was no excuse to forgive him his loathsome character.

"How did you know Barosso worked for Rockefeller. He never made it obvious even to the inner circle in New York."

"Who do you think brought him into the diplomatic post from Brazil. Think, corporate interests, fertile soil for industrial secrets, come on keep up!" mocked the spy.

"Ford?"

"Second gear, well done."

"What was his interest in Barosso, then."

"Oh dear, do I have to spell it out, for god's sake."

"Yes," insisted Toto, "You do!"

"Rockefeller needed your little reparations number stopped. Used the black sheep, Prentice, to deliver your *coup de grâce* in the shape of dirty dealings, knew your previous with Barosso, used his enmity of you to organize a bribed reporter to ask the question and then bring final embarrassment at breakfast the next morning with that bit of Brazilian skirt to rub it in for good measure. If I got paid for all the tarts used to bring a man down I'd have been able to write off all the losses I incurred in the crash. You though, were destroyed, written off, end of story. Bankers served, crash on track and the world set for inevitable change."

"Hold on. You mean you lost your shirt in the crash?"

"Bloody near drained me dead," replied Dansey.

Toto laughed aloud. He could not believe the great spy could have been so foolish as to have not seen what, for anyone paying attention, was flagged a mile off.

"So how is it with all your info and inside detail, you missed the sitting duck of all sitting ducks, Dansey?"

For the first time Toto saw embarrassment appear of the face of his opposite number.

"In retrospect you're right. I ought to have known. I just got caught up, thought I could beat the system and whoosh!"

Toto was glad to have all his pieces of jigsaw confirmed yet what still concerned him was Dansey's depth of intelligence into the American scene. About to pose the question when the spy, having sipped tea, spoke.

"You went and started to pick yourself up, sniff around and use your bloody skills to begin asking the right questions. Got us all in a flurry."

"Us all?" snapped Toto. "Who do you mean?"

Dansey had slipped. He swiftly backtracked. Toto was having none of it.

"What do you mean by us all, Dansey? Were you working your American connections in industry, your corporate resources? Is that it?"

Toto began to get very angry. He saw the sniveling interference of an operative, whether head of services here in Italy or not, fast moving into overreach.

"Look old man, of course I've assets in the high rollers in America, how else can we help keep tabs on the global situation?"

"You know those very same assets are the ones controlling their own interests with the bloody Nazis, no doubt also the Bolshies and every other crooked establishment around town."

Dansey aware of some of Toto's research, realized it had dug far deeper.

"How much do you know, Albert, I'm sensing what you do know may hold a greater threat to your well-being than chasing pots of gold others have earmarked."

The heat of the day, protected by the wisteria cover and a soft breeze wafting through the terrace, was more pleasant than the heat Dansey generated. Toto smelled an uncomfortable familiarity with a trait his counterpart was famed for. Viciousness, double dealing and callous disregard for fellow operatives. His intuition told him to be on his guard.

"So what do you think I know, then?"

"What you may know and why it's so sensitive must be laid against reasons why certain things are taking place and by whom. If you're just bumbling into knowledge you happen upon and sticking pins into patterns forming, it may very well land you in trouble. That's all I can say."

Toto pushed him.

"So what if I'm sniffing down the right hole and smelling dirt?"

"Beware you don't become the hunted, that's all I'd warn you against."

"What if I'm already the hunted, what would you say to that?"

"Then you're smarter than I thought, if you've escaped your tail."

"So they *are* tailing me, are they?"

"I didn't say that."

Toto looked disgusted.

"Did you not? Then my ears must be so full of wax I heard nothing."

Dansey's anger was rising.

"It really would be best for you if you'd heard nothing, however I fear you've already got hold of far too much and are past the point of no return."

"So why did you bloody well step in and save me in Brazil."

"Fuck it. Old times sake?"

"Bullshit! Why?"

"Because you're a good operative, I respected you. You never went to university like all the other poofs and pompous old-school types and yes, you've proved yourself."

Toto was furious. This man was so twisted, so Machiavellian, he hardly knew what truth came out of his mouth.

"Was that all?" Toto spat back.

Dansey looked at him. Took his spectacles off his nose, polished them, huffed on them, polished again and looked out over the valley as he replaced them and in a far softer tone replied.

"I'm attracted to you."

Toto shot to his feet, strode round the table, placed both hands in his trouser pockets and leaned right forward, till his nose was inches away from Dansey's face. He stared deep into the little shit of a spymaster's face.

"You know what, you pathetic creep, you little queer, I've had just about all I can take from you. Keep your sexual preferences, your manner disgusts me, the company you keep is as evil and malevolent as this world needs. No wonder so many in the service loathe you and your disgusting little ways. You think I'm afraid of you? Good God, man, I pity you."

Dansey visibly shrank into his chair. He had never been so spurned with such venom in his life. He had known some terrible errors he had made but this was turning out to be a misjudgment too far. He had a single option: to attack.

"You know the power of the machine you're up against, don't you?" he hissed.

"I know and I also know the power the force I have at my back holds. Laying those two alongside each other, all I see is mine is so far taller than yours, as to dwarf it."

Agent Z was nonplussed. He had no idea who or what this wild card was talking about. Was he bluffing? Were there forces out there more powerful than the ones he worked for?

He challenged him.

"You know why I'm based in Rome?"

"Well, it's not because you love fine arts and want to be close to your hail Marys, is it?"

Dansey sniggered nervously. The pansy in him wilted conspicuously. But he rose again, this time in cobra form.

"I'm in Rome, at the ear and eyes of the Vatican. The Holy Roman Empire never expired, never was defeated."

"Bloody hell, Dansey the classics scholar, what ever next?"

"The dots you're trying to string together, they'll only make sense when they form the holy trinity. Haven't you worked that out yet?"

'There's a trinity that's rising and it's in deception, division and bloody war." Toto shot back, emphasizing each part.

"You've forgotten the form behind all that has to be the rock, the pillar and guiding principle initiating it all. Therein lies the true power. You lot see it as the hidden hand, the wizard behind the curtain. That Frank Baum of yours who stole your name for his wretched dog, he knew. That's why the Wizard has been so successful for us to laugh in your faces, to show you the truth in plain sight, under the guise of entertaining you and you all fell for it!"

"Used to bug me Baum stole my name but frankly what I am about to expose will shoot his story into a reality none of you want exposed."

"You think we're just going to let you publish and be damned. You think we haven't already considered your pathetic attempts at exposure?"

"I know one thing: my history."

"What's that supposed to mean?" Dansey asked, lost for a moment.

"Ah, no wonder you get jealous of a good education. If you'd given yourself one you'd know in all mankind's history, selfish, greedy, arrogant and tyrannical rule never lasted, never won the day. You may build your power into what passes as an unassailable tower of strength but it'll fall as comprehensibly as this Roman Empire fell and the British one with it, from within."

"You forget we've the all-seeing eye, the single vision of the power of Rome, the Church, the City of London, where Norman reigns and the Federal Reserve in Washington. We've governed all the money, the industry and even pesky revolutionaries who felt so exceptional breaking from the Crown."

"You think that's your power? You've no idea what lies beyond the dimensions of human hubris. At your peril you'll drag your vision forward until you face the blindness you've created in that eye."

"You're good with words, Albert but we have the magic, we hold the people in our grasp. We are the illumined."

"Dansey, *you* are the deluded. People may be asleep, they may retreat into cells of petty security but nothing wakes a man faster than waking from a nightmare and recognizing its ephemeral nonexistence."

Toto backed off, turned and walked over to the edge of the terrace. He looked out over the city that brought into being creativity, inspiration, art and culture. So much nourishment began to feed the human psyche, nurture the imagination of millions down the centuries and show many how beauty touches hearts and changes worlds. This was a movement calling time on the ridiculousness of human arrogance.

"You think all the renaissance birthed can be wiped out by your power? You think the human spirit so weak?"

"Who sponsored that revival, who was it that paid its development?"

"So it's all down to money?" Toto spat back.

"He who pays the piper calls the tune," replied Dansey.

"That tune always remains the remit of the piper. He can change it at a stroke. The money may look like the force ruling but the right music inspires revolution. True revolution is never in the pay of the powers that be."

Dansey realized he had given it his best shot.

"So you're committed to carry this through, your revolutionaries' attempts to change our world?"

"You're right there. *It is* your world presently, yet no matter how much you control information, feeble minds and those asleep, it will never be your world. It was never yours to begin with and criminality never got away with it, no matter how large an ego it developed."

Dansey got up, walked over to Toto who, turning ninety degrees, faced him. The researcher saw a pathetic figure of a man, whose powers and influence were fast fading. His loathing for the man turned to pity.

"You'll be dead within the week," Dansey predicted.

"We all die one day," retorted Toto.

"Your family, that brilliant young mind of a son of yours, he'll miss his father."

"That he will not."

"Does he care less for you than that?"

" You can never kill an idea and you can never separate truth from itself," Toto flashed back.

"So it's au revoir, friend." Dansey responded calmly.

"Adieu more like, and I never counted you as a friend," he replied bluntly, turning sharply and walking off the terrace into the house.

Dansey was left a lonely figure amongst the beauty of the mimosa, the sweet smelling honeysuckle and cold tea left on the table. All he retained for company was the dark aura of spite and vindictiveness he carried.

It was time to put the latter into action.

CHAPTER FIFTY TWO

Toto had his answer as to where the true triangulation of evil resided. It was a complex weave, yet he had all the time in the world to work on this, alongside his heart Faviola. Before he could reach Genoa, there was one commission he had to complete.

Heading to Florence and its central terminus, he found the express taking him to Milan. Before boarding the train, there was contact across the Arno needing to be made. Depositing his bag with the left luggage, he retained one with him. From the station he moved swiftly towards the River Arno and across one of her many bridges to the Via dei Serragli. Here he found a large courtyard entrance, into which he disappeared, making certain no one followed him.

He mounted two floors of wide steps and knocked on a beautiful old timber door. In moments the lock shifted, a bolt moved sideways and the door opened cautiously. As soon as his face was recognized, he was ushered in the door closing promptly.

"Signor Trapman, I'm so glad to see you," whispered the old, yet noble Contessa. "How are your treasured sisters and brother? It's been so many years since we all met in Pau."

Toto was happy to see this old family friend, so well and with all her senses intact.

"How can I help you, child," she said, forgetting he had very much grown since they last met.

He allowed her little eccentricities. This was always how he had considered the Contessa, ever since their families met each summer in Pau.

"I would hope you could make sure this small packet gets to my son, Adrian, in London. It's all addressed."

"Of course," she immediately consented.

"Also could you telephone this number and alert them to my imminent arrival. They will know what to do as your husband has briefed them. I would do it myself but I have to be so careful as I have people who would wish to trace me and their ears and eyes are everywhere."

He handed her a piece of paper.

"Did they follow you here?"

"No, I took a circuitous route, checking at each bend."

"My husband did inform me you were working on something our great

347

leader would disapprove of immensely. Anything grating his sorry head I'm all for," she admitted with far less decorum than one of her title might be expected to utter.

"These are rotten times, yet I hope we'll soon be through them. Now I must rush as the train to Milan is about to leave."

The Contessa embraced Toto, as if he were one of her own wishing him god speed and the guidance of the Holy Mother.

He exited the courtyard below, scanning each side of the street and then weaved his way back to the terminus. His journey to Milan was, as far as he could ascertain, free from unwanted eyes.

Before boarding the train for Rome, Dansey also had an assignation to fulfill. There would be no Contessa involved on his. It was a briefing with members of the Department of Political Police.

This force, ostensibly created to keep tabs on political dissent, had in various parts of the state struck up excellent relations with Dansey and his officers' needs. On a freelance basis, various members, under the radar and for bonuses they never declared on any tax returns, executed commissions. It was to a house near the Basilica San Marco he headed and met one such group of freelancers. Led into an ornate front reception, with busts of emperors, princes and an eclectic array of medieval potentates of their era, he waited.

Out of a side room stepped a confident, well-groomed figure. He greeted Dansey in an excellent American English accent.

"Claude, it's a pleasure to meet you again. It's been a little while since we met in New York but I know we both have risen from the ashes and serve our respective purposes with pride."

"That we do," replied Dansey as he moved to shake hands with Aaron Kersh, a once successful trader on Wall Street, emigré from Prussia and now heading up a European control mechanism.

His presence here in Italy coincided with a call from those whom both he and Dansey dealt with in the States. In his role as contract killer, he had been commissioned to deal with a small business matter needing closure. To that end he had several of his men follow the business asset across Europe. Unfortunately it had recently been reported back two of them had suffered a very poor connection at the Gare du Nord. It was relayed to Dansey that, in the event of not being able to complete his own transaction with said asset it would be beneficial to all parties if he passed the assignment to Kersh and several of his assistants to complete. His meeting with Kersh passed that baton.

Fortunately for Toto the meeting near the Basilica held a small social pause within it, enabling him to be free of interference and being tailed to Milan. However, having followed an elderly Contessa back from posting some mail, one of Kersh's men had extricated Toto's itinerary along with a telephone number alerting them to the fact an extremist group in the Lake Como area were still currently active. As the poor Contessa breathed her last, Kersh's small troupe made their way to Como.

Toto meanwhile made his connection and was well on his way to a meeting with the Contessa's husband, Count Spindollini and a group of activists made up of several members of a resistance organization, engaged amongst other things in uncovering the role of the Vatican in relation to the elite money interests Toto uncovered across Europe and the States.

A small house beside the lake, bordering Bellagio was the agreed meeting place. The members, including the Count, awaited Toto with anticipation. His work, reputation and successes went before him and now with the triangulation of DC, The City of London and the Vatican open to full investigation and under the spotlight by an array of small groups around the world, it was finally down to briefing the Italian arm on approach and process. For this reason Toto had made this his last stop in Europe before heading to Genoa and one final boat trip back to South America.

His arrival was received with much celebration. The Count greeted him warmly and asked after his wife.

"She was in good spirits when I visited before coming here. What a ball of energy for her age," Toto shared.

"That's good and you were not followed at all, either there or on the way here?" Spindollini asked anxiously.

"No, all clear."

"Good. By the way why would she feel a second call to me having confirmed your arrival was necessary? Can you explain that?" he asked.

"Second call? I've no idea. Is she prone to forgetfulness?" Toto asked, with a little concern.

"Not at all. It's strange. Anyway let's get down to business."

The group spent several hours discussing the way forward, how they would remain in contact and how any relevant information might be passed to Toto. Having covered a lot of ground they broke for a light supper. The weather fine they all decided to eat *al fresco*, where the table was laid with the view of Como an idyllic backdrop to their hopes and plans.

As they took their places, the telephone rang. One of the men took the call. The line went dead.

"That's really strange, there was no one on the other end," the young man relayed to the assembled group. Spindollini looked across to Toto.

"Do you think the two calls are related?"

Toto mystified, scratched the side of his head. One of the activists who had been out front came running towards the front door.

"*Attenzione! Arrivando!*"

Before he could explain further, a bullet struck him in the head and he fell dead across the entrance.

"My God, someone knows we're here," Toto yelled.

He reached for his suitcase and grabbed his revolver. The Count and several others pulled firearms out from various secretion points on their persons and from side cupboards. It began to look like a full-blown raid by the DPP.

Several of the group took up positions on the first floor, where the vantage point offered an excellent angle to pick off anyone raising their heads above cover. Toto pulled out Brighton's handiwork and began splitting it into various component parts.

The Count looked on.

"What's that?"

"Our advantage," replied the Englishman.

"What can we do with it?" inquired the Count, nervously.

"We can blow at least some of them to hell, on a one way ticket!"

Toto proceeded to show the Count and another fellow who admitted expertise in explosives how Thomas's little pieces of magic worked. Around them the shooting holding the attackers at bay, intensified.

"You see this whole kit breaks into slender strands of explosive capacity, enough, my friend told me, to take at least three people out completely or maim them for life, so since we have six, used well we should repel these criminals. Toto slipped one into his pocket and proceeded to show the others the small clockwork short fuse acting as timer.

"By pulling the cord it gives the user vital seconds to either throw it or dispose of it into the fray."

The young expert grinned.

"*Bellissima!*" he sighed, as any hot-blooded Italian would do, spotting a beautiful woman across the street.

Shots still rang through and around the property.

One of the assailants popped his head a little too high above a gardenia bush and was dispatched to his maker. Almost immediately a cry from upstairs indicated retaliatory action.

"Toto, my friend, you need to get the hell out of here!" Spindollini screamed.

"I'm in it as well," he replied.

"You're the asset needing to live, under all circumstances. This is not your battle. Come, go!"

The Count tugged at Toto's arm and dragged him away to the back exit. Before he went, Toto scraped up extra rounds, envelope and paper lying in the case. He stuffed it into his pocket and fled.

With a hurried *ciao* thrown at those remaining, he was out and running towards the shoreline.

The Count, covering him, suddenly dropped like a dead weight. Toto turned to see his old friend lying motionless behind him. As much as he wanted to reach down and pull him with him, shots flew past, too close for heroics.

He had to get away.

Scrambling over the wall of a nearby house, he dropped down onto an old mattress left behind it. Picking himself up, he raced on. Ahead he could see a dinghy in the water. What he also saw as he twisted his head to track if any one followed was a well dressed, heavy set figure wielding a machine gun. The last time he had seen anything like that was when shown a trophy Neily had been given recovered from a Capone raid.

He ran faster. With a wall fast approaching needing to be leapt, he brought all his strength to bear on one huge final jump. He assaulted the wall as if fresh out of army training camp. It felt good, yet almost immediately a hail of machine gun fire rattled across his path. He ran towards a huge bougainvillea bush and launched himself into it, hoping it broke through to the water's edge.

It did not. As he attempted raising himself he felt the barrel of the machine gun in the back of his head.

A voice spoke.

"Turn round, you piece of shit."

Toto made no sense of the American accent he heard. He knew better than not to turn.

"You piece of shit," the voice repeated. "We've been chasing you across the continent and you've gone and bruised two of my boys bad," the holder of the gun spat out.

"The contract on you just run out, now all that's left is for me to sign off."

The hunter grinned.

"Who the fuck are you and who contracted me out?"

"How quaint! The little Brit boy wants answers," his assailant mocked.

"You gonna tell me?" returned Toto, mocking the goon's accent.

The gangster prodded him with the butt.

As Toto waited, he studied the face of the gunman. Something looked familiar, but he was damned if he could place it.

The man looked at him with a sickly grin.

"We got some mutual friends in New York. They got fed up with you constantly popping up when they thought they'd taken you down. Pesky son of a bitch you seem to be."

Toto began to realize, this was the job they had previously tried to finish him, courtesy of Barosso.

"I'm hard to pin down," he retorted.

"Don't look that way just now to me," the gunman prodded him again.

"So who the hell are you anyway, big man?"

" Kuterkin, Aaron Kuterkin."

Toto scrambled through an ancient memory bank. *Kuterkin, Kuterkin*, he repeated silently.

"That's a Khazar name, Kuterkin. You Prussian?"

The Khazar went ballistic.

"Call me Prussian? he yelled. "I kill Prussians for breakfast."

He lent over and spat on the ground.

"That's what I think of Prussians."

"Must've emigrated then to the States," Toto threw back with no respect.

"In ninety-three, shoveled coal on the Lucania to make sure I did. Made a fortune on Wall Street."

Toto's mouth dropped at the realization why he looked familiar. He remembered below deck on that trip.

He goaded his assailant.

"I was the lad knocking into you, remember, being shown round below? You got off with a single suitcase dockside. Slipped away. Spotted ya!"

Kuterkin looked at his prize. His mind rolled back the years. Pissed his quarry wanted to reminisce, yet marveling at a coincidence nearly fifty years old. Still pointing the machine gun, he replied.

"O.K. I got it. That was you, was it?" he questioned with almost a hint of sentiment.

Then swiftly dropping the act.

"Lots of Prussians on that boat. You Prussian?" he demanded viciously.

Toto knew better than dig himself any deeper. That would seal his fate.

"English, as they come!" Toto swiftly responded.

The other grunted.

"Well who the fuck cares, I'm gonna kill you anyway. That's my job and I love it."

Things now looked a little awkward, Toto accepted that. Looking for a stall, he assessed the scenario and for some stupid, idiotic moment he thought of Edwin Carewe. He even mystified himself, as here at death's door he turned to Hollywood. Oh, well if you're going to go out on the dream machine you might as well have the best director guiding you, he reasoned.

"You heard of Edwin Carewe?"

Kuterkin looked blank. He grunted a second time.

"No, who the fuck's he?"

"One of Hollywood's finest. Directed a great movie, Resurrection, you catch it in New York?"

"What the fuck, I'm gonna waste you and you start quizzing me on films. You wanna be a fuckin' movie star?" Kuterkin spat out.

" Make it quick, speak your last before I send you to hell?"

"It was Carewe who made the film of my gold claim, ring a bell?"

The Khazarian blinked, remembered handing Prentice the false stock and then put two and two together.

"You're the patsy we set up! What an idiot, falling for that cheap one," Kuterkin exploded in mirth.

Toto, polite as ever with nothing to lose, also laughed.

"So next I suppose you gonna tell me, you got the gold, right?" Kuterkin shot back with derision and no laughter.

"No, I'll leave that to my friend the Count behind you. He'll fill you in."

Take that cheap one, he thought.

Kuterkin turned round to wipe out the Count. Toto realized the oldest pantomime joke in the book had worked its magic, whipped his hand into his pocket, pulled the clockwork cord on the bomb stick, stuck it in the Khazar's pocket and ran like greased lightning, putting as great a distance between him and his executioner as he could muster.

Kuterkin turned back, having found no one, raised his gun, aimed it precisely at Toto's skull and pressed the trigger. The nanosecond between the trigger pressure applied and the end run of the clockwork timer was enough to blow the Khazar to kingdom come and allow Toto to reach the rowboat.

With all his remaining strength, he rowed frantically away from the mess of blood, destroyed bougainvilleas, house side and body parts.

As he lengthened distance of boat to shore, two remaining gang members, alerted to the blast, came running down to the shore. The light was fading. The sun's warmth of the late summer evening swiftly extinguished overtaken by fast approaching storm clouds. He kept rowing in between emptying his gun back to the shore. Bullets flew back and forth, until he was drained of ammunition. Searching his pockets for more bullets, the envelope and note fell out. He looked down at them and smiled.

Just then a bullet connected with his fingers in the left pocket. He whipped it out, loaded it and stood up, kicking a discarded, empty wine bottle away. Pointing at one of the two figures on the shore, he aimed and fired. At the same moment he felt a searing pain rip through his shoulder. It threw him off balance and back. Cordite from all the rounds littered a small cushion in the bottom of the boat. The cushion was the last thing he brushed before falling backwards into the water.

The remaining figure on the shore saw the target fall, turned to his dead companion who had received a bullet between the eyes and cursed the Englishman. He turned back. There was no one, just a floating skiff. That comforted him. He would report back the asset neutralized. Despite heavy losses, he got his man and now the reward. The house above had taken heavy casualties, though several lived to carry on.

The first flash of lightning seared across a cold gray metallic sky and lit up the envelope and note lying in the bottom of the drifting boat. It carried a simple few hand written lines:

"I've filled my pockets with pebbles, my belly with a bottle of Chianti and slipping over the side will place a bullet in my head, so as to be no bother to anyone."

It was signed, Toto.

POSTSCRIPT

At the beginning of May, 1936, Adrian Trapman, Vice Consul at Addis Ababa, knew the Italian advance and imminent fall of the city had encouraged the Emperor to take flight. As many British and foreign men, women and children remained stranded and exposed to the ensuing rioting and chaos, he single handedly began to evacuate by open lorry as many as he could take on each ten mile round trip. Over five days, through erratic and mortal rifle fire from rioters, he saved many lives.

His actions were recorded and in early September of that year he took his girlfriend Anne for a short holiday in Greece, visiting good friend and colleague, Patrick Roberts, now the British Charge d'Affaires at Athens, but formerly of Addis Ababa.

A beautiful sunny morning, the eighth of September, heralded the perfect day to motor down gently to the coast.

All three piled into Patrick's car and wound their way through olive lined, twisting roads, leaving Athens and passing through Ekali making their way up to the hills, towards the coast. As they motored past a small monastery, Adrian decided to break the news of his new posting as Vice Consul at Baghdad. The others were thrilled at this prestigious assignment.

Sitting in the front, as Patrick drove, Adrian could not have been happier. Shortly to marry Anne, they both relished this break before the assignment.

The car negotiated a long winding bend. Several sharp cracks alerted all three and Patrick swung round to catch where it came from. The car veered off the road at speed, as he tried regaining control. The front of the vehicle slammed into a large olive tree. The men were flung forward hitting the steering wheel and windscreen respectively. Both were killed instantly, with Anne left unconscious.

The bullets creating the punctures on both back tires went unobserved, as did a figure fleeing swiftly from the monastery behind them.

The New Year's Honors List of 1937, had King George VI award the British Empire Medal to Adrian Sidney Gilbert Reginald Trapman, Vice-Consul at Addis Ababa for Gallantry - posthumously.

ACKNOWLEDGMENTS

There are so many who deserve acknowledgment:

Toto, Louis, Leila, Willy and the whole von Meister clan. Nikola Tesla for his genius, Frank Baum for stealing Toto's name. Those now dead who played their role and brought us round again to face reality today. Craig Pruess for unswerving support for years, having my back from the get go. So many helped in small and large ways. If you feel you did, then you did and have my gratitude. Christopher Little, whose literary credits are all time top draw, I acknowledge his gold encrusted advice to make this the first book. I bow low in gratitude. To my immediate family, with special thanks to brother Chris, encouraging me to carry out the imprecations of our father to tell the story of Toto, on handing me the files, notes and heritage. This is for them, their grandchildren and their children's children. My father John and mother Lois for life, I return my love and for Nan, teaching us all unconditional love. Chris Street, for his author's ear. For all those never believing it would leave the Dream state, your doubts were the fuel proving Realities live. Larry Wilson, for sharing the true hero's journey, of lightness, fun and joy. Ginny, Carol, Gillian, Peter, Chris, Susan, Jennifer and Véronique whose support, laughter and patience egged me on. Mark Victor Hansen, for motivation and rubbishing a title. Robert Sachs for a working title causing a replug and editorial wisdom. A multitude of writers, journalists and Toto kin who refuse to sell their souls. Katherine Fenton for so much. Richard Hammerton whose eyes, ears and advice polished, crafted and brought it home. Finally Virve, my love, my wife and life. My joy, my stick clearing blocks, her constancy, belief and trust encouraging me to reach the tape, allowing me to trust the inner Toto, my intuition and helping begin and continue a journey I came here to finish.

THE FREEDOM CYCLE

The Freedom Cycle is a heptalogy (seven) book series tracing the journey of an idea, sponsored, projected and interpreted by the hero's journey.

DREAMS AND REALITIES - You've just experienced it!

ANGEL OF REDEMPTION - A visitation from an angel foretells the three outcomes of a newly birthed state of freedom. Across the centuries the third and ultimate outcome plays itself out. A fully corrupted Empire of Control, eager to complete its plans is challenged by the fully awakened Outsiders. Will the Angel of Redemption be called upon to visit once more?

INHERITANCE OF CAIN - Millennia of control through manipulation of spiritual realities, reveal the true face of evil. Its resurgence in an horrific and terrifying modern form challenges the very nature of what is considered to be human. Is there still time for the hero to intervene against this inheritance?

TREE OF LIFE - If the sum of who we are is charted in individual genealogy, then these stories become a map guiding us towards an ever growing Tree of Life and illumination of true purpose. If the future is written in our genes how then can we write that into the stars?

VORTEX OF THE VEIL - A multidimensional, ever more complex matrix. Beyond the Veil it is time for evolution to take center stage and become! A call goes out for heroes. Will it be heard?

MIND OF GOD and **THE FREEDOM FACTOR** are mysteries unfolding, with heroes coming face to face with ....

For more on the whole series please visit www.thefreedomcycle.com
The remaining titles in the series to be published: (With license to change!)
THE ANGEL OF REDEMPTION
INHERITANCE OF CAIN
TREE OF LIFE
VORTEX OF THE VEIL
MIND OF GOD
THE FREEDOM FACTOR

Find out more **www.thefreedomcycle.com**

ABOUT THE AUTHOR

Jonathan L. Trapman has written since aged 9. His first novel The Bull got fair marks at school and marked him out as an author in need of improvement.

Defying his early detractors he began his professional career as a photojournalist, working for some of the top titles in Fleet Street at the time. Amongst them the London Times, Daily Express and a very short and boring stint with the Sun newspaper. Having been exposed to the amount of propaganda and half truths demanded from photo/journalists in the '70s and 80s, he decided his soul was worth more than shekels earned from the news rooms of corporate cronyism.

Marking his further career becoming one of the industry's foremost photographers he enjoyed getting to know the world, its peoples and a far wider vision of life on earth on others' behalf and at others' expense.

He has appeared on TV and radio including the BBC, France Inter and online radio. He has been invited to speak at creative and literary conferences across the globe.

In the early 2000s in partnership with his wife he accomplished several translations of foreign writers. The most enduring, endearing and ground breaking has been the first ever, in nearly 1000 years, translation of 10th century Sufi founder and mystic saint **Hoja Ahmed Yassawi's** *Diwani Hikmet (Divine Wisdom)* poetry and sacred verse.

His magnum opus **The Freedom Cycle**, an ambitious seven book project of which this book is its first, is set to evolve over the next several years.

Jonathan presently lives in Somerset, UK.

Lightning Source UK Ltd.
Milton Keynes UK
UKHW020631141021
392201UK00015B/1080